The Meeting
A Traveling Romantic Thriller

G.T. Rodrigues

Copyright © 2023 G. T. Rodrigues

All rights reserved.

ISBN: 978-1-7368583-2-5
Creative Book Writers

DEDICATION

This story is dedicated to everyone.
Everyone who treats his or her fellow humans with love.
And there is love in everyone.

(And to our Moms)

CONTENTS

1	Potato Patch	1
2	Ferry Building	5
3	Sausalito	13
4	Pelican Inn	20
5	Charleston, SC	32
6	Boneyard Beach	41
7	Napa Valley	47
8	Cape Fear	59
9	Kill Devil Hills	71
10	Redwoods	90
11	Appalachian Trail	112
12	Looking Glass Falls	128
13	Sautee Nacoochee	139
14	Route 66	154
15	Alice's Restaurant	171
16	Half Moon Bay	189
17	Mavericks	209
18	Año Nuevo Island	223
19	Twin Peaks	230
20	The California Missions	246

21	Steep Ravine	255
22	Carmel-by-the-Sea	280
23	Point Reyes Station	299
24	Alcatraz	328
25	Lighthouse	349
*	Prologue to The Call	372

INTRODUCTION

Sam was the girl every girl wanted to be. Beautiful, genuine, giving and full of adventure. But she was done with her life in Charleston, heading off in her little black convertible across the country. Ranger was just amazing. Handsome, smart, talented and tough. Captain of everybody's team. Living the dream by the California coast … Then, they met.

The Meeting is an adventure, a traveling romantic thriller, book one of a five-part series about finding love, finding yourself, living this one shot at life, and the people we meet along the way. Ranger and Sam only wanted good for everyone. So, how could things end up the way they did? Come on, let's take their incredible journey together … Are you ready?

The Meeting ... read with an open world.

Hey, Romantic Travelers!

You and yours can explore the spectacular places and things you read about in Sam and Ranger's trip through **The Meeting** as well ... Just click on the links in the digital text to see them. You can also get your favorite travel shoes on, open **The Meeting** Trail Map below, and get out and see the places for yourselves!

The Meeting Trail Map

https://www.google.com/maps/d/u/0/edit?mid=1TZofX9CEcApmLwxl__dUyefT064&ll=34.586076118125 99%2C-106.76957218799981&z=5

Follow the footsteps of all five couples from **The Meeting** traveling romantic thriller series:

Sam and Ranger in **The Meeting**

Owen and Abby in **The Call**

Jett and Faye in **The Engagement**

Ellyse and Andre in **The Kiss**

Stone and Daisy in **The Surrender**

Most importantly, may your journey lead you to the greatest adventure of them all ... **LOVE**

1 POTATO PATCH

Did you know? The word *fathom* means depth, usually depth in the ocean, one fathom equaling 1.8288 meters, or exactly six feet. Originally though, *fathom* meant *something that embraces* or the *outstretched arms*, which on an ordinary man, arms wide open, measure just at six feet.

Hence, a *fathom*.

Have you ever been to San Francisco? It's really beautiful there. The next time you go, if you will, take a look out beyond the Golden Gate to the Pacific Ocean, north past the low, craggy peninsula where the Point Bonita Lighthouse sits. There, about a mile offshore, lurks a peculiar stretch of ocean called the Potato Patch.

Barely twenty feet deep in spots, the Potato Patch is several square miles of shallow water on top of a reef called the Four Fathom Bank, itself a segment of the great San Francisco Bar, the horseshoe-shaped expanse of reef that begins north of the lighthouse, runs out about five miles west of the Golden Gate, then bends back toward shore south near Ocean Beach in the city … just there beneath the surface in that spectacular view you see from the windows of the historic (and romantic) Cliff House restaurant.

Anyhow, right down the middle of that giant horseshoe reef runs the narrow, fifty-five foot deep commercial shipping channel leading into San Francisco Bay. If you were in a helicopter, here is where you'd want to be to get the best bird's eye view of the huge ships sailing in and out of the bay every day. Colossal vessels like the Benjamin Franklin, the largest ship ever to pass through the Golden Gate, longer than four football fields and nearly as large as the Empire State Building … or the Queen Mary 2, with its seventeen decks and four thousand passengers, which docked here during her grand voyage around the world several years back.

Things so big they can only arrive when the tide is right.

Now, I say *lurks* because the Potato Patch is quite the hazardous place. Very tricky to navigate. Swells from the North Pacific cause enormous, unpredictable waves sixty or eighty feet high to haunt its waters, especially in winter, making it a final resting place for many a ship and sailor, even to this day. Legend has it the Potato Patch got its name because of all the Irish potatoes lost overboard from ships pounded in the surf or grounded on the reef there during the Gold Rush. Others claim the name comes from the topography of the reef itself, a large, flat section of ocean floor with protruding knobs and gnarls all over, resembling potatoes sprouting from the ground. Either way, ships traveling in and out of San Francisco Bay must stick to the main shipping channel or hug the coast and steer around it ... or risk losing it all.

The place is that nasty.

Here ... is where we find our hero.

His daredevil father had paddled with the legendary Tsunami Rangers kayakers back in the 1980s. That's where he got his water skills ... and his nickname.

Ranger was good at everything else too, it seemed ... 6-foot-3 and muscular, with long arms and an athlete's waist and legs, captain of the rugby team at his alma mater, the University of California at Berkeley, he ran cross country just for the fun of it. People in the know said he looked a lot like New Zealand All Blacks rugby star Sonny Bill Williams, maybe not as much in the face as in the physique.

And he was certainly a gentleman like Sonny Bill. Did a little boxing on the side like him too.

All being said, Ranger was pretty awesome.

The main wave at Potato Patch was still a couple hundred meters out, but it looked as big as a building already, and Ranger aimed his solar-colored Dagger Nomad kayak straight for it. *Swooosh! Swoosh! Swooosh!* The rhythm of his paddles was quick, and strong.

By the time he got there, however, the ocean had settled. Now a pretty dark blue of thick, smooth swells rolling by quietly underneath his boat. Great white sharks swam out here, Ranger knew it, and the fog had not yet fully receded back over the Gulf of the Farallones, west towards their main feeding grounds, the Farallon Islands.

For most anyone, the view out here, out to the open ocean or back to the rugged shore, might look beautiful, but today it was eerie. Forlorn.

Like you weren't supposed to be out there at all.

Like you were lost at sea.

Ranger sat and scanned the water.

A couple minutes went by ...

Then out of nowhere, a monster rose up behind him.

Ranger began paddling.

Swooosh! Swoosh! Swooosh!

He stroked firmly against the wave's sucking ebb in front of him in order to catch the beast, the rear of his kayak elevating immediately, and so steeply, that the nose of the boat buried into the wall of water forming below it.

Whoomp!

The nose made a loud, hollow sound as it popped free, but as soon as he started to descend, Ranger felt the surge double up underneath him, a second huge breaker bursting out of the face of the first. It cast him into the air, discarding him into a free fall the rest of the way down to the pit at the bottom.

Sppplllaaaaaassssssshhhhh!

Keeping his balance and digging his oar in, Ranger swept left, paddling hard down the line onto the mass of water's now peeling face.

The giant roller curled over the top of him, and he vanished into the four-story barrel of green-gray.

"Yeaaaaahhhh!"

Boooooommmmmmm!

The thing spat him out just as it exploded.

As he slowed, bouncing up onto the monster's whitewater shoulder and flinging the saltwater from his hair and eyes, rainbows lighting up the cool, wet air behind him … Ranger looked back to witness what he had just escaped.

Wow.

It was a warm, sunny day. Saturday morning. Middle of December.

Ranger didn't know it yet … but it would be a day that would change his life forever.

2 FERRY BUILDING

A quote: "Three things in human life are important ... the first is to be kind; the second is to be kind, and the third is to be kind."

Henry James

Ranger paddled his way back to Rodeo Beach, where his car was parked.

He had a couple things to do before the big Christmas party tonight.

Every year, he and a couple college buddies got together, rented a really cool place and hosted the holiday bash. They invited family and friends, business associates, all kinds of people, even ones they'd just met who might be able to use a little of the season's cheer. There was always great food, music, dancing, and gifts for everyone under a spectacular tree. Last year, the affair was at the Claremont Hotel, a hundred year-old resort in the Berkeley Hills, with its renowned gardens and spa, and stunning views of San Francisco Bay at sunset. The year before that was the Top of the Mark, the 360-degree penthouse lounge of the Mark Hopkins Hotel at the top of San Francisco's Nob Hill.

This year, it would be in Muir Beach, north of the Golden Gate, at a quaint oceanside 1600s English country style bed and breakfast called the Pelican Inn.

Ranger unzipped his glideskin wetsuit and warmed up in the sun for a minute. Then, with his right hand, flung the kayak up onto his shoulder.

Perfectly proportioned, he really was an impressive sight to see.

"How's it going?" Ranger greeted the strangers he passed in the parking lot, then arrived at his car, a West Coast gray 1964 Chevy Chevelle Malibu SS convertible. He toweled down, secured the kayak onto its rack, then took the top down and jumped in, beginning the zigzag drive back over the Marin Headlands ... towards home.

Great music.

One of the best views in the world.

Weekend traffic was already heavy on the headlands near the Golden Gate Bridge at the Battery Spencer scenic overlook. A carful of tourists -- mother and kids in *I Heart SF* caps, cameras ready, and the father behind the wheel -- was stuck on the turnoff trying to get back onto the road, but nobody was letting them in.

"Go ahead, my friend." Ranger smiled and waved a big arm out his open top for the car to go in front of him. The dad smiled and waved back. As the Volvo pulled out, the kids pointed to Ranger's cool convertible, snapping some photos and waving as well.

Ranger continued along the bay, past the famous sea lion statue, by all the cute restaurants, and parked at the Sausalito ferry landing. He was catching the 11:20 boat into the city.

In a recent survey, international travel journalists and photographers called the ferry ride from Sausalito to San Francisco the *second most exciting such ride in the world*, with only the Star Ferry in Hong Kong, with its spectacular city skyline views as the backdrop and local fishermen in boats plying their trade right there in the harbor in front of you, rating higher.

The weather was perfect, so Ranger took an outdoor seat on the multi-deck MV Marin.

Shortly after departure, he noticed a young lady he'd seen on the boat several times before, always sitting quietly, arms folded across her pack, listening to something in her headphones. She was bigger, and had short sandy blonde hair, wore jeans and a sweatshirt usually, and was obviously blind. And on occasion, Ranger observed, she'd crack the most heartwarming smile, apparently when she got to a part in her headphones that she liked. Quickly though, as if she didn't dare impose on anyone else who might be looking.

She was one of those people, it seemed, that nobody ever noticed at all.

So today, Ranger decided to say *hello*.

"Excuse me ..." he said as she pushed buttons on her device. "I have to know what you're listening to that makes you smile like that, 'cause I could stand smiling like that too."

She hesitated, surprised. "Oh ... It's Tom Jones." Her voice was wary.

"Tom Jones ... alright!" Ranger replied, enthusiastic. *"It's not unusual to be loved by anyone ..."* he sang, low, so nobody else could hear. "That Tom Jones?"

She cracked a smile and nodded.

"Fabulous choice."

"Thank you ... My grandmother used to listen to him." She spoke softly.

"Family favorites are the best. My grandfather always liked this guy named Jimmy Smith. He played the electric organ. So ... now I like him too. Makes me feel connected." The ferry sounded its horn and began pulling out. "Thanks for sharing. My name is Ranger."

"Hello ... I'm Dee."

Dee was shy, but Ranger had a way of making you feel pretty instantly at ease, so the two ended up chatting all the way to the Ferry Building.

An important transportation hub since 1898, before the two landmark bridges were built over the bay in the 1930s, the San Francisco Ferry Building bedecks the city's waterfront, there on the Embarcadero at the foot of Market Street. Its 245-foot tall clock tower modeled after the great Giralda at the Seville Cathedral, earth's third largest church, and its facade, French Beaux Arts. Today, the Ferry Building continues on as a busy passenger terminal, but it's also been renovated into a bustling marketplace, with more than fifty artisan shops, cafes, eateries, and novelty retailers, and a top-notch open-air farmers market several days a week.

Dee was meeting her best friend there today. On the boat, she told Ranger all about Annie. About how the two of them had met in the first grade, and how Annie moved away to Maine in junior high. About how hard-working and determined Annie was. How she had invented an app in college for a senior project and ended up making a mint from it. And how she'd recently moved back, and all the things they'd been doing since to catch up.

Oh, and how over-the-top outgoing she was.

"She talks to everybody," Dee told him. "And she'll try almost anything, at least once … Skydiving, stage diving at a U2 concert. Diving with sharks …"

You could tell she really loved her best friend.

"My grandmother used to call her *Annie the Unstoppable*."

It made Ranger smile.

When the boat arrived, the two of them walked together from the dock to the marketplace, outside Frog Hollow Farm, Dee's designated meeting spot. Annie wasn't there yet.

"It was very nice to meet you, Ranger. Thank you for the conversation." Dee stuck her hand out to shake, then found the wall with her cane and backed up against it.

"Likewise, Dee. It was fun sailing with you." He started to go, then turned around and offered, "Do you want to look for Annie? I'd be glad to help."

Dee checked her vision-free phone. "That's okay ... Thank you. She's probably running late. She always calls five minutes before she arrives ... I'll just wait."

Ranger searched the crowd around him.

"We'd hear her before we saw her anyway." Dee's lip quivered as she cracked a smirk.

"Oh, really?!" Ranger laughed. "That's funny! Annie the *Uncontrollable*, right?"

"*Unstoppable* ..." Dee giggled out loud.

They both chuckled.

"Well, Miss Dee, I'm going to go pick up a few things ..." Ranger took in the air. "I can smell 'em already."

Dee searched around with her eyes. "Yes, it does smell good," she said, firmly on the wall and out of the way.

Ranger paused a second, then offered again, "Come on, you have to at least try the cheese. Everybody does. It's really *unbelievable*!"

"Okay ..." Dee replied, pausing. " ... I guess it would be wrong to pass up ... *unbelievable* cheese."

"Yes, it would be ... *unimaginable* ... Almost *unforgivable*."

"Well, alright then ... shall we?" Ranger set Dee's hand on his shoulder so she could follow, and they pushed off to taste a bunch of great stuff. Cheeses from the Cowgirl Creamery, salami from his friend Dean at the Golden Gate Meat Co., coffee from Blue Bottle Coffee, sourdough from Acme Bread. They even braved the crowd at Humphry Slocombe to try some of the mind-blowing ice cream flavors -- Secret Breakfast, Chocolate Sea Salt, Brown Butter, and Lime Basil, all of Ranger's favorites.

Then, Dee's phone rang.

"Hi, Annie ... Yes, I'm here ... I'm at the ... Humphry Slocombe ice cream shop right now."

Ranger could hear Annie's effervescence right away on the other end.

"Well ..." Dee continued, "I've been walking around with this nice person I met on the ferry ... tasting a bunch of stuff." She spoke quietly, almost embarrassed.

Annie's volume increased.

"His name is Ranger ..." Dee whispered. "... Yes, he's a guy."

"Alright, Dee Dee! Woo hoo, right on! I'll be there in two minutes, then ... Does he have a friend?" She giggled loudly. Ranger could hear her clearly now.

"Annie ... stop it."

"I'm kidding, Honey Dee! ... Love ya! See ya in five! Taste something totally *scrumptious* for me!"

"Love you too. I'll be at the meeting spot." Blushing, Dee hung up.

"*Uncontrollable*," she said.

As predicted, they heard Annie about fifteen seconds before they saw her coming around the corner. Dee introduced her.

"Woo hoo! Nice to meet you, Mr. Ranger!" Annie grabbed his hand and squeezed it tight.

"Hi, Annie. I love your energy ..." Ranger told her and gave her a hug in return. She giggled.

Ranger always made it a point to compliment people he saw were kind, generous, positive, or who did their jobs well, things like that. He wanted them to know they were not unnoticed. That they were appreciated. And, he was a hugger. He hugged everyone, and when he hugged you, you knew it ... Like you were family.

The three of them, Annie, Dee, and Ranger, talked and walked and laughed out loud on their way out of the Ferry Building, to the Embarcadero where Annie's driver was waiting.

"I hate to part company with such a handsome man, Ranger, but you know, the day awaits!" Annie announced. "We're off to do some serious Christmas shopping at Union Square ... When can we see you again? It's an absolute must, and soon!"

"Well, Dee and Annie," he returned, "If you're free this evening, a couple of my friends and I are throwing our annual big Christmas party at the Pelican Inn in Muir Beach. We sure would be honored to have you."

"Really ... Christmas party at the Pelican Inn?! Heck yes! I've always wanted to see that place!" Annie was thrilled. "Umm ... What time shall we be there?"

Dee looked in her direction a bit apprehensively.

"Starts at 7:00, dinner is at 8. There's gonna be dancing, and gifts, and everything will be taken care of. We reserved the whole place. All you have to do is show up."

Annie seemed almost unable to contain herself. "That sounds fabulous! I've been telling Dee Bee she needs to start getting out more. Have some *funnnn*! ... This is perfect."

"But, I don't ... have anything to wear ... to a party, Annie," Dee hesitated.

"Dee Dee Darling, we're going shopping at *Union Square*! You're gonna be Cinderella at the ball tonight when we're all through with you ... Both of us ... We're gonna be knockouts!"

"Well, we'll see you there then ..." Ranger smiled. "I look forward to it."

Ranger was pleased they could make it.

They all hugged and said goodbye, and he set off to pick up a couple more gifts. For Annie, he ended up getting a gift bag of goodies and gift cards from the shops he and Dee had just visited, so the two of them could come back and taste together. And for Dee, he got the best portable speaker system he could find so she could listen to Tom Jones as loud as she wanted, whenever she wanted, especially at home in Marin City where she grew up with her grandmother, who was no longer with her.

Ranger was grateful he had said *hello* to Dee on the boat today. She and Annie were really wonderful people, and it was refreshing for him to hear all about their friendship.

He hoped the Pelican Inn would be a fun and memorable time for the both of them ... Something they could really enjoy and remember together.

Even if neither of them would be able to see any of it at all.

3 SAUSALITO

Did you know a dog's emotions develop similar to those of a human child? They learn to feel excitement, and stress, contentment, fear and anger, suspicion, joy, and affection. Research also shows they stop there, however. Never learning adult things like pride, disrespect, or disdain.

Shopping bags in hand, Ranger boarded the ferry for home.

He and his brindle American Staffordshire Terrier Bernard had a two-story floating home on Liberty Dock at Waldo Point Harbor in Sausalito, and they loved it. It was here Otis Redding stayed for a couple days back in June, 1967, rented one of the houseboats, and wrote the first verse to one of the all-time classic American songs. Rumor has it he sat out on the deck, strummed his guitar, and sang the first couple of lines to himself over and over. His manager later said this was the time in his life when Otis began looking more introspectively, thinking about what was important, about change, and about love. And you can hear this in the tune. No singer had done a song with soul like this before. People around him thought it a bad idea. Too melancholy, they said, but Otis insisted. He told them it would be his biggest hit.

It went:

Sittin' in the morning sun

I'll be sittin' when the evening comes

Watching the ships roll in

Then I watch them roll away again, yeah

I'm sittin' on the dock of the bay

Watchin' the tide roll away, ooh

I'm just sittin' on the dock of the bay

Wastin' time

I left my home in Georgia

Headed for the Frisco Bay

Cuz I've had nothing to live for

And look like nothing's gonna come my way

So, I'm just gon' sit on the dock of the bay

Watchin' the tide roll away, ooh

I'm sittin' on the dock of the bay

Wastin' time

Looks like nothing's gonna change

Everything still remains the same

I can't do what ten people tell me to do

So I guess I'll remain the same, listen

Sittin' here resting my bones

And this loneliness won't leave me alone, listen

Two thousand miles I roam

Just to make this dock my home, now

I'm just gon' sit at the dock of a bay

Watchin' the tide roll away, ooh

Sittin' on the dock of the bay

Wastin' time

(whistling)

Six months later, he was gone in a plane crash, and *Dock of the Bay* went to number one.

Ranger thought about the upcoming night.

He, Richie, Julian and Dan had some quite lively plans for the festivities.

Richie was an all-American guy from a small town, nice as can be, strong as an ox, down-to-earth, a real stand up gent. Julian was the party guy of the bunch, taller with a darker complexion, and changing his hairdo often to match the fashion he was sporting at the time. For tonight's party, he was going with a high pompadour hairdo, clean shaven, with a 70s chevron moustache, square-framed Cutler & Gross specs, a designer fitted black tux with gray accents and peaked satin lapels, red plaid shirt, matching socks, black bow tie, and Jimmy Choo patent leather loafers with the shiny logo accent bar across the vamp ... He was pumped. Dan was the ladies' man. All the girls loved him. Chiseled jaw, honey voice, with a smile that lit up the room, clean cut with naturally messy brown hair, and a strong physique. Daniel was cool.

As men go these days, all three of Ranger's rugby buddies were really stellar guys.

Also coming as Ranger's guests were a handful of work associates; his trainer at the gym Schalk, who also doubled as Bernard's sitter when

Ranger was out of town; Ms. Elodie-Jane, the spirited little French lady who lived four doors down on the Liberty Dock ... and Carolijn, a Dutch transplant with whom Ranger went to summer performing arts camp as a teenager. They got to be pretty good friends, graduating high school together, and staying in contact with their group through college, when they'd go dancing on the town over holiday breaks, and once acted in a local production of the 1930s Cole Porter musical-at-sea *Anything Goes*.

Ranger starred as Billy Crocker, and Carolijn, the apple of his eye, Hope.

They had a lot of good times together.

The ferry ride back from San Francisco was nearly all the way full. Christmas shoppers filled most of the seats. You could tell by the red and green bags everywhere.

The trip was pleasant, as usual ... except for the one couple sitting up on the upper deck. They were younger, probably late twenties, and they were loud, using a significant amount of inappropriate language. The guy was sprawled out in one seat, arm and jacket hanging over into another, sneaker up on a third; and the girl, on and off her phone the whole time.

They were making passengers uncomfortable.

The boat pulled into the Sausalito Ferry Landing about 3:20 pm, and people from the top deck began to make their way down to get in line to exit. Deckhands prepared for docking. With no hesitation, and as loud as they had been the entire ride, the couple from upstairs strolled past everyone already in line, stood alongside those at the front, and waited there for the doors to open, engaged with their electronic devices.

An older married couple, in their late fifties perhaps, about ten people back from the front, took notice of their violation. "There's a line, you know?" the wife muttered to her husband, not really intending it to be heard.

But, the woman did hear it.

She looked up, and found the wife. "You got a problem?" she inquired aggressively.

Nobody said anything. With half the boat watching now, her guy glared back at the couple, and anyone else who dared, "That's what I thought ... Shut up, then."

He was quite the intimidating figure.

Heads shook, and eyes dropped to the floor.

Then, seconds later, the smug line cutter was surprised (shocked, really) to feel his personal space ... interrupted.

A strong hand came to rest on his shoulder.

"These people were here first. Why don't you come on back to the end of the line with me."

Ranger was cool, and clear, as he looked the guy square in the eye.

"Pffffff ... And you are?" he scoffed.

"The guy who's gonna see that you make it to the end of the line ..."

"Umm ... Do you work here, or something? I don't see no uniform?" the woman piped in.

"Man, get outta here before I ..." The guy attempted to swipe Ranger's hand away, but it didn't move. In fact, it went from resting on his shoulder to clenched tightly just beneath his chin, with most of the collar of his sweatshirt balled up inside it.

With one arm, Ranger moved him out of the line.

"Listen, sir ... You have been extremely inconsiderate since you've been on this boat. You have your feet all over the chairs. Your language is foul. There are kids and families here. Then, you cut in front of all these good people like you're the only ones on board ... You're not getting off first."

The man quickly understood the weight of Ranger's words, through the weight in his fist and the purpose in his eye, and the woman looking on realized as well that her man was not going to win this battle ... if he chose it.

They about-faced, and walked together to the back of the line.

More than a few of the passengers smiled, exchanging wide-eyed glances of amazement, and a handful of them gave the *thumbs-up*.

Outside, the deckhands completed their docking maneuvers, opened the gangway doors and manned the ramp, wishing all the passengers a good evening and Merry Christmas.

The ferry-goers went on their way.

And Ranger drove the mile-and-a-half along Bridgeway and the shoreline ... home.

"Whooaa! You big old baby, you!"

Bernard was excited to see Ranger. He'd been out on the second floor deck almost all day, playing with the seagulls. Bernard didn't bark much, thank goodness, because he'd annoy the neighbors, who were out on their decks a lot too during this kind of weather. Actually, when he did bark, it sounded more like talking. He'd ramble on to the birds, spinning back and forth as they circled overhead. Then, he'd grumble as he fell asleep in his doghouse, just to let them know he was still watching.

On either patio, Ranger and Bernard enjoyed sitting, watching the sunrise, or taking in the view over to Belvedere Island, or tracking the boats as they came and went in the bay out past Tiburon and by Angel and Alcatraz Islands. The first floor deck was a resort lanai, built to specification like the ocean villa terraces at the Ayada Resort on Maguhdhuvaa in the Maldives, where Ranger had visited two years ago -- complete with the stone plunge pool, deck-level ocean hammocks, and stairs leading down to the water. The only difference, Ranger's veranda was enclosed with floor-to-ceiling glass doors, which could be opened in any direction, or closed completely to keep company inside comfortable on those not-so-tropical Bay Area evenings. The second floor deck was simpler, with a rocking chair, a table, and the doghouse.

A place where a man could do some real thinking, and a dog could chase the gulls.

Ranger sat up there the rest of the afternoon with Bernard, and tea, contemplating the day.

Watching the tide roll away.

4 PELICAN INN

"Home is where the heart is," said Roman naval commander Pliny the Elder, and his heart was on his ship. The irony is he went aground trying to rescue a woman and a friend, perishing in Pompeii during the 79 A.D. Vesuvius eruption. His advisors had advised him to stay at home.

The Pelican Inn sparkled, decked in elegant white lights and boughs of holly everywhere.

Dan had a friend from the Union Square Macy's do the decorating for the party every year. It was kind of a tradition. She and her friends would come out the day before and transform the place, then at night, break out the Ganz Kissing Krystal and Mark Roberts ornaments, sip hot buttered rum punches, and trim the tree. "Oooooh, that's pretty, Danny!" they'd coo when he'd reach up to set the lighted star of Bethlehem on top.

The dark wooden tables, chairs and floors of the rustic dining room glowed in the bright lights. But, the focus of the room was the semi-walk-in fireplace, designed with seats in it, and the words FEAR KNOCKED AT THE DOOR. FAITH ANSWERED. NO ONE WAS THERE inscribed across its head-high mantle. Spectacular! A charming covered patio adjoined the dining room, and both areas were set for dinner. On the menu: Gigi's Sotto Mare clam chowder; cheese boards of English blue stilton, white cheddar, Cotswolds, and jams; a half dozen Point Reyes miyagi oysters with mignonette and lemon (Julian loved them); pastry-wrapped and seared filet mignon; carving board turkey; bourbon yams and garlic mashed potatoes; port cranberries; and English bread and sticky toffee, among other goodies.

Twelve Days of Christmas hors d'oeuvres and an array of spiced and chocolate holiday drinks featured in the cute pub style bar. The charming round tables and stools, benches and window ledge seating, paintings, and country trinkets adorning the walls made you feel like you were in England, and in the spirit. The ten-foot Noble Fir was from an Apple Hill farm, and all the presents were there under it. Beyond the pub was a chamber called the *snug* -- a cozy parlor with a fireplace of its own, wingback chairs, an overstuffed couch, and piano.

Johnny Mathis was singing in there. *It Came Upon a Midnight Clear.*

The guests began arriving at 7:00 pm, on schedule.

Every year, Ranger and the boys hired a local dance outfit to help greet the guests, and serve, and put on a dance performance later during the party. They'd always dress up, this year coming as angels. This evening, they met guests at their cars, welcomed them with a frolic, and escorted them into the inn, where the hosts awaited with stocking stuffers and hugs.

"Ranger, *c'est absolument magnifique!*" Ranger's eighty-two year-old neighbor Elodie-Jane entered with her angel. The bellboy reached for her faux fox stole to hang in the coat room, and she briskly smacked his hand away. "I shall be keeping this on tonight, young man ... I'm not quite as hot-blooded as I used to be, mind you."

He smiled.

"But, perhaps I shall let you have it when Ranger takes me to dance a bit later." She smiled.

Ranger winked at the attendant.

"Ms. Elodie, I will most certainly be seeking you first for the dancefloor, young lady."

"*Fantastique!* I do have my dancing shoes on, you will know!" Ms. Elodie proclaimed, excited. She poked her little leg out to reveal an adorable vintage ruby suede bow pump.

"Wow. Like Claudette Colbert," quipped the coat check angel. "Could stop traffic."

Ms. Elodie did a twirl. "Or give you a kick in the shins." She winked at them both.

Ms. Elodie was a tough little old lady. Ranger had offered to bring her to the party tonight, but she'd insisted on driving the twisty Highway 1 route herself.

She had become deeply independent since losing her beloved Higginbotham last year.

Suddenly, another familiar fun-loving voice rang out from the porch. "Alright, we're here ... Let the party begin!"

"Almost, ladies. Just a couple more steps and we'll be inside," their angel guided.

"Oh ... yes. Of course. We knew that."

"Stop." The other voice whispered.

It was Dee and Annie, stepping cautiously into the doorway, holding for instruction.

"Okay, we're here. *Now* the party can begin!" the angel declared.

The girls most definitely had done some shopping, and came dressed up for the occasion. Dee had on a shiny red satin dinner dress and matching mid heels, her short hair pulled up in a baby bun with green and red ribbon; and Annie, shorter than her friend, wore a crimson and emerald sequins gown, sunglasses with reindeer antlers for rims ... and a mistletoe-topped Santa hat that read *Ho! Ho! Ho! Now Kiss Me!* across the front.

Ranger greeted them. "Dee, Annie ... Welcome! So glad to see you ... How are you?"

"Oh ... Hi, Ranger. Thank you," Dee replied.

"Woooo, hooooo! Helloooo, Ranger! We're doing awesome!" Annie belted.

Ranger patted their young angel on the shoulder and mouthed to her, *nice work, thank you*. Then, he gave Annie and Dee hugs. "Merry Christmas! Let me introduce you to my friends, and your hosts for the night, Richie, Dan, and Julian."

The guys gave the ladies warm hugs, then Dan kissed Annie on the cheek, several times, alternating left and right like they do abroad.

"Wooo. What big muscles you all have ... Ooohhh, my goodness ... Well, hello to you too!" She was taken off-guard by Dan's extra greeting.

"Just read your hat," he told her.

"Oh, Dee, have I died and gone to heaven?" Annie giggled ecstatically.

"Annie ..." Dee sighed again.

"Well, Annie, you were right. You both look absolutely stunning this evening." Ranger said. "We're so glad you're here." The boys handed each a small, neatly-wrapped gift box.

"Have a blast tonight!" Dan and Julian took their hands to lead them to the dining room.

"Can I take these?" Richie asked about their canes. "You won't be needing them. You'll have escorts all evening."

The girls handed them over, and he checked them into the coat closet.

And off they went.

All the guests had arrived by 8:00, dinner time, including Schalk with his trainer friend Sara. Ranger's work partners Cheslin and Duane, and some associates visiting from South Africa named Eben and Lodewyk. Richie's wife Liz and her very best friend Stacey. Two great guys, Ma'a and Sevu, coaches from the High Street Boys and Girls Club in Oakland, who taught Dan what it really meant to reach inner city kids when he did a rugby camp there last summer. A handful of Julian's business acquaintances: Rhys, Maro, Courtney and George ... And, Ranger's friend Carolijn.

She arrived about 7:45 pm, escorted by a couple of gregarious angels, and her new fiancé, a fellow by the name of Rob Shaw. Ranger didn't know. He hadn't seen her in over a year. Nonetheless, he and the boys greeted them both with gifts and hugs.

"Good to see you." She smiled.

Dinner was sumptuous, and afterwards, staff cleared the room while everybody moved to the pub for presents. Hugs and laughs and tears were all around. Liz opened her gift to find the new Teva Ahnu Sugarpine boots ... for her upcoming hiking trip; Sevu and Ma'a, courtside seats to the Warriors game; and Dee got her portable speakers.

The guys got Dan one of those new Onewheel fat tire all-terrain electronic skateboards ... along with an assortment of Jockey underwear.

"Wow! How'd you guys guess?! ... The only two things I need to survive!" He was pumped. "You know what I'll be doing tomorrow!"

"And exactly what you'll be wearing doing it!" Julian held up a pair of the briefs.

The girls could hardly contain themselves.

Ranger went last. He unwrapped a matching pair of oversized, hand-painted *kulhads* (earthen tea cups from India), then a slick Moonraker telescope (to use out on his deck), and some silk pajamas with big crimson hearts on them. A pair for him, a pair for Bernard, and one additional pair.

"Aaawwwww!" Ranger held them up.

"Is that third pair a medium?" One of the girls shouted from the corner, her friends bursting out in giggles. The boys all elbowed Ranger too.

Just then, a remix of the hit *Last Christmas* by George Michael began on the loudspeakers. "Merry Christmas, everyone!" Julian whooped. "We're so glad you're here and ... let's dance!" The hosts, along with the angels, grabbed guests and led them out onto the floor.

"Yoo hoo, Ranger ... over here!!" Miss Elodie called out, waving her hand in the air.

"Let's go!" Ranger swooped her up.

And they Boston-waltzed all over the room, to the delight of the crowd.

Just like that, the Pelican Inn was magic.

The dance segment of the party was a tradition, and each year the boys did it differently. This year's theme: classic R&B. Videos for songs like *Used to Be My Girl* by The O'Jays, The Whispers' *And the Beat Goes On*, and Michael Jackson's *Don't Stop 'til You Get Enough* were projected onto the walls, and they danced with all the guests, doing the moves from each of them. They played the hits from Nat King Cole, Lou Rawls, and Gladys Knight & the Pips, and weaved in live video from each of the rooms so people could watch themselves dancing the night away.

Everyone was having a ball. Even Dee got out there and boogied a little.

It was when the angels were performing to a version of *All I Want for Christmas Is You* that Ranger noticed Carolijn and Rob withdraw into the snug. They didn't look happy.

Ranger followed and found Carolijn sitting next to the fire, Rob standing next to her.

"Hey, you guys alright?"

"Oh ... hi, Ranger. Yes, just taking a break from all the fun." She hardly looked up.

"Yeah, it really is a great party," Rob commended. "You boys do an outstanding job."

Rob Shaw was a good guy. A big man, but gentle. And good-hearted. Not the smoothest operator by any stretch, or the best dancer in the world either, sort of goofy with two left feet. Certainly no match for Carolijn, but he tried hard and was really friendly, a real talker ... and that's what she loved about him. He wore his heart on his sleeve, and gave it all he had every time.

"Thanks, Rob," Ranger replied. "I'm really glad you guys are here."

Carolijn looked to her fiancé, then back to Ranger, realizing he'd come to see why they'd left the pub so abruptly.

Rob decided to defer to Carolijn. Let her handle it.

"Hey, honey buns, how about I let you and Ranger catch up, and I'll take a walk outside? ... Scout a route for a midnight walk on the beach a little later." He winked at her.

Carolijn smiled. "Sounds great, dear."

He kissed her on the head, shook Ranger's hand, then walked out the snug's back door. "Love you, sugar dumpling," he said.

"I love you too, babe."

It was quiet for a minute, almost an uncomfortable silence, before she spoke again.

"You know, Ranger ..."

His eyebrows raised.

"I loved *you* for a long time too ... All those years."

The logs in the fireplace crackled.

"Oh, yeah? ..." Ranger said back, caught off guard.

"Yeah," she continued. "All those days we spent together ... and the summers. All the nights just cracking up on the phone."

"Yeah, that ... was really great."

"You never realized I was in love with you?" Carolijn looked squarely into his eyes.

"Carolijn ..."

"Even that day at Steep Ravine?"

Ranger and Carolijn had gone hiking one day at Steep Ravine Trail on Mount Tamalpais, and Carolijn just grabbed him, kissed him as they neared the bottom and Stinson Beach. But, that was as far as anything ever went between the two of them. In fact, that day marked the time almost exactly when their relationship began to change.

Suddenly, a cheer came from the pub area next door, breaking the bar of silence.

"Ranger, you know, you're the most amazing man I know. You always know what to say. You're the smartest guy around. You're strong, and kind, and you'd give your last dollar to anybody who needed it ... But, I don't know if any of that matters ..."

Tears started to well in her eyes.

"Maybe it was just me."

"Carolijn ..." he said.

"Anyway, that's why I went away ... It was too much to stay."

She sat up, wiped her eyes, and straightened her dress.

Just then, the door from the pub eased open; it was one of Julian's work acquaintance Hooper, along with another guy named Michael. Michael's eyes met Carolijn's, then Ranger, then with a smirk, he turned back into the pub.

Ranger looked to Carolijn, back to the door, then down at Carolijn again. "You know that guy?" he asked.

"Yeah, he's the reason we walked out of there." She looked annoyed.

Ranger turned and faced her.

"Rob and I were dancing, having a good time, and I noticed that creep started looking at us ... We both saw it ... We'd look away, whatever, then I'd look back, and he'd be staring again, talking to his stupid friend. Then, he pointed at Rob and started laughing. Rob didn't see it, but I did. So then, Rob goes to the restroom, and I'm at the bar, and the loser comes up and starts talking to me, like, *Hey, how ya doin'* ... *Nice moves out there.*'"

Carolijn could be pretty feisty at times, and she was definitely a show woman, so, when she described Michael, it was pretty funny, with her exaggerated body language and voice ... But she was upset. Ranger could see it.

"So, Rob comes back and sees the guy and says to him, you know ... *Hello, can I help you?* And the guy just looks at Rob and is like ... *No, I don't think you can, pal* ... With that same smirk he had on his face right now. That's when we came in here."

Ranger just stood and listened to what Carolijn was saying.

"Rob's not a confrontational guy, but I will definitely say something … so, I figured it was best to just walk away. You know?"

Carolijn looked defeated, again, and Ranger felt bad. He had not liked seeing her like this. The last thing he wanted was to see her hurt.

Just then, Rob wandered back into the snug through the same door he had left, exuberant about something … just as Julian burst in from the pub.

"Hey, babe. Guess what …?" Rob started.

"Ranger! There you are! Come on, brother, we're on! Sorry … Come on, everyone!" Julian cut him off.

Carolijn and Ranger exchanged glances, then he turned and hastened off with Julian.

Carolijn got up, and Rob followed her out of the room.

All the hubbub and ruckus was because the hosts were doing their annual performance. This year, Richie had a little surprise for his wife Liz, a song and dance by the boys to her favorite song … *My Girl* by The Temptations.

The four of them, Richie, Dan, Julian, and Ranger cleared some room, and accompanied by the angels, lined up four-across in front of the shimmering tree.

"Hey, everyone!" Richie announced on the microphone, "Grab your honey for this next one, if she's here. And if not, come and dance with us anyway!"

He took Liz by the hand and ushered her up front. Ranger, Julian, Dan, and the angels welcomed her as she sat in the special chair, beaming ear to ear and blushing bright red.

"I love you, baby!" Richie told her through the microphone, in a steamy smooth R&B tone. "Merry Christmas, sugar ... This one's for you!"

The lights went out. The music began. And the boys started dancing.

Dun ... dun, dun, dun, dun, dun ... Dun ... dun, dun, dun, dun, dun!

I've got sunshi-i-i-i-i-i-ne ... on a cloudy day!

As soon as the spotlight hit the boys, everyone got up and cheered, all over the Pelican Inn. If you've ever seen the Temptations perform *My Girl* live, then you know just how cool the dancing is. But, this one, with Richie singing the lead, and the boys pouring on the moves in the background, and Liz beside herself in that chair, seemed even *better*.

Talkin' bout my girl ...

The guys hit their final pose, and the crowd went crazy.

Richie hugged his wife and planted a giant kiss on her, and most of the men in the room did the same, including Rob Shaw with Carolijn, out there in the middle of the floor.

With Michael watching them.

The party continued on pretty late into the evening, finally winding down around 1:30 am. By almost every account, it was a dazzling celebration. The boys had all of the bedrooms rented out upstairs, so people who wanted to stay and avoid the undulating drive back over the hill were welcome. Although most of the guests went home, about a quarter stayed. Some enjoyed the short walk out to the moonlit beach, some retired to the bedrooms, but most just hung around, talking and laughing over a nightcap or late night snack.

In the morning, there was a great English breakfast of bangers and scones, and peppermint hot chocolate for everyone.

When all was said and done, every guest had checked out of the Pelican Inn by 11:30 that next Sunday morning.

But it wasn't until about 7:00 am two days later, on that Tuesday, however, that a fishing charter discovered Michael Roman's body floating face down in the Pacific.

About three-quarters of a mile offshore.

5 CHARLESTON, SC

Abraham Lincoln's primary goal was always to keep the Union intact, despite slavery. But when the Confederacy seceded, that was too far in his eyes. They lost the war, and slavery went with it.

Sam parked her black 1953 Siata 208CS Stabilimenti Farina Spyder convertible along the Battery promenade, grabbed a pen and paper, and jumped out. The history of it was: her grandfather Tommaso gave her that car about five years ago, after having tinkered on it for decades before that. His father, Sam's great-grandfather, had been a part-time technician for the Italian auto parts and tuning shop Siata during the War, before the company started making its own line of cars, about the time Tommaso was born. And, when he was younger, *Nonno*, as Sam called her grandfather, worked for them too, fixing up Barchetta Sports, and Abarth 750s, and Springs and Dainas, and 208Ss, which, as *Nonno* always told her, the great Steve McQueen used to drive. *Nonno* worked two other jobs during that time as well, jobs that even better reflected his wonderful, kind-hearted personality: 1. Gianduiotto apprentice: the candy maker master-in-training who uses the hazelnut chocolate spread *gianduja* to make the famous upturned boat-shaped chocolates native to the Piedmont region of Italy; and 2. attendant to the sick and infirmed at *Piccola Casa della Divina Provvidenza* (Little House of the Divine Providence), better known as the *Cottolengo*, a centuries-old Catholic charity house located in the quaint Aurora section of Turin called Borgo Dora, where he grew up, and where he met his sweetheart, Sam's *Nonna* Giulia. Today, Borgo Dora is known for its *Balon*, an outdoor flea market held in the neighborhood's beautiful, narrow and twisted streets, and for the *Cottolengo*.

Anyhow, *Nonno* Tommaso was a sweet old man, and he gave her the car.

Nonno and *Nonna* had saved their pennies and now were living the good life south of Turin, on the Cinque Terre, in just the prettiest seaside village you ever saw, called Manarola.

He still tinkered with engines from time to time. Fiats mostly. That's where Sam learned to work on cars.

Truth be told, she wanted to be just like him one day.

She hoped to have a career that helped people too, and made them happy. And, she dreamed of having a beautiful house on the coast, like her *Nonno*. Perhaps one like these antebellum estates along the promenade here on East Battery or lining Murray Boulevard, but somewhere right on the beach, like Teahupo'o, or Zanzibar, St. Ives or the Florida Keys. For now, though, she had to settle for a one bedroom apartment on King Street, a block down from the Mellow Mushroom, the best pizza restaurant in town, where she was an assistant manager and server.

Not for long, though, because Sam was leaving Charleston.

She took a seat on a park bench among the Columbiads, the smooth bore, large-caliber, muzzle-loading cannons that once guarded Charleston Harbor. Out there in the water was the infamous Fort Sumter, site of the first shots of the American Civil War. April 12, 1861. Many never realized that it wasn't Confederate troops occupying Fort Sumter at that time, when South Carolina and six other states decided to secede from the Union and form their own nation called the Confederate States of America, but it was the Union Army, the North. They had abandoned their vulnerable position at nearby Fort Moultrie several months earlier, moving into Sumter in an attempt to be better able to control the entrance to the harbor. This was the United States of America after all, and they needed to keep the Union together. The Confederacy did not comply, however, and fired on the Union garrison at Sumter for nearly two full days. 4003 Confederate guns and mortars bombarded the fort from every direction, beginning in counterclockwise order, one single shot every couple of minutes. The infidels even utilized the dreaded *heated shot*, cannonballs emblazoned red hot in the furnace, to shell the Yankees and burn most of the wooden structures in the fort to the ground. History has it that many of the socialite citizens of Charleston gathered along the waterfront and on the grand porches of these beautiful homes, and toasted the assault. After thirty-four hours, the Union forces waved the white flag ... and surrendered.

No-one was killed in the fighting at Fort Sumter, but two Union soldiers did lose their lives, ironically, in an artillery explosion during their ceremonial 100-gun salute to the U.S. flag ... a concession the Confederates allowed as part of the Union surrender.

Then, the defeated Union troops took the *Fort Sumter Flag*, its thirty-three stars and thirteen stripes ... and left the South.

"Okay, what do I need to take with me?" Sam thought out loud.

Only the essentials.

She looked out over the water, tapping her pen to her lip.

And, what are the things I want to try to accomplish? Appreciate? Enjoy?

Every single day.

She opened up her journal and started to write.

- *Get out, go for a walk, and see something amazing*
- *Keep a good journal, and take lots and lots of pictures*
- *Enjoy something fun to eat, no matter the price, or the calories*
- *Meet at least one extraordinary person, and tell them why you think they are*

- *Be kind to everyone & grateful for the journey each and every day*

Sam thought to add *And never, ever look back* as the final entry, but she refrained.

She didn't want to be reminded of Charleston, or Damien.

She'd moved on, past the fact that he wasn't right for her. Past what had happened. She was ready, and looking forward, and positive. Excited about her fresh, new start.

Sam worked her last shift at the restaurant that Saturday night, the manager Marcus instructing her to take her last hour off, paid, and not worry about cleaning up. So, her best mate Sally walked her home. About half an hour later, though, Marcus called. He told her he needed her help with something and asked if she minded coming back.

Of course, she didn't, so Sam and Sally walked the block-and-a-half back.

When they arrived, Marcus was waiting outside with a gift in his hand.

Aww ... How nice, Sam thought to herself.

The restaurant was dark inside, and she was about to ask, when ...

Surprise!

The lights burst on, and Sam saw through the glass the whole Mellow Mushroom filled with co-workers and friends, her favorite customers and locals, all in party hats, blowing on streamers like it was New Year's Eve. An enormous sign stretching from wall to brick wall: *Bon Voyage, Sam! We love you!*

Sam stood stock still, her eyes welling up.

Samantha Amaris was a tough girl, didn't cry much, except for the really important things. She had too much else to do. She grew up in Margaret River, Australia, after her Italian father moved there for work and met her *mum*. She remembers being a bit of a tomboy, playing cricket and footy, of all sports for a young girl, starting when she was about five. She also remembers playing in the sand at the beach almost year-round, with her friends, especially her *best mate* Oola, a sunshiny little aboriginal girl whose name meant *red lizard*. "Oola … So *coola!*" she always called to her.

The family transplanted to North Carolina when Sam was twelve, again close to the water, in a town called Kill Devil Hills, on the 200 mile long, often less than a mile wide string of barrier island coastline called the Outer Banks. The place where the Wright Brothers took their first powered airplane flights in December, 1903. (The town didn't exist yet back then, so Kitty Hawk, not Kill Devil Hills, is listed as the world famous, historic first flight site … though it's located about four miles north of the actual spot the flights took place.)

Sam loved it there.

First Flight High School, an odd name because both the Wright Brothers were dropouts, had yet to open, so Sam commuted the 16 miles to Roanoke Island, to Manteo High School. And, she did everything there. Student government vice president; editor of *Sound to See*, the school's monthly newspaper; star of the Redskin cross country, soccer and surf teams. And, best of all, member of the mighty board game club.

The board game club was her favorite.

They took their games on the road, visiting the old folks in the assisted living community, kids in the hospital, and their specially-abled friends at the Dare County Extension Center, where they brought a lot of joy. Sam often thought how her pal Oola, the little *red lizard*, who loved to give, and share, and go, just like her, would have been a great board game club member too.

And a great Manteo Redskin.

Anyhow, North Carolina was also where she met Damien.

Sam teared up as she entered the restaurant, seeing all those faces.

She'd spent most of her life serving others, in high school, taking care of her sick mother, the restaurant, Damien. She'd never really done anything at all just for herself. And, that was okay. But, now she'd decided it was okay too if she did. Just a couple things … Like take some time and replenish on this trip, and one day have that house on the beach.

That's it.

That's all she wanted.

"Where exactly are you planning on going?" Sally asked when Sam finally had a chance to slow down for a minute.

"You know, not really sure." Sam hadn't told anybody anything in detail about the trip yet, because she hadn't planned much yet herself. "But, I do have a few things on the itinerary."

"Okay, let's write them down then, girl … on this napkin." Sally reached for a pen out of an order pad holder, "Because this one needs to know where her very *best mate* is gonna be!" Sam didn't have much of an Aussie accent left at all, but you could definitely hear it when she said things like *best mate*.

And, Sally loved saying stuff like that.

"Righty, then. Let's see … First, I'm going for brunch with my *best mate* Sally in the morning." Sam smiled. "Then, I'm going home for a couple of days." Sally started writing it down. "Umm, I'll be in Durham

Wednesday night, and ... oh, Sautee Nacoochee for Christmas ... Eureka Springs, Arkansas, after that ... and the plan is California by New Year's Eve."

"Sautee Nacoochee ... Ooooh, Sammy!" Sally got all big-eyed.

Sam rolled hers.

"What's his name again?"

Sam used to have a friend at Manteo, a nice guy she ended up going to junior prom with, who now owned and operated the bed & breakfast called Lucille's Mountaintop Inn & Spa, in Sautee Nacoochee, Georgia. He'd recently phoned, and left her a message.

It was an open invitation to come and stay, anytime, on the house.

There was a panoramic view of the Blue Ridge Mountains, he said, she just could not miss.

Sam thought it might be a good time to go.

"Totally not like that, Sal." Sam balked. "He was just a friend ... nothing more."

"Okaaayy ... But, you never know ... His place sounds fabulous."

Sam shook her head and smiled.

"I'm obviously very excited for you, Sam," Sally went on. "I think it's a great decision you made."

Sam paused, then looked Sally in the face, more looking through her, and Sally looked back, her expression more like a mother than a friend.

"You mean going on this trip, or leaving ... you know?" Sam asked.

"Well ... both, if you put it that way."

Sally knew Sam didn't want to talk about it, because Damien had been trying to contact her almost every other day to get her to change her mind, and she was sensitive about it.

It had been hard for her.

"You can't stay with a selfish, arrogant, heartless guy like that, Sam ... Plus, he's a cheater." Sally let herself go. "It's great you're doing something like this. For you ... I wish I was!"

"Yeah, I know," Sam responded, more than a little resigned. She looked Sally in the eyes ... "It's not love when they don't love you back, huh?"

Sam thanked everyone, and the crowd had mostly said their goodbyes and gone when Sally proposed they do one last round and get out of there. "You've got a big day tomorrow, girl." She cleared the table, then shoved the napkin itinerary into her coat pocket.

"Can't forget this!"

The girls went around, bid farewell to the stragglers, first downstairs, then up, and on the patio out back, then they started to leave.

As they descended the double-section rear stairs leading to the dining room and the exit, they stopped.

There was some sort of commotion happening midway across the dining room floor.

Marcus, along with a couple of the servers, appeared to have had intercepted this ... woman, who looked angry. They were holding their hands up, trying to redirect her the other way, back towards the front door. She was tall, and thin, with beyond-the-shoulder white-blonde hair covering most of her face. She also had on a long, black hooded raincoat.

And black sunglasses.

The noise from the bar made it difficult to hear what they were saying.

Suddenly, Marcus raised his voice. "It's a private party, ma'am ... I'm sorry!"

Then, as if in slow motion ... the woman turned, and saw Sam and Sally standing there, halfway up the stairwell.

Marcus and the other employees looked too. The woman glanced towards Sally for a second, then shifted her head to Sam, her face mostly hidden behind the sunglasses and her hair, and the collar of her coat ... But, you could see her mouth, smeared bright red in lipstick, was distorted.

She then turned for the front doors, and left.

"What was that all about?" Sally asked Marcus.

A little taken aback, he said the woman was standing outside, looking in through the glass. And, that when someone unlocked the door to let somebody else out ... she walked in. Marcus stopped her and told her it was a private party. Then, she became very upset.

Marcus looked at Sally, and then Sam.

"She said she was *looking for someone* ..."

6 BONEYARD BEACH

People desire faith and love more than they want reason or science. Freud was wrong.

Sally spent the night at Sam's. She'd planned to sublet the apartment while Sam was gone; it was a good deal because the rent was cheaper than where she was in Sullivan's Island, and the commute to work much shorter. Sam didn't know when, or even if, she'd ever be back to Charleston, so Sally taking over her lease was probably the best thing for everyone.

Today was the first day of her trip, and Sam was eager to start the things on her to-do list. First, she wanted to enjoy a good meal. When she was with Damien, he always tried to make her feel subconscious about her appearance, most likely for control purposes, making comments about what she wore, what she was eating, her hair, makeup, whatever.

Starting now, she would never be concerned about any of that stuff again.

It was a late fall heat spell in the South, so the girls took the top down in Sam's car and drove just outside of town to a restaurant called The Fat Hen, in Johns Island. It was a local favorite Sam had read about that served delightful French Lowcountry dishes made with ingredients from the surrounding farming community. Sam ordered the cheese plate, crème brûlée French toast, and some bacon cheese grits. And Sally, fried green tomatoes, BBQ brisket & macaroni cheese open faced sandwich, and pommes frites. They laughed and ate and had the best time.

After brunch, the girls complimented the servers, took photos with the chef and the menu, posed for a few out on the porch under The Fat Hen sign, then drove back to King Street, parked, and got out. It was understood that neither of them would make it a long goodbye, so they exchanged a couple of *okays* and *see you soons*, hugged, and went opposite ways. Sally waved, standing there on the sidewalk with a key in the apartment door and a hand over her mouth ... and Sam waved back, tears in her eyes, watching her best mate once more disappear in the rear view.

It was nice as the Siata headed north on U.S. Route 17, across the Arthur Ravenel Jr. Bridge, one of the longest cable-stayed bridges in the Western Hemisphere, and towards *home*.

She realized there wasn't much left there, in Kill Devil Hills, but she wanted to go anyway ... *Might as well start from the beginning*.

Sam also realized she'd already accomplished three of the five things on her list for today, and the fourth was probably happening right now via a heart-shaped note she left on the refrigerator door:

Dearest Sally

Although I met you many years ago

I wanted to tell you today how special this meeting has turned out to be for me

You have been my biggest supporter, and my closest friend, in all the good times

And through the pain

I will always be there for you, like you have been for me, and I just wanted to tell you

You are the best mate in the whole wide world ... and I love you

See you again soon ...

Sam

Sam had changed her number so only the people who really needed to could reach her. She checked her phone. The urge struck suddenly to hit the button and call Sally right now, but she knew it would only be sadness on the line, and possibly a *What the heck am I doing? I'm turning around right now and coming back.*

So, she drove on. She still had her walk to do today anyway.

The following is what she had read about the place where she was heading:

If you're reading this, you've probably never visited Bulls Island. You haven't been on the ferry for the eco-tour that takes you through the breathtaking estuary. Or taken that first step onto the island, map in hand, quietly anticipating the start of your adventure. You've never walked down Alligator Alley or soaked up the beauty of Boneyard Beach or sat still at the viewing platform to witness Black Skimmers feeding.

It's time to go.

Sam had been looking forward to it for a week.

Bulls Island is located just forty minutes north from the bustle and charm of Charleston ... but a universe away in terms of access to solitude. There were loggerhead turtles there, bottlenose dolphins and bald eagles, 293 species of birds, and of course the alligators. 5,000 acres of stunning coastland, sawgrass marshes, minks, otters, bobcats and deer. What Sam wanted to see most, however, was the jewel of the whole place, Boneyard Beach. A three-mile stretch of sand at the northeast corner of the island that was literally a forest stranded in the surf.

Sam arrived at the Bulls Island Ferry early in the afternoon. She decided to do the eco-tour, which was thirty minutes, then the boat dropped her off on the island ... She felt excited, and nervous, and emotional all at the same time. With no cars on the island, and a very limited number of people, Sam could wander the trails without much worry of hazard, aside from the alligators, of course.

So she pulled her hat down, disembarked, and started walking.

It wasn't long before she caught her first glimpse of the open Atlantic waters to the north. She was close, so she took a deep breath, put her head down, and pressed on.

Then, there it was.

The surf at Boneyard Beach is constantly sweeping the sand away out into the ocean. Scarecrows of trees that have grown there for centuries have literally lost their ground. With the sun setting, it was one of the most stark and gorgeous things Sam had ever seen. Hundreds of sun-bleached oaks, and cedars, and pines, stranded and half-submerged, washed away in the waves.

What a perfect symbol this was going to be, she thought, reading about it a few weeks ago. A place to renew, and connect, and say goodbye to the past.

Goodbye, Charleston. Goodbye, heartache. Goodbye, Damien.

But, as she stood there, what she saw was something else.

> *Once was a beautiful forest, now reduced to a wasteland of dead and dying trees by the cruel and unrelenting sea.*

She felt remarkably alone.

With the sun vanishing overhead, Sam had just enough time to take a few more photos, then get back to the ferry by dark.

Her rest stop for the night was Myrtle Beach, an impressive tourist destination with every possible kind of attraction, from places like Broadway at the Beach and Barefoot Landing, to Sea Screamers and Skywheels, swamp tours and boardwalks, ocean piers and pelicans, and beachfront hotels as far as the eye can see. It was a two hour drive to Myrtle Beach, but the trip seemed much longer tonight.

"Get it together, Sam," she told herself.

A glint from passing lights reflected from her phone, which lay there in the darkness of her passenger seat.

She glanced over at it.

"Thurston, play some music."

A song came on. A beautiful one. Lush, with beautiful instruments and a beautiful voice.

It was one of her favorites.

> *Take me now, take me anywhere you're going*
>
> *'Cause I can't stay here, I won't make it long*
>
> *And this piece of my soul you're controlling*
>
> *In this time and this space where we belong*

She turned it up, and started singing.

> *You're breathing is quickening*
>
> *Take my lungs I owe you*
>
> *Lost and cold now*
>
> *There's a place in my arms I can keep you*

Tears filled her eyes.

> *A billion stars and here we are, the same bit of dirt holding our weight*
>
> *And before it drags us under, I can make you feel young again*

As the last few dark miles of Highway 17 rolled by outside, Sam clutched onto the wheel. Why wasn't she feeling any better?

This trip will be so good for you. You're so much better off without him. Her friends all told her. And, they were all right.

But, the one thing she really wanted. Always wanted. The only thing that matters.

What she had hoped for in Charleston, but was never there ... still wasn't.

Sam arrived at her Myrtle Beach hotel, the Ocean Creek Resort, at 11:00 and checked in. Then, she settled into a long bath.

Afterwards, she decided to go down outside, take a walk across the footbridge out back, across the creek, and onto the beach. Leaned back in a lounger, she opened her journal, and scratched a check mark next to each of the five items on her to-do list for the day.

Then, she sat and watched the ocean.

Just after midnight, before she got up and went back in, she added one last thing to her list.

- *It's okay to fall in love again today*

7 NAPA VALLEY

In the Bible, sulfur is known as *brimstone*, and *Hell* is said to smell of it. Chemically, sulfur bonds with many elements. It is soft, yellow, and under extreme heat, it melts and looks like blood. Love, on the other hand, is pure, strong, and does not falter under pressure. It is sweet-smelling, every color, and it never fails.

Moral of the story: Avoid sulfur. Pursue love.

Ranger got back before noon Sunday morning, and Bernard was thrilled. He had made plans to visit a few friends this week to drop off some presents before Christmas on Friday, and Bernard was going with him.

Every year during the holidays, Ranger and Bernard went to visit a boyhood friend of his, Francois (Frans for short), and his family, if they were in town. Ranger's and Frans' families were close as the two of them were growing up. The boys played sports together, and the dads coached, while the moms did their pottery and paintings, acting in the local theater, and raised horses. Frans was a good guy, for the most part, despite always trying to be more than what he was. Ranger had to protect him more than a couple times because his mouth kept getting him into trouble. You know, writing checks his body couldn't cash.

Ranger absolutely loved Frans' parents, though ... Especially now, that he was all alone. And, they loved him. He was *family*.

There was only one problem: they were all USC folk, the University of Southern California, and Ranger was Cal. Rivals to the end. It made for good banter at the dinner table.

Frans had invited Ranger and Bernard to stay in one of his parents' plush vacation homes, built up onto a wooded hillside overlooking the town of St. Helena, in the Napa Valley. Ranger was looking forward to it.

So, he packed a bag and headed to the convertible.

Bernard was beside himself to go. He loved sticking his face through the open window, smelling all the smells, and mugging at all the passers-by.

The two of them made their way up the 101 north to Highway 37, then to the 121 and 12 into Napa, and finally to the Broadway of all wine country routes, Highway 29 and the Silverado Trail.

Open for travel in 1852, the Silverado Trail started as an old silver and wine trading route. Famously, bandits like Black Bart, who was known to leave taunting but humorous poetic messages behind at the scenes of his 1880's stagecoach heists, plied their trade here. About a century later, Stag's Leap Wine Cellars (one of forty or so wineries along the trail, and two-hundred in the valley) made the area famous again by claiming first prize in the *Judgment of Paris*, a tasting competition crowning the finest of French and California wines, with its 1973 vintage Cabernet Sauvignon.

Before settling in, Ranger made a stop at the fanciful Long Meadow Ranch farmers market, a renovated barn on Main Street in St. Helena, and picked up some goodies for the stay. Then, he and the dog drove west about a mile, past the old cemetery and Sulphur Canyon, up the access road to Frans' parents' house.

As if the drive up there wasn't amazing enough, the house was out of this world. A big sunny orange villa, modeled after a seventeenth century Bavarian hunting *schloss* (manor house), it looked more like a chateau than a vacation home. The majestic lawn out front was terraced beautifully, with a fifty foot Roman pool of the gods stretched across it. Animals on pulpits made of stone played all along the promenade balustrade. There were spires spanning the roof and rounded turrets at its corners, and an amazing regal deck encircling three quarters of the five thousand square foot estate's main level.

Inside, eighteen foot tall French doors ushered you into the living room, with its thirty-six foot tall ceilings. There were nine fireplaces throughout, and marble hearths, bedrooms fit for kings, and bathrooms with terracotta floors and walk-in showers you could spend all day in unwinding.

"Wow." Ranger told Bernard as they stepped out of the Malibu.

Bernard agreed, taking off and galloping across the massive lawn.

"Good idea, boy. Let's go for a run."

Ranger had some energy to release as well, after last night, so he dropped his things inside, slipped on some gear, and grabbed Bernard's leash ... although it didn't look like they'd need it because it seemed improbable there was another soul around for tens of miles in the hills behind them.

Finding the trail, they took off uphill into thick groves of live oak, Douglas and incense fir. Bernard was great in that he could run with Ranger all day, and Ranger kept up with him, who was fast. They followed the long switchbacks up the mountain west of the *schloss* for about half an hour, then scaled a rocky path next to a small creek, Ranger pausing to take in the panorama back east of the valley and town, and Bernard sloshing further upstream into the wood, playing in the water.

"Look at this view," Ranger breathed, turning to find Bernard, who wasn't there.

It was suddenly all quiet ... As he stood there, Carolijn's words from last night, from the snug, for whatever reason surfaced in his mind.

> *I don't know if any of it really matters ... None of it matters ... Nothing matters, without ...*

Then, all of a sudden, *Wooooooooooo!*

It was Bernard.

"Here, boy!" Ranger called. He recognized his dog's tone of distress and strode up the path.

It was really strange at times, it appeared Ranger did things physically kind of superhuman. The way he climbed up something so fast, or jumped over something, or made the incredibly dangerous look so easy. If you saw it, you'd say to yourself, *Did he really just do that?*

Ranger got to Bernard, who was standing there at uncertain threat, focused on the bushy ledge directly above him, and halted to assess. Bernard was aware that Ranger had arrived, but didn't dare remove his eyes from that ledge.

Snarling, he took a few steps left towards his master, and ten feet above him in the bush, footsteps followed.

What was that up there?

Ranger moved slowly towards Bernard and the ledge, lifted his shirt, which was already off, and held it spread above his head. Then together, they moved slowly away, both growling. The footsteps followed a few more seconds, then stopped, and Ranger and the dog retreated back down along the stream until they reached the main trail again.

Ranger put Bernard on his leash and started the lengthy trek back down the switchbacks, south first, making the first hairpin, then turning back to the north.

Where is it? Ranger surveyed the hill above them, then the trail again.

And, there it was ... twenty feet in front of them. A mountain lion just off the path to their left, crouching with its long teeth exposed.

Ranger and Bernard skid to a stop, almost toppling over each other.

The lion stared them down, then for some reason, turned and darted back up the hill, straight up. Ranger wasted no time resuming his sprint downhill. They were still probably twenty-five minutes away from the house, and he could hear the cougar *screeching* and *scawing* in the distance.

They made the hairpin turn to the right and bolted on.

"Huff, huff, huff."

They paced steadily down, then ... *SWIPE*! A giant paw slashed out of the brush and grazed Bernard, who somehow detected it a split second before and leapt in an attempt to avoid it, somersaulting over the lion, who proceeded to fly across the path right in front of Ranger ... They were like two speeding trains that had just averted a head-on collision. Bernard landed violently, sliding on his ribs and back across the rocks at the side of the trail, but he regained his feet. The mountain lion rolled, twisting end over end two rotations, only to right itself and locate its targets immediately. And re-establish its attacking stance.

"Come on, boy!" Ranger commanded, and they took off again.

He glanced back at the hill and saw the cat going up it once more, then down at Bernard, who was bleeding.

Ranger contemplated cutting straight down the mountain because the lion appeared to be intercepting them along each switchback, but the brush was thick and the slope was steep. So, he decided to stick to the trail, picking up a couple fist-sized rocks to use in defense. And, they continued running.

Sure enough, as they reached the midpoint of the next section, there the big cat was again. This time, however, a little farther up the hill, watching.

They made the next turn, and the same thing happened, then again on the ensuing couple of switchbacks until the lion wasn't there anymore.

"You okay, boy?" Ranger wiped the blood from Bernard's wounds as they got to the house. Thankfully, they were only superficial, just scrapes and scratches.

Woooo! Bernard yelped, but Ranger knew he was alright.

The two of them sat out on the porch for a while, keeping one eye on the hill behind them. The sun was across the sky as Ranger got up to shower. He still had a busy night ahead. He was on his way to meet Frans for dinner, and then visit Frans' parents after that.

The Chateau Montelena Winery in Calistoga was hosting the pretty fancy private dinner, and Frans had asked Ranger four or five times over the past few months if he would come. Less than half an hour drive north, past the historic Beringer Vineyards and Charles Krug, the hot springs and Old Faithful Geyser, the beautiful ivy-draped 1880s castle was ready for a dazzling night.

The dinner was a celebration. Like Stag's Leap had done in the red wine category, Montelena had won top honors for whites at the Judgment of Paris with its '73 Chardonnay. A big deal in wine circles.

The event was packed with Chardonnay lovers and hobnobbers from all over, and when he got there, Ranger met some of them touring the estate with Frans and his girlfriend Sophie.

"Pretty sweet spread, huh, Ranger?" Frans gushed. "You know, babe," he turned to Sophie, "Ranger and I have been pretty much best friends since like … when we were in diapers. Huh huh!" He laughed. "Back when I was pinning his butt in the playpen. One, two, three!" He pounded on a barrel as they strolled the wine cave beneath the chateau.

The best Frans ever was was third string on the junior high wrestling team.

"Awww … That's sweet, babe. You're so … studly."

Frans reached up to give her a kiss.

She was taller than he, pretty much by a lot. One of those part-time model types in heels. He sort of looked like a little boy next to her, in his striped pastel jacket, cotton white pants and loafers sans socks.

"So, buddy, did you get a chance to do anything exciting at the house today?"

"Well, nothing much ..."

Montelena was a lovely place, remarkable really. The caves. And, there were paths leading out to a lake called Jade Lake. There was a temple garden and crooked footbridges connecting a couple of islands to the main property. Chinese legend has it that evil spirits are only able to traverse water in straight lines, so the crooks in the bridges.

The rusticated stone chateau itself was amazing too, built into the hillside with thick walls. Montelena was modeled after a Gothic castle gatehouse, complete with battlements, parapets, crenels and merlons, narrow archer windows, and a large wooden arched front door where the spiked portcullis would have been. The works.

One could marvel at the place for hours, and many people tonight were. But, not Ranger. Not tonight. He wasn't into it, and Frans could tell.

"Anybody hungry yet?"

He wrapped up their tour of the winery cellar, then directed Sophie and Ranger to their fancy table in the middle of the courtyard. As if on cue, a trio of young ladies approached and joined them. More model types. Friends of Frans.

He and Sophie proceeded to kiss them all repeatedly on all of their cheeks.

"Ranger, these are my friends ... Aprele, Heather, and Atlee." Frans announced.

Ranger rose and had his cheeks kissed as well.

"Ladies, Ranger was just enlightening us about how he fought off a mountain lion today on his run behind my parents' house … I mean *really*, Ranger? Wow!"

The girls all *wowed*. Ranger instantly regretted telling them.

"That lion better be thankful he didn't run into me, huh, babe?" Frans looked to Sophie. "'Cause we'd be having cougar tartare with the Chardonnay tonight … Am I right?!"

Most of the table laughed.

"I bet it would have tasted like chicken!" One of them added.

Brilliant.

Ranger muscled through the dinner, the girls asking him inconsequential questions and telling frivolous stories, and Frans' expression losing hope by the second. It was obvious he was trying to set his buddy up, a *thank you* perhaps for putting up with him all these years, but more than that, a chance to give the man who had *everything* something he didn't yet have.

For once, Ranger would be like him. *Any one of them you'd like. Take your pick, buddy.* But, it wasn't working.

"Hey, guys, I've had a really enlightening time tonight, and I appreciate each and every one of you." Ranger had this way of never actually lying with his words. "Frannie, I love you like a … little brother." Frans' grin turned straight, and he sat up taller in his chair to save face. "But, I've got a date to meet your parents in about half an hour."

The table sat there and stared.

"Sophie, Aprele, Heather, Atlee … You all have a magnificent evening."

And, just like that, Ranger was gone.

Frans' parents were out at the White Barn tonight, a gem of an 1872 estate that was once Civil War General Erasmus Keyes' home and winery. Now, it serves as an all-volunteer, seventy-five seat performing arts venue that donates all of its proceeds to charity. Just the cutest little place, with a white picket double staircase outside, deck for square dancing, and nineteenth century bucolic charm inside, it looked beautiful in the clear night air.

You can see it there at the end of Sulphur Springs Avenue, down the hill from where Ranger and Bernard were staying.

Frans' mom was singing in a Christmas concert with the Saint Gabriel Celestial Brass Band, and his dad was serving dessert and drinks in plastic cups and paper plates during intermission in the back.

The performance was a delight. Inspiring. There were couples there all over the audience, mostly older, some holding hands, and some just sitting. Ranger smiled as several of the gentlemen nodded off, arms crossed across their laps and programs still in hand, eyeglasses slipping down the slopes of their noses.

But it was okay, because when they awoke, their wives were still there beside them, snapping their fingers and tapping their toes to the music.

Ranger sat near the back, close to Frans' dad, who manned the refreshments table dutifully even while the performance was going.

After the show, they were all able to go outside to the deck to catch up.

The three of them hugged, and laughed, and reminisced, like they did every year. As far as each was concerned, this was family.

Of course, Frans had already phoned his mother earlier about the mountain lion incident, so they conferred about it. "It was probably protecting its cubs. That's what we mothers do, you know." She told Ranger, holding his hand with both of hers, like mothers do.

They'd already figured Frans would try to fix Ranger up sometime on his trip to the valley. Mom had made a comment at the dinner table recently when Frans and Sophie were there, about Ranger and wondering if he'd fall in love and get married one day. Frans' eyes lit up like a Christmas tree. So, they guessed he would invite *one* of Sophie's friends tonight.

They just didn't realize he would be so generous.

"Forgive him, Ranger," she entreated. "He's only trying to be useful. Trying to do something so you'd look up to him for once." Dad chuckled. "He's getting on pretty well with Sophie. They're good for each other, and he's very proud that she is with him. You know, Ranger … love knows no bounds."

"Yeah … not even for our wonderful Frannie."

Frans' father stepped in closer.

"You know, tonight was like the *Judgment of Paris* meets the *Judgement of Paris*," he said. Frans' father explained …

The *Judgement of Paris* is a story in Greek mythology where Zeus hosted a marriage celebration for the hero Peleus and his wife, and Eris, the goddess of discord, was not invited … Zeus figured she'd probably ruin the party for everyone. So, in her indignation, Eris threw a golden apple with the inscription *FOR THE FAIREST ONE* on it into the party. Three goddesses claimed the apple, Aphrodite, Hera, and Athena, and they asked Zeus to choose which of them was in fact the fairest and should have it. Zeus wanted no part of that decision, so he passed it on to Paris, an impartial Trojan mortal.

The goddesses then bathed in the springs of Ida, and took their turns trying to persuade Paris to choose them. Hera offered to make him royalty over all if he chose her. Athena offered him abundant wisdom and military skill. But then, Aphrodite, the most cunning, offered to give unto him the most beautiful of all the women in the world, Helen of

Sparta, if he selected her. Paris chose Aphrodite, and Helen, who was delivered to him ... stolen from her husband Menelaus, king of Greece.

The Greeks were furious ... Their expedition to retrieve Helen in Troy was the mythological story of the cause of the Trojan War, and the legend of the Trojan Horse.

"The *Judgement of Paris* has been the muse of many a famous artiste, you know, Ranger." Frans' father informed. "Botticelli, Rubens, Renoir."

Frans' father was never really into art all that much, but he studied it because his wife was. He'd study all the masterpieces and the movements because *she* enjoyed it.

Because he loved his wife that way ... and she loved him for it.

He winked at her as he finished the story. And, she winked back.

"Our son proved tonight he's both a wine aficionado *and* master historian all at the same time. And he didn't even know it!" Dad joked and the three of them laughed together out loud.

Ranger and Frans' parents exchanged gifts there at the barn, as their time this year together would be quick. The parents were heading on a trip to the beautiful and remote Brazilian Ilha Fernando de Noronha in the morning.

Ranger thanked them so much for their hospitality, and their love. He hugged them good, and went on his way up the hill.

And, there was good old Bernard, waiting patiently at the end of his long leash on the deck. He was excited. He knew it was Ranger as soon as he saw headlights coming up the road. Funny how dogs can always tell it's you by just the slightest of familiar sights or sounds. Ranger joined him on the porch, and sat, and opened the gift he had just received.

Of course ... a USC Trojan horse Christmas tree ornament. Unbelievable. Frans' father was assuredly smiling down that hill right now.

Ranger thought about the day, the past two, staring off into black Sulphur Canyon below. Carolijn, Rob, Frans, Sophie, Frans' parents, and the words Frans' mother had just whispered to him as she hugged him goodbye ...

Find love, Ranger ... and never ever let it go.

He just sat in the rocking chair out there on the porch. It was 11:00, Sunday night. He was heading north tomorrow, and was glad to be leaving Napa this time.

In the dark of the warm winter night, Ranger could see the glowing eyes of the critters darting back and forth in the shadows of the brush. Animals doing what they do to survive, and it made him wonder. Out there in the world, this world of selfishness, and heartbreak, and regret. Everything he'd seen, even at home in his own family.

Could something be different out there for him?

8 CAPE FEAR

Generally, the bigger the star, the faster it burns up, and the shorter its life. The brightest stars ... they burn out, exploding into supernovas or black holes after only a few billion years. Smaller stars, like our sun, they are wiser, managing the balance between heat and gravity much better, and lasting much longer ... They often shine for ten billion years or more.

"Hey, Schalky!"

"Ranger!"

"What's happening, my man?"

"Just finished my *Schalk's Senior Sizzle* class where I mix Pilates with tribal dance to give my *more experienced* clients a deeper cardio burn ... (in the background) Super job, Mr. Phipps ... You're a tiger! ... See you next week! Don't forget to do your stretching!"

Schalk's voice was always a welcome sound coming through Ranger's sound system.

Schalk was great. He loved helping people. All people. Fitness first-timers, old ladies, muscle dudes, kids. He was the same with *everyone*, kind and accepting. Schalk was in top shape too, energetic, with a million dollar smile. Most of the time he wore a headband over his blonde hair, which was more brownish on the sides, and fluffy, with sideburns, and both longish *and* balding on top. But, his sort of funny look only made him more lovable. He was certainly a good friend to anybody who wanted one.

"That sounds awesome! Tribal dance? I *really* need to get in for some of that. Lower the age limit just one time for me?"

"You got it, pal!"

"Right on. Hey, buddy, just wanted to let you know I'm leaving for the Russian River today, and I'll be back Wednesday to get ready for Christmas Eve dinner!" Schalk was always available to house sit for Ranger. He loved staying on the water, plus he never traveled anywhere far because of his dedication to the gym. He had a key to the house.

"C'mon, really? Are you serious?" Ranger mumbled to himself. A car had sped up behind him and was now right on his bumper.

"Say again, buddy?" Schalk asked. "(In the background) Okay, see you later, Mrs. White! You're an animal! Keep up the good work, okay?!"

"Oh, nothing, Schalk. I just have this tailgater … Listen, I'll see you at the dinner. Thanks for watching Bernard. You're the best, amigo."

"Okay, cheers, Ranger. Anytime. Peace be with you, brother."

"Yep."

There aren't a lot of places to pass on Highway 29, and the white SUV wasn't backing off, which was a problem, because Ranger didn't appreciate aggressive people … Or, people who caused problems, or treated others badly, or mean people, or rude, or selfish, or vain, or people who felt they needed to put others down to feel better about themselves.

And, people who acted like they were the only ones who mattered in the world.

It was difficult for him to just let that kind of behavior pass.

So, Ranger took his foot off the gas. In the mirror, he could see the woman, talking on her phone, holding it up to her ear, with her French tip nails and salon hairdo, become agitated. She had to brake so quickly and firmly that the front end of her vehicle dipped out of sight beneath Ranger's rear view. Her expression was inflamed, and her mouth began letting Ranger know exactly how she felt about his move ... but, she still didn't back up.

Ranger continued to slow down, and the woman became so incensed, she attempted to pass him across the solid double yellow line, but an oncoming pickup truck forced her to brake and swerve back into her lane.

There was a stop light coming up, as they had reached the little valley town of Yountville. Traffic was heavy coming the opposite direction, and the shoulder on the right was too narrow to use, so Ranger went ahead and decelerated practically to a complete stop, hundreds of feet back still from the signal. The woman was beyond furious.

As the dueling cars crawled up to the red light, Ranger got out.

The woman looked galled at first, then terrified to see the big man approaching her Lexus. She glanced to the right, then back, as if to gauge if there was space enough for an escape, but before she could even try, Ranger was at her door ... And, as coolly as he had stopped, he removed the chewing gum from between his nonchalantly clenched teeth, stuck it to the sheet of paper he was holding, and pressed the paper squarely into the middle of her vision on the windshield. He had written on it in bold, black marker:

You are operating a deadly weapon.

PAY ATTENTION and DO NOT TAILGATE!

Thanks (smiley face)

Ranger returned to his car, and as the signal changed, he drove away.

The woman got stuck at the light.

Sam got a bit of a late start hitting the road in the morning. She took the opportunity to be on a South Carolina beach one last time.

Plus, for some reason, she wasn't real anxious to get back to Kill Devil Hills.

She felt much better today than she did almost all of yesterday, though. It was a brilliant, warm Monday morning, and she had plans to see two of the more extraordinary places along the coast over the next day-and-a-half.

Cape Fear and Cape Hatteras.

Sam crossed the border into North Carolina on Highway 17, the Ocean Highway, making it through the town of Carolina Shores by noon. She was bouncy, and the music was good.

So good it caused her to not notice the dark vehicle riding *her* bumper down the fast lane. Eventually, she glanced up and spotted the car, switched on her blinker and moved over into the slow lane.

"Oh, sorry." She was embarrassed.

Then, she looked into the mirror again, and ... *What?* ... The car was right behind her again.

Close.

It must've tried to pass on the right, she guessed, *and I cut it off again when I moved over.*

"Wooops. Sorry ..." she said to herself and quickly moved back to the left.

The car pulled up alongside the Siata, door-to-door, and stayed there for about 30 seconds. Sam looked over and waved, mouthing the words, *I'm really sorry*, but she couldn't see inside the black Infiniti because of the tinted windows. All she could make out was the silhouette of a figure looking back at her.

Sorry. Sorry, Sorry ...

Sam felt bad.

The car sped off.

Pirates like the intimidating Blackbeard and the gentlemanly Stede Bonnet once patrolled the waters off Bald Head Island and its infamous Cape Fear, where Sam was headed. Before them, Native Americans inhabited the area as a seasonal retreat, much the way vacationers do today. Their midden sites, or shell mounds, formed from harvested oysters and other shellfish, have been discovered all around the island's beautiful creek estuaries.

At the southeastern tip of the island is Cape Fear, where the water sinks off into the ocean, the beginning of thirty miles of shifting and disappearing, then re-emerging sandbars called Frying Pan Shoals, which have made the waters treacherous here for centuries.

Cape Fear has earned its name.

Sam exited Route 17 and drove into Southport, an endlessly romantic village and setting for dozens of television shows and movies. She rode the ferry boat over to the island so she could visit Old Baldy, the state's oldest standing lighthouse, have lunch there, then take her walk for the day along the beach to the point of the cape.

Built in 1817, Old Baldy received a fresh coat of whitewash from the lighthouse keeper every couple of weeks. However, when its lamp was retired from 1935 to 1988, the lighthouse fell into disrepair, and large chunks of white stucco began falling from the tower. Various Samaritans after that came to try to re-stucco the structure's weathered surface, but used such a variety of plasters and paint colors that it produced the unique hodge podge brown and tan look the lighthouse is known for today.

Now, Old Baldy stands proud as the patchwork of all its caretakers' big-hearted intentions.

As Sam walked over to the keeper's cottage to purchase her ticket and climb the 108 steps, five landings, and one ship's ladder to the top of the lighthouse, there weren't any other visitors in sight anywhere around the lighthouse grounds.

Except one.

Sam got her pass and headed out.

She dialed the number for the audio narration to begin her self-guided tour, then took the walkway across the historic property towards the lighthouse's front steps.

From the opposite end of the walkway, the other visitor arrived and entered the lighthouse door behind her.

Inside, Sam made her way up the steps and the rungs pretty quickly, and as she climbed, could hear faint footsteps of somebody climbing below.

She reached the lanthorn room. The stranger came in shortly after.

It was a young woman.

Maybe twenty or twenty-one, she was wearing a sand-tone hooded jacket, no makeup, knee-high suede boots with fur tops and buckles, and a grey knit beanie.

"Hi!" Sam greeted her.

"Hi."

Sam and the girl strolled around the room separately, both surveying the land and the spectacular view of the cape to the East.

"Are you from here?" Sam asked.

The girl nodded. "Are you?" she said back after a second.

"No. Well, kind of ... from North Carolina by way of Australia, but I live in Charleston now." That actually wasn't even true any longer, Sam realized.

"Yeah, I can hear your accent." The girl spoke rather softly.

"Yeah, cheers." Sam replied with a sunshine smile. "Where are you from, exactly?"

"Right here ... Southport. Been here all my life."

"Wow! You're lucky. This place is so gorgeous."

"Yeah ... It's small, though. Sometimes gets pretty ..." She paused.

"Well, I'm the lucky one, then," Sam said. "I can now say I know someone from one of the most beautiful and lonely places in the world ... My name is Sam." She extended her hand.

"Nice to meet you. I'm Abby."

She almost smiled.

They looked out over the wild landscape.

"You see that other lighthouse, over there on the other side of the river?" Abby asked.

"Yes."

"That's the Oak Island Lighthouse ... It's the brightest lamp in all of the United States?"

"No ... Wow! I did not know that."

"It's true ..." Abby went on, "but the lighthouse itself isn't very pretty."

They both gazed over at it.

The Oak Island Lighthouse was a tall structure, kind of looked like a factory smokestack, painted dull gray on the bottom, drab white in the middle, and faded black at the top.

"Yeah ... right," Sam agreed.

"I always liked Old Baldy much better growing up."

Sam smiled.

"It's like that one has the big flashy light and all," Abby continued, "but once you see it, you know, all of it ... it's not that great."

"And Old Baldy," Sam said, recognizing. "Although it's been through a lot ... she's more beautiful because of it."

They both stared across the river mouth.

"A she's the same color brown you wore today." Sam pointed down to Abby's jacket.

The two shared a smile.

"Hey, are you busy this afternoon?" Sam asked. "Would you like to join me for some lunch?"

"Actually ..." Abby paused, "That sounds good ... I haven't eaten in days."

Sam hesitated, then figured she'd save the big questions for later. "Fantastic! Where do you recommend? ... Anywhere, my treat."

"Well, since we're here on the island, we can go over to the Shoals Club. I used to work there in the summers, and my parents are members. The food is good."

"Sounds great. Can I walk on the beach from there afterwards?" Sam asked. "I walk every day."

"Oh, sure. You can walk from the club all the way back here, if you want. And, you'd be going into the sunset, which is definitely one of the best things about this place."

"Perfect!"

"It's a pretty long walk, though, like three or four miles."

"Even better!"

"Alrighty, then … Settled!"

It was clear Abby was starting to feel much better.

The two girls drove out to the Shoals Club in one of Abby's family's ultra-nice golf carts. That's how people commuted out here on beautiful Bald Head Island. They enjoyed an exquisite lunch of scallops wrapped in bacon with maple-pepper glaze; butternut squash, chorizo and feta salad; and short rib quesadillas with caramelized onions and red apple, and the chef picked up the tab.

Abby was apparently one of her favorite guests.

"Yeah … So, that's the story."

Abby had just finished telling Sam all about the boyfriend who'd just recently dumped her. How affectionate and caring he was in the beginning, then how one day he just changed. Like his light faded out all of a sudden, and he went to date another girl.

Sam completely understood.

The two of them ended up having the best time together.

Abby turned out to be so witty, and energetic, and she had a really compassionate heart … totally different from the sullen figure Sam had first encountered. She told Sam everything, about her childhood, and her friends, and her family, and all the hobbies and sports and things she was into. It was kind of like she was a younger version of Sam.

Or, her little sister.

Time was passing by, and Sam still had to get her walk in before dark, so she asked Abby if there was any chance she would like to join her.

"I'd love to!" she bubbled.

So, the two walked out to the tip of Cape Fear, where the sand slinks away into the water, with its diabolical intentions, and they took a bunch of photos, then started the healthy walk back towards Old Baldy. The chef had arranged for a couple of the country club attendants to return Abby's cart to the lighthouse, so it would be waiting for them when they arrived, and before they left, Sam wrote a note for the boys to take back to the chef, telling her how great the food was.

And, how grateful she was to have met her today.

And, on the long beach of the cape, Sam told Abby all about her journey, and Damien.

"So, you're just doing it, huh? … Aren't you afraid, even a little bit?" Abby asked.

"Yes, and no. I mean, I was nervous when I first made the decision to go, then I wasn't afraid at all when I was planning it … As a matter of fact, I was totally excited. Then I was scared all over when I left yesterday, and now that I'm gone, I'm totally not afraid again … Does that make sense?"

"*Totally* … I *totally* get it," Abby replied.

"You know," Sam continued, "It's like … we do what we do because that's what we want. And, if we want something different, then we need to do something different. If you want a different outcome, you have to prove it … And, that means you have to prove it to yourself."

Abby studied the setting sun, focusing in on Sam's words.

"There's a function to all our behavior. Sometimes we choose the same old thing simply because we don't walk far enough past it to see something else ... Each step of my journey, I'm finding, is helping me get beyond the past, you know ... Abby?"

She turned to look at her.

"I know what I was with Damien ... and, I want to find out what I can be without him."

Sam realized, as clearly as the orange and red and purple colors lit up the sky, that her unplanned, unscripted, and unexpectedly enjoyable efforts to help Abby feel better today were doing miles and miles and miles to help herself. She hadn't felt this way in a long time, because of the joy she'd been allowing Damien to steal from her.

"I get it, Sam ... I really do," Abby told her, tears of enlightenment filling her eyes.

The girls reached the bend in the beach at the river mouth, on the end of the island where Old Baldy was. They took more pictures, hugged, and exchanged phone numbers.

"I appreciate you, Abby," Sam said.

"And I appreciate you, Sam!" Abby's spunk seemed like it had to be nearly all the way back. "You know ... I bet the pirates around here were a lot like you."

"Oh, yeah?"

"Yeah ... They weren't afraid either. They just went for it ... Take no prisoners."

"I think that's the only way, *mate!*" She smiled at her new friend.

Sam spun around and peered back behind them, back toward the east, toward the cape ... then looked ahead out to the west, and the traveling sun, and she felt good.

No conflict with what she was doing. No second guessing. No confusion.

No fear, and no dark times going this way, she thought to herself. She looked up at Old Baldy, then at Abby.

"You know ... you look beautiful in brown."

Sam and Abby hugged again, then parted ways.

9 KILL DEVIL HILLS

Ancient Chinese Secret:

1. Victorious warriors win first, then go to war. Defeated warriors war first, then hope to win. *The Art of War*

So, be confident you have the victory, no matter what.

2. If it is obvious your current strategy is leading you to defeat ... retreat. Don't surrender. Don't compromise. Just escape. *The Thirty-Six Stratagems*

In this case, run for the *hills***, and save yourself.**

There's this 60-foot tall granite monument perched atop a 90-foot hill less than a mile away from Sam's family home. The engraving on it reads:

In commemoration of the conquest of the air by the brothers Wilbur and Orville Wright, conceived by genius, achieved by dauntless resolution and unconquerable faith.

The day was December 22, just five days after the anniversary of Orville and Wilbur's historic first flights over a century ago. The brothers' first flight attempt lasted 12 seconds, and went 120 feet; the second, 12 seconds and 175 feet; the third, 15 seconds and 200 feet, and the fourth, a triumphant 59 seconds. 852 feet. And, had Wilbur flown a wee bit further, he might have landed in what was now Sam's front yard.

The Wright brothers took off from knolls of shifting sand dunes back then in 1903, but the fortified embankment that stands at their launch spot today is a 90-foot tall mound called ... Kill Devil Hill.

Sam reached Roanoke Island, where her alma mater Manteo High was, at noon on Tuesday afternoon. Instead of making a left onto the Virginia

Dare Trail and traveling the fifteen minutes or so home, however, Sam went right, south on Cape Hatteras National Park Road, and drove the almost fifty miles to the famous cape and lighthouse.

Cape Hatteras Lighthouse was truly one of the most beautiful things Sam had ever seen. Her parents had taken her here when she was fourteen years old, and even then as a carefree ninth grader, she adored the place. Maybe it was because her *Nonno* and *Nonna* were with them. They couldn't take their eyes off of it. With its red brick base and jet black lantern room, and most of all its 210 feet adorned in black and white spirals to the top.

The colors of *Nonno's* beloved *calcio Italiano* (soccer team) ... Juventus of Turin.

Nonno always said this was one of his favorite sights in the whole world.

Sam was honored today to drive the white sandy beach of the National Seashore, from the lighthouse to Cape Point and back, top down, just like with her grandparents years before.

She remembered how they held hands the entire way.

Back on the highway, she called Sally.

"Hey, girly, whatcha doin'?" Sam was happy to hear a familiar voice.

"Sammy!" Sally was excited as well. "Getting ready to go into work. What about you? ... Where are you?"

"Just leaving Cape Hatteras Lighthouse, heading into town," she answered. "Probably gonna stop by the old favorite Tortuga's Lie for dinner."

Sam had never taken Sally to see the place where she had spent most of her teen years. Matter of fact, she hadn't been back with any of her

Charleston friends at all. But if she had, they would've no doubt gone to Tortuga's Lie. Sam always loved the place. They served the best homemade chocolate chip cookies, there was a beach volleyball court out in the back, and she always appreciated the fact that there were turtles (*tortugas*) in the name.

She enjoyed volunteering with the turtle protection programs on the Carolina coast.

"That sounds great, woman! I miss you so much already, and it's only been two days!"

"I know ... How are things there?"

Sally gave her the rundown, which was a lot of the same old stuff, which was strangely comforting for Sam, who literally had no idea what each next turn had in store for her.

They chatted until Sam reached Nags Head, where the restaurant was.

"Hey, didn't you say you were headed into work, Sal? That was like half an hour ago."

"Pfffft. They can wait. I'm going in on my day off to cover dinner, anyway. I'd much rather be chatting it up with my best friend!"

"*Good onya*, my *jooggy-boonk*!" (Aussie, meaning, *good stuff*, my *good friend*.)

"Whoaa ... what! What does that mean?!"

"I'll send it to you with some pictures tonight. Get to work, and say *hello* to everyone for me. I love you, girl!"

"Ooohh-kaayyy ... Love you too, girl!"

They hung up.

"Oooh, time to walk."

Sam saw the sign and pulled over at Jockey's Ridge State Park, 426 acres of the tallest active sand dune system in the eastern United States. She used to love coming here to fly kites and sandboard with all her friends.

Today, she grabbed her tablet and decided to trek over the dunes soundside to shoot some video of the park, the town, and the seascape below. Just before shutting the camera off, she extended her index finger into the shot, pointed towards the ocean, and disclosed, "Right about there … is our old house."

She hiked back to the car as eventide took over.

Screeeeeech!

Out of nowhere, just before she got to Tortuga's Lie, a car pulled out and nearly broadsided Sam's little roadster from the right.

"Hey!" she protested out loud.

The road was well lit, and there was no reason it shouldn't have seen her.

Sam sure saw it, though.

That's strange … she thought.

The car looked exactly like the black Infiniti she'd tangled with on Highway 17 yesterday. Same tinted windows, same South Carolina plates.

It tore off in front of her, north up the road.

Down south, in Sam's apartment on King Street, Sally swung open the refrigerator door, then gazed up to find the heart-shaped note Sam had left, and the Mellow Mushroom napkin with Sam's itinerary scribbled on it, the two of which she'd scotch-taped together and affixed to the freezer door so she could see them each time she got something to eat or drink.

But ... they weren't where she had left them.

They had moved.

Instead of on the right side of the upper door, they were in the middle of the lower one.

How did that happen?

Sally stood there for a second and looked around.

Then put them back where they were before.

Sam wasn't thinking about encountering anybody extraordinary (for her checklist) today, first, because it was getting late, and second, she really wasn't that excited to be home in the first place.

But, she reminded herself to keep a positive attitude.

Out in front of Tortuga's Lie, she parked her car and went in.

Oh, my goodness! She squinted to make sure the person she saw as she came through the doorway was who she thought it was.

"Wow ... It is him." Sam walked up as the man finished settling his check, his wife and kids heading towards the restroom.

"Hi!" Sam waved. "You probably don't remember me, but I remember you. You're Jack from the surf school."

"Uhh, hello." Jack turned to find her.

"I'm Sam. I was a counselor at one of your summer camps years ago!" She smiled. It's great to see you. What are you doing here at Tortuga's?

Isn't your school down in Wilmington?"

"Yes, yes it is. But, we're up here doing our Christmas camp with Dare County this week." Jack could see the excitement in Sam's eyes. She wanted to hear. "You know, surfing, camping, gift giving with all kinds of folk. Special needs, at-risk, the blind, hearing impaired, medically-fragile, victims of abuse, wounded warriors, kids, adults, families, volunteers, celebrities, everyone. We sure could have used you, Sam. Are you still surfing?"

"Well, not so much anymore. Or, at all. I kind of gave it up when I moved to South Carolina ... But, I'm heading out to California this week, so ..."

"Hey, right on. That's where I'm from originally. Spent quite a bit of time in Half Moon Bay. You should definitely do that," Jack encouraged. "What's in California for you?"

Sam hesitated.

"Just taking the lid off."

"Hey, you remember that ... That's awesome. *Opening up your mind, heart, and soul*, right? He finished.

"For sure. I loved working with those kids. It was one of my favorite things ever!"

Jack's wife and family returned from the restroom, and he introduced them. Sam told them all how much she always valued the impact Jack made on her and her desire to help others, especially back in school.

Before she met Damien.

They all enjoyed hearing it.

"Sam, call me up anytime you need a job. I'll always have a place for somebody like you."

"I definitely will!"

Jack and his family gave Sam a big hug and posed for a few photos for her memory book. Then, they wished her luck, much continued *stoke*, and left.

Suddenly, it felt pretty good to be home.

Sam took a seat in the dining room and ordered a bowl of their wonderful Hatteras style chowder, along with the honey habanero BBQ Bajan bacon cheddar burger and some fries, and of course a couple of the Tortuga's Lie chocolate chip cookies she loved so much.

They were especially good tonight.

She sat there, all alone, and wrote in her journal.

A lot of memories and emotions coming back.

Up the street, at the Glenmere public beach access, on an elevated wooden walkway leading out to the beach, is the Little Red Mailbox. Folks come from all over to visit.

Written in black paint on its red aluminum front door ...

LEAVE A NOTE OF HOPE

Sam had a message she wanted to leave before settling in for the night at her former home, so she took one of the pink heart-shaped notes from her bag, penned a few words, drove over and placed it inside.

Making sure to raise the tiny outgoing mail flag for pick-up.

The note read:

Although it seems you lost your way, and I know the road was hard

Today and for the rest of time, please know that you are loved

Out there in the night on the walkway, Sam listened to the sound of the waves for a while, then returned to her car and drove the last bit up the street.

Then, there it was.

The single story home, raised on stilts, built in the shifting dunes of the sand, was hers now. Her parents left it to her, but nobody lived there anymore. It was a vacation rental for coast-goers year-round. There, with its tucked away entrance, and back doors leading to nothing but the beach and the surf of the Atlantic.

There, at the end of Avalon Drive.

Before it was emptied out, Sam recalled, a painting occupied the wall opposite the front door as you walked in. A lithograph called *The Last Sleep of Arthur*. The painting was of medieval King Arthur of Britain, with his attendants, lying there on the island of Avalon, mortally wounded by Mordred after the Battle of Camlann.

But, that painting had not always been there.

When Sam's family first moved in, what hung on that wall was a shining, life-sized replica of King Arthur's legendary sword Excalibur … That was when Sam's parents were still together. Sam's mother told her that the sword represented the endless protection of their Camelot. A symbol of hers and her father's impenetrable love.

But, it didn't last.

Sam's dad had the sword removed, swapped out for the painting once the trouble started.

He had done his research, and found that, in lore, the mythical island of Avalon was not only the place where Excalibur, the legendary Sword of the Stone and defender of Camelot, was created, but was also the place where King Arthur, noble ruler of Camelot, went to die.

The most painful part for Sam was that the reason King Arthur had battled Mordred in the first place was that Mordred had usurped the crown when Arthur left England for France to confront the man with whom his queen Guinevere was unfaithfully in love.

His right hand, and chief knight of his Round Table, Sir Lancelot.

Not unlike what happened in her house.

Sam climbed the front steps and entered the house, then stood frozen there in the dark until her memory informed her what to do. *Drop your keys on the counter, walk through the living room, and open the sliding glass doors so that the familiar sound of the water soothes you. Then, deep breaths.*

Then, she turned on the lights.

Everything in the house was different, except for the ocean sound, and the basic layout. She could walk that house in the dark with her eyes closed still, if she needed to.

The ocean did work to soothe her, and the sterile pastels and bamboo of the touristy decor lightened the moment a bit as well. But, it looked strange in there, like a funny catalog.

This was definitely *not* her home anymore.

Tired from the long day, and without any desire to reminisce, Sam decided to get to bed. She was up and out of here early tomorrow morning anyway, so she poured herself a glass of water, walked down the hall to the room she slept in for years, changed, and got under the puffy covers.

And retrieved her journal for what she thought were the day's final notes.

About ten minutes later, a car pulled into the driveway, its lights bouncing up into Sam's window as it neared.

"Who is this?" Sam muttered to herself, peering through the blinds.

The person, who was wearing a dark jacket with the hood pulled up, exited the car quickly, then ran up the stairs and delivered five or six stiff raps to the door.

Sam's bedroom was straight down the hall, going left from the house's front entranceway. With her door open, she could see anyone who entered the house as soon as they came in. Unable to sleep, Sam witnessed her mother stumble in that door too many late evenings, then slip away in the other direction to sleep it off on the opposite side of the house. Towards the end, she'd watch her father return even later, after searching throughout the night for his wife.

Knock! Knock! Knock! Knock! Knock!

Sam looked again to try to identify the car, but couldn't. It was too dark.

Then, a voice called out, "Sam … Open up!"

"Oh, my gosh …" she spoke to herself. "What is *he* doing here?"

She hesitated, then got up and cracked open the door.

It was Damien.

"Sam."

"Damien, what are you doing?"

He paused, with a desperate, pleading look in his eyes. "I had to come see you, Sam … before you left."

Sam stood behind the pine front door, which was open just enough for him to see her face.

"I couldn't just let you go, Sam ... Not yet ... Not like this."

Sam was surprised to see him standing there under the dimness of the single porchlight, but then again, not really. But, she was concerned.

"Damien, how ... did you know I was here?"

"I ... uhh," he stumbled. "Sam ... That's not important."

"Um ... Yes, Damien ... It is. The only person who knew I was here is ... Sally."

Damien thought about whether or not he would answer the question, and decided not to, his eyes dropping down to his leather brown Ferragamo shoes, dusted up from the sand in the driveway.

"Sam ... I love you. It's that simple, and there's nothing else for me to say."

There was no response.

"Please ... can I come in ... just for a minute?"

Damien had been trying repeatedly to call her, until she changed her number. Then, he showed up at the restaurant several times as Sam was getting off ... and she'd seen him, but turned and walked away before he got close. The other time, Sally went out and told him to just quit trying, because Sam had moved on from him.

That was the last time she had had any contact with him, before tonight.

She hesitated.

It was just for the sake of courtesy that she opened the door all the way and let him in. Because she just wasn't hard enough to turn him away, though she knew she should have. She retreated to the dining room area, arms wrapped across the front of her in her robe, standing there in her slippers.

She motioned for him to have a seat.

"Can I have something to drink?"

An assortment of sodas and waters were in the fridge. She grabbed a couple cans of Coke, then sat and waited for Damien to speak.

"You know, Sam ..." He popped the can open. "I still remember the moment I first saw you, right there, on Avalon Pier."

He pointed.

"You had on that sun hat, and that yellow sun dress, riding on that spray-painted cruiser ... Do you remember?"

"Yes."

Sam remembered it well. Her mother had bought her that dress, and she wore it that day, for her.

Damien tilted forward, extending his hands part way across the table.

"I remember it like it was this morning ... That's how special it was to me, Sam."

He went on. "You know? That whole, entire day ... and our dinner that night at Jolly Roger's. Those are the things I think about now ... And our first trip, on that boat the next day, holding your hand on the dock that morning ... I was so excited."

Just then, a gust of wind riled up and blew something across the deck out back.

Sam got up, walked over and looked, then closed the slider and locked it as he continued.

"And our first kiss, seven days later. I was counting. Those are the times I want back."

Sam did not look at him as he spoke.

"I really do love you, Sam. And, I was wrong ... And, I meant to tell you that all those years ... but I didn't. And, I'm sorry for that."

An uncomfortable pressure came down on both of them.

After a pause, Sam spoke.

"I was really ... shocked at first, when you showed up here tonight. But now ... I think I'm okay."

He searched her eyes.

"And I appreciate what you're saying."

Damien was handsome. Good-looking, in a boyish sort of way, but he never came across as trustworthy. Sincere. The way someone you're supposed to be close to is supposed to be. Even that day at Avalon Pier, looking back, Sam could see it.

Though, back then, she knew very little about those kinds of things.

So, she just trusted him.

Now, however, things were different.

She looked him in the eye.

"But, I appreciate it for you ... not for me."

His head dropped.

She continued.

"I know you've been trying to reach me. And I hear what you just said. And I understand that you say you want to try, and that things would be different ... but it's not for me, Damien."

Damien found the words harsh on his ears.

"Listen, Damien," Sam reached her hand towards his. "I thought I loved the beginning too. And, I really wanted it. Our relationship. Us ... And, things were good."

She sat back, and so did he.

"But, after a while, it changed. It was like the real you started coming out more and more ... And, I wasn't sure you loved me anymore. Or, that you really ever did."

"Sam, we were young."

"Yeah, I agree ... But, we got older."

Everything went silent in there, as the two of them went wordless. Everything but the wind.

"Then, the weeks away at work started. And the parties ... And, everything else. We stopped being us ... It was just you."

They both sat there, clutching their drinks. He knew what was coming.

"Then, there were the other girls."

"Sam, I never saw anybody ..."

"It didn't have to be that, Damien ... It was the constant looking, the noticing, up-and-down ... and thinking I didn't notice ... And, all the comments about how you wanted me to look, or what I needed to wear, to make *you* happy, or me somehow worthy."

Damien seemed stuck, almost annoyed, as if he wanted to respond like he probably would to anybody else: *C'mon, are you kidding? ... Every guy does that.*

"And then ... the phone call."

Damien twisted in his seat. Sam could barely say it.

Her expression turned pale.

"I have absolutely no idea what that was, Sam. You *know* that ... I've tried to tell you a thousand times."

Sam was referring to an incident that happened one night last October at Magnolias Uptown Down South restaurant downtown, in Charleston. Sam and Sally were giving Sally's sister a tour of the city that evening, and they were headed to the waterfront when Sally noticed Damien inside the restaurant at a window-side table. Surprised, the girls went in. Sam asked Damien what he was doing there, and he said he was waiting for his partner Teddy. To discuss some investment plans over dinner.

Sally looked skeptical. She never liked Damien anyway, didn't trust him ... and he knew it. Right then, Damien's phone rang, and without even glancing at it, he extended it to Sally ... as if to say, *Answer it and talk to Teddy yourself. Then once and for all, mind your own business, and stay out of ours.*

Sally took the phone, pressed the green button, and lifted it to her ear.

And, her face went white.

In what was a flash, she hit the phone's speaker button and then stood there, mouth open. It was a woman's voice ...

> *Damien? ... Are you ready for me? ... Damien? ... Are you there? ... Damien?*

Damien snatched the phone from Sally's hand and hung it up. Then, immediately tried to call the number back, but it was private. He tried to call Teddy, but he didn't answer either. The girls left the restaurant, shocked, as Damien sat there, stunned.

That was the last time she ...

"It was already over by then, Damien. Like I said, all that other stuff. The years of it were just ... not in the picture of what a relationship is supposed to be, at least for me."

The truth finally settled onto Damien, like a shipwreck to the Atlantic floor.

"How can this be so easy for you, Sam?" Damien let go one last salvo of his hope.

"Not easy ... It's just clear to me." She looked him in the eyes. "You just can't love someone with everything you have inside ... when they don't truly love you back."

That was it for Damien.

"I should go to bed." Sam got up. "I wish the best for you, Damien. I sincerely do."

He remained with his head down.

"You can let yourself out."

Damien sat there for a second, then placed his can of Coke on the table, next to Sam's ... got up, got in his car, and drove away.

Sam retired to her room.

There was a certain peace in the air all of a sudden, and Sam fell asleep right away.

But, the wind picked up steadily over the course of the night.

Perhaps that was the reason she didn't hear the front door as it opened.

She'd forgotten to go back and lock it after Damien left.

The next sound was crystal clear, however ...

Clinkety - clink - clink - clink - clink!

One of the empty Coke cans Sam and Damien had left half-empty on the dining room table crashed to the floor.

Sam awoke instantly, propped up, and peered down the hall.

"Damien?"

She squinted as her eyes adjusted to the moonlight reflecting off the floor in the entryway. She could see the can, and a puddle of soda splattered on the tile ... and the front door wide open.

And, there, stood a figure, squarely, looking down the hallway into Sam's open bedroom ... a figure she processed, quickly ... and identified.

It was the woman from her party in Charleston ... the one the managers had stopped on the dining room floor ... She recognized the silhouette of her long jacket, and her hood ... and her blonde hair.

Sam jumped up to her feet, and said nothing.

The woman began walking towards her, lipstick red pumps clicking on the hard tile surface. Sam leapt to the door and slammed it shut just before the woman could get there.

She locked it.

"Who are you?! ... What do you want?!" Sam called out.

No answer.

After several long and disturbingly still seconds, there was a gentle knocking on the door. Sam instinctively began grabbing her things and shoveling them into her bag.

Silence.

Then,

Bang!!

One harsh knock struck the barrier separating the two.

"What do you want?!" Sam's voice began to quiver.

"Open the door." The voice was faint, calm, eerily so.

Seconds passed, and ...

Bang!!

Another forceful blow.

"Oh, my gosh!" Sam was fraught, and crying now.

"*Please* ... Open the door." The voice was deeper now.

Sam surveyed her escape, and peeked at her phone. It was just after 4:00 am.

A jack-and-jill bathroom connected Sam's bedroom to the next bedroom down the hall. From there, her parents' old room was all that remained before a sliding glass door that led to the deck, and the beach off of that.

Sam made her move.

She slung her bag around her shoulder, and in her robe and slippers, slipped through the two rooms and out into the hallway. She glanced back quickly to locate the woman, who did a slow-motion quarter turn to the right and faced Sam as she began to run. Frightened, Sam bolted to the master bedroom, flung the door open, and slammed into the sliding door at the back. Then, she reached for the lock, but it wasn't there, in the spot she remembered it used to be ... She could hear the footsteps resume, coming down the hall.

In that split second, Sam remembered that the locks on the doors had all been changed. And, she had to recall where this one was ... which she did, and dropped to the ground to unscrew it. The footsteps entered the room just as Sam got the lock undone.

She jumped up and looked back.

In the streak of moonlight coming in, she saw the long fingers in bright red nail polish reaching out for her.

"Aaaagghh!" Sam screamed and whipped the glass door open, the red fingers scraping down the back of her robe. She leapt off the wooden deck and ran out onto the beach, slippers flying into the pitch black air, and sprinted up and over the rise in the dune.

And, went left along the water.

A good distance from the house, she looked back and could see, under the streetlight, there at the end of Avalon Drive, the black Infiniti backing out from her home's driveway, and speeding away.

10 REDWOODS

Cognitive Dissonance is a theory about human motivation. It says: tension occurs when we have two thoughts that are dissonant, or don't match up. Example: "We think world hunger is a terrible thing, but we walk right by it every day."

Dissonance is supposed to be unpleasant, therefore, we are supposed to be motivated to reduce it.

Sam called the police and reported the incident at the old house as she drove out of town. They said they'd go out and look, get some fingerprints, and let her know what they found. She wanted to call Sally, but it was still too early. She'd call in a few hours, from the road, west a ways down Interstate 40.

The incident replayed over and over in her mind, and as she drove, she was spending more time checking the rearview than watching the expressway out ahead of her.

Finally, she called. It was 7:30 Wednesday morning.

"He-l-l--o." Sally's voice was groggy.

"Hey, Sal … It's Sam."

"What's up, Sammy? You okay?"

"Uh … yes … Not really."

"What's going on?" Sally woke up quick.

And, Sam told her about Damien, and the other visitor.

"Sally, how did Damien know I was here?"

Sally paused. "Sam, the napkin was moved, the one with your plans, on the refrigerator, and I didn't move it. I noticed it last night. I was gonna call you, but I didn't want you to …"

"Oh, my gosh …. Sal. Have you been locking the deadbolt?" Sam asked.

"I thought so."

"The deadbolts are new, but Damien still has a key to the bottom lock. I never got it back."

"Oh, Sam. I'm so sorry."

"But, who was that woman, Sally? … What does she want?"

"You know, Sam …" Sally hesitated for a second. "Maybe it was the one, from …"

Sam checked her rear view again, her eyes tearing up.

She was scared.

Ranger drove north along the 101 to meet his workmate Duane up the Russian River way. They were hiking today in Armstrong Redwoods State Nature Reserve with Duane's two sons Jan and Faf. Duane was the rugged mountain man type, big and strong, great beard, invariably in boots and a flannel this time of year, and he was huge on country hospitality. He invited Ranger up every holiday season to enjoy a good home-cooked meal, and get out into the Sonoma County outdoors with the boys.

They met around 1:00, Monday afternoon.

"Hey, Ranger! Great to see, brother." Duane gave him a big bear hug.

"Hi, Mr. Ranger!" Faf called out.

"Merry Christmas, Mr. Ranger!"

The boys jumped out of the pick-up, a 1967 6-cylinder, 3-speed on the column, turquoise Ford half-ton they called *Stormer*. Ranger loved that truck.

Duane was a true outdoorsman, and a brilliant analyst. The best anywhere with numbers, and he was training the boys to be the same. He was teaching Jan and Faf about the earth, its ecosystems, and its endless variety of resources. They supported wildlife organizations, and every year they purchased the California Explorer pass with the ultimate goal of visiting all the state's 250+ national parks, beaches, preserves and landmarks.

Faf could name them all for you if you wanted.

"Hey, Mr. Ranger ... Did you know that the *sequoia sempervirens*, the redwoods of course, are the tallest living things on earth and can reach the heights they do because their roots grow wide instead of deep, so they're able to absorb more of the water from the riverbeds and watersheds of the valley?" Faf asked.

"No, I did not." Ranger walked side-by-side with the youngster, from the car into the Armstrong Grove, impressed by how he talked more like a little man than a 7 year-old.

"Yeah, their roots go only five or six feet deep into the ground, but they grow out up to 100 feet from the trunk, and they intertwine with other trees' roots and even fuse together so they can share water, which helps them stand against the forces of nature ... like drought, or high winds, or floods."

Faf nodded his head assuringly as he talked.

"The tallest tree in this park is right up here, Mr. Ranger. It's called the Parson Jones Tree ... 310 feet tall." Faf leaned forward, looking around Ranger to Jan, who nodded back.

"Yeah ... so that would be," he calculated, "3720 inches, more than 103 yards, or taller than the Statue of Liberty, or the equivalent of, hmmm, let's see ... 38 of the largest California grizzly bears ever measured, 8 feet tall, Mr. Ranger, standing one on top of the other."

He paused to let Faf catch up with the numbers.

"With two *teensy-weensy* 3-foot baby bears at the very top rummaging around for berries." The 9 year-old said in a funny voice to make his little brother laugh.

It was fun.

"Yeah, but they're not gonna find 'em 'cause redwoods don't grow berries, silly little cubs." Faf mimicked his older brother. "They're down here in the huckleberry, and thimbleberry, and salmonberry, and Himalayan blackberry bushes ... Right over here!"

They were both giggling away now, and Duane winked to Ranger, who found himself quite entertained. The sound of their boots scratching and thumping down the hard dirt path.

When Jan spoke again, it echoed, as they were getting deeper into the forest.

"Yeah, they're never going to find the berries anymore, Mr. Ranger." Jan looked up at him. "On account of the California grizzly being extinct."

"Oh, yeah?"

"Yep, the great bear on our state flag? ... Gone. Gold Rush and the vaqueros killed them all. Last one was seen around Sequoia National Park in 1924."

Thump, thump, scratch, scratch, thump, scratch, scratch.

It was really beautiful out there.

"Mr. Ranger?" Faf's voice rang out.

"Yeah, Faf."

"Did you know that the *largest* tree in the world is in Sequoia National Park?"

"No... I didn't."

"Yep ... the General Sherman Tree, a giant sequoia. It's over 274 feet tall, 27 foot wide, 56,000 cubic feet of volume, and 3,200 years old."

"Yeah, Mr. Ranger," Jan added, "And that's still not as old as Methuselah, or the unnamed ancient bristlecone they found in Inyo National Forest that replaced Methuselah as the *oldest living thing* in the world ... 5,067 years-old! ... We're going there next year!"

The boys looked back and forth at each other again, then up to Duane.

"*Da-a-a-a-d-d-d*?!"

"Well, hmmmm ... Let me think ... That would make old Methuselah's older brother ..." Duane closed his eyes, raising a finger to his brow as to build the suspense (although the boys knew he had the data already computed in his head) " ... 50 centuries old, of course ... but a mere sapling at the dawn of recorded history in Mesopotamia ... and precisely the same age as (*drumroll*) ... 532,432,800 *dolania americana*, the animal with the shortest lifespan known to man (about 5 minutes long) living back to back to back to back to back. One poor little bugger right after the other."

"Whoa! ... Dad! Good one!!"

Faf and Jan were astounded.

"Dolania Americana? ... What are those?!"

"Well, it's a species of mayfly from the southeastern part of the United States. Apparently, in June in South Carolina, just before dawn, the nymphs rise to the surface of the coastal creeks, lakes and rivers, come out of their skin, and fly off to mate. Males fly around then fall from exhaustion, and drown in about thirty minutes, but the females mate right away, deposit their eggs into the water ... and are dead within five. Neither lives long enough to even see the sunrise."

"Awww ... Poor things." Jan said.

"Yep ... A very short but meaningful life."

"That's so cool. Are there mayflies here in California, dad? ... Can we study them sometime?" Faf implored.

"Of course we can, son."

Duane hugged his boy and winked over again.

They arrived at the Parson Jones Tree, which they stopped to admire. Ranger took pictures, and Faf and Jan watched through his viewfinder as the redwood towered above.

"This is incredible ..."

"Yep, Mr. Ranger," Faf continued. "It's the tallest tree in the park. And, did you know the tallest tree in the world is about four hours north of here? A redwood called Hyperion. 380.3 feet, but researchers say another one, Paradox, is growing at such an incredible rate, 7.4 inches per year, that it will overtake Hyperion by the year 2031."

"380.3 feet, Mr. Ranger." Jan smiled. "Wanna give it a try?"

"Oh, okay." Ranger was caught a little off-guard, but he liked math, and he'd seen a few nature shows, so he gave it a go.

"Okay, so that would be, let's see, just over ... 4560 inches. 126 and-a-half yards. Right at ... uh ... 116 meters. And, just about nineteen fully grown bull elephant seals, 20-footers, swimming around Drake's Bay ... at Point Reyes, where there's a colony of them, of course? And, they're all lined up, one right after the other, playing ... follow the leader ... No, no ... choo-choo train ... No, no. I got it! ... They're dancing a conga line! With one little baby Spanish Mackerel leading it out front .... You know, for the *point three* ... of the 380.3 ..."

Jan and Faf looked at each other, snickering.

"And ... Spanish ... for, you know, the conga ... thing."

Duane did his best to not bust up as the boys shook their heads.

"Uhh, okay. That was ... really interesting, Mr. Ranger," Jan tried to keep a straight face.

"Yeah, not too bad ... I guess ... for your first time."

They all three looked at each other. Ranger recognized what was happening.

"Except," Faf piped in, "when exactly would an elephant seal ever dance with a mackerel? He would eat it for lunch."

Jan immediately cracked up.

"Faf!"

"Sorry, dad."

They all stood there under the Parson Jones in the momentary silence.

"And, isn't the conga from Cuba anyway ... not Spain ... But, who's really counting? ... I mean, if a mackerel wants to do the conga, let him conga ... Who am I to say?"

Jan coughed up his gum.

"Faf!"

"Sorry again, dad."

"That is a good point, though." Jan mumbled under his breath.

Duane shook his head, and they all four laughed.

In less than a half-mile, they arrived at the old Colonel Armstrong Tree, the oldest redwood in the park. 1400 years old. And, after that was the start of the more strenuous hiking they'd be doing today. It was utterly beautiful out, and Ranger loved taking in the fresh air.

"Ready, Mr. Ranger?" Jan smiled as he showed the way to the open trail ahead.

"Yep, let's do it."

"*Conga*, anyone?" Duane called.

"Yeah!" The boys made music sounds and latched on behind him.

Ranger, with a big grin, did the same.

Ranger and Faf followed *Stormer* in the Malibu, top down, to Duane's cabin in Monte Rio, where Duane's wife Libby and father-in-law Heyneke (Grandpa *Hank*) were cooking dinner.

"Hey, guys!" Libby was ecstatic, she had hugs and kisses for everyone.

"Ranger, it's so good to see you!"

Heyneke gripped Ranger's hand and pulled him in. "*Velkommen*, my *sonn*."

He always liked Ranger, a lot.

Heyneke was from the colorful island town of Alesund, in Norway, from a family of 14 kids. Libby had a total of 11 brothers and sisters herself. The local joke was that when Heyneke's family planned to show for the annual *Den Norske Matfestivalen* (Norwegian Food Festival) in Alesund, vendors would spread the word in advance so there would be enough food, and the sheep would hear it and escape into the streets so their heads would not end up on the extra plates of *smalahove*.

Which was ironic because nobody in the family ate *smalahove*.

"It's good to see you, my *sonn*," Grandpa Hank whispered in Ranger's ear.

The group milled around, laughing and catching up, until Libby rang the family dinner bell, an actual bronze bell hanging outside the foldaway patio doors. She called everyone to the 12-foot Redwood Burl dining table, which they had crafted out of a fallen tree they acquired near Arcata, and the boys told Libby and Grandpa Hank all about their day.

"And the elevation gain over the whole hike, since we took the East Ridge Trail back, was over 1100 feet." Jan reported.

"Yeah, and you know what? ... That's like 106 ... and *nine-sixteenths* ... 10 and-a-half foot Sasquatches doing a Norwegian folk dance on top of each other's heads ... " Ranger winked. "Angry ones, too, 'cause who'd want a smelly pair of size twenty-sevens all in your face?!"

The kids burst out in laughter.

"You're getting better," Duane commended under his breath.

Ranger and the boys started a little dance.

"Well, you know what's taller than all the trees in the world?" Grandpa Hank announced as the reveling settled down.

He made sure his eyes met everyone else's around the table.

"What, Grandpa?"

Everybody was listening.

"My love for you all."

"Awwww ... Grandpa."

"That's sweet, dad."

"That's so nice, Grandpa Hank."

Heyneke's rosy red face and white beard lit up in the light from the stone fireplace.

"You see, my children, every good man needs just two things in his life." Hank continued. "Two things ... Faith and family."

The family gave him their undivided attention.

"See, a man has to believe in something ... A dream, a vision. And, he must put everything he has into making that dream happen ... This is his faith. And then, he passes the fruits on to the people he loves, and those who love him. The people who believe in him. His family."

He smiled at each one of them. "Without these things, a man is *nothing*."

Ranger listened.

The crackle of the fire, and the sound of *Silent Night* coming in from the kitchen, and the timbre of Heyneke's voice made for a poignant warmth in there.

"Life is short ... And, it can be taken away at any time ... Too often, the greatest things are right there in front of us, and we miss them. Then, it's too late."

He turned to the Faf and Jan.

"Boys, what do we always say?"

They sat up in their chairs. "Give it all you have today, for tomorrow holds no guarantee!"

"That's right!"

Just like the mayfly ... Ranger thought to himself.

"Well, *takk for maten* (*thanks for the food*)," Heyneke offered and sat back in his chair.

"*Takk for maten!*" They all echoed the sentiment.

After dinner, the adults enjoyed some tea, and more conversation, then cleaned up while the boys played and got ready for bed. Ranger had made reservations for a couple nights at the well-appointed Village Inn down the road, on the Russian River, and he was getting ready to head out.

He liked the solitude up here. In the morning, he was renting a kayak and paddling out to the ocean and back, and he planned to get a run in on the mountain roads before that.

"*Tusen takk!*" Ranger hugged everyone and thanked them all in Norwegian.

Then, he walked out to his vehicle.

Morning came early.

Huff ... huff ... huff ... huff ... The rhythm of his Asics gliding up the Bohemian Highway was four times as fast as his breathing.

Seeing Ranger run was really an awesome sight.

He got his kayak at around 8:00 am, the attendant doing a double take as Ranger flung the boat above his head with one arm only and toted it to the water's edge. Then, he got in and started paddling the nine or so river miles to the Pacific. Past the hamlet of Villa Grande, past Sheridan, Duncan Mills, under Highway 1, through Jenner-by-the-Sea, and into the tranquil estuary leading out to the beach. Ranger made it to the river mouth, where the ocean surf was big.

Double overhead today. He loved it out here.

The Russian River was a real waterman spot, wild, rugged and tranquil all at the same time. You can watch seals being born out here, or surf, or hear stories of great white shark attacks right off the beach. Abalone diver and spearfisherman Rodney Orr was hit here when one of the estimated 2500 white sharks still around this, the *Red Triangle* area of Northern California, took his head and shoulders into its mouth, lifted him out of the water high enough that he could see the ocean rushing by below, and carried him along for tens of meters before letting him go. Mr. Orr survived the attack, like he did his previous one years earlier at a notorious white shark breeding ground south of here in Tomales Bay, escaping that one with just a couple teeth punctures to the face and the back of his neck.

On the paddle ride back, Ranger stopped in for lunch at the River's End Restaurant & Inn, the place billing itself as a *luxe unplugged* experience, that is, no cell service, no internet, and no *New York Times* at your room's doorstep in the morning.

Just fine dining on the river and breathtaking ocean views from your cabin on the bluff.

Afterwards, Ranger paddled his boat east upstream, and arrived back in Monte Rio at 3:30, retreating to his room to settle into a long shower.

He was planning on spending the evening out tonight, exploring the town of Guerneville, five miles upriver.

Guerneville, California. Former logging town established in the 1850s. Before the majority of the redwoods were cut down, the valley surrounding Guerneville was one of the densest biomass regions anywhere on the planet. That is, this area had more life growing in it --

with all the trees, plants, and animals -- than any other place on God's green earth.

The Pomo Native Americans lived in the valley as a summer destination, calling it Ceola, meaning *shady place*. As the trees fell, however, the village acquired its first English name, *Stumptown*.

Then, immigrant Swiss businessman George Guerne arrived, took over the town's sawmill, and the town took his name.

Ranger had read that one of the only groves of true ancient old growth trees remaining in the entire region was the Armstrong Grove, where he, Duane and the boys hiked yesterday, about four miles away.

Pretty sad story, Ranger thought.

But, the big trees weren't the only sad story around Guerneville today.

"Hello ... Hi." Two young women passed Ranger as he walked up one of the side streets off the main River Road in town. They pirouetted with another glance and a smile.

As Ranger continued up the hill, he noticed a little dog across the street, in the garden near the steps of St. Elizabeth's Catholic Church, sitting there just staring at him.

"Hey, little guy!" Ranger called. The dog was perched on some blankets, tail wagging as Ranger jogged over ... "Whatcha doin' over here all by yourself?"

Something rustled underneath the pile of sleeping bags.

"Just *tryna* get some sleep, sir. But, thank you for the concern."

The man's voice startled Ranger. "Whoa ... Sorry. I didn't see you there."

"Accustomed to that, sir."

The black and white pup stood to its feet.

"I see you have met Cecil. He much happy to meet you ... Always is."

A man emerged from under the mound of blanket coverings. "Please to meet you as well, sir. I am Lwazi." He pointed to himself, humble and friendly.

"Uh, thanks ... I'm Ranger." He waved. "Well, I guess I'll let you two ... get back to sleep."

"Yeah, he my little friend." Cecil began licking all over the man's bearded face. "You are my good boy! Oooooo! Hoo hoo!" Lwazi's giggle made Ranger laugh as well. Lwazi was older, thin, sixty-five or seventy, with gray hair and a beard, and spoke with a pretty good accent. "Okay, goodnight. It was a pleasure to meet you, sir Ranger."

He and the dog retreated back under the sleeping bag canopy.

Ranger took a couple steps, then turned ... the good nature of the man drawing him back.

"Uh, Mr. Lwazi? Not sure if you're hungry, but would you like anything to eat, you and Cecil? Cecil wiggled out, tail going like a tiny rocket again. "I'm heading down to get some dinner, and maybe I can pick something up for you."

Lwazi sat up.

"Why, thank you, sir Ranger ... Yes, I am quite hungry, and am most certain Cecil is as well. We have not had much this week."

Week? Ranger thought. *This man thinks about how much he's had to eat by the week?*

"Hey, Mr. Lwazi, if you'd like, I'd be happy to treat you two to dinner. Why don't you join me in town? Anyplace you like. I'm not from here, so I could use help choosing. It would be my honor, for you and Cecil."

It was neat to witness a man's face go from empty, lonely and outcast to the realization that somebody just took the time to care about him.

"Yes, that would be great … Thank you."

Ranger, Lwazi, and Cecil, tucked away in Lwazi's oversized jacket, proceeded into town. They chose the hip and bustling Boon Eat + Drink, and took their seat for some supper. They had a great time, and talked for hours. Lwazi turned out to be such an interesting guy. He was from the KwaZulu-Natal province in South Africa, and had been in America for the last twenty-plus years, since the *war* ended there.

He told Ranger all about the country, its natural beauty, its people, and about apartheid. About how he lost his entire family in that awful explosion. And, how instead of retaliation, he chose to heed Mandela's plea for peace, and forgave.

But, remaining there was just too painful. The memories too difficult to bear.

So, Lwazi found his way here, and eventually to California.

He settled into the shadows of Guerneville, he told Ranger, just about five years ago, completely cut down and checked out from life … except for his little buddy Cecil who woke him with a lick on the nose one morning while he slept in an alley.

Cecil was Lwazi's little *Armstrong Grove*.

"Here you go, my little *umngani* (friend)," Lwazi whispered as Cecil popped his tiny piebald head out of his master's coat for a bite. The little chihuahua was loving it. He got to have some Point Reyes blue cheese, and some tasty truffle fries, and quite a few bits of the slow braised pot roast that Lwazi had ordered.

He used to make pot roast for his family back *home* every Sunday.

"You ever think about getting up on your feet again, Lwazi. Maybe getting involved in something you care about? ... Having a home again?" Ranger asked him.

"You know, sir Ranger, so funny you ask this. I have this dream just a last evening. I dream ... *I hope my family no see me this way.*"

He paused.

"You know ... Even though they not here anymore, I still hope they not a see me."

Ranger listened.

"I no want a them see me this way."

"Because they're your family." Ranger said. "And, you're their father."

"Yes. You a understand, sir Ranger?"

"Yes, Lwazi ... Yes, I do."

They smiled.

"I am so very grateful you come along, sir Ranger."

Ranger choked up. Lwazi was such a good person, and their time together so wonderful, there had to be something he could do.

Ranger told Lwazi that he was going home tomorrow, and that he would love to help him. Maybe take him to county services in San Rafael to help him get into some programs.

Develop a purpose. Restore some faith.

Ranger offered to reserve Lwazi and Cecil a room for the night, but Lwazi politely declined.

He did, however, take him up on his offer for tomorrow.

They started walking back.

"So, I'll meet you right here in the morning," Ranger confirmed.

"Yes sir, sir Ranger."

"Just *Ranger*." He smiled. "See you tomorrow then, my friends." Ranger pet little Cecil (who licked him back) and gave Lwazi a big hug.

The man probably hadn't been hugged in over twenty years.

Then, he started back down the hill.

Right then, the two young women Ranger had passed walking, just before he noticed Cecil, whizzed by, driving a firecracker red Jeep Backcountry. They waved again and yelled *hello*, heading east down the main drag.

The one in the passenger seat looking back over her shoulder until the four-wheeled drive disappeared around the bend. Ranger waved back.

The next day, they arrived in the city of San Rafael, and parked outside the Marin County Department of Health and Human Services building. It was 9:30 Wednesday morning.

"Okay, Lwazi. I've been thinking … Since you've decided to make an investment in yourself, how about I arrange a place for you to stay, so you can do all the things you need to get connected and get going out here?"

Lwazi sat still in the car, staring back at Ranger.

"You go inside and get all the information, and I'll take Cecil and find you a hotel close by, and some places you can eat and enjoy yourselves. Sound good?"

Lwazi's eyes glazed over. "It would be my honor, Ranger."

"Alright then … Sounds like a plan."

Lwazi began tearing up. "You will see, Ranger. I will do it. For my family. For myself and you. And, to give it back to others. I will do it ... You will see, sir Ranger!"

He headed inside, excited and waving as Ranger and Cecil drove away.

Ranger located a pet-friendly extended stay hotel just down the street, then mapped out the bus route to the supermarket and Montecito Plaza stores near the canal waterfront. Then, they found a pet playcare called Planet Canine right next to the services building so Lwazi could drop Cecil off when he had things to do.

And, a place little Cecil could meet some new doggy friends.

Ranger returned about an hour later and checked Lwazi in at the hotel. Afterwards, they stopped to drop Cecil off. Lwazi read the first part of the brochure aloud while they waited:

They come to play. They run around. They sleep. They make friends and at the end of the day they feel happy, loved and part of a community. Heck, they're ready to put on a show ... about how great it is to be a dog with other dogs!

"This is perfect, Ranger."

Cecil ran right in and began playing.

Ranger rode the bus with Lwazi to the marketplace, then they returned to the services building for Lwazi's appointment with the social workers.

"Okay, my friend, I'll meet you at Whole Foods around 4:00 then. We'll get some groceries, then pick up some clothes for you, and we'll be all set!"

"Yes, sir!" Lwazi went in, full of confidence.

Ranger stopped at Whole Foods to pick up stuff for the Christmas Eve dinner tomorrow at his house, then took the 101 freeway the half hour home. Bernard was there waiting, happy as ever to see him.

Ranger unpacked, played with the dog, caught up with his messages, then relaxed out on the deck until it was time to go back.

By 4:20 pm out front of the Whole Foods, Ranger realized Lwazi was nowhere to be found.

Then, he heard the sirens. He knew something was wrong.

Across the street from the market, there was a school ... San Rafael High School.

It was here, fall of 1971, that five teens boys, innocuously calling themselves *The Waldos* because they always hung out by a certain wall, found a map ... a map that supposedly led to an enormous marijuana crop located somewhere out on Point Reyes National Seashore. The *Waldos* decided then to start gathering daily on campus at the statue of Louis Pasteur, at 4:20 pm to try to go find the crop, commencing each journey with a smoke at the monument.

They called the routine *420-Louis*, then eventually just *420*.

Now, decades later, marijuana associates itself with the number 420 all around the world. It's a time to smoke, 4:20, a counterculture holiday, April 20, and a symbol for a generation to celebrate. States like Colorado, for example, now produce *419.99* mile markers for their roads and highways because the *420* markers keep being stolen. People live by the motto *It's 4:20 Somewhere* and smoke all day long. And, the clock at the *Summer of Love* hippie mecca street corner of Haight and Ashbury in San Francisco is perpetually frozen in time at ... you guessed it, *4:20*.

And, now, *420* was the reason Lwazi was being sped away in that ambulance.

Ranger ran over towards the commotion at the high school. There was a small crowd dispersing.

Ranger asked a few people what had happened, but nobody knew. Then, as he started back towards the market, through the empty parking lot along the side of the softball field, a voice came up from behind him.

"Mind if I walk with you, sir?"

It was a young man, probably 19 or 20, clean cut and handsome.

"No, what's the problem? Did you see what happened back there?"

The boy said nothing. He glanced back at a car that was pulling up behind them in the lot. Ranger saw the car too.

"They beat him up … They're the ones," the boy spoke.

"Beat who up?" Ranger asked.

"The homeless guy … Keep walking." The boy kept on, straight ahead, head down.

"Was it an older African guy with a beard, and an accent?" Ranger asked right away.

The boy began walking faster. "Yeah … He was sitting on the bench. They were after us … and he tried to help."

"Owen!" A guy in the car called the boy. "Come here."

Ranger stopped and turned around to face the car.

The kid, *Owen*, hesitated, figuring it was probably safer to stay than walk away on his own.

"Can I help you?" Ranger proposed, assessing who, and what might be in that white sedan. He could see there were four individuals inside.

"Not talking to you," the voice responded.

"Well, he's not coming over," Ranger stated clearly.

The front passenger door opened, then the other three, one by one. Four men emerged, clearly years older than Owen, and in all probability not from the same neighborhood. Ranger checked each one of them out as they took a couple steps towards.

"Owen ... You're coming with us."

What was going on here?

Just then ... Owen took off running, and the guys hurried back into the car and sped off after him. Ranger watched closely as they jetted off into the early night.

Ranger got to the hospital just before 5:00. A nurse met him outside the emergency room.

"Sorry, sir ... The patient is not available right now."

Ranger was calm, but shook up inside. "Can you give me any information ... at all?"

"No, I'm sorry. You can leave your name and contact information. Someone will notify you." The nurse gave Ranger a pad of paper and a pen. "So, you say the patient has no family ... no next of kin?"

"Yeah, no. That's correct ... Nobody." Ranger wrote on the pad and gave it back to the nurse. "Okay, I'll wait to hear ... Thank you," he said.

That night, Ranger took a blanket and sat outside watching the lights on the bay.

"I don't know, boy," he sighed, petting Bernard on the scruff of his neck.

Please let Lwazi be okay, he prayed.

"And, what about that kid, Owen?" Ranger asked the question. Bernard licked him in return, twice on the cheek.

What was he doing? Who were those guys? And, where is his family?

"I just don't know."

He thought about the last couple of days.

Family

Some are strong, like the Armstrong Redwoods

Some, chopped down and ripped up from the roots

And far too many, their young are like seeds, scattered in the wind on the hard, dry ground

Thirsty for any place to accept them … Anywhere to grow

Anywhere to belong

It was 10:00 Wednesday night, two days before Christmas. Ranger struggled to get to sleep.

11 APPALACHIAN TRAIL

In the animal world, females select mates who most stimulate their senses. The most colorful male guppy, the loudest green tree frog, the flashiest dancing grouse, the fiercest bull elephant seal. Males for the most part take anything they can get.

Sometimes, however ...

I'd never let my family get that way.

It was Ranger's last thought before he fell asleep. By the time he woke up in the morning, the message light was blinking on his phone.

Back in North Carolina ...

"Sam ... Durham, Lucille's, Eureka Springs, and some other places were all on that napkin. You don't think she'd follow you to any of those, do you?" Sally's voice was concerned.

"Well, I'm in Durham now, and I'm not stopping ... She must have been looking for Damien. Following him." Sam was trying to figure it all out. "Sally, I'm not sure how, but do you think you can find a way to figure out who that woman is? ... I need to know."

"You and me both, Sammy. Yeah, I'll figure something out ... I'll get it done."

"I love you, Sally. Thanks for being there for me."

"Always, girl. You know it ... Listen, feel better. Relax. Forget about last night. Enjoy your trip. You have some great things coming up. And you're free. Damien got it, you said, right?"

"Yeah, I think so."

They said goodbye.

And again, Sam instantly felt really alone. She'd never driven west of Durham, so the road for her would be untraveled from here on out. She passed Greensboro on the 40 and was nearing Winston-Salem, and wished so much she could talk to her grandfather right now. *Nonno* would know exactly what to say.

"I need to get out and walk," she told herself.

Sam pulled off the highway so she could get a look at the map and choose a destination. The Blue Ridge and Great Smoky ranges, parts of the Appalachians, were just up the way. She scanned her tablet, and right away found where she wanted to go.

A place called Grandfather Mountain.

She sat in her car there for a few minutes and read about it.

Grandfather Mountain rises 5,946 feet above the sea in the pretty Blue Ridge Mountains, one of the thirteen provinces of beautiful ranges that form the great Appalachian chain, which reaches from central Alabama in the south up to Newfoundland in eastern Canada. The Appalachian Trail (AT for short) is the legendary hiking route that stretches from Georgia to Maine, spanning an amazing 2,200 miles and 14 states. It's the longest foot-traffic-only walking path in the world. *Thru-hikers* traverse the AT all in one season, most of them traveling from south to north, from spring to late summer or early fall, following the white painted *blazes* that mark the path.

Hundreds of shelters, campsites, and towns dot the route along the AT, places where many of its 3 to 4 million annual hikers experience what they call *trail magic*.

Trail magic could be anything. Any kind of gift or assistance from strangers along the trip. Home-cooked meals, a cup of coffee, a ride into town during inclement weather, a shower, or a couch to sleep on for the night. Or, a simple *C'mon ... You can do it!*

The record for the solo fastest thru-hike on the AT is held by a woman ... just over 54 days. Before taking on the famous byway, this record holder reported having been out of shape, weighing over 200 pounds, and having had never backpacked before.

But, she went for it nonetheless.

Inspired by the accomplishment, she took on the other two legs of hiking's Triple Crown -- the 2,600 mile Pacific Crest Trail, from Mexico, through California, Oregon, and Washington, into Canada; and, the 3,100 mile Continental Divide Trail, that goes from Mexico to Canada along the Rocky Mountains.

On her way to do that hike, she stopped for a detour in Damascus, Virginia, during the town's summer festival, and attended an Appalachian Trail hiker reunion. It was there that she experienced her bit of trail magic, meeting a man thru-hiking northbound.

She said:

> *We all know where this goes. Girl has adventure. Girl meets boy having similar adventure.*
>
> *Love at first sight ... It's the Prince Charming part of the fairy tale.*

The two completed the Triple Crown together.

Then, they got married, settled into a cute apartment together, and pursued their careers ... but there was one problem, the woman wasn't happy. She wasn't quite sure of the reason, but she found herself in a huge crisis. She said she'd achieved absolutely everything in her fairy tale, but she was miserable. She reported that it took *a lot of tears*, and *introspection*, and the *love and support* of her husband to figure out why.

The answer, she determined, was that she realized she was living someone else's fairy tale. Patterning her life after an ideal that had been presented to her since she was a small child ... but it wasn't what made her happy.

So, she divorced, sold everything she owned, quit her job, and went hiking again.

Sam read all about Grandfather Mountain, the Appalachians, and the famous hiking trail. She figured she'd be able to see the area of Damascus, Virginia, where the woman met her *Prince Charming*, as the town was only 50 miles north of the mountain, and the view from the mountaintop was supposedly a hundred miles on a clear day.

And, it made her think.

What ever happened to the hiker's husband?

What about him? Did he find his fairy tale as well?

The Appalachian Trail had been conceived specifically for hiking by a forester and conservationist named Benton MacKaye, after he too lost his wife.

His in 1921. She drowned herself in New York City, in the East River.

It made Sam wonder.

They were married

The hiker, and the trail builder's wife

Why did they leave?

Was it even ever love in the first place?

If it was love, it would have lasted.

That's what her *Nonno* always told her.

It's black and white ... Love never fails.

She jotted notes in her journal, then hustled into the Hobby Lobby, where she was parked, and picked up some beads and a leather cord to make a bracelet. Black and white beads.

And vowed that the Appalachians would mean something different for her than they did for the others.

Sam arrived at the state park and began walking, instinctively looking over her shoulder from time to time.

She was still in a daze from the night.

The place was rugged, and spectacular, with many of its landmarks high and exposed. Some of the highest wind speeds in history, some over 200 mph, had been recorded here, but today the air was breathless, and the sky crystal clear.

And, the views from Grandfather Mountain's sheer bluffs and rocky outcroppings were jaw-dropping.

Sam drove to the park's famed Mile High Swinging Bridge, the highest footbridge in the country with relation to sea level, which offered an amazing 360-degree view of the region, while suspending you high over a chasm.

She wandered out onto it.

The bridge's capacity read 40 souls, but there were only ten or twelve on it along with Sam. Standing alone, she gazed out to the horizon, in the direction Damascus would have been, and thought about the hikers who might be there today.

Suddenly, a gust of wind hit the bridge, out of nowhere, rocking it. Everyone taking a step back from the railing. A couple people decided to get off and get back to solid ground.

Then, it went away.

"Look, you can see the skyline of Charlotte over there." Sam heard a voice that was still on the bridge, down from she was, towards the sun. "That's over a hundred miles away!"

She gazed out towards the panorama to see it.

"And, did you know Grandfather Mountain is home to 73 endangered species of plants and animals?" The voice continued.

This time, Sam could hear it was the voice of a child.

Right then, a second quick and powerful gust slammed into the 228-foot long apparatus.

Vroooooooommmmm! Squeeeeeaaaakkk! Squeak! Squeak! Squeak!

"Whooaa!" Some people gasped, then came the aftershock of human footsteps scrambling for the catwalk exits.

But, Sam stayed where she was.

"It's okay, Mama ... It's alright." The small voice promised as the wind subsided.

"And you know what else, Mama? At the very, very top of Grandfather Mountain, up there, there's a tiny patch of trees called southern Appalachian spruce-fir ... An *island* of them."

Sam glanced over and could finally see through the glare the source of all the park trivia, who she could now tell narrated with a Spanish accent.

It was a short, dark-haired boy in a blue jean jacket. His back was to Sam as he spoke. So, Sam smiled over to his mother, and she smiled back, but she looked uncomfortable.

"And, Mama ... there's a really endangered species that lives in those trees, on that island. Right up there." He pointed to the mountaintop. "It's called the spruce-fir moss spider ... There are only a couple places on earth where it still exists."

Sam looked up there.

"Do you think the little spider can survive, Mama? ... I do. I do."

She smiled.

Suddenly, another violent burst of wind smashed into the bridge, so furiously it seemed to blow the span completely sideways. In that split second, Sam felt her feet leaving the deck, her back teeter on the rail, and her upper body starting to go over. Amidst the screaming, she managed to curl forward and drop to her knees as the bridge returned to upright.

The child's mother fell flat, straight onto the galvanized steel walkway floor boards. The boy helped her to her feet, then turned and held out a hand to Sam.

Impossible ... Sam recognized it right away. The boy was wearing a black and white soccer jersey under his jean jacket ... Juventus ... just like the one *Nonno* wore. And, the one he had gotten her when she was a teenager ... It was packed in her bag in the car right now.

"It's just a little wind," the boy told Sam. "Don't worry. Everything will be okay."

"What's your name?" Sam asked before the boy and his mother hurried away.

"My name is Agustin." He shook Sam's hand.

They had made it safely back to terra firma, and people were heading for their cars.

"Hi, I'm Sam." Sam shook his mother's hand too.

She was shorter, and a little roundish, but her steps were quick getting off the bridge.

"Hi, hi ... I am Corinna ... Wooo, *zat* was not so much fun."

Sam agreed. She looked down at the boy. "You sure did a good job helping your *mum* ... and me too. Thank you. That really made me feel better."

"You're welcome!" Agustin replied. "Bridges are usually a lot more stable than they seem."

"And you sure do know a lot. I was listening to all your facts out there. I learned so much. Thanks for that too."

"You're welcome. Thank you." He was chipper.

"Yes, Agustin is very *inteligente*. His papa is *Porteno*, which makes him, how you say, genius! Agustin wants to be environmental scientist when he grow up. He already twelve now. Oh, my *leetle* baby grow up so fast!" Corinna pinched, and squeezed, and hugged her son.

"Mama!" Agustin sighed, giggling.

"What's a *Porteno*?" Sam asked, surprised to hear Agustin's age. He was small for twelve.

Agustin explained. "It's a person who's from a port city. We're from Buenos Aires ... Argentina ... where *Portenos* consider themselves smart and fancy people. But, we are not really like that. Mama just thinks it's funny. Papa's family is actually from Italy."

"And, we are not rich like *Portenos* anyway," Corinna announced with a shrug. "But, *dis* okay ... We are happy!" She did a little *chacarera* (Argentine dance).

Sam laughed. "You know, my grandfather is from Italy. He has a Juve jersey just like yours, Agustin. And, I have one too, right there in the car. I *love* your shirt!" She gave him a double thumbs up.

"Thank you, Sam! Yeah, I love the *Bianconeri* (white and black)! My papa used to play with Gigi Buffon when he was a boy. He's a really cool guy, my papa says. Do you like to play soccer?" Agustin asked.

"I love it!" Sam answered, and Agustin grinned big.

"Where are you from, Sam? Do you come from close by?" Corinna asked.

"Well, I was born in Australia, I lived on the Outer Banks, and South Carolina, but I'm traveling around the country right now. How about you?"

"We live in *ze* town of a Hot Springs. About one hour and half from here. It is where *ze* hot mineral springs are ... *Oooooo, bueno onda*! Feels so good! Soak in *ze* jacuzzi and having massage! Especially after day like today, *mina*, right?!"

"Wow, that sounds good." Sam imagined it.

"Maybe you can come, Sam! Mama, can Sam come? We could kick the ball," Agustin asked.

"Sure, mijo ... After what we just a go *trew*, Sam like a family. Please, Sam, come if you like. We have room for you, and we work at hot springs, so I take you *zere*. You are very welcome *en nuestra casa*!"

"That sounds great! I'd love to visit your hometown. I'll come for the evening, and then be on my way in the morning. Thank you so much for inviting me!"

"Good, you can follow us." Corinna gave her a hug. Agustin smiled. "We make one stop on way, for Agustin."

Sam nodded.

Then, they got in their cars headed to US 221 south.

The drive through the Blue Ridge Mountains was remarkable. Sam noticed everything now. They rode through several quaint small towns, then pulled off the parkway after about thirty minutes or so on the route.

It was just after 2:30, Wednesday afternoon.

"Come on. We hike," Agustin told Sam.

They walked the trail about a quarter mile, and then heard the sound of pounding water. They had arrived at a waterfall.

"This is Linville Falls." Agustin shot video with his tablet. "The most photographed falls in all of the Carolinas. It's 90-feet tall and flows here into beautiful Linville Gorge."

Agustin spun slowly to capture the canyon's steep walls.

"Notice the contrasting colors of the oaks, hickories, and birches, and also the white pines and green hemlocks."

Sam and Corinna watched, impressed, as Agustin narrated. "You are so good at that, Agustin." Sam complimented, and he thanked her.

"Agustin make video journal. He has so many already. He is amazing!"

Corinna was proud.

The three got to Hot Springs, to Corinna's modest stone house, around dinner time.

"Okay, we eat! You are hungry, Sam?" Corinna asked, excited.

Sam realized she hadn't eaten a bite all day. "Yes! I'm famished."

"*Vamanos.* To *ze* kitchen!" Corinna handed Sam an apron, got one herself, and went to work. She guided Sam as they began preparing a most incredible dinner: asado with a chimichurri salsa, choripan and provoleta grilled cheese sandwiches, quince jam empanadas, and salted caramel dulce de leche chocolate pots.

It was *fantastico*!

"So, now we go take a hot springs, yeah?!" Corinna declared after they cleaned up.

She was such a joyful lady, tons of spirit. A lot different from the nervous wreck she'd been on the bridge.

Sam was really appreciative to be around her and Agustin.

Corinna worked in some capacity at the resort, so she was able to get them into the spa without any kind of reservation. The staff was thrilled to see the three of them and greeted Sam with warm hospitality.

Agustin played on his computer in the office as the two ladies went in to change.

"So, first we start with exfoliate!"

The girls did a rosemary mint sugar scrub and oil full body rejuvenation, then a hydrating herbal body wrap with a head and neck massage, a facial, and a full body rub down. Afterwards, they walked outside by the river for a 104 degree mineral water soak in the ambrosial wooden jacuzzi hot tubs.

"You know, Sam, people been coming to *zese* springs for a long time ... First *ze* Cherokees, *zen* American settlers in 1778 ... now *turistas* y *excursionistas*, like you." Corinna poured some waters. "It was ... how you say ... popular stopping place during Revolutionary War, and today it's a popular for AT ... you know, Appalachian Trail."

"The Appalachian Trail is nearby?"

"Yes, Hot Springs is *on* AT."

"Wow ... I did not realize that."

Corinna was reclined now in the hot, pumped-in spring water, lemon slices covering each of her eyelids. Sam laid back too.

"This is so totally relaxing, Corinna," she said. "How can I ever repay you?"

"*Hermana*! It's such a pleasure to meet you!" Corinna smiled. "After *ze Grandfather* bridge ... we are like ... bonded forever!"

Sam closed her eyes ... She hadn't slept in almost a day, but she wasn't tired. Perhaps it was the smell of the forest, or the massages, or the water tingling her skin. She thought about Corinna's words ... *bonded forever* ... and wondered where her husband, Agustin's dad, was.

In fact, she'd been wondering about it all evening, but had been hesitant to ask. "So, Corinna, is it just you and Agustin here in Hot Springs?"

"Oh, no! *Choo* kidding?! I have daughter who is 6. Her name eh Cecilia. And, a two dogs, Sánchez and Landajo ... And goldfish. Agustin love a goldfish. He name Fernández Lobbe."

"Oh, cool ..."

"Then, of course," she went on, "my fantastic, wonderful, kind, handsome, incredible, loving, super-hot husband Castrogiovanni Marco Leonardo Sergio Alessandro!"

Sam's eyes went wide open.

"And *zis* just *hees* first name!" Corinna laughed. "He is at Cecilia Christmas play in Asheville ... She play a *leetle* drummer girl. So cute! ... Agustin and I a go last night."

A spa attendant came to ask the girls if he could get them anything.

"How 'bout you, Sam? You have a family?"

"Just my grandfather."

Corinna held the lemon slices in between her fingers. "*Aye*, Sam."

"It's okay. I'm used to it, and he's great." Sam smiled. "Sounds like you have an awesome family, though!"

"Oh, yes ... *Zees* for sure."

It was perfect out there, under the bright stars, in the middle of the Blue Ridge Mountains, the sound of the water coming around the curve of the French Broad River.

In their little corner of Madison County.

"Corinna, can I ask you a question?"

"Yes, of course, my dear."

"Um ... When you first met ... *Castro* ... *gi* ..."

"*Castrogiovanni*," Corinna helped her.

"Yes. Thank you ... Castrogiovanni."

The attendant came back with their wine glasses.

"How did you know ..." Sam continued, "You know ... he was the one for you?"

"Hmmm. *Thees* very good question." Corinna sipped her Montepulciano. "I tell you ..."

She moved in closer, sunk down into the water so only her face above her chin was out.

"I read it in magazine when I first a learn English."

It was humorous the way she moved.

"First, it's in *ze* eyes." She pointed with her index finger to her own eyes, back and forth. "Yessir ... Uh huh. *Ze* way he look at you ... From *ze* eyes *choo* know if he really into you." She smiled. "Not, ze *I's* ..." She then pointed her finger to herself just below the water level. "He cannot be about he self ... I *zis*, I *zat*, I, I, I ... *La, la, la* ... Always about *heem* ... *Nup* ..."

She wagged that finger back and forth. "He not *ze* one for you."

Sam smiled.

"Next, he must be a *real* ... Honest, responsible, have *ze* good friends, *ze* good family value. Good a job. He a like *ze* kids ... And of course, he want a marriage."

Corrina raised her plump little hand, and Sam looked to her bare ring finger.

"Ooops ... my ring being ... a how you say? ... Resize." She giggled.

Sam giggled too.

"And, last ... It no hurt if he make a you *leetle* bit excited. *Choo* know? ... You a look at *heem*, and a *ooooowie, wowwwwie*! He make you a *leetle* hot inside, like my Castrogiovanni."

Sam blushed.

"*Oooh*, Sam ... You have a zees four *ting* ... Then you have ... a FIRE!"

Corinna leapt up out of the bath, water spraying everywhere.

The young attendant ran over.

"Wups ... No *zis* kind of fire, Alec ... *Everyting* is okay."

They all laughed.

"Anyways ... magazine say *dees* how you know, Sam ... I a never forget."

Corinna relaxed back down into the tub with her wine.

Sam watched the river go by for a second, thinking about what Corinna had just told her, and it made a lot of sense. How to look for love, if that's what you wanted.

Damien would have never even passed the first step.

"And, you know most important *ting*, Sam?" Corinna added.

"Yeah ... What's that?"

"You must be same for *heem* ... *Becuss* love ... It go a *bote* ways."

Just across the river from them, across Bridge Street, down the Appalachian Trail a little bit, is a rocky summit ridge that overlooks the town of Hot Springs, and all its little charms.

It's called Lover's Leap.

Corinna had asked, and Sam was able to stay in one of the resort cabins near the trail ... She was thrilled about that. And, in the morning, she got up and hiked to the top of the ridge, before Corinna, Castrogiovanni, and the kids came over to say goodbye.

Agustin shot some video for his journal of Sam and him kicking the soccer ball around, both in their black and white Juventus jerseys.

Nonno Tommaso would have loved it here in Hot Springs! She thought.

At Lover's Leap, Sam got some video for her new friends.

> *Hi, everyone! It's Sam!*
>
> *Thank you so much for yesterday!*
>
> *Grandfather Mountain, the awesome nature lessons, the incredible dinner, the spa, and the AT*
>
> *It was one of my favorite days ever!*
>
> *Most of all, thank you, Agustin, for making me feel safe, and at home*
>
> *And Corinna, for teaching me about love*
>
> *I hope it's as clear for me one day as it is for you!*
>
> *You all are so wonderful*
>
> *And, I am grateful forever*

Sam felt refreshed, redeemed.

"*Chau! Suerte!*" The family called to her as she drove away.

12 LOOKING GLASS FALLS

"There are two kinds of people in the world: Those who believe there are two kinds of people in the world, and those who don't."

R. Benchley

It was Christmas Eve morning, and Sam decided to stop just south of Asheville at the world renowned largest home in the country, the Biltmore House. *Christmas at Biltmore* is huge; there were so many dazzlingly decorated Christmas trees and festive holiday happenings inside the stunning estate, it made Sam's head spin. The tradition of *Christmas at Biltmore* has been around since George Vanderbilt, the horticulturist and art collector son of the Vanderbilt family, first opened his country home to family and friends Christmas Eve, 1895. Sam took video of the gorgeous 34-foot Fraser Fir featured in the mansion's banquet hall ... It was impressive, and it was a fabulous day to be there.

The air was a little colder today, not like the winter heat wave that'd been hitting the Carolina coast the past week. Perhaps there was a storm coming in.

Sam had already enjoyed a *forever* memorable walk this morning on the Appalachian Trail, but she was in the mood to explore some more. So, she chose to take in Looking Glass Falls, as she had time, and there weren't any other plans until Christmas lunch, and dinner, tomorrow with Louis in Sautee Nacoochee, which was only two-and-a-half hours away.

Looking Glass Falls is named after nearby Looking Glass Rock, which got its name because water freezes on its sides in the winter, then glistens in the sunlight, making it resemble a mirror. The falls were truly gorgeous, at least as beautiful as Linville yesterday, and they made Sam think. She pulled her tablet out from her pack, looked into the camera, and with the falls in the background, filmed herself.

> *This is Looking Glass Falls, in the Blue Ridge Mountains of North Carolina. It's so beautiful here!*
>
> *I've learned a couple of important things this week that I want to remember.*
>
> *A couple things that, when I look in the mirror, for the rest of my life, I want to see in myself.*
>
> *One ... Every person is good. Some just might need help taking the lid off to see it.*
>
> *Then, they will be able to enjoy life, and help others.*
>
> *And two ... every person deserves love. They just need to be ready, and know how to find it.*
>
> *F ... FIRST, it's in his eyes*
>
> *I ... Not in the I's*
>
> *R ... He's got to be REAL*
>
> *E ... It's okay to be a little excited*
>
> *Then ... You have FIRE ... And then, there can be LOVE*

Sam smiled, picturing Corinna. Then, she added ... *But, it has to go both ways.*

She clicked the camera off.

After Looking Glass Rock, she hiked out onto Upper Looking Glass Cliffs, and then watched a group of intrepid teens slide down a 60-foot boulder called Sliding Rock, soaking wet, on their bottoms, down the 11,000 gallons per minute Blue Ridge Mountain flow. In summer, Sliding Rock, and about twenty other natural swimming holes and water slides close by (one's even called *Bust Your Butt Falls*), stays packed with people lined up at the railing, eager to take the plunge. Today, only a half dozen or so were braving the chill.

"Hey, lady ... Why don't you come try it!" One of the boys called out.

"Yeah, right!" Sam called back.

"C'mon ... Live a little!"

Sam stood there on the wood platform bridge above the pure natural pool at the bottom, in the middle of this forested wonderland, and thought ... *You know, the kid's right. Why not?*

"Okay! ... I'll do it!"

One of the boys got out to film it, while the others escorted her to the top of the rock ... And, in her soccer jersey and shorts, she took the slide.

Wooooooooooooooooooooo! Hoooooooooooooo!

Ranger woke at about 8:00 Christmas Eve morning and saw the message on his phone, hoping it would be some news about Lwazi, but it was his friend Richie:

Hey, Ranger! [Hey, Range!] Liz and I wanted to wish you a Merry Christmas, pal! [We ... wish you a Merry Christmas! We wish you ... Liz sang in the background.] We're on our way to the airport. We'll be on that Milford Track in New Zealand for the next week or so, so we'll be out of touch. Absolutely hate missing the party tonight. What are you guys making this year? What are they making, babe? [Masala and sandwiches!] Oh, man! Can we cancel the trip? [Richie!!] Yeah, they only allow 40 hikers in a day there in Fiordland, so we gotta go. Anyway, have a great holiday, my friend. We love you, and we miss you already! Cheers, Range! [Love you, Ranger!] Click.

He got up and drove to the hospital. On the way, a nurse called with

Lwazi's room number. He went right up to see him.

"Hey, my friend. How are you feeling?" Ranger patted Lwazi's shoulder.

"Like million bucks!" Lwazi's grin was bigger than ever on his heavily bandaged face.

Ranger was pleasantly surprised. "That's great, but you're looking a little rough, pal."

"This, Ranger? These are merely scrapes, the doctor tell me. They fix me up, and now I feel a brand new!" The nurse walked in to check Lwazi's dressings. "How is Cecil? Is he doing okay, my little *umngani*?"

"I saw him last night running around with his new friends ... *and*, when I called this morning, the sitter said he was having a *slumber party*, asleep on top of an Olde English Bulldog named Oxford. The guy said Cecil was actually snoring, he'd been playing so hard!"

Lwazi cracked up. "Yes, Cecil does this ... snoring! Hoo hoo hoo hoo ... Ooh!" His face hurt.

"Everything looks good, Mr. Lwazi. Your abrasions are healing up very nicely. Doctor says you'll go home today, young man." The nurse's name was Anna-Lena. "Our friend here took a few bumps and bruises, but he's going to be just fine," she reported to Ranger.

"Yes, I cover, but some blows I block real good, with face." Lwazi winked.

Anna-Lena rolled her eyes and smiled.

"Only *ting* is ... Deez men take gold necklace ... One my wife give me day before she go."

Guests began showing up at the Liberty Dock at 7:00 pm. Elodie-Jane met everyone at the gate with reusable gift bags custom-printed with

Joy to the World and filled with all kinds of Christmas treats. The idea was that Ranger's friends were to invite people who would otherwise be alone at Christmas, prepare a fun meal for them, play games, listen to Christmas music, and do some gift giving. Then, they'd celebrate again with the same guests on the 4th of July.

Ms. Elodie co-hosted with Ranger and assigned cooking stations for the night's meal, which was chicken tikka masala with mint, mango, and chopped red onion chutneys made from scratch, naan and puri; Pittsburgh Primanti Brothers-style sandwiches with fresh cut Molinari Deli pastrami, capicola, and genoa salami, stuffed with homemade fries and coleslaw, tomato and a hunk of Cowgirl Creamery cheese; Christmas plum pudding; with holiday slush punch and candy cane hot toddies to drink.

"Okay, Danny and Folau, you're doing the masala right here! Merry Christmas! Duane, you and Madison are on fries! Schalk, Sara, Carlin and Jay Jay, you're preparing chutneys there! Heyneke and Perry, you handsome men, you have the pudding here!"

Elodie loved the Christmas and 4th of July parties. She dressed up for them and everything. Tonight, she had on an elf stocking hat, red glitter bow tie, and jingle bell slippers.

"Ranger, you, Mr. Lwazi, and Anna-Lena are doing the punch, okay, darlings! Joyeux Noel, everyone!"

Julian and his guest Dawn, a widow who lived on his street across the Bay on Alameda, doubled doing the slaw and the music. They played classics like *O, Little Town of Bethlehem*, and *It Came Upon a Midnight Clear*. And, everyone played holiday charades, using Christmas words only. You should have seen Lwazi attempt to act out *Hark, the Herald Angels Sing* ... Somehow, Schalk was able to guess what all those gyrations were.

"I never hear of angel name *Harold* before!" Lwazi complained. It was hilarious.

The guests ate, drank, and sat outside on the lanai with Bernard and Cecil, and shared memories of Christmas past. Nurse Anna-Lena was so thankful that Ranger had invited her. She was new to California; her whole family still overseas in Sri Lanka.

After dessert, Ranger raised his glass to toast the special guests:

Merry Christmas, everyone! Ms. Elodie and I are so thankful you are all here!

We all ... Elodie, Dan, Julian, Duane, Libby, Grandpa Hank, Schalk, Sara ... all of us ...

Want you to know that we care about you, and we love you!

The world is a better place because of people like you ... Merry Christmas, everyone!

It was a fun party.

Sam thanked the boys for her experience at Sliding Rock. It was well worth the brief chill, and the wet clothes and hair. There were four of them, nice local kids, Kieran and Dane, and brothers Jordie and Beauden. They were all going off to play college football next year, Kieran and Dane at Newberry College in South Carolina, Jordie at Wingate University, and Beauden heading to Tennessee to be a Tusculum Pioneer, all faith-based colleges in the South Atlantic Conference.

They snapped a handful of goofy photos with her, and Sam hopped into her car. "Alright, boys ... *Hooroo*!" she called as she buckled up. "That means *see you later* in Aussie."

"See ya, Sam!" "Nice to meet you!" "*Hoorooooo*!" The boys yelled as she drove off, waving.

Sam was hungry. In the mood for Italian food. Driving through the scenic Sapphire Valley, she came across Osteria del Monte Ristorante Italiano, which she'd read had been recently called the *best Italian in the mountains*. The restaurant was darling, a marigold-colored home-style cottage with red currant shutters and pine green trimmed roof arches.

In Italy, an *osteria* is a restaurant that offers simple food and wine. Menus are usually short, with an emphasis on local specialties such as pasta, grilled meat or fish, and food is often served at shared tables. It's traditionally less formal than a *trattoria*, which is less formal than a *ristorante*. Osterias are more akin to a *bottigliere*, where patrons can take a bottle or flask and refill it from a barrel, or an *enoteche*, which focuses especially on the wine … This place had the feel of both, osteria and ristorante, hence the name, Sam guessed.

For Christmas Eve, the place was packed. Sam had just beaten the crowd in when she took her table for one in the corner.

"Hi, welcome!" Sam's server, a young girl named Martine, arrived at her table.

"Hi!" Sam replied with a delighted smile. They chatted for a minute or so. Turns out Martine was headed to the same college as Kieran next year, Tusculum, but she didn't know him.

Sam ordered the *petto di pollo parmigiana* with a side of *penne alla vodka*, with tomato cream sauce spiced with crushed red pepper, and finished with parmesan.

Molto saporito!

"We'll have the *Barbaresco*," a young man ordered two tables over. He was a red-haired fellow, late twenties, seated with another guy, dark haired and olive skinned.

"Where are you from?" Sam heard Martine ask as she returned with the wine and two glasses.

"Australia!" the redhead replied, which caught Sam's attention, and she glanced over, the dark-haired one noticing her glance and returning it with a smile.

"Here ..." the dark one answered, still not focused on his own table.

Sam nodded, then continued her *pasto*.

The darker guy raised his glass and nodded back. "Cheers!"

A little later, Martine returned to Sam's table, this time with a glass of wine and something written inside a napkin. "The gentleman over there asked me to give this to you," she said.

Sam looked over to the table, the American eyeballing her. "Oh ... Okay. Thanks, Martine."

She opened the napkin; it read ... *You are absolutely stunning! What are you up to later?"*

Sam smiled. She tore off one the heart-shaped notes from her pad, thought for a minute, and started writing back.

"Sam ... Can I get anything else for you?" Martine came back after a bit.

"Well, Martine, the dinner was fabulous, and your service was even better. Just one thing. Would you drop this off to the gentleman at the table over there? Oh, and feel free to read it before you do."

The note read:

> *Thank you for the compliment. Maybe try to get to know a girl first before asking her out, though. Personality and mind. That's what's stunning in a person. Anyway, all the best to you.*

Sam paid her bill, took a picture with Martine and the manager, then left the osteria, leaving the full wine glass at the edge of her table to be returned to sender ... And continued on her way to Georgia.

Ranger spent Christmas Day at home with Bernard, like he had every year since his parents had been gone. Today, however, another guy with a dog would be joining them.

Lwazi and Cecil spent most of the morning and early afternoon at Ranger's, Lwazi really enjoying watching all the Christmas television programming, and Cecil and Bernard playing outside with the gulls. The men reminisced about the day before.

"So, tell me again about the necklace they took, Lwazi. What was it?" Ranger asked at lunch.

Lwazi looked over at Cecil, who was jumping, trying to get the birds.

"Yes … It was golden heart my wife and children made by hand in friend's blacksmith shop. The gold come from my grandmother. Just big lump, you know? So, they melt it down for necklace. My wife and two children were at shop day after they finish, to say thank you … *Boom*. Shop is bombed … They *tink* they make knives in there to fight, I hear after."

Ranger listened.

"So …" Lwazi continued, "I wear necklace to remember … Remember wife, children, grandmother … all of them."

For the first time, Ranger saw a tear in Lwazi's eye.

Lwazi and Cecil were ready to head back to the hotel by mid-afternoon. It was time to rest. Ranger packed up some leftovers for them, drove them back to the hotel and walked them up to the room.

"I'll come by tomorrow, my friend. You call if you need anything, okay?"

"Thank you, Ranger." Lwazi was very grateful. "Merry Christmas."

Ranger took the onramp to Sir Francis Drake Boulevard, just a couple hundred feet from Lwazi's hotel. And there, to his left, loomed the oldest prison in California, San Quentin. Ranger looked over at its walls.

Built in 1852, San Quentin is the only death row remaining for male inmates in the state, and the largest death row in the country, its nearly 750 condemned almost as many as Texas and Florida combined. Between 1893 and 1937, 215 were executed at San Quentin by means of hanging, and after that, 196 in the gas chamber. But, in 1995, use of gas was ruled *cruel and unusual*, so lethal injection became the method of capital punishment. Between 1996 and 2006, 11 were terminated at the prison this way.

Recently, a new 230 square-foot lethal injection chamber was constructed, complete with three separate viewing areas for victims, family, and the press, replacing the old single-view one fifth its size. And, it's ready for use. Ready for the 125 or so who tortured and murdered their victims, the 175 who murdered children, and the 45 cop killers.

Ranger passed by the prison, then took 101 north to San Rafael.

Driving by the high school, he noticed people gathered by the Louis Pasteur statue ... It was 4:15 pm.

He pulled onto Mission Avenue and parked, then walked slowly half way over to the spot, where some sightseers were taking photos. Then, as if by some pre-arranged twist of fate, the four men he encountered a couple days ago strolled up near him among the trees. They didn't see him at first, as it appeared they were surveilling the unwitting tourists.

Ranger approached them.

"Hey, fellas ..." he spoke, looking each one of them in the eye. "I have a question for you ... You remember that old homeless man you beat up the other day?"

The four turned and faced Ranger.

"That was my friend ... and I'm gonna need his necklace back."

The men eyed one another, then spread out into a semicircle, appearing to remember Ranger and the encounter with him on Wednesday.

"What did you say, man?" the shortest one challenged. It was then that Ranger saw Lwazi's heart of gold around his neck ... They closed in.

One of the guys, the bigger one, took a sudden half-step forward, not clear his intention, and Ranger knocked him down with a powerful blow to the chin. Seconds later, the other three were all down too, two by way of punches, and one via a brief wrestling match after having attempted to dive at Ranger's legs and tackle him.

A couple of them rolled around groaning in the pine needles, and the other two laid silent.

Ranger crouched over the one who spoke, ripped the gold heart from the collection of jewelry under his collar, and secured it in his pocket, then stood and looked over the four, sprawled out there among the trees of San Rafael High School ... and thought to himself:

The world would be such a better place without people like you in it.

Ranger checked to see if anyone was watching, returned to his vehicle, and drove off.

13 SAUTEE NACOOCHEE

> "And now here is my secret, a very simple secret ... It is only with the heart that one can see rightly ... because what is essential is invisible to the eye."
>
> Antoine de Saint-Exupéry, *The Little Prince*

Sam drove the hour-and-forty-five minutes to Sautee Nacoochee, Georgia, since she had a room for Thursday and Friday nights. She pulled into Lucille's Mountain Top Inn and Spa just after 10:00 pm.

Louis had the Mountain Suite reserved for her, all expenses paid, and it was out of sight ... king bed, private screened in porch with mountain views, living room, sitting area, dining table, fireplace, wet bar, bathroom with double vanity, bubble massage tub with mountain views, separate shower with rain-can shower head, secluded deck off the bathroom with outdoor shower, and flat screen televisions. Wow!

Sam felt alive after two uplifting days on the road, but was also beat tired. She washed up, got in bed, and began reading through her journal. Her eyes were weary ...

Down a rock trail, on a romantic cobblestone overlook, two wooden chairs with a connecting table offer the best view of the Blue Ridge Mountains on all of Lucille's property. Sam sat and waited for Louis, sipping a virgin Georgia Peach and reveling in the scenery. She wore her gorgeous daffodil and black beaded, flowy dress, and pear drop earrings, with her hair down and pulled behind one ear.

"You look really nice ..." Louis announced as he approached on the pebble path behind her. Sam blushed. They walked inside the inn and were seated for lunch.

The food was good, and everything Louis said was really funny. Sam laughed and laughed. A small band began to play, and guests started dancing on the lovely wood floor in the middle of the room. There were couples of all ages, everyone dressed so nicely.

"Do us a favor, Sam …" Louis requested with a riveted smile.

"Okay …" she responded.

"Go up to your room. There's a gift waiting there for you."

"Okay …" She replied, wondering what it could be.

Sam walked the stairs up to her room. There were couples hurrying down, passing her on either side, giggling and laughing and excited, heading to the dancefloor.

Sam opened the door to her suite. There resting on a tray on the bed was a boutonniere, and a golden yellow daffodil corsage.

"Hmm. Okay …" she said to herself as she walked over to them.

The sun was going down, and it was dark in the room. A last couple's set of shoes scampered by towards the music. Sam watched their shadows in the light coming in from underneath the door. Then slowly, one final pair of steps clicked up the hallway.

Stopping just outside her room.

Sam focused back on the flowers. They were pretty. There were long pins for fastening on the tray too. She picked up the items, walked to the door, and rested her hand on the knob. Then opened it and returned downstairs.

Louis was waiting on the dancefloor.

"Pin it on?" he asked.

Sam started to feel warm. She pinned the boutonniere on him as he started to spin her slowly by the waist.

"Huh?"

Louis' face was all of a sudden much older, and wrinkled.

"Okay, now yours."

Louis laughed as he spun her, raising the corsage and pin to her dress. Sam could no longer see any of the faces in the room. Like they all went black.

Then, she was startled as she spotted Corinna standing outside one of the large windows, in the darkness. She looked troubled.

"What ...?" Sam mumbled to herself.

Louis continued his odd laughing, and the daffodil and pin were getting nearer and nearer to her chest. In the blur, Sam saw Sally standing outside now.

She was yelling something, but Sam couldn't hear it. The music was too loud.

"Almost got it ... Sam!" he roared.

She spun faster and faster, and her head fell back, so she could see out the window again. This time, Corinna and Sally were together there in the dark, outside a big glass door, waving for her to come to them.

They were panicked.

Sam wasn't able to break away.

Then, from the opposite direction of her two friends, it happened ... The *woman* appeared ... in the coat and sunglasses. And, she began walking towards Sam ... like in the house. With each revolution, she could see that the woman was closer, and closer, and Louis kept laughing, and the noise kept getting louder.

The hands and flower and the pin getting nearer. Sam was paralyzed.

She began to cry.

Then, the music and spinning stopped, and the room went dark.

"Got it!" his calm voice whispered. Sam froze, looking down at the hands, and the daffodil pinned to her chest. Then, she looked up … but it wasn't Louis anymore … It was *her*!

"Aaaaaagghhh!!" Sam woke up screaming. It was 3:30 am.

8:00 am: the lights in the suite were still on from the middle of the night. Sam was pretty groggy, but she got her walking gear on, went out on the grounds, and stretched anyway. She wanted to get out early because of the day's plans.

First, she headed through the forest to the historic Nacoochee Mound, down by the Chattahoochee River. The mound was a near 2,000 year-old reminder of the Mississippian Native Americans who once lived all up and down this region and used the mounds for all kinds of things, like public townhouses, dances, temples, and the residence for the chief. They lived inside some of the mounds and used some as burial sites.

75 of them were found inside the Nacoochee mound when they discovered it.

From there, Sam walked along the Unicoi Turnpike back to town, where the inviting Sweetwater Coffeehouse was having a Christmas morning gift exchange for anyone who wanted to stop at their adorable front porch. Sam got a chai latte, and bought one of the store's signature *Sleepless in Sautee* mugs. She got to talking to a nice lady named Shelley, who worked at the well-known Old Sautee Store nearby, and they walked over together so Sam could see inside.

"This is so cute!" Sam signed, as Shelley was deaf. She was so hospitable, happy as a bug in a rug to show her new visitor around the historic 1872 shop.

"Whoa!" Sam jumped as she passed the big, funky looking troll perched on the counter.

"You think that's scary, Sam? Come see the *wampus*!" Shelley smiled. She showed Sam a wooden crate outside the store that had cage wire over the top and a tail sticking out of a hole on the side. This, legend had it, was the dwelling place of a rare and dangerous local animal called the wampus.

Sam was cautious as she looked in.

Then ... *whaaammm*! ... the wampus jumped out at her.

"Uuggh!" Sam screamed.

Shelley patted her on the shoulder, chuckling.

Post adventure, Sam picked up some of the renowned Farmer Cheese at the shop, a jar of Georgia Peach Preserves, and some of Sautee's own Greenstone Soap Company all-natural, handmade bars to use in her spa bathroom at the inn. She chose the Kudzu & Grits with Cedarwood and Lemongrass, and the clove-scented ones.

"Thank you so much, Shelley." Sam was gratified. "This was such an unexpected treat!"

"You're welcome, Sam. It's so nice you found us." She gave Sam a warm hug. "We like for everyone to have the opportunity to be together with someone on Christmas," she smiled. "Now, it's off to presents at home with the family for me."

What a great idea, Sam thought to herself about the coffee get-together as she rambled up the road back to Lucille's. She unwrapped her soaps, prepared a bath, got in, soaking up the glorious mountain view from the luxury of the tub.

Sam waited for Louis by the two wooden chairs he had arranged as their meeting place. Though she appreciated the scenery, she didn't sit, like in her dream.

"Hi, Sam," he announced, walking up on the rock path behind her.

"Louis." Sam turned and gave him her hand.

"It's very good to see you. Welcome ... and Merry Christmas."

Louis took her hand, paused, then pulled her into a hug.

The last time Sam saw Louis, he was a skinny high school junior dressed in a black tuxedo, gold bowtie and cummerbund, and a gold and black boutonniere she had pinned to his lapel. Those were Manteo High's colors. They had classes together, ran on the track team, Louis did distances and Sam was a sprinter, and were both members of the board game club. Junior prom came around, and neither of them had a date, so they agreed to go together, as friends. Prom was on the evening of the last day of school before summer, and when it was over, Louis went home, and moved out west to Monterey, California, the very next day. His family had purchased a bed and breakfast in the charming coastal town of Carmel. Louis had learned the business while he was there, and was now the owner and proprietor here at Lucille's.

Anyway, that was the last time.

Louis did look older, but not that much. He looked good, and filled out nicely since Manteo. He had on a gray chambray suit jacket, a nice pair of jeans, some casual oxfords, and a touch of some men's fragrance that smelled quite good.

"Merry Christmas to you too, Louis."

"How was your drive in?" Louis kept one hand on Sam's shoulder.

"Really nice … The mountains, and valleys, and everything have been so gorgeous."

"And last night … how'd you sleep?"

Sam hesitated a split second. "The room is … also so gorgeous. It's way too much, Louis. You didn't have to do that."

Louis' eyes got a little bigger, and he sort of swallowed a gulp before he responded next. "To be honest … I was kinda really excited to … I mean, my goodness, it's Christmas Day, and Sam Amaris was coming to visit … After all these years? … This was pretty big for me."

"Louis, thank you … That's really nice."

It's funny how easily seeing someone again, even a picture, can transport you back in time, in terms of feeling those old feelings again.

"Well, okay, Sam … How 'bout some lunch? Are you hungry? I'd love to hear all about you and what you've been doing." Louis broke the pause in the conversation and opened his stance towards the inn.

Lucille's was dressed up really elegantly for Christmas Day. Louis had a special holiday bouquet of flowers arranged in the middle of their table set just for two, which was away in the corner of the dining room, near the big windows overlooking the outside deck … opposite from where they sat in her dream. The wait staff arrived *tout de suite* with a variety of treats, among them a tray of Lucille's favorite desserts, gooey chocolate butter bars, banana cake with slow-cooked caramel icing, and cream cheese frosting carrot cake.

"Do you still like your dessert first, before everything?" Louis asked, his eyes excited.

Sam smiled, warmed inside. "Yeah … most of the time I do."

That was the one and only time she'd ever ridden in a limousine, the night of junior prom. Louis had arrived at 5:45 pm at her house, she still remembered the time, and her parents peeking out the dining room windows at the car, and the boy who was taking their daughter. (It was the last time Sam recalled seeing her parents in the same room together.) They didn't look good, either one of them, but they were so proud of her.

Then, Sam moved away to Charleston the next year, a day or two after graduation.

And, sadly, that was the end of home as she knew it. Sam never saw her parents again ... and she never got a chance to say goodbye.

Anyway, Sam ordered dessert first for dinner that night, and Louis loved the idea of it.

"Excellent!" They dug in. Louis proceeded to tell Sam about the good stuff she was tasting, and about all the great places Lucille's bought their food and ingredients and local wines.

The main lunch dishes started arriving at the table.

"Wow ... I'm not gonna have any room for dinner tonight," Sam professed.

"Good, Sam." Louis genuinely looked pleased. "You deserve it ... You know I still owe you, right?"

"Oh, yeah ... how's that?"

"11th grade ... English class."

That's when Louis and Sam met. For their final project in that class, the teacher divided the students into random groups of four. They had to read the classic novel assigned to them, rewrite the story so it took place there in their home setting of the Outer Banks, and present it in front of the whole class as a play.

Sam, who was always a great student, was saddled with three stiffs as partners, he joked ... A kid who skateboarded all day long and did little else with his brain, named Zack. Then, this long-haired, flannel-shirt wearing anti-social ruffian sporting a full beard, named Todd ... and Louis.

Their novel, *The Great Gatsby*.

"Oh, my gosh!" Sam recalled. "That was so much fun."

"It was pure torture ..." Louis offered his opinion.

"What do you mean? You guys were great! ... Zack played Nick Carraway *and* every other background character at Gatsby's parties, so he had to read narration while jumping in and out of all those crazy costumes we made." Sam remembered the detailed production well. She was so good at writing, creating, and organizing, and bringing out the best in others. "The whole class, and Mr. Milton, thought he was soooo funny! ... And Todd, playing Tom and Myrtle at the same time. Remember that? He was excellent! ... He really blossomed after that play. You know, lots more outgoing. That was fun to see."

"Yeah, the wig ... with the voice ... and the beard ... That was a great idea, Sam."

"I think so too. And you ... You were such a sweet Gatsby. You did a fantastic job."

Louis' eyes dived into Sam, and the memory.

She never quite realized the reason Louis played such a great Gatsby was because that's how he really felt ... About her.

"It was all you, Sam ..." Louis confessed, arriving back at his original point. "You got us all together to read the book ... which was a miracle in and of itself. You wrote the whole thing. I was such a terrible writer ... I couldn't help. You directed us, did all the costumes and the set stuff, and you even thought to bring refreshments for the class the day we performed ... You were perfect."

Sam let go a modest smile as Louis leaned forward.

"And you were such an awesome, and wonderful … and beautiful Daisy."

A server arrived at the table and asked if they needed anything more.

"No, thank you, Ashley," Louis answered.

It was then that Sam realized Louis had extended across the table, his hand covering hers.

"No … All set … Thank you," she told the server, then looked back to Louis.

"Anyway …" he said, "I owe you for that."

A red light used to flash in the night … there at the edge of the sand, in the open space between Sam's house and the Avalon Pier.

Perhaps to alert drivers of the coming end of the road, or beachgoers the end of their day in the sand. Either way, for Louis, its purpose was to illuminate Sam as she walked from her job at the pier arcade home each evening.

Louis lived in an extravagant home on the other side of the Virginia Dare Trail from Sam, there at the end of Avalon Drive, and he watched her walk by that light almost every night. Until the day he left.

The light was still there when he returned home that next summer, after they graduated, and he was hoping to find Sam and tell her how he felt.

Something he'd failed to do while he was there, or in the letters he wrote from Carmel.

But, she was gone.

Her parents were gone too.

Louis stopped by Sam's house that summer, after they graduated ... but it was empty.

And, nobody in Kill Devil Hills had any idea of where she had gone.

Like she had just disappeared.

And had it not been for a chance night out for pizza one night by a bed & breakfast reviewer he knew from out West, who told him she'd just met someone from Kill Devil Hills, this lovely blonde server ...

Louis would have likely never seen Sam again.

They finished their lunch, reminiscing about old Manteo stuff, and refrained from talking about anything after that.

Too much heartache for such a nice Christmas Day.

Then, the two stood up and shared a warm embrace.

"Well, that was ..."

"Sam." Louis cut her off. "I'm very thankful ... to be able to see you again."

It started to rain outside. A storm had ended up coming after all.

And, before Sam could say anything, Louis went on, "I'll contact you before dinner tonight. Just to confirm, okay? ... Your eyes look tired. You should get some rest."

"Okay."

Sam *was* tired. The night, the days before, and all the food and drink had crept up on her. Louis picked a rose from the vase on the table and put it in her hand.

"Merry Christmas, Sam." He looked her in the eyes, then turned and headed towards the front desk of the inn. Sam traipsed slowly up the stairs to her suite, crawled into the soft, comfortable sheets of the bed, and curled up.

"What time is it?!" Sam jumped up in bed.

How long have I been sleeping?

Dinner was surely coming soon.

"What am I doing here?" she sighed.

Sam glanced over at the light coming in under the door. There was an envelope lying in it.

She walked over, still in most of her clothes from lunch, and opened its flap.

It was a note from Louis.

Dearest Sam,

I say dearest because you occupy a very special place in my heart

In my life

And I'm so glad I was able to thank you today

For English class, and so much more

Because of the impression you have made on me

On my life

The joy, and the goodness, and spirit I saw in you everyday

The wonderful person I knew, until that last day of school

Did so much to give meaning, and purpose, and perspective

To my life

And I know tonight, and forever in my heart

That because you took the time to be my friend, and shared your light

That you have changed me for the best

Forever

And you probably never even knew it

But I also realize tonight, by the look in your eyes

That although you have been all this for me for all these years

That I have never been the same for you

Even though I had hoped in the smallest way maybe I could be

I fell in love with you, Sam, and it just grew and grew after I left

You had no way of knowing

And I'm sorry for that

Don't worry about dinner tonight, I am so thankful for the wonderful lunch we did have

And thanks again for everything. I'm so glad I got the chance to tell you

I truly hope every bit of the best for you, Sam

Maybe we'll see each other again one day, in some other place and time

I hope so

Enjoy your travels!

It was good to see you again

Cheers, Louis

Just like that, it was done.

Sam felt bad, and she cried. Not because of the letter, or that Louis was gone. Everything he said, she realized, was true ... But because feelings hurt sometimes.

Why had love caused her so much pain? she thought. Her parents, Damien, and now Louis. She sunk back under the covers, staring at the peach-colored rose on the bedside table ... the one he had given her.

Manteo High School is located on an eighteen square-mile chunk of the Outer Banks chain called Roanoke Island. Its name was the name of a Croatan Native American chief who had befriended English colonists after they landed there in 1584.

Queen Elizabeth had intended to establish the first permanent English settlement in the Americas on the island, and commissioned writer/explorer Sir Walter Raleigh to found it. After three years of struggles, fighting with the natives and the lack of food and supplies, 115 additional pioneers were dispatched to the island to establish the settlement for good. But, the struggles didn't stop. Fearing for their lives, the Roanoke colonists sent a boat back to England to report about the unstable situation. And, 118 settlers stayed.

90 men, 17 women, and 11 children, including Virginia Dare.

The first English child born in the Americas.

However, when commander John White and his men made it back to the Roanoke Island colony several years later, they found nothing there.

No houses, no forts, and not a trace of any of the 118 people.

All that was found was the word *CROATOAN* carved in the post of an old wooden structure, and the letters *CRO* scratched into a nearby tree.

The mystery of what happened to those colonists on the Outer Banks was never solved, and the Roanoke Colony is now known in history as the Lost Colony.

Every summer since 1937, in a scenic amphitheater built on the spot of the actual events, on the water, just a few miles north of Manteo High, their story is played out every night.

A company of over 100 actors, dancers, singers, and technicians create a magical evening for your whole family. Gather clues from the colonists as you are immersed in epic battles, haunting Native American dances, elegant costuming, and beautiful music in this enormous stage production. The Lost Colony brings our nation's oldest mystery to life all around you.

Experience a night surrounded by the mystery of The Lost Colony!

Sam performed in *The Lost Colony* a couple summers while she lived up there.

She loved it. She always played one of the happy, dancing colonists.

Totally lost, however, is how she felt about her former home now.

No ties left ... Little sign she was ever there.

Louis probably felt the same way too ... after today.

14 ROUTE 66

In many cultures, the man's calling is to love his wife, safeguard his home, and provide for his family. The woman's calling: to support her man fully, keep the peace, and care for her children before herself.

Oh, how often we get it wrong.

Sam got up early the next morning and hit the road. She didn't feel right staying at Lucille's, or Sautee Nacoochee, any longer than she had to. Plus, she was driving twelve hours today, straight to her next destination, the town of Eureka Springs, Arkansas.

Before leaving, Sam wrote Louis a note thanking him for everything he did for her, and said.

And, she said she hoped to see him again one day as well.

It was Saturday morning, the day after Christmas.

Sam drove through Atlanta and into Alabama, past Mount Cheaha, the highest point in the state, by the Talladega Superspeedway, and stopped in downtown Birmingham for a break. She got a sandwich and a frosted lemonade from the *Chick-fil-A*, then pulled over by a quiet park to eat, and walk.

Across 16th Street, she saw a most beautiful Baptist Church and four little girls playing double dutch on the sidewalk alongside it. She watched them, and told them how amazing she thought they were. And, they invited her to jump in.

She did, and had the best time.

"Bye, Sam!" They cheered and waved as she drove off in her little black convertible.

Half Moon Bay, California ... that's where Sam decided her destination would be. After that, she really had no idea. Jack had spent a lot of his time surfing there, growing up out west, and it was such a beautiful place. So, she planned to be in the water there, New Year's day.

Sam crossed into Mississippi, then Tennessee, drove through Memphis and Little Rock, Arkansas, and finally into the Ozark Mountains to Eureka Springs. She'd read all about Victorian style village, *The Magic City*, *The Stairstep Town*, and its cute, steep winding streets, no two of which meet at a 90-degree angle, and all the fun and festivals that happen there around the year.

Sam had dinner at the 1881 Crescent Hotel, visited the 67-foot Christ of the Ozarks statue and The Great Passion Play amphitheater, then started back across the town to her room, the *Lofty Lookout Treehouse* at the Original Treehouse Cottages resort -- the most awesome treehouse cabin you ever did see, complete with an en-suite heart-shaped whirlpool tub, and surrounded on all sides by deck-to-ceiling windows and the beautiful Ozarks forest.

In front of the town's iconic Flatiron Flats building, she came across a woman laboring up the street's hilly steps. "I love your shirt!" Sam said, assessing if she was okay.

"Oh, thanks ..." The woman looked up, still hunched over, fifty-five or sixty years-old in a tie-dye green and red T-shirt, Christmas visor over her blonde permed hair, and white cotton shorts and a fanny pack. "I'll tell you, this town is pretty and all, but these streets ... I'll tell ya."

"I hear you." Sam commiserated. "Nothing *flat* about this place. Where are you from?"

"Flat ..." she gasped. "Omaha, Nebraska. How 'bout you?"

"Heading to California." It took her a second to say.

Sam asked the lady if she wanted a walking partner, since she was heading the same way. Turns out her name was Jeanne; she was in Eureka Springs with a couple of her *Homeaha* girlfriends taking in the Christmas Festival.

They visited a different town every year for the holidays, sometimes with their husbands, sometimes without.

Jeanne was out by herself tonight because she loved to walk, she said.

She just wasn't very good at it here in these hills.

"Thank you, my dear," Jeanne looked better as they arrived at her hotel, the Peabody House B&B. "It's so much easier with a partner. I'll tell ya."

"You are so welcome." Sam smiled. "Does your husband walk with you back in Omaha?"

"Oh my, no, Sam," she replied. "He just sits in that old chair and watches his beloved '*Skers*" (short for Cornhuskers, the University of Nebraska sports mascot).

Sam smiled.

Jeanne invited Sam for breakfast the next morning with her group on the hotel veranda, and Sam met them. And, before she left, she encouraged Jeanne to start a walking group back home with her friends, and their husbands. They'd make tie-dye shirts for everyone, pick out different routes to walk, and try to include a hill or two sometimes, for practice. Then, they could end their walks at some fun restaurant ... for lunch, or dinner, or dessert. Even to watch a Cornhuskers game together.

The ladies loved the idea.

They all hugged, and Sam walked once more across those Eureka

Springs streets to her car, and headed west.

It was Sunday morning.

Ranger returned home and sunk into the hot tub on the first floor lanai. The jets, the steam, and the cool air coming off the bay were therapy for him.

It had been an eventful 48 hours.

In the morning, he planned to check on Lwazi, then finish planning a hiking and diving trip down on the central coast. It was a good time to get away for a while.

"Knock, knock!" Ranger tapped on Lwazi's hotel door. He could hear Cecil jumping on the other side. Lwazi opened up, and there stood Ranger, holding the golden heart in his hand. "Here you go, my friend," he said.

"Ranger! How you do this?" Lwazi choked up. He took the heart into both of his old hands.

"I found the guys and got it back … Had to be done."

"They give it back to you?" Lwazi looked into Ranger's eyes, and quickly understood their message … *Sometimes it's better not to ask.*

Ranger's phone rang, it was Anna-Lena. She was calling to check on Lwazi too, and to thank Ranger again for the party Thursday night. Ranger asked if she was free for breakfast.

"It sure is nice what you've done for Lwazi," Ranger told Anna-Lena.

They sat down at their table at Mama's on Washington Square in San Francisco.

Ranger thought he'd take them to the place voted *best breakfast in the city* nearly every year for the past forever long. They all shared the Californian M'omelette, Pan Dore french toast, and North Beach Mama's benedict, the chef dividing the dishes up specially for them.

"Yes, you know … back home in Sri Lanka, the nurse comes to check on you at home too. Night and day. This is the custom I know."

Lwazi smiled, warmed inside, as Cecil popped his head out for a syrup-covered treat.

"Plus, I feel like Lwazi, and you, Ranger … you are my friends now."

The three of them shared laughs, and memories made over the past couple days. Anna-Lena insisted on helping Lwazi get set up with housing and any necessary services the upcoming week. She knew all about that stuff … It was social services who'd welcomed her, and helped her start down the path to becoming a nurse when she arrived in California, with nothing and nobody.

"You two are great role models," Ranger told Anna-Lena and Lwazi, walking back to the car. "Where you've been, and what you're doing with your lives … I'm grateful to know you."

They both smiled.

And walked a little taller after hearing that.

It was another stunning Saturday afternoon on the coast. And, Anna-Lena asked if they could take the top down on the Malibu for the drive home. Ranger was happy to oblige.

He couldn't help but notice her expression in the passenger seat, and Lwazi's in the back, pure joy as they headed home back over the Golden Gate Bridge, the wind in their faces.

He guessed that neither of them had experienced a drive like this before.

Ranger said goodbye to his three new friends at the hotel, Cecil launching a surprise lick attack to the face as he picked him up for a snuggle. He told them he'd catch back up with them later in the week, sometime after his hiking trip, and the New Year's Eve party at the Ritz-Carlton Thursday night in Half Moon Bay.

Then, he spent the rest of the day at home with Bernard.

Planning and packing for the outdoors.

Sam got to Amarillo, Texas, around dinner time and she was hungry.

It was a long haul through Oklahoma, but it gave her time to think. She'd wondered if Sally had been in contact with Damien at all ... and she wondered about Louis.

The radio had been advertising most of the day about how some local was going to be at The Big Texan Steak Ranch tonight to take on what they called the Texas King world steak eating challenge, and try to beat the current record, held by, of all people, a 125-pound mother of four from Sacramento.

Here was the deal:

Anyone able to finish the Texas King, a 72-ounce (4.5 pound) steak, buttered roll, baked potato, three fried shrimp cocktail, and salad, in less than an hour got the feast for free. You pay $72 up front, then get your money back if you succeed. The record, held for 21 years by a former major league baseball pitcher, was 9 minutes, 30 seconds. Then in 2008, the new record was set by that really likable Joey Chestnut guy, who won all those Nathan's hot dog eating contests on 4th of July at Coney Island in New York ... 8 minutes, 52 seconds. Then, in 2014, the little lady professional eater came along, set the new mark of 4 minutes, 58 seconds, and demolished her own record the very next year, 4 minutes, 18 seconds ... polishing off two more Texas Kings right after, for a total of 3 in less than 20 minutes.

Most Amarilloans leave the Big Texan to the tourists and the college kids, preferring joints like Tyler's Barbeque, the Coyote Bluff Cafe, Huds, or the Golden Light Cantina on the old U.S. Route 66. But tonight, the one-and-only Big Gar, was here to claim the title for himself, the town, and Texans everywhere.

He and his wife Kay had been on the radio throughout the afternoon promoting the event, and the couple's colorful personalities sounded too good to miss.

"And now, ladies and cowboys!" A twang rang out from a skinny man in a ten-gallon, holding the microphone. "Here's your man of the hour! Your champion cattle rustler and Nashville recording star! Former Olympian, councilman, and friendly neighborhood dentist! ... Big Gar, and his wonderful wife Kay!"

"Wow?" Sam said as she waited for her own 8-ounce filet, advertised as the *tenderest* you'll ever have.

Sam couldn't see very well from her booth, with all the people and the TV cameras around crowding in as the event began, but when the crowd went wild for those couple of minutes, *whoopin'* and *hollerin'*, then quieted, and then let out that collective groan, she deduced there would not be a new Texas King crowned tonight.

As her meal arrived, the people were already disassembling, and Sam could see Big Gar sitting there now, in front of a cyclone of food dishes, with Kay standing there beside him.

She got up and walked over.

"Hi ... Just wanted to let you know I kinda have this goal to meet someone extraordinary ... everyday ... So, *hello* to you both ... I'm Sam."

"Well, howdy, Sam." The large man looked up from under the brim of his Cavender's palm leaf Ponderosa hat, "I'm Big Gar ... This is my lovely wife Kay." As dejected as he surely felt, he still beamed a hearty smile.

"It's a pleasure to meet you. I heard you all on the car radio driving in today, and I thought you both were so delightful ... I can see why the crowd loves you so much."

"Why, thank you. That's very kind of you ... Sad we didn't bring it home for *The Rillo* tonight," Gar looked to Kay. "But, we'll get 'em next time. Won't we, honey skunk?"

"Sure will." Kay kissed him on the cheek, which spurred on that big toothy grin again.

"Nice try, Gar! We still love you! Blow Sand Blow!" A family called as they headed out.

"Blow Sand Blow!" he returned. "That's the motto for the Amarillo High School Sandies." Turned out Big Gar and Kay emcee their football games on Friday nights as well.

"So, where ya headin', Sam?" Kay asked as Sam was about to return to her table.

"California ..." she answered.

"Hey, alright ... We road tripped out there one time too! Remember, my little cuddle-dilla?" Gar reached over and pinched Kay in the roll on her side, and she giggled.

"Back in 1985 ... Last year of the ol' Route 66."

Kay reeled off a couple places they had stopped to see along the way.

"Kick in the britches, wasn't it, baby doll? It was our honeymoon!" Big Gar reached down with both hands in order to loosen up his *Texas to the Bone* belt buckle.

"You goin' it alone, Sam? ... Nobody travelin' with ya?"

"Nope ... All by my lonesome."

"Well, that could be a good thing, little darlin' ..." Kay winked at her.

"Yeah?" Sam replied. "How is that?"

"Been married before, Sam?" Kay asked back.

"Me ... no, ma'am."

Kay and Gar both smiled, with a sincerity like right then Sam was kin.

"Then your honeymoon still has the chance to be *once-in-a-lifetime* special," she smiled ... "Way it should be."

"That's right," Big Gar added. "Not like us ..." He tucked a new napkin into his shirt collar. "See, Sam, we've both done it all before, and if I have one regret in my life, that's it."

Kay put her arm around her husband's big shoulders. "Ya see, honey, Gar's the one for me, sure as the sun sets on the prairie in the evenin' ... And if we'd just waited for each other the first time 'round, until we was sure. I mean one hundred 'n' fifty-five percent Texas certain ... we'd a had that *once-in-a-lifetime* honeymoon too."

"Woulda gotten it right the first time." Gar nodded, eyeballing the chow still on his table.

"No dogfightin' with your ex's, or heartbreaks, or messy divorces ... To be cowboy honest, that's the reason I had to work so many jobs in the first place."

"Not to mention the kids." Sam could feel the regret in the big man's eyes.

"Yeah, we do a little presiding over matrimonies 'round here too ... you know, on the side," Gar added, which didn't come as a surprise. "And we always tell the interested parties the same thing ... We say, *Hey, spend some time together 'fore you go off decidin' to fix the ol' hitch ...*

Especially if this ain't your first rodeo. That way, you know better if your little rustler there ... truly is the one for you."

"That's what we did ... waited a year ... And after that, we was sure." Kay smiled to Sam.

"Then, we went to California!"

Big Gar looked to the time on his wristwatch, and down at the remainder of his Texas Kings, then resumed chawin' away at the meat. Finally, after a bit, he raised his napkin.

"59 minutes, 42 seconds!" The voice boomed over the Big Texan Steak Ranch loudspeakers. "Congratulations, Big Gar, all three of your Texas Kings are on the house!"

There was a smattering of applause as the host handed Big Gar and Kay their $216 back, and a few patrons hustled in to snap photos. Sam found herself clapping pretty hard too.

"Looks like you got 'em this time after all," she said.

Kay and Gar smiled, then wrapped her up in big hugs. She felt tears filling up her eyes.

"Yeah ... But you, Sam ... You get 'em the first time ... Know what I mean?"

"Yes ... yes, I do."

Sam wiped her eyes, turned and headed for the door. When she got there, she looked back. Kay and Big Gar were standing by their table, arms around each other, waving.

And, Sam mouthed the words to them ... "Thank you."

Ranger loved waterfalls. He always wanted to see the falls at Julia

Pfeiffer Burns State Park, and now that he was staring right at them, he couldn't believe what else he was seeing … three adult gray whales in the mouth of the beautiful small cove, about 100 feet offshore. Unreal!

He was 35 miles south of Carmel, 10 south of Big Sur.

It was Sunday morning.

McWay Falls stood there, 80 feet tall. It used to flow directly into the Pacific year round, but landslides in 1985 created the positively sublime beach that the waters pour down onto today when the tide is low. Granite cliffs, endless evergreens, riparian mystic Redwoods, serene flowers, and a perfect cove and falls made this place, as Ranger's research described it:

Like Fantasy Island, only better, as this is real.

Ranger hiked the afternoon, up McWay Creek to Canyon Falls, up the steep Ewoldsen Trail, through meadows, thousands of years-old giant trees, streams and ridges, up nearly 1500 feet to access some of Big Sur's most spectacular coastal vistas. He returned before dinner, and got to his environmental campsite, from where he could see otters playing in the cove, brown pelicans diving for fish, and pods of gray whales migrating south for the winter.

He had fixed camp, made some dinner, then settled in to work on his fully rugged tablet when a message popped up from Julian and Dan, who were in Abu Dhabi for New Year's, and to see the stopover for the Volvo Ocean Race, an 8-month, 40,000 mile yacht sprint around the world that happens every four years.

They were having the best time, of course.

Ranger combined their message with footage from his hike and made a cool mini-movie, which he enjoyed doing to remember the day.

To remember the good times.

He chuckled as he scrolled through a few old ones ... The boys' surfing trip to Tavarua ... some of their best rugby rivalry games ... and dancing at the Christmas party last week.

There were none of his family, though.

Until the day he left, Ranger's dad had always been a good dad.

Being out in the wilderness, like out here, was his father's favorite thing in the world to do. He'd bring the kids, Ranger and his two older sisters, and camp, and hike, and dive, and find all kinds of new and exciting ways to play in the surf. It's where he and Ranger thrived.

But, Ranger's mother was never into it all that much.

To Ranger, it seemed his mother regretted ending up with his dad. Like he was a mistake. She'd put him down, his lack of scholarly sensibilities, and the way he spoke sometimes. *Forgive him, he's from the other side of the tracks*, she'd beg her art group friends every once in a while, in front of him, and the kids. By the end, his parents hadn't spent a night together in the same bedroom for the better part of ten years, Ranger guessed.

Neither Ranger nor his sisters could ever quite determine what exactly catalyzed the failure, but it was always a pretty cold feeling around the Gabriel house. You see, mother was boss, and everyone mostly went along with what she said.

Until his dad left, then the family completely dissolved.

Ranger's mom moved to France, she'd always wanted to, and his sisters both left for the east coast, diving into their careers, administering their own relationships, and blaming their father fully for the breakdown. Ranger tried to stay in contact with his dad for a while, but it mostly faded, as the demands of his new, younger wife and her children increased. Now, Ranger calls him a couple times a year just to say *hello*.

But, he always felt for his dad, deep down.

Maybe he should have been more of a leader.

Ranger continued editing his film clip. He'd add more in the morning after his scuba dive in the underwater preserve at Partington Cove, which he read would be amazing, and possibly very hazardous. He titled the piece *Central Coast, December*, and mixed in some music to it. The song he chose made you feel like you were there, on the coast, among all this beauty and wilderness, or under the water ...

Sometimes I see the vision ... Sometimes you know I don't

Oh how I wish it would show me ... Only the things that I want

I kept desiring context ... The air was heavy and cool

Everything so delicate ... As I watched you walk into the room

I really want to make it so right ... For us to belong to the night

Just falling apart

We could follow the water

Sam had a 10-hour drive to her next stop, so she took off before 7:00 the next morning. She wrote Sally a good, long message and sent her a bunch of pictures the night before, and asked that Sally write her a good, long message back. She'd read it after she checked into her hotel for the night, so she could concentrate on driving, and enjoying her journey ... in case there was any alarming news.

She cruised right through New Mexico, just north of where outlaw Billy the Kid did his thing, and met his end in 1881. Where the first nuclear weapon ever was detonated in July, 1945, as a test, less than a month before the bombs were dropped on Hiroshima and Nagasaki. This one was named *The Gadget*, and was the same design as *Fat Man*, which hit Nagasaki.

Little Boy hit first over Hiroshima.

200,000 people lost their lives in these atomic explosions, but experts say casualties would have been much higher with a ground invasion of Japan.

And she drove by Roswell, or more precisely, Corona, where a government balloon went down in 1947, prompting an investigation that concluded it was an alien spaceship crash, with alien bodies recovered, and an attempt by the feds to cover it up.

Then, on to Seligman, Arizona, for dinner at the Route 66 roadside attraction Delgadillo's Snow Cap Drive-In. Big Gar and Kay had recommended the place and told her to order the *cheeseburger with cheese* or the *dead chicken*, just as the signage in there advertised.

The guy behind the counter, John, was hilarious.

He was the owner, along with his sister, and the son of Snow Cap's famous founder Juan, who started building the place in 1953, mostly out of scrap lumber from the nearby Santa Fe Railroad yard. Sam told John that Big Gar had a picture up somewhere in the restaurant, one from his Olympic days, and that she would have to locate it to see what sport he did.

John knew it instantly and took Sam to its laminated home under one of the tabletops ... the one where Big Gar and Kay sat on their honeymoon.

Sure enough, there he was, hair slicked back, on a cliff in Mexico, in a Speedo and waving the American flag.

"Diving?!" Sam blurted. "I would have never guessed that in a million years!"

Sam ordered a *Dble Patti Juan in a Million burger, w/chz*, of course, a *Route Beer 66*, and sat to eat out by the old Snow Cap 1936 Chevrolet with all the horns and decorations on it and a Christmas tree in the back. She noticed an older man, dressed in a tweed jacket and ascot, hair combed back, shoes shined, sitting alone, holding two cherry dipped cones.

He kept looking down the road, to the west, like he was waiting for someone to arrive.

"Hey, John!" A parade of 1920s and 30s Ford roadsters went by honking their horns as John emerged out of the restaurant. He waved and gave them all a big two-finger peace sign, then walked over to where Sam was sitting.

"That's funny ... Dad liked Chevys!" He pointed over to the collection of vintage Chevrolets parked out by the funky, kitschy outhouse. He'd brought over for Sam one of Snow Cap's favorite classic desserts, a *banunu split*.

"Thank you, John!" She was excited.

"For our first time customer ... We appreciate you." John smiled and started back inside.

"Hey, John." Sam called. "Can I ask you? Do you know that gentleman sitting over there with the two ice cream cones?"

He nodded.

"I was just curious ..."

"His name is Mr. Jonah." John looked over to him. "He's one of our long time customers."

Sam sat, waiting to hear more.

"He lost his wife ... probably twenty-five or thirty years ago now. Comes here every Monday and orders two dipped cones ... one for her, one for him ... like they used to do."

Sam's forehead wrinkled a bit. She paused. "Does he think ...?"

"Nope ... He knows she's gone, from here. But he says he's keeping the regular schedule, until they can pick it up again in heaven ... Doesn't miss a week."

"Wow. That's ..."

"Totally cool, right?"

"Yeah ..."

"And you know what else is awesome?" John went on. "He says people always try to tell him, *It's been so long, Jonah. Why don't you allow yourself to date, remarry? Don't stay lonely forever.* And you know what he tells them ...?"

Sam's eyes got big. "What?"

"He says ...

How am I going to eat ice cream forever

Sittin' at our favorite table in that diner in heaven

With the love of my life,

My wife ...

And another woman?

There is only one.

So, Mr. Jonah keeps the routine."

Sam finished her *banunu split*, said goodbye and thank you, and took a picture with John, then walked over to where Mr. Jonah was sitting.

She introduced herself and asked if she could take a picture next to him.

"It would just be super to have a photo with the greatest husband in the world," she said.

He obliged, put on his straw fedora, and smiled big for the camera.

Mr. Jonah was happy.

Heart totally full, Sam gave him a hug, and a kiss on the cheek, then got back on the route.

She got to her hotel, unpacked, washed up, and reflected on the day.

> *Maybe if dad wasn't too busy to do things with mom*
>
> *And waited on her the way Mr. Jonah does*
>
> *She wouldn't have ended up where she did.*

The thought of it saddened her, and gave her hope all at the same time.

By the time Sam cozied into her bed for the night, she realized she still hadn't heard back from Sally.

15 ALICE'S RESTAURANT

> "We don't yet see things clearly. We're squinting in a fog, peering through a mist. But it won't be long before the weather clears and the sun shines bright! We'll see it all then …"
>
> ***The Message***

The truth of the matter was that Damien had no idea who the woman was on the other end of the line that night at Magnolias. Didn't have a clue.

Sally couldn't figure it out either.

She'd tailed Damien a few days over the week, but didn't see anything out of the ordinary. She went by his house when he was home, and hung out by his work downtown … nothing.

Sally got back to the apartment at 8 pm Sunday night after walking around Charleston a bit. Even by Magnolias. She threw her keys and phone on the counter, flopped onto the sofa, and got to pulling off her brown leather knee-high riding boots and striped toe socks.

Then, began talking to herself …

"I'm just gonna walk up to that no good cheater and say it right to his face … Hey! … Stalker! … Why don't you just tell us who that creepy woman is you're covering up, buddy?!"

Sam's best friend was pretty scrappy.

"Oh … and another thing … Leave Sam alone already! … She doesn't love you!"

Sally paused, the apartment still mostly dark … There was a noise in the hall, like a thump.

She looked back to the door to see if she remembered to twist the lock on the deadbolt ... or if she'd forgotten again ... but there wasn't enough light to see.

"And give us back that key," she whispered.

An uneasy rush filled her body.

Sally jumped up, hurried over, one sock still on and one on the couch, and bolted the door.

The hall was quiet now.

She flicked on the dining room light and walked down the dim hallway into the bedroom, then re-emerged, wrapping herself in a robe.

"Wonder when Sam's going to call ..." She mumbled to herself.

Before returning to the couch and finishing her socks, Sally stopped by the kitchen, and the refrigerator, to check for a snack. She gazed straight ahead at the napkin she and Sam had written out, which was magneted in its original spot ... the right side of the freezer door, and read the only still relevant information printed on it:

California for New Year's

She opened the lower door and looked in, but there was nothing inside good enough for a Sunday night alone in front of the television. Then, she remembered she had an unopened pint of *Ben & Jerry's Blondie Ambition* ... buttery brown sugar ice cream with blonde brownies and butterscotch toffee flakes ... waiting for her in the freezer. She grabbed a spoon, opened the freezer door, pulled the lid off, and dug out a big scoop. And then one more. Her head dropped back and she closed her eyes.

Mmmm ... Sooo gooood

It was when she re-opened her eyes that she saw the pair of black leather work shoes, standing on the other side of the freezer door from her.

Before she could do anything, see who it was, move away, defend herself ... Sally was being attacked.

She tried to put her hands up and fight back, but was knocked sideways down to the floor with very strong force. The attacker grunted, and hit Sally repeatedly, in the side of the face, and back of the head, until the whole place faded dark.

The last things she heard were the sound of objects sliding off the counters all around her, and the thuds as they hit her in the body and head.

And the grunting.

She lay there slumped, unconscious and bleeding from the scalp and ear.

Ice cream spilled all over the floor.

What Sally had failed to realize ... All the time she was following Damien around this week, somebody else had been following her.

Diving at Partington Cove is so potentially dangerous that you're required to have a permit, and a buddy. Ranger found a dive buddy for the morning online, a burly islander guy named Manasa, with a thick, full beard, and big barrel chest.

Sure didn't look like a diver.

Ranger parked up on Highway 1, and he and Manasa walked down the steep trail together, over the footbridge, past the *no cliff diving sign*, and through the 60-foot redwood-lined tunnel that cut through the rocky point leading out to the Pacific. At the start of the 1900s, mules pulled carts of tanbark oak through that tunnel to ships waiting in the cove below, which reportedly also served as a landing for liquor smugglers during the Prohibition era.

The waves in the cove were pretty calm, though Ranger had read they can get real gnarly. The guys finished suiting up, checked their gear, went over a few basic buddy hand signals, and without much more than that ... they were in the water.

The ocean was blue and beautiful. Ranger and Manasa descended slowly along the steep granite walls, discovering some impressive looking marine life, like 4-foot lingcods, males, with their giant mouths and pointy teeth protecting their nests. Starfish and sea otters. Huge, spiny cabezon with heads the size of basketballs.

Manasa was amazed, like a big kid. You could tell by the thumbs ups he kept giving Ranger.

They'd been down for about half an hour when ...

Whoa! What is that?

Some sort of fish cruised by beneath them. It was about 3 feet long, striped and spotted, brilliant, and moved like a shark. Ranger followed above it towards the throat of the cove, out towards the open sea. All of a sudden, it turned left, quickly, towards the dark opening of what appeared to be a cave -- hourglass shaped, half above the water line and half below.

And ...

What on earth?! ... Wow!!

A big skate, like a stingray but more triangular, about 6 feet in length, whooshed by along the same path as the first fish. Ranger turned to Manasa, whose eyes looked as big as the spots on the skate's back, and the grin surrounding his regulator mouthpiece just as wide. He couldn't believe it. Skates usually stay in deeper water, much deeper than in the cove. This one must have been out of sorts some kind of way.

Ranger entered the mouth of the cave, where he'd seen the little spotted shark wiggle in, and readied his camera. He found the shark, stationary on a jagged ledge of the cave wall. In the camera light, the stones around the fish glowed deep green, perhaps they were jade, which can be found here on the Big Sur coast.

As Ranger snapped some photos, the shark began fluttering its tail and fins, and swaying back and forth on the ledge, kind of like it could hear the camera, like it was dancing with it. Ranger looked back to Manasa, who was silhouetted in the big greenish ocean behind him. *What a treat?* He was thrilled. He switched the camera to video, and right after that ...

Poof!!

The small shark puffed up like a balloon, threatened, its bloated body twice its original size. Ranger sensed something else in the cave behind him, rotated, and found the big skate just a foot from his face. The panicked animal thumped into him, nearly knocking his mask off. In a flash, the swell shark propelled away, out of the cave, towards the far side of the cove. The big skate flopped 180 degrees, bouncing off the wall, and followed it.

Ranger managed to capture most of what had just transpired on camera, and as the discombobulated skate swam away, he noticed Manasa waving and pointing in the corner of the frame. It was a bigger shark, a broadnose sevengill, probably 8 feet long, but it looked much bigger gliding in front of the entrance of the cave.

It veered right, with its rounded prehistoric head, like it was in pursuit of prey ... the skate, or the swell shark, or maybe both.

A strong wave surged into the cove, then another, and Ranger signaled to Manasa that it was probably a good time to head on up. The two surfaced at the dive flag, the onset of a swell bobbing them up like tops.

Then, in one swift movement, holding onto each other, they kicked one time and elevated up onto the rocks.

Just as large waves began crashing into the cove.

Neither of them could believe what they had just seen.

The guys proceeded to peel off their gear, then Manasa unpacked a tasty lunch to share. Fiji style bread, kumala stew, pudding, and kava. They talked and laughed together for over an hour. Manasa told stories about each of his apparently very entertaining 14 children, and it turns out his wife was one of the front desk hostesses at the Tavarua Resort where the boys had just stayed on their surfing trip.

He spoke of her with a glow on his face … a jolly woman, with a huge, gapped tooth smile, and a contagious giggle. Ranger remembered her well.

Manasa raised his cup of kava, and Ranger did the same.

"You come back visit again someday, my friend," Manasa smiled. "You be our guest!"

"I'd like that," Ranger replied. "Very much."

They toasted … "Bula!"

Then …

Woooof!

A sound came from the water like a dog barking. It was the little spotted swell shark, releasing the air it had taken in. The guys stood up, excited to see it.

Then, they noticed the skate circling around too, right beneath it.

Both creatures looked perfectly okay. Like the threat of the sevengill was gone.

The two men packed their stuff and walked back up the Tanbark Trail, above the treetops, to the highway. Looking up the hill, the mountains seemed to go straight up to the sky. They loaded their cars, gave each other a big hug, and said goodbye.

Ranger promised Manasa he'd see him again ... as a guest back at his home in Fiji.

The drive up Highway 1, across the Bixby Bridge, to the Point Lobos State Natural Reserve was especially stunning today. Ranger spent the rest of the day hiking the coastal trails and shoreline, discovering hidden coves and a multitude of wildlife.

After dinner, he checked into his Monterey hotel.

Sam crossed the border into California about 9:30 Tuesday morning.

She felt butterflies as she drove by the welcome sign, for some reason.

There still wasn't a return message from Sally. And, she hadn't answered her phone either. Sam was looking forward to telling her she'd be in Half Moon Bay New Year's morning ... actually surfing in the Pacific.

So, she figured she'd just wait to hear from her.

She motored through Barstow, Tehachapi, and Bakersfield, onward to Interstate 5 north, and could feel the dryness in the valley air.

It was different out here than it was on the east coast.

The convertible then turned west onto Highway 46 near Lost Hills ... by Blackwell's Corner, the gas station there at the intersection of 46 and 33.

Also known as James Dean's Last Stop.

Although Sam was never into Hollywood movies that much, and she'd never seen his films, she knew that James Dean's last movie was a 1956 classic called *Giant*. She'd also read that before *Giant* wrapped filming, James Dean had done a public service announcement ... reminding motorists to mind the road and to drive safely.

It was just 25 miles up the road from that stop, two weeks after he delivered that message, that Dean was lost in the crash.

The driver of the other car said he never even saw him.

Sam passed right by the spot of the accident, there at the junction of Highways 46 and 41 ... the plea made by the 24 year-old actor to young drivers repeating in her head ...

Take it easy ...

The life you save might be my own.

Sam got her first close-up view of the Pacific Ocean from Highway 1 at Moonstone Beach, just past the scenic town of Cambria. Waves were crashing, and it was absolutely gorgeous. She parked at the head of the mile-and-half long boardwalk that parallels the coast there, pulled her sweater snug around her, drew the waist tie, and started walking.

There were people all along the beach. Some playing down by the surf, a few were jogging, and some just strolling hand-in-hand.

Sam looked out to them, and realized she hadn't spoken a word yet to anyone all day.

She stepped off the wooden walkway, removed her Keen Coronado sneakers, and headed towards the water.

Can you believe Damien and I never walked on the beach together?

Not once ... Ever?

What a rip-off, she thought to herself.

How could she have given so much to him, and not have seen what he was giving in return? … He really never even tried.

Not until after it was too late.

It was unbelievable how lonely she felt right now.

Sam's bare feet hit the cool of the wet sand; she turned north and kept on walking.

Then, she heard a voice.

"I'm looking for moonstones!"

She looked up to see a little girl, probably four or five, standing there looking at her.

"I found two already!" The girl held out her hand so Sam could see.

They were silvery and white with beautiful swirling patterns and a pale light reflecting from their centers.

"Those are beautiful …" Sam told her.

The little girl smiled, then gazed up into Sam's face, like kids do when they're studying you. "If you look hard enough, you can find one too."

"Come on, Sam. Time to go!" The little girl's parents called out to her, gathering their things and turning back for the boardwalk.

Sam's eyes widened as she heard the sound of her own name.

"Try over there!" the little Sam directed as she ran off to her family, pointing to the surf about thirty yards away. "Bye bye!"

"Bye … *Sam*." Sam watched as the girl packed her stuff into her little red and white striped backpack. She waved … and Sam waved back.

It was almost dark, that time when both the sun and moon shared the irreversibly dimming sky. But, still enough light for Sam to search the ankle-high surf where the girl had pointed, and to happen upon a nice-sized moonstone somersaulting right up to her feet.

She held it up and examined the glow in its center.

"Wow," she smiled, then started back for the car.

Sam stopped for dinner at the Moonstone Beach Bar & Grill, right there along the seaside, where she ordered Tom's soup and salad, and relaxed outside by herself to eat. After that, she checked into her room at the Fogcatcher Inn a few doors down.

Out on the hotel deck overlooking the ocean, she wished she could have said something more to little Sam … At least tell her *thank you* for the moonstone, and for talking to her.

And that her name was Sam too.

Ranger woke, did some push-ups in the room, and headed out for breakfast at his favorite Loulou's Griddle in the Middle on Monterey's commercial pier. He loved the warm, homey feel there. There was a training run happening today at the popular Skyline-to-the-Sea Trail, a near 30-mile route that tumbled down from the Santa Cruz Mountains to the ocean at Waddell Beach, north of Santa Cruz, and Ranger was excited to do it.

He took the Pacific Coast Highway to California 17, then State Route 35 to the Saratoga Gap, and arrived. He knew most of the run organizers from his UC Berkeley cross country days, and they were thrilled to see him. So, he chatted for a while, got the course particulars, laced up his ASICS FujiEndurance trail runners, and started off.

On the trail, he thought about the past week, and about his family. And, he realized that the life he'd learned from them was not necessarily the life he had to be resigned to himself.

That a life with love was much better, and much more fulfilling, and right, for everyone. And, it was something he could see ... for himself.

Like the beach and the Pacific down the trail in front of him.

Ranger reached the finish line in just over three hours. He'd run by forests of coastal evergreens and old growth redwoods, lush ferns and chaparrals, sandstone formations and 65-foot misty waterfalls.

3,000 feet of elevation gain, 6,000 of descent, and wildflowers galore ... It was spectacular.

Shuttles were set up to transport people the hour back up the mountain to their vehicles. Tomorrow in the afternoon, Ranger would be checking in at the Ritz-Carlton Half Moon Bay, a guest of his old rugby pal Tanaka, who was hosting a New Year's extravaganza for his charitable foundation at the luxury oceanfront resort.

So, he'd have one more morning to hike and explore before heading over.

Ranger called to check in on Schalk and Bernard at the house before his cell service went out in the hills. Then, he drove over to his campground, and set up the tent for the night.

He slept well into the next morning.

Sam was up before sunrise.

She made a sarsaparilla tea, and walked out barefoot onto the deck to catch the first light. Curled up in a wicker chair, she ran the stone she'd found in the waves through her fingers, and stared out at the ocean. The rock felt rounded, and irregular, with a notch on one side and a blunted point on the other, and when the sun burst over the coast range behind her, she held it up so it could catch the sun's rays.

It glowed right away.

Sam hadn't noticed yesterday, but her moonstone, with its unique and abstract perimeter, and its swirled white streaked patterns ... was shaped roughly like a heart.

It was exquisite, and cool. Really quite perfect. It gave her goosebumps.

Sam got herself ready, skipped breakfast altogether, jumped into the Siata, and took off. Yesterday was a really lonely struggle, and she wanted to get past it as quickly as possible. She looked forward to seeing the California coast today, but was mostly just ready to get to Half Moon Bay and begin this new chapter in her life.

Ranger packed up camp around 9:00 am, enjoying an easy pace this Wednesday morning. There was something he really wanted to see today, so he took to the trail to get there.

Giant fallen trees cross Bridge and Aptos Creeks many times in the Santa Cruz Mountains, and Ranger had a blast traversing every one he could. At Maple Falls, there was one huge trunk that extended out about 25 feet from the trail into the falls, 20 feet above the ground. Bold souls shimmied out and took photos sitting on the log, but it was definitely a risk.

Ranger, in his infinite skill, leaped out onto it and proceeded to tightrope walk to the end ... all the way into the mist of the flow still pouring down from the rains a couple weeks ago. He turned the video camera on and panned around, down to the pool below, then up to the top of the 35-foot falls.

With the camera still rolling, he then half ran, half somersaulted back off the slippery trunk and got onto the trail.

We could follow the water ... The song was still stuck in his head.

Sam motored north up Highway 1, by the places she'd read about a couple nights before. Hearst Castle, the elephant seals at Piedras Blancas, and the ocean cliffs at Ragged Point. She saw the hang gliders and treasure hunters at Jade Cove, and pulled over to watch surfers along the expanse of Sand Dollar Beach, with 5,155 feet of Cone Peak shooting straight up behind her, from the sea to the top of the Los Padres National Forest.

A half hour later, she parked and strolled down to the platform overlooking McWay Falls at Julia Pfeiffer Burns State Park, where Ranger had been three days before.

It was 10:00 am.

Rounding the final curve coming up to the breathtaking Bixby Bridge, Sam realized she hadn't yet taken a single photo since arriving in California. Amidst all this beautiful scenery, it hurt her to be alone. She started to cry ... Everything felt so far away for her now.

Sam pressed up the Big Sur coast, past picturesque Carmel and up the Monterey peninsula, a place so perfect that many people around these parts call it ... *God's Country.*

Ranger reached the sign along the wooded Aptos Creek Trail a little after 11:00 am. It read:

EPICENTER

Loma Prieta Earthquake

MAGNITUDE: 6.9

DATE: 10/17/89

TIME: 5:04 pm

LONGITUDE: 121.88°W

LATITUDE: 37.03°N

The scene in the Forest of Nisene Marks is stunning here, and eerie. Giant 2,000 year-old redwoods and robust Douglas firs ripped out of the ground, crisscrossing each other like stacks of pick-up sticks.

And quiet.

Ranger passed another sign informing him that the San Andreas Fault was directly beneath his feet, and reminding him not to get eaten by mountain lions, which made him chuckle; but the vast chasm left by the quake, visible as you scrambled alongside the Aptos Creek canyon, and the obvious landslide areas where the cliffs had crumbled were a little more sobering.

He followed his GPS to the true epicenter of the quake, a remote place up on a forested slope, off the beaten path. This is what he had come to see. Where the great Pacific Plate meets the North American, and where the rupture occurred, a dozen miles below the surface, shaking the ground for 15 seconds, but suspending time for so many forever.

63 people lost their lives that day. 3,757 were injured.

Ranger took one photo, then reached down into a small crevice in the hillside, dug out a chunk of striated sandstone, and slipped it into his pocket to keep as a memento.

Sam stopped at a filling station for gas. A little, grey-haired man came out to meet her.

"Heading up the coast?" he asked, noticing the plates on her convertible.

"Yes," Sam nodded.

"Well, just heard on the radio ... been a rockslide this side of Año Nuevo. Highway's closed."

Sam opened the door and stepped out, and started to ask ...

"Gonna need to go up the 17 to the 35 and back down if you want to get back to the PCH," the bearded man instructed as he pumped her gas. "Where ya headed?"

"Half Moon Bay," Sam replied.

The old man finished up screwing the gas cap in and gave a smile. "That's nice."

He turned, then started back toward the shop.

Sam checked her phone for a signal so she could access her map, but there was none.

"You'll see the signs," the attendant said, without looking back.

"*Ooh kaay* ..." Sam whispered to herself, doing a double-take.

Ranger took his pack and shoes and shirt off, and enjoyed a refreshing shower under the cool gush of pretty Five Finger Falls, a high, wispy stream that cascaded down a vertical rock face into an intimate little grotto. After that, he hiked back to the car and started making his way over to Half Moon Bay.

He took Skyline Boulevard (Highway 35) a winding two-lane road that runs from Highway 17 in the Santa Cruz Mountains to Highway 1 in San Francisco, following the ridgeline and offering those who drive it unreal views of the Pacific coast on one side, Silicon Valley on the other, and the San Francisco skyline as you go farther north ... A great road to drive.

Ranger remembered Skyline Boulevard well from his childhood. His family came here often, to the El Corte de Madera Creek Open Space Preserve, where his mother served as director of habitat restoration, and his dad built trails.

And the place where the family came to eat, Alice's Restaurant.

Alice's was a real treat ... An eclectic rustic cabin, built in the early 1900s as a general store, then purchased by a lady named Alice Taylor in the 1960s, and renamed after herself and the now classic 1967 anti-war, anti-authority folk cult song *Alice's Restaurant* by Arlo Guthrie. It had a fabulous wrap-around deck, a great bar, great music, and a big backyard property that led to hiking and equestrian trails, and endless miles of wilderness all around everywhere.

If you looked the place up, here is what you would find:

Alice's is a little slice of bliss among the redwoods. It's a place where families, motorcyclists, hikers, equestrians, Silicon Valley entrepreneurs, writers, musicians, locals, and visitors can all come together to enjoy a great meal. Whether you want gourmet burgers and sweet potato fries, or one of our scrumptious scrambles, or homemade pie, you can find it here.

Ranger parked out front, with all the cool cars and bikes, and entered the front patio area. It was crowded for 3:00 on a Wednesday, but you never really had to wait here at Alice's. You just looked around for a seat, and took it, which was nice, because Ranger was hungry.

And a little stiff.

The 30-mile run yesterday, and all that hiking had made his legs shaky.

"Whew ... not as young as I used to be," he groaned as he squatted into a picnic-style table on the side deck and opened up a menu, nodding to the older biker couple who were seated at the other end.

Ranger felt good being here now. He hadn't been back in a while, because of the memories.

They hurt too much.

This was such a great place to be as a youngster, running around, playing in the forest with Frans, and Carolijn, and his sisters. And, it was the only place Ranger could remember seeing his parents happy, together at the same time.

And the menu still looked so good.

The *Jalopy* burger, smothered in BBQ sauce, bacon, Jalapeno, grilled onions & jack cheese. The *Le Mans*, with sauteed mushrooms, grilled onions, and Swiss. The *Harley*, loaded with bacon, sausage, grilled onions, cheddar and jack, and the ⅔ pound *Hog*, with avocado. Brisket sandwiches smoked for 12 hours, pulled pork, BBQ ribs, grilled chicken sandwiches, mahi tacos.

Like the song says, *You can get anything you want ... at Alice's Restaurant.*

Just like when he has eleven, Ranger ordered dessert first. He got raspberry cheesecake, with a sauce made from scratch and fresh berries, *and* he got the chocolate molten cake, with two scoops of Humboldt Creamery vanilla ice cream.

Oh, man, was it awesome.

As he ate, Ranger watched the variety of patrons around the restaurant, and he pictured his mom, whom he would always find out back trotting around on her jet black Percheron, or painting with her college girlfriends; and his dad, who would hang out in the front, chopping it up with all the bikers and classic car buffs.

Although the kids watched their parents drift painfully and steadily apart over the years, like a receding tide, there were a lot of good times here.

Ranger ended up having the Norton burger, named after the British motorcycle company, with the Point Reyes bleu cheese, and bacon. And, he watched the people taking pictures out on the *Group W* bench.

In the song *Alice's Restaurant*, a young Arlo Guthrie sings about being arrested for littering on Thanksgiving Day, 1965, when all he was trying to do was help his friends Alice and Ray by dumping their trash over a cliff. The Vietnam War was going on at the time, but because of his crime, authorities determined Mr. Guthrie was morally unfit for the draft and service to his country.

He was made to sit with the others whose *kind* they didn't like ... on the *Group W* bench.

After incriminating him there, they asked him one final question ...

> *Kid, have you rehabilitated yourself?*

It was clear he had not.

It was exactly 4:13 pm, on the other hand, when Ranger's rehabilitation, for everything he had lacked, everything he had missed growing up, for all the heartache and faults of the family, came complete.

He stood up from the table, and felt both of his knees buckle underneath him. Was it his legs, from the run? Or another earthquake?

No. Not either ... It was Sam.

16 HALF MOON BAY

The moon is a permanent satellite of earth, and though we see it both night and day, and a *full* one every month, still only 59% of it has ever been visible from our planet's surface.

Sam was clutching the moonstone in her right hand when she saw Ranger out on that deck, and she lost her breath for a moment. They smiled at each other for what seemed forever, then against gravity, Sam backed her way into the front door. Ranger suddenly felt dizzy. He went down the stairs and walked right by Sam's parked car, and she watched him out of the big window as he wandered ... finally finding his Malibu.

He got in, then proceeded to drive around in a near complete circle, without realizing it, twisting his neck to try to see into the bright reflection of the restaurant's glass. And, it was only by chance and autopilot that he managed to find his way safely back onto Highway 35 north towards State Route 92.

Who was that girl? He thought to himself every mile along the way.

Sam had a huge lump in her throat.

It was December 30.

The sun took forever to settle over Half Moon Bay that evening.

A Scottish bagpiper was playing out alongside the cliffside 18th hole of the Old Course at Half Moon Bay as Ranger checked into his oceanfront suite. Tanaka really went all out at these events, and this New Year's Eve at the Ritz-Carlton was to be no exception.

In college, Tanaka was a pretty good, albeit overly vocal scrum half for Cal rivals St. Mary's, and after Ranger knocked him unconscious with a big hit during a match their junior year, then helped him off the field as he was waking up, Tanaka knew from that point on he needed to have Ranger on his side as an ally, not an opponent.

Cal won the game; Ranger was happy to oblige. The two became good friends after that. They did some business stuff together, and Ranger and the boys helped out with some of Tanaka's charitable projects. And, they still got together to play a little pick-up footy on the weekends every once in a while.

Beneath all the big, well-to-do personality, Tanaka was really a good guy.

He had showered and cleaned up by the time his friend showed up to his room.

Knock ... knock ... knock ... knock ... knock!

Ranger opened the door, and as soon as he did, Tanaka hit him with a *duck and clean* move, a rugby technique where one goes low to try to knock his opponent backwards off the ball. Tanaka challenged Ranger with a stunt like this every time the two of them got together, however it never worked.

For a split second, Ranger considered letting Tanaka get the best of him, just this once ... but then decided against it.

As Tanaka grappled his legs, Ranger wrapped his huge arms around his buddy's torso, rolled backwards, and gut-wrench suplexed him about six feet into the air, crashing him headfirst and sideways into the center of the luxury California king bed.

"Whoooaaaa!" Tanaka yelped as his skull and neck twisted into the mattress.

He stumbled to his feet, and a couple steps to the side, pretending like he wasn't stunned, and laughing, came over and gave Ranger a big bear hug.

"Dang, Ranger! ... You still got it, man! ... How you doing, buddy?!"

"Good ... Fantastic ... How are you, my friend?"

"Couldn't be better, man!"

(Not exactly true considering how that little scrummage had ended up.)

"Business is great! Family is terrific! And married life treating me very, very good!" Tanaka pulled his skin-tight, lavender polo shirt straight and regathered his focus. "You know, Krystyna is running foundation now."

Tanaka had come to California for college directly from Japan, and his father, one of the wealthiest men in Osaka, started the foundation for him so he'd never forget to practice the cherished Japanese custom of *Kikubari* while he was here. *Kikubari* meaning to be others-centered, giving ... Selfless, not selfish.

Which was good, because Tanaka needed reminding growing up.

"No, I didn't know that. That's really great. Good for both of you guys."

Krystyna had been the director of the performance group Ranger hired for their Christmas parties, and last year at the Claremont, she'd spent most of the night helping Tanaka learn the moves to all the songs. She noticed him trying, but his abject lack of rhythm was so profound that she felt bad and went over to rescue him.

The rest, as they say, was history.

They ended up making a great couple, both incredibly outgoing people. Ranger and the boys flew over for their fairy tale wedding in romantic Kyoto last summer.

"She have a really cool stuff planned. Wait until tomorrow night, Ranger ... You gonna see!"

Tanaka walked out onto the suite balcony overlooking the eighteenth green and the sea as the bagpiper was finishing up his effervescent set.

"It gonna be a night none of us ever gonna forget!" Tanaka took a big breath of the fresh salt air.

"Can't wait ..." Ranger replied.

Tanaka turned to Ranger. "So happy you here, buddy. I just wanna make sure room is good, and you have everything you need."

"It's really nice, Tanaka. Too much, really ... Thank you ... And, I'm honored."

"Okay, then! We meet tomorrow morning for the breakfast. 9:00 sharp!"

"Looking forward ..."

Tanaka went back in, pausing to straighten the section of comforter where he had landed. "Okay, my friend ... I see you," he said.

"Okay ... Give Krystyna my best."

Tanaka left, and Ranger sat down, pulling the chunk of Loma Prieta stone from a wrinkle in the blanket Tanaka had missed. He had smoothed it out and removed the tiny bits of earth stuck to it while he was in the shower.

It was beautiful.

With all its stripes and layers, and colors and curves.

"It was so wonderful to meet you, Sam ... You're just the sweetest girl in the world!"

"Thank you, Naomi ... No. I think *you* are amazing."

It was good that Naomi came and sat at her table. Sam had been sitting there in a daze. Also, Naomi ended up inviting Sam to the big charitable event she was attending tomorrow night on the coast, and Sam accepted.

Before leaving, the two decided to take a photograph together out on the *Group W* bench ... Sam's first photo in California.

"I'll see you around 7:00, then." Naomi hugged her, wiping the tears from her eyes.

"Yes you will," Sam replied.

Sam's GPS was finally working, and it guided her directly to Half Moon Bay and the cottage she was renting for the week. A big master suite in a private home, with its own entrance, one block from the beach, and walking distance to the village's charming downtown.

Photos of it had shown a cute, raised four-poster bed, and the owner had written that there were bicycles and surfboards available to use. Sam was lucky to get it on such short notice, and at such a great price.

She settled in, then ported over a lounge chair to the serene bluff overlooking the beach, and sat there in the heavy, cool air.

Alice's ran through her mind ... *Who was that man?* she thought to herself.

The feeling ran through her all over again out there on that pretty, low-rise cliff. Like a gigantic wrench grabbing her insides and twisting them into a pretzel ... but in a good way. Like when you're on a really fun roller coaster.

This had never happened to her before.

The way he looked at her, as if he knew her. Knew everything about her.

And like she knew him.

Like they were experiencing the same exact thing, at the exact same time.

Why didn't I say something?

Anything.

"Stupid," she mumbled, and sat there, staring at the sea.

It was close to 10:00 when Sam decided to turn in for the evening. It had been a long day, and she was tired.

"Where is Sally?" she asked out loud, digging her phone out from the bottom of her bag. She called again, but there was no answer, so she sent a message as she got the hot water going in the walk-in shower.

SALLY, WHERE ARE YOU ???

She hadn't heard from her best mate in four days … It just wasn't like her.

Swelling in the brain (or cerebral edema) occurs when fluid collects in the brain tissue, causing the pressure inside the skull to rise, and the flow of blood and oxygen the brain needs to function to restrict. Breathing tubes are utilized to supply the brain with oxygen, and to remove the harmful carbon dioxide.

It was likely Sally's tube would be removed soon, because the swelling in her brain had begun to subside.

She remained unconscious, though.

The doctor was explaining all this to her sister, who'd arrived from Boston to the intensive care unit yesterday morning. Marcus, from the Mellow Mushroom, was there too.

It was Marcus who had found Sally lying there … in that mess in Sam's old kitchen on Monday. He had walked over and checked on her because she didn't show for work that morning.

And, it was fortunate he did, the doctor said, because the swelling was serious.

Charleston police interviewed Marcus yesterday, and what he told them confirmed their investigation. This had not been a burglary gone wrong. The apartment was not ransacked. Sally's purse and wallet were still on the couch where she had been sitting.

Everything outside of the kitchen was found undisturbed.

The only thing they couldn't find was her cell phone.

Sam fell deeply asleep that night. Perhaps the roar of the waves coming through the open window helped put her out. But at 1:50 am, her phone vibrated hard on the rustic wooden nightstand next to the bed. Its bright green glow lighting up the room. Sam woke right up. She reached over, grabbed the device, saw it was text from Sally, and sat up, perplexed.

It just asked back ...

Where are you?

Sam looked around to collect her bearings.

The room looked surreal in the light of the phone, kind of like in a movie when they use the night vision on the camera. Everything stood out. The only darkness was the square hole of pitch black in the open window.

Sam focused back on the phone and began to type.

I'm in Half Moon Bay. Rented a cottage right on the beach.

Sally, what's been going on? Please call me and let me know everything's okay.

Call me now if you can, or answer your phone. I have so much to tell you.

She almost hit the send button, but paused a second, and added one more thing.

I wish you were here.

Then, she waited for about half a minute and tried to call again.

It rang five or six times, then went to voicemail ... again.

Eventually, the green light of the phone faded out, and so did the room. The only illumination now were the stars over the Pacific, becoming visible one-by-one outside.

Sam closed her eyes.

On the cocktail table in front of the white Victorian brocade couch inside Damien's loft, Sally's phone went dark too. The caller ID had just read ... *Sam.*

If you stood there, down on Broad Street in the middle of Charleston's old French Quarter, and looked up that split second at Damien's apartment, you would've seen the dark figure, with the ghost white face, standing there just inside the big bay window.

Then, see it move quickly away towards the door.

The next day was the doldrums for Sam and Ranger both. Sam stayed in bed until noon, burying herself under the big white comforter, not coming up for air even one time. Ranger met up with Rudy Rios and some other old friends over lunch. But he wasn't really there. Had it not been for the party tonight, he would have driven home to Sausalito and Bernard, and his deck on the second floor.

Sam ended up walking along the coastal trail, to Poplar Beach, Half Moon Bay State Beach, up to Venice and Miramar, and back. After that, she started getting ready.

She arrived at the magnificent Ritz-Carlton to meet Naomi. It was early, just before 6:00 pm, so she took a stroll around the grounds before the sun set all the way. It wasn't cold at all. In fact, it felt almost balmy. So, she stayed out for a while.

Until the moon was well on its way towards the booming ocean at her northwest.

"Hi, Naomi ..." Sam's Aussie accent sounded warm, and the two hugged as she passed through the doorway into her room. "You look so nice." Naomi was still young, early forties at the most, but she seemed a bit older than that for some reason.

"Thank you, Sam. I don't think I've worn ..." She paused mid-sentence and her eyes went to the floor.

Naomi was in a floral dress that looked about fifteen years ago, her gel-held hair showing gray at the temples, and the gloss white mid-heels she wore were scuffed in more than one spot. You could tell this kind of stuff wasn't customary for her. However, as uneasy as Naomi looked, Sam was equally or more natural and graceful. She had on a flowing dark royal purple evening dress that an up-and-coming Florida fashion designer, a gal named Essence, had made for her, the two just happening to meet at a popular beachside restaurant in Clearwater Beach called Crabby's Bar & Grill. They had such a good time talking, about life, and girl stuff, Essence ended up taking Sam's measurements right there at the table ... then sent her the dress in the mail two weeks later. It was a gorgeous piece of couture, knotted in the front, strapped around the neck, long and wispy, and open in the back.

It was the only dress she brought with her.

Sam had her hair up with a wide, loose braid on top, and a cute, high ponytail, and wore the Pomellato Luna earrings her *Nonna* and *Nonno* had given her for her eighteenth birthday.

As Naomi looked up again, she saw how dazzling Sam really was.

"Sam, you are so pretty," she said, tears falling away, and a smile finding its way to her face. "I'm really happy you're here."

"I'm happy I'm here too," Sam answered, touching her hand to Naomi's shoulder.

"Let's go have the best year we can ... Both of us."

Naomi took a deep breath, picked up the sweater from her bed, and the two headed off down the hallway to the elevator.

The ballroom at the Ritz-Carlton is the largest of its kind on the Northern California coast, and it was decked out for the event. Giant white hydrangea and rose bouquet centerpieces in three-foot tall crystal vases on the tables, custom blown glass chandeliers and gorgeous golden pendant lighting everywhere, and cool, vintage Old Hollywood spotlights.

Arriving guests were shown to their tables, and at 8:00 sharp, the festivities began.

Music played, and an ensemble of servers, dressed really cool in '40s crepe and gabardine, wavy hair, matte makeup, suspenders and Cuban heels, emerged through the main doors. They whizzed around filling up everyone's glasses, greeting the guests by name, ballroom dance stepping as they came and went.

"Evening, Naomi. So wonderful to see you!" ... "Welcome, Sam, to a most magical night!"

Then, they served the first of an extraordinary twelve-course *Kaiseki*-style dinner, *sakizuke*, an appetizer dish similar to the French *amuse-bouche*, for which Krystyna ventured outside traditional Japanese and chose a wonderful creamy parmesan panna cotta.

After that was the second course, *hassun*.

"C'mon, c'mon!" Then, the servers scampered over to the old-fashioned microphone on the dance floor, and with golden spotlights and ballyhoo, opened the show:

Welcome, everyone, to a Vision of New Year's, past and future ... We hope you enjoy it.

And, thank you for celebrating the New Year with us ... here in unforgettable Half Moon Bay!

Sam and Naomi's table was more towards the back of the room, near the main entry doors, so they had to sit up to see as the crew kicked off an incredibly fun swing dance routine, pulling guests out from the crowd to join in as they went.

Of course, Tanaka was one of them.

It was very entertaining.

Even Naomi tapped her fingers along to the music.

Sam was happy she was there for Naomi, who had nobody to go home to anymore either. She looked over at her, and recalled the promise she had made to herself at Looking Glass Falls.

Always help others to take the lid off ... so they might enjoy life and help someone else along the way.

Yesterday at Alice's, Naomi had told Sam about the day she learned what joy really meant in life. The day she met her husband. She was new in town in San Rafael, in line at the market. Check stand number two. She said she'd never forget that. He said *hello*, and they talked.

That afternoon, and many times afterwards, he told her ...

You know, you can tell a lot about a person by just the smallest of their gestures.

And that it was just the way she was standing there in line right then, and the way she told the clerk who bagged her things *thank you*. That it was simply the tone in her voice ... and the way she looked at him just before he spoke to her.

He could tell she was a beautiful heart.

She told Sam never in a million years had she ever considered that someone would fall in love with her like that. Especially at first sight. That wasn't supposed to be for her. She just wasn't the type. Nobody had ever pursued her, or showed any interest.

Not like what happens with all the other girls.

That day, however, the other thing Sam had reminded herself at those falls in North Carolina, came true for Naomi.

That *everybody deserves love.*

Naomi's husband was exactly right about her, standing in line at the supermarket that day, and she would love him forever because of it.

They would love each other.

It was 9:00 when the servers escorted everyone back to their seats, then paired up for the next part of the show, a rumba to the holiday classic by Ella Fitzgerald.

> *Maybe it's much too early in the game*
>
> *Aah, but I thought I'd ask you just the same*
>
> *What are you doing New Year's*
>
> *New Year's Eve?*
>
> *Wonder whose arms will hold you good and tight*

When it's exactly twelve o'clock that night

Welcoming in the New Year

New Year's Eve

Maybe I'm crazy to suppose

I'd ever be the one you chose

Out of a thousand invitations

You received

Aah, but in case I stand one little chance

Here comes the jackpot question in advance

What are you doing New Year's

New Year's Eve?

It was very romantic.

It made Sam think about Ranger ... again.

For probably the five hundredth time today.

And at his table up front by the stage, Ranger sank back into his chair.

Anyhow ... That's how the night began.

Neither Sam nor Ranger ate very much, but no one really noticed. The room was dark, plus the evening never quite slowed down. There was all kinds of stuff, even a funny skit about New Year's traditions around the world. Silly things people do to try to gain health and good fortune, like throwing plates at friend's doors, and buckets of water out of windows, eating grapes, hiding knives ... and hoping that the first visitor to cross the threshold of your front door after midnight is a tall, dark-haired, handsome young man bearing gifts.

At 10:00, presentations for the foundation were well under way.

Onstage, Krystyna was introducing two former rival gang members named Israel and Ihaia, who were about to perform, with Tanaka, an original song/dance they called *Together I Can*. That was the name of their project too, where next month, they'd start bringing kids from all over Northern California to the foundation's hi-tech campground in the coastal hills near Lagunitas for weekends spent together rapping and dancing, recording music and movies, dirt biking and hiking ... and learning new things, like how to play cricket, and cook Thai.

And how to treat each other well.

A handful of other outstanding projects followed, then it was Naomi's turn.

Krystyna called her to the stage.

It took her a second to get started. "Hello ... My name is Naomi Jacobs." But once she did, she was going.

"And, in just one month, each class had its own project up and running in the community."

"Then, I get a call ... out of nowhere." Naomi turned to her left, towards Krystyna, who was standing next to her with the most enthusiastic smile. "Krystyna heard what we were doing, somehow, I don't know how ... and asked if she could help."

Naomi talked about a venture she started at her local elementary school where each class, with parents and staff, created an ongoing project to help make the world a better place. One class did activities with the elderly, another, neighborhood clean ups, one did wellness events with the less fortunate, like *Pizza & Pilates in the Park* and *Mini Marathon Movie Day*, where families, the homeless, the mayor, whoever wanted, walked together a healthy stretch to take in a movie and lunch. Those who could treated those who had little.

And, one class sent gifts and letters to soldiers overseas.

She told the story of how her husband served in the Armed Forces over in the Middle East ... and was lost in combat two winters ago.

And how that destroyed her family.

"We were caught completely off guard ... He went off to duty again. And we just thought he'd come back one day, like he always did before. And things would go on. Like normal."

She paused.

"But, he didn't come back this time ... And, we were never able to spend time with him again."

Krystyna put her arm around Naomi.

"That's why we emphasize so much parents doing these projects right alongside their kids. And that's why the projects never end. They go on every year ... So, the opportunity for us to spend time together, for parents to spend time with their children, never ends."

She managed a smile for the crowd.

"I watched my son Owen just disappear before my eyes ... I haven't seen him for months now. You see, we think we know our children ... I mean, they are, and always will be, a part of us. But unless we continue to reach out for them, understand them for who they are, and offer to share their experiences alongside them, as much as we can ... We only see so much."

It was quiet.

"So, Krystyna called me and said, 'Naomi, if you can do all that at one school in San Rafael, do you think, together, we can do it in schools everywhere?!' ... And, I answered, 'Heck, yes!' So ... we dreamed, and planned, and decided to ask our students from Owen's old school to reach out and write letters to the students in the village where my husband went down, and ask them if they wanted to join our project … And they said, '*Baleh!*' … Which means *yes*! So, we sent them some technology, and now, the students are communicating every day. And, we're helping them, with their parents, build projects in each of their classes too!"

"And, with Naomi leading the way," Krystyna added, "we'll keep the project growing, from schools like Owen's, to schools in the Middle East … to schools all around the world!"

The guests stood and cheered.

And didn't stop until Naomi made it all the way back to her table.

"That was *sooo* good!" Sam got up to meet her, trying to choke back the feeling of sadness, and joy, and conviction hitting at the same time.

They exchanged a few words, hugged each other, then returned to their seats.

Ranger was backstage with Rudy Rios during Naomi's speech. They were changing, and warming up for their presentation, which was next. Out of his slate bespoke Huntsman jacket and necktie, Ranger was now in a black tight-fit Canterbury base layer top and matching compression leggings, and he looked ripped.

Rudy Rios was in great shape too. In fact, he looked a lot like Ranger.

Except that he was missing both legs below the knee.

He was a police officer who'd been injured in an attack … And now, more than ever, he realized he could do anything.

And they were demonstrating that for everyone out there tonight.

As she sat back down, Sam noticed the dull red glow of the message alert blinking on her phone inside her little Meredith Buck knitted leather pouch under the table.

She checked it and saw she'd missed a call ... from Sally.

"Excuse me for a second, Naomi." She got up and stepped out just as Krystyna came to introduce Rudy and Ranger.

"C'mon, Sally. Answer your phone." Sam roved into the restroom and to the lobby trying to connect a call, but the ring was choppy and she couldn't tell if it was going through.

So, she sent a text.

Sally, you there?

I'm at a party at the Ritz-Carlton Hotel on the ocean.

Trying to call. I think the reception is bad.

Call me back!

She paced the resort foyer, then the courtyard outside, waiting to hear something.

It was coming up on 11:00 pm.

Inside, the ballroom was in full swing. Rudy and Ranger's exhibition had everyone so fired up it nearly brought the house down. There was a live band onstage, playing all the best songs from everybody's younger days, and many of the guests were now letting it loose out on the dance floor.

It was the last hour of the year.

"See you out there, man." Rudy Rios had already changed and was ready to join the party. Ranger was still half-dressed.

"Thank you, brother."

He was honored to have a friend like Ranger. Someone you knew had your back.

"Always."

Ranger took a seat as Rudy left the room.

It bothered him that people could ever get to a point where they would attack good people like him. That we'd ever live in a world where people could treat each other so badly.

Ranger thought about everybody he had encountered the past couple of weeks.

And he thought of his own parents.

He felt an overwhelming sense of love, and wanting to be loved. And since yesterday late afternoon, the person he wanted at last to be loved by.

It was Sam.

She was all he could think of.

Happy New Year, Sal. I'll try you again in the morning.

Sam abandoned hope that she would reach Sally tonight and returned to the ballroom. Naomi noticed her coming in through the doors and went over to meet her.

"Hi, Sam. Everything okay? ... I'm over here talking to some really nice people who want to help with the project. Come meet them."

As they walked over, a couple of the dancers intercepted them, and dressed them both up with a supply of party favors for the countdown to midnight, which was in fifteen minutes. Naomi got a shiny silver foil top hat that read *Happy New Year*, some oversized star-shaped plastic sunglasses that lit up with flashing lights, streamers and noisemakers.

Sam got balloons, and necklaces, and a cute glittery gold tiara.

One of them asked if he could take their picture.

Click!

Click!

Ranger noticed the flash out of the corner of his eye as he re-entered the room. It was all sort of a daze in there for him with all the revelry, coming from that quiet back area.

He looked down at his watch and considered turning back ...

But paused where he was.

The lead singer of the band, a lively young fellow with a pleasantly energetic raspy voice, announced that upcoming was the final song of the old year, and that it was going to be a good one.

Nearly everybody was on the dance floor now. The ballroom had transformed from classic and elegant to much more modern while Ranger was out backstage. There were lasers and cool fiber optics everywhere, images and video of the guests projecting all over the room.

The band started up.

Dunnn ... Dunnn ... Dunnn ... Dunnnn!

> *I'm gonna wait 'til the midnight hour!*
>
> *That's when my love comes tumblin' down*
>
> *I'm gonna wait 'til the midnight hour!*

When there's no one else around

I'm gonna take you girl and hold you

And do all the things I told you

In the midnight hour!

Then, Sam's picture came up on the screen.

And Ranger saw it.

With how beautiful she looked, you'd never tell she didn't want to be in that room either.

17 MAVERICKS

"Wild horses couldn't drag me away."

The Rolling Stones

You do all kinds of crazy and cool things when you're in love.

Do you remember?

Sam realized she'd much rather be at the ocean for the start of the new year than inside at that party.

Actually on the beach, at the water's edge.

So, she wished Naomi *Happy New Year*, told her she'd be right back, and left her with her new friends there in the ballroom. Earlier, on her walk, she had come across a stairway south of the hotel, along the coast side trail, leading down the cliffs to the beach below, which was stunning ... like a secluded stage, with the bluffs soaring overhead, and rugged points of land north and south jutting out to frame in the half-mile expanse of sand.

The full moon lit her path to the top of it.

As her toes hit the sand, Sam heard the pop of fireworks and cheers from the resort above. It was New Year's. On the beach all by herself again, she turned north and started walking. It was bright out near the water, once she got beyond the pitch black shade of the cliffs, and the ocean was peaceful ... at least between the periodic sets of pounding surf.

It was breathtaking out there.

"Happy New Year ..." Sam resigned to herself. She picked up a couple rocks and threw them one by one far out into the Pacific.

"Sam!"

A giant wave exploded onto the shore, and Sam thought she heard her name.

She turned and looked, but didn't see anything, gathered her dress, picked up her shoes, and started back down the beach.

"Hello?"

A she got closer in, she cut on a diagonal across from the water to the staircase. A solitary couple emerged in the distance, but they turned left, and faded off southward down the beach. As Sam neared the cliffside, and the threshold between the shadow and moonlight, she sensed someone else was there.

Waiting for her.

She could almost hear the breathing.

It was tense all of a sudden. Then, suddenly …

"Sam!"

Ranger appeared out of the dark.

Sam froze, eyes wide open, dress in one hand, shoes in the other, and dropped them both.

"Oh … my … gosh."

She stared, frozen into his eyes.

"It's you …"

Ranger stopped, motionless himself for a good handful of seconds, then rushed in and wrapped his arms around her, and Sam sunk into his strong embrace.

And, it felt amazing.

She just couldn't feel herself.

"Hi ..." is all he said.

It was so impossibly exciting.

"How ... did you know I was here?" Sam asked as they went back up the stairs together. Ranger told her about seeing her picture, and finding Naomi, who told him where she was. They walked back to the resort talking about the night, and the day, and the day before, and passed the hotel, and kept walking. They talked, and laughed, and smiled, and listened, and hugged several more times, then found a quiet corner inside and shared stories about each other's lives until well after 5:00, when they decided to say goodnight ... until they'd see each other again in a few short hours to surf the jetty.

Wow.

It was still dark as Sam pulled up outside of her rented cottage.

And quiet.

She went inside, dropped her things, and sat for a minute at the edge of the elevated bed.

It had been an unbelievable night.

She thought about it all as she changed, and washed up, the glint of a smile coming over her face more than several times in the bathroom mirror.

Then, her phone rang.

It was from South Carolina.

"Hello."

"Hello, is this Samantha Amaris?"

"Yes ..."

"This is Detective Murray of the Charleston, South Carolina, Police Department."

Sam turned sideways away from the mirror, suddenly concerned.

"Ms. Amaris, please listen, and try to stay calm ..."

"Wha ..?"

"We have reason to believe you might be in some danger right now."

Sam's heart dropped.

"Ms. Amaris ... can you hear me?"

"Uh ... yes," she was whispering now.

The detective continued. "Okay. Are you in a safe location? ... Where are you?"

"Yes ... I think so. I'm in the cottage I rented."

"Are you alone?"

"Yes ... Yes, I am." Sam looked around the room, what she could see of it from the entrance of the bathroom area.

"Okay," the officer continued. "Ms. Amaris, have you noticed anybody following you at all ... or any kind of strange activity today?"

"Uh ... no. What do you mean?"

"Well, we received notice from Dare County Police in North Carolina about the attack you reported last week. It appears your attacker may have followed you to California."

The feeling in Sam's arms and legs left her, for the second time tonight.

"We also believe it's the same individual who broke into your apartment last Sunday and attacked your friend Sally."

"What?!" Sam responded. "Sally? ... What are you talking about?"

"I'll explain later. We're sending an officer to your location right now. Ms. Amaris, what's the address of your cottage?"

Sam's head was immediately spinning.

She hesitated for a moment ...

"Ms. Amaris ... can you hear me?"

"Yes ... officer. I have to find it." She kneeled and started searching through her travel bag.

"Um ... How did you know where I was?" She asked. Her voice was shaking.

"And why do you think ... I'm being followed?"

"Sally's cell phone was missing from her apartment after the incident. We traced several calls on it to your phone over the past twenty-four hours or so."

He paused.

"Ms. Amaris, as of last night, that phone ... and yours ... are pinging off the same tower."

A chill came over Sam that was shocking. She scrambled faster through her bag.

"Officer, would you hold for a second while I find the address in my phone?"

"Yes."

"I know it's Ocean …"

Sam stood up and held her phone out in front of her.

And as she did …

The woman was there. The one who attacked her. Her face in that black window at the far side of the bed.

But, Sam didn't see her.

That moment, as she pushed the buttons on her phone, seemed to take forever.

Then, Detective Murray broke the silence …

"Ms. Amaris … Are your doors locked? … Ms. Amaris?"

"I'll check right now."

The door at the foot of the bed leading out to the bluff was closed and locked, but Sam looked startled to find the window wide open. She hurried to close it and fasten the latch.

Then drew the curtains.

"I have the address," she whispered to the officer.

"Okay … go ahead, Ms. Amaris. I'm ready."

She turned slowly toward the front of the cottage, raising her phone again as she did.

"Okay …"

"I'm at 221 …"

In a gradual progression, the focus of Sam's eyes went from the bright light of the screen, to the darkness of the entranceway to the bungalow, to something in it.

It was her ... standing there.

Inside the front door ... Sam could hear the breathing.

The woman came instantly towards her.

She was tall, and in that same black trench coat, and her hair blew back as she closed in ... So, Sam could see her face clearly. Her lipstick was smeared, and her jaw protruded, abnormally so, almost deformed in its structure ... And she had no sunglasses on this time.

Her eyes were scary.

She held something in her clenched fist, but Sam couldn't make it out.

A chair crashed to the ground.

The woman reached the foot of the bed, unleashing a grunt, and a piercing, shrill shriek. Out of pure instinct, Sam reacted, raising a foot and kicking her in the upper mid-section, staggering her for a second and causing her to drop whatever it was she was holding ... which clattered to the cold, hard floor.

Then, Sam sprinted by her to the door.

But she followed as Sam ran barefoot through the trees into the front yard.

"Help!" Sam let out a scream, and as soon as she did, sideswiped a guy riding a bicycle down the middle of the empty street.

"Whoa!" He screeched on the brakes as Sam went spiraling to the pavement.

She twisted around just in time to point to the woman coming up fast beside him.

Right at her ... with a large block of firewood raised above her head.

In a flash, the man jumped up and over the bicycle, and tackled the woman to the ground.

"Arrrrgghhhh!" ... *Thump*!

Sam started to cry.

Off in the distance, in the direction of the blood red sun peeking up over the coastal range, the hum of police sirens was heading their way.

"And what are *you* doing here, sir?" The officer inquired with a matter-of-fact yet affable face.

His name badge read *Laidlaw*.

"Well ... I wanted to bring her ... flowers." Ranger was simple, unpretentious in his response.

"So, you rode your bike over ... at 6:00 in the morning ... to bring flowers?"

"That's correct, officer." Ranger caught Sam's eye and smiled.

The bouquet Sam had cradled in one arm, her other hand was over her mouth, was a little beaten up on account of the collision out on the road. However ... it was undeniably beautiful. All wildflowers he'd picked on the way over. Fairy lanterns and pearly everlasting, and bull clover, and shooting stars, and forget-me-nots.

"My car was blocked in, so the valet kid let me borrow his bike."

"Ooh kay ..." Laidlaw shifted the focus over the top of his glasses from Ranger back to Sam.

"So, then she came at you here?"

"Yes," Sam replied.

"And then what happened?" He proceeded, scribbling into his notepad.

"She screamed ... like this awful roar."

"And ...?"

"I ... kicked her."

He looked up again, eyebrows raised.

"And then you ran for the door?"

"Yes."

Ranger stood there listening to Sam, really just completely captivated by her. She glanced up at him, snapping him back to reality.

"So, what happened next?"

"So, I ran out this way." The three of them walked out through the yard to the narrow road. The other houses didn't seem so far away now in the morning light. "And that's where I crashed into ... Ranger."

Officer Laidlaw glanced at them both. He got it, what was going on.

"And you both fell."

He picked up the chunk of wood.

"The perpetrator approached, with this here piece of timber raised overhead?"

Sam nodded.

"And then, Mr. Gabriel, you got up and took her down."

"Yes, sir. That's right."

Officer Laidlaw scratched a few more notes then returned the pad to his chest pocket. "Okay then, Ms. Amaris, I gotta tell you I'm real sorry about your ordeal here this morning. Half Moon Bay doesn't see stuff like this very often. You must be pretty distressed ... I suggest you try to relax, get some sleep, and we'll follow up with you later today when we get an idea on a possible motive."

He was looking again over the top of those glasses.

"Sound good?"

"Yes, Officer. Thank you very much."

Laidlaw then turned to Ranger. "Well done, young man, for being here to take care of her."

He popped Ranger on the tricep and looked at his hand like it hurt it.

"Glad you didn't tackle me," he smiled.

"You two have a nice day." He began to walk away, then turned back. "And, Happy New Year ... to you both."

Ranger stepped in and Sam held onto him in a long embrace. He started to ask if she wanted to postpone surfing for now so she could get some rest, but she stopped him.

"I don't want to leave you," she said.

Sam and Ranger had both been up for over 24 hours now, but neither was tired. Not at all. So they decided to go and get some breakfast ... and talk.

It just seemed like they could talk all day.

They took Sam's car for Mexican at cute Cafe Capistrano in town and ordered omelets, and discussed the woman a little bit, but Sam couldn't really figure out who she was at all ... or why she was doing what she was doing. Laidlaw had promised to get a message to Sally, who he was informed was going to be okay, but was unavailable in an undisclosed hospital bed location right now.

Sam stared at the man sitting in front of her at their tiny table in the corner as they ordered.

What a wild mix of things she was feeling.

When they got back to the cottage, not sure who said it first, but they thought it would be fitting to ride the beach cruiser together back to the hotel and return it to its owner.

And, although she was worried sick about Sally, Sam still wanted to do what she'd promised herself she'd do today. Go surfing.

Ranger assured her they'd get anything she needed to go, so she stuffed her bathing suit into a tiny bag, and they took off, starting with Sam on the seat behind Ranger holding on, then arriving at the resort with her atop the handlebars.

They were smiling about something as they rode up to the young valet attendant out front.

"Thank you *very* much for the bike, Josh." Ranger placed his hand on the boy's shoulder. "You'll never know how important it was."

He gave Josh an extraordinarily big tip. Then, they went inside.

Waves at the Princeton Jetty were playful that day, and there weren't very many people out.

Ranger was amazed at how well Sam could surf.

And she felt secure in his presence.

Farther out, past the breakwater west of the harbor, beyond Pillar Point and the rocks ... was Mavericks, the legendary surf spot.

After about an hour out there in the safety of the harbor, Sam asked if they could go see it.

A friend of Jack's, a local guy named Jeff Clark, rode the giant here by himself for fifteen years before the world found out about it. Clark had watched it for a couple of winters, studying the break closely and preparing himself, and one day in 1975, when the conditions were perfect, he told his friend:

We gotta go out there ... Today's the day.

Clark's friend replied there was no way he was paddling out there with him, and that he'd call the Coast Guard to tell them where he last saw him.

But Clark wanted it. And he went.

It was low tide when Sam and Ranger got to Mavericks Beach, so you could walk on the reef almost all the way out to the rocks. The rocks where Clark hung on for his life in the raging whitewash for the better part of an hour after a wipeout out there a few years back.

A handful of people were there tide pooling, and a white-haired German shepherd was running around, splashing in the puddles. Out at the end of the land, waves were breaking over the reef, but the spot where Mavericks goes off, a quarter-mile offshore, was flat.

Along the way, there was a crevice in the reef through which the ocean ebbed and flowed, and a narrow gap you had to leap over to get over to the other side, closer to the big rocks.

A man was standing there with a bucket.

"Hi ... Hello." Sam and Ranger announced as they approached.

He was an interesting type. Strong yet simple looking, like a friendly cattle farmer. Slightly receding hairline and a little gap between his front teeth.

"Cheers!" he replied.

"Happy New Year," the two smiled, and the man stepped aside so they could cross.

Ranger jumped, then held out a hand for Sam to follow. She readied herself and leapt.

The man beamed back from across the little channel. "Happy New Year to you too."

It was about 3:30 pm. The sun was moving fast towards the skyline of serrated rocks at the edge of the exposed reef. It cast a golden glow.

"It's a little scary out here." Sam watched the waves coming in from multiple directions, appearing to be significantly higher than the level of their heads. The boulders between them and the open Pacific somehow keeping the waves at bay.

"Do you want to head back?" Ranger said to her.

Mavericks was right there, right on the other side.

"No …"

Suddenly, the waves out beyond the big rocks calmed, and the violent splashing subsided. And, the ocean looked as if it was withdrawing a little, quietly, back to where it came from.

And … *Boooooooooom!*

Ranger lifted his head towards the sound, which was like a giant river rapid coming up quickly around the bend … and saw the top of a wall of whitewater rushing in.

They were so far out there.

Before she could blink, Ranger jumped to Sam and lifted her into the air, her legs flying up around his waist. Then with arms clasped under her, he bounded up the huge boulder in front of him. The water coming in seemed twice as high as Sail Rock now, which was the last piece of land between them and the ocean. Beyond that they could see Mavericks. Out of nowhere, it was erupting.

You know, maybe it was the way all the other people farther in on the reef were running away, scrambling for safety, or the way the late afternoon orange sun reflected in the spray around them. Or, the magic of the day and the night before … But right then at that moment, with Ranger hanging on, Sam holding onto him, and the water trying to separate them from their hold on that rock …

And the way they looked at each other. It seemed almost as if they were the only two people left alive on earth. Just them … the only ones in the whole, wide world.

18 ANO NUEVO ISLAND

"A billion stars and here we are."

Copeland

Ranger found a place to have an early dinner, out on the deck at Sam's Chowder House, overlooking the harbor. They could hear the waves peeling off the Princeton Jetty where they had surfed earlier today, only a couple hundred yards away.

Mavericks was out there beyond that over Sam's shoulder to the west.

Ranger had planned to check out today and head back north to Sausalito, while Sam still had five more days paid at the rental cottage on Ocean Avenue. But, neither thought it a good idea for her to stay there another night.

Sam really had no idea what she was going to do.

She just felt happy being with Ranger … exactly how they were right now.

"Thank you," she told him, "for everything you've done."

"You are totally welcome," he said.

She blushed, then …

Beeep … Beeep … Beeep

Her phone began to ring.

"Hello?"

"Hello, Ms. Amaris. How are you doing? It's Officer Laidlaw."

"I'm doing fine, Officer. How are you?" She felt herself cringe a little on the inside as it suddenly flooded back in.

"Fine as well. Listen, it's been a little slow going over here, but I wanted to get you updated. Our perp hasn't said a word all day, and she has no ID on her either." His voice was matter-of-fact, as usual. "I got in contact with Charleston, and it looks like your friend Sally is going to be able to give you a call tomorrow, as per the doctor's orders. Then, we might be able to get somewhere with this case."

"Okay, that's good. Thank you, Officer Laidlaw."

"Don't mention it ... Anyway, you might want to stick around the next couple of days while we work this thing out. Did you have any plans going you needed to get squared away?" Laidlaw's voice was soothing, plus looking across the table at Ranger, the man who ended all of this with one takedown, made her feel safe.

Oh, my gosh! She was warm all inside as Ranger smiled at her.

"No, not really ... I just need to find another place to stay. Don't really think I could sleep in that place again ... you know?"

"Right ... I understand. Listen ... Why don't you let me take care of that for you. My wife is really big on the tourism scene around here. She knows everyone ... And, I mean *everyone*. That woman likes to talk, if you know what I mean. I bet she can make a couple phone calls and get you a place. I'll have her call you right back, if that's okay with you."

"Uh ... yeah ... definitely. That would be great. Thank you very much."

"Don't mention it ... Alright, then, look out for her call, and I'll give you a buzz tomorrow ... Sound good, Ms. Amaris?"

"That's perfect ... Thank you, Officer Laidlaw."

"Not at all ... Good night, then."

The waves picked up again, as a smooth, focused set moved in. Sam and

Ranger both looked over to see it.

"Good night, Officer."

Ranger and Sam went to pick up the rest of Sam's things out of her car, which they had left with Josh to take care of at the Ritz-Carlton, and the two of them drove in the Malibu to the accommodations Laidlaw's wife had set up. A resort 30 minutes south called Costanoa. Turns out the owner of the rental cabin and the manager at Costanoa knew each other and were able to arrange a swap. Sam didn't have to do anything.

Ranger called Schalk to let him know he wouldn't be there tonight, which wasn't a problem as Schalk and Sara loved it at Ranger's, and their two chihuahuas Kurtley and Rob loved playing with Bernard. They were having a great time.

"Ranger, did you know that this place, Costanoa, gets 30 to 40 more days of sunshine per year than Half Moon Bay or Santa Cruz, and it's full of deer, fox and bobcats ... and there used to be grizzly bears there?" Sam read from her device, the screen lighting just her face with darkness everywhere else. "It says Spanish explorer *Sebastian Vizcaino* described this part of the coast as *swarming with wild, large sea beasts*. She looked up at Ranger with big eyes. "Whales, sharks, seals, orcas ... It says he named the point where the elephant seals are mating *right* now *Punta de Año Nuevo -- Point of the New* Year -- when he discovered it New Year's Day, 1603 ... You can see it from the cabins."

The two of them rounded the bend at the Pigeon Point Historic State Lighthouse Station and continued south on the Cabrillo Highway another four miles to the Costanoa Lodge. Mrs. Laidlaw had told Sam she would be in one of their coastal studio cabins, which was good because it had a queen bed and a pull out trundle, a deck, a kitchen, and access to all the amenities of the resort. It was the only room they had, and it was absolutely perfect.

The clock in the lobby read 8:30 pm as they checked in.

New Year's Day.

Maybe it was the day, or the circumstances, or the fact that neither of them had slept for a day and a half now, but the next three-and-a-half hours, if you asked Sam or Ranger, were the most wonderful, strange, heart-pounding, and romantic either of them had ever lived.

"Sam, I'm happy you'll finally be able to get some rest, and talk to your friend Sally tomorrow ... and hopefully get some answers." It was so strange for him to be in this little four-walled room, with this girl he felt so close to, and barely even knew.

His heart was racing just being there.

"Yeah, I guess we should try to sleep," Sam responded. She was feeling the exact same way.

She took a few things out of her bag, then looked over to Ranger as she turned toward the bathroom door. "I suppose I'll take a quick shower, then. Uhh, would you ... like to go first? ... You can go first, if you'd like?"

"No, no, no. You go, Sam ... And, take your time. I'll go after you ... I'll just be right out here."

"Okay ..." She smiled through the lighted crack of the doorway.

He smiled back.

Click. The door closed.

Ranger took a deep breath, then inspected the room. He went out onto the deck outside and could see the lights of the other cabins, the lodge, tent bungalows off in the distance, and the glimmer of the ocean to the southwest down the hillside. It was extremely dark, and at the same time brilliant, as everything was lit up by the bright night sky.

Back inside, he closed the blinds, double-checked the several locks on the inside of the front door, then arranged the trundle bed he'd be sleeping on between the glass slider leading to the deck and the queen bed in the middle of the room.

Aside from the sound of the water running, it was quiet. *How could anybody ... be trying to hurt her, of all people?* He wondered to himself.

Ranger pulled the chunk of smooth sandstone from his bag, along with some of his nighttime things, and set them on the table next to the futon chair. As he sat there studying the stone, the water from the shower turned off, and Sam came out, bundled in her huge robe, her hair wrapped in a towel, and the fluffy white and grey faux fur slippers Sally had gotten for her from Pottery Barn before she left, on her feet.

Ranger stood to his. "Uh ... How was it?"

Both of them still had New Year's Eve, walking on the beach, surfing, salt water, hiking at Mavericks, and that fight still on their physical bodies.

A shower was just what they needed.

"It was nice ... You're going to love it."

"Okay ... I can't wait, then." Ranger picked up his things from the table, nodded to her, then started towards the bathroom, stopping at the corner of the bed in front of where she was. "All the doors are locked, and the blinds are shut ... and, I'll be right in here."

He stepped in, placed his hand on her shoulder, and kissed her on the cheek.

Oh ... my ... gosh.

You know, it *was* in the way he looked at her ... into her eyes ... Kind and protective, selfless and honest, excited like a child lost in the experience of this whole thing since it started the other day at Alice's.

It was all in the eyes.

What Sam saw was everything Corinna had talked about, but so much more than she had imagined it would be.

She wasn't sure how much time had passed before she had gotten dressed, dried her hair with the towel, and then heard the water turn off.

Click. Ranger came out of the bathroom

He was wearing a dark T-shirt and long pajama bottoms that were nearly identical to the top Sam had put on, with her sweatpants and slippers. Red and a dark-colored plaid flannel.

"I made tea for us …" Sam said as she stood there with two oversized cups in her hands. She set them down as Ranger came over to her, arms wide open.

It was about 11:30 pm when Sam rolled over and whispered, "Ranger, are you awake?"

"Yes …"

She pulled herself to the edge of the bed, in all the fluffy comforters and pillows, so she could see over to the area of the trundle bed where Ranger was, but it was dark.

"I haven't slept at all," Ranger said.

A giggle blurted out of Sam, which made Ranger laugh too. Neither of them had slept. They'd just been lying there in the blankets.

"Wanna go for a walk?" Sam asked.

"That sounds great!"

Click. The light came on, and the two of them were immediately up.

They smiled. As Sam went over to get her shoes, she saw the sandstone under the light on the table, went over and picked it up.

It was pretty and felt a lot like hers.

It was so bright under all the stars there at Costanoa that evening that Sam and Ranger were able to explore some of the trails leading away from the property just by moonlight. Eventually, they came across a few Adirondack chairs overlooking everything from the hillside they were on all the way down to the coast.

Punta de Año Nuevo was right in front of them, clear as day, with Año Nuevo Island there just offshore.

They sat down … Sam placed her hand in Ranger's, and in the other hand, she held both of their stones. Ranger did a 360 to survey the surroundings … Under those billion stars, there they were, just before midnight, the first night of the year.

"Sam …" Ranger said, turning to her. They kissed as he whispered something in her ear.

19 TWIN PEAKS

"Friendship is born in that moment when one person says to another 'What! You too? I thought I was the only one.'"

C.S. Lewis

Naomi hadn't heard from her son in months now. The last message she had received read, *Mom, I'm okay*. So, the text that came Saturday morning was big to say the least.

Happy New Year, Mom. I miss you. Hopefully, I can see you real soon. Love, Owen

---

Over the course of their long weekend together, Ranger and Sam had gone on long walks on the beach, hikes in the hills, and had visited the elephant seals down at Año Nuevo several times. Laidlaw called on Saturday, like he promised, but still didn't have much to report. Just that the woman who had attacked Sam and Sally was still being detained and wasn't getting out anytime soon.

And, she'd said only one thing since being placed in police custody over 72 hours ago.

One word not too surprising to either Sam or Sally at all ...

Damien

She'd repeated it several times.

Sam was glad to talk to Sally, though they decided not to talk about the incidents too much. Sally could hardly remember anything of hers anyway. Sam had also decided not to say anything about Ranger just yet either, considering everything Sally had been through recently.

She'd tell her soon, though, as soon as she was feeling much better. She really wanted to.

Really, she wished the rest of it would just all go away.

It was Monday morning, and Ranger and Same were headed up to Sausalito.

Home.

"I've had a great time this weekend …" Ranger whispered to Sam, with Josh standing there, Sam's keys in his hand, and the little black Siata pulled up.

"Yeah … It was like the best camping trip ever," she smiled.

Which was true. Sam and Ranger in their pajamas, sharing hot chocolate, telling stories … some funny, some adorable, some adventurous, some heartfelt … sleeping good, Sam in the big fluffy bed, Ranger on the trundle, dreaming the same dreams at night, being together.

Grateful for these first three days of the year.

"Thank you, Josh." Sam took her keys, and Ranger's hand. "I'll follow you, then."

"Sounds good."

He hugged her, and they got into their cars, driving off to the coast highway, north.

Sam had opened her journal for the first time since New Year's Eve sitting out on the deck of the cabin that morning, and she'd read the daily checklist she'd written for herself two weeks and two days ago on the promenade by the cannons overlooking Charleston Harbor.

Get out, go for a walk, and see something amazing. Enjoy something fun to eat, no matter the price, or the calories. Meet at least one extraordinary person, and tell them why they are so. Keep a good journal of your experiences, and take lots and lots of pictures. Be kind to everyone, and be grateful for the journey, each and every day.

And the one she added the next night in Myrtle Beach.

It was incredible everything from the list that had transpired between that time and now.

Except she hadn't taken many pictures. Just the one on the bench at the Alice's with Naomi.

The thought of pictures with Ranger excited her.

She asked if they could stop for a few.

At points along the way home, Ranger pulled over, with Sam behind him in her sports car, and they took a bunch of photos. At Pigeon Point with the lighthouse high above their heads, barefoot on the sand at Gray Whale Cove, and among the stones of the labyrinth up on the cliffs at Lands End, above all the shipwrecks in the mouth of San Francisco Bay.

Then, they pulled over and parked at Vista Point on the north side of the Golden Gate Bridge and watched the boats go by in and out of the city.

Sam had never seen a view quite like that before.

It was about 3:30 pm when Ranger walked out onto Liberty Dock, under the wooden canopy of the main entrance way, with Sam by his side. Schalk and Sara were out in front of the floating house to greet them.

"Bring it in for some love!" Schalk pulled Sam in for a giant bear hug, Sara's big, welcoming smile lighting up the already sparkling day on the bay. Ranger had called to let them know he was on his way, and that he'd be bringing company.

Other than that, he hadn't been on his phone at all the last several days.

All of a sudden, the front door swung open and Bernard came barreling out. "W-w-whoa!" Sam burst out laughing as he vaulted past her into Ranger's arms.

"Berna-a-ard, my boy!"

Rarrr rarrr rarrrr rarrrr rarrr, Bernard told Ranger all about it.

They all laughed, then the five of them went inside.

"Schalky, thank you so much for taking care of everything. Sara, you guys are the best." Ranger was happy to be home. "C'mon, boy," he told Bernard, "let's give our guest a tour."

Ranger, Sam and Bernard strolled the first floor of the house while Schalk and Sara hung in the kitchen. The place was spotless. Schalk took such good care of it when he house-sat. Ranger whispered to Sam to see if she wouldn't mind taking Schalk and Sara to dinner as a thank you.

She gave a big thumbs up.

"Hey, guys! We want to take you out to dinner … Are you free right now?!" Ranger called down from the top floor balcony.

Schalk nodded to Sara. "Yeah, sure we are! That sounds great!"

"Right on!" Ranger answered, the turned to Sam. "I know just the place … We can even bring Bernard."

Sam thought it was pretty cool to be at a second restaurant on her trip named after turtles. Elegant on the inside, with a great outdoor space, a mini park for kids and dogs to play, and a performer's stage overlooking the San Rafael Yacht Club and harbor, across the creek from Montecito Plaza, and San Rafael high school, all on the edge of the bay, Terrapin Crossroads was nice.

She wondered how they came up with the name.

"You know, his clients just love him." Sara was telling Sam about Schalk, the combination of his big, wide smile and simultaneously long and balding golden hair glorious in the patio area where they were, waiting for their entrees to arrive.

Sara had ordered the spice rubbed fish tacos, Schalk, southern fried chicken with honey and homemade hot sauce, mashed potatoes and corn on the cobb. Sam got Bolognese pasta with house made pappardelle and parmesan, and Ranger the Terrapin cheeseburger topped with white cheddar and tabasco onion rings.

It was so good.

"He just gets it ... He believes in them, and gives them hope," Sara smiled.

The place had just opened, and it was Monday, so there weren't many people there yet as a couple of the workers and some older gentlemen passed by their table.

"You and Ranger should come for a class," Sara offered.

"Yeah. I told him we really want to do the *Senior Sizzle*." Ranger did a little move, and Schalk did too.

"Or maybe my *Booty Bustin' Bachata*!" He winked as he took a big bite of his fried chicken, then stood, singing in Spanish:

>"Màs, màs, quiero, màs ... Move your bod-dy!"

They all cracked up.

Then, out of the blue ...

>Bweeeeeeeeeeeeeeer chugga chick chick ... Bwaaaa waaa waaa wooooooooom!

A loud guitar sound came from down by the water, and the guys who had just walked by, some ex-hippie looking dudes, were up on the stage.

They started jamming.

"Right on!" Schalk whooped.

Not too long after, they started to sing.

> *I know you rider, gonna miss me when I'm gone*
>
> *I know you rider, gonna miss me when I'm gone*
>
> *Gonna miss your baby, from rolling in your arms*

It was cool. Just like that, a concert gratis on an unseasonably warm day on the water.

"Hey, is that …?" Schalk turned to Ranger.

"I think so."

As the band ended, Ranger's table, who'd been bobbing and tapping heads and feet all along, stood and applauded, which caught the attention of the bass player.

"Thank you, thank you." He called into the mic. "You young folk sure are welcome to come up and join us here for this next one."

They started up again. Drum, then guitar.

> *Duht … duh duht … duht … duh duht duh!*
>
> *Duht … duh duht … duht … duh duht duh!*

"Heck yeah!" Schalk jumped up and grabbed Sara by the hand.

Ranger looked to Sam, and she nodded, smiling.

As the musicians grooved, people from all around the harbor, and even across the canal, were looking over to see what was going on.

The song was so much fun.

> *I wanna tell you how it's gonna be*
>
> *You're gonna give your love to me*
>
> *I wanna love you night and day*
>
> *You know my love not fade away*
>
> *You know my love not fade away, not fade away*

Folks started spilling in through the back door of the restaurant and a gate on the side, realizing who was on-stage, while Schalk and Sara and Ranger and Sam were dancing.

> *My love is bigger than a Cadillac*
>
> *I try to show you but you drive me back*
>
> *Your love for me has got to be real*
>
> *Your gonna know just how I feel*
>
> *Our love is real, not fade away, not fade away*

It was a blast ... Schalk and Sara went back and forth doing moves, then Sam and Ranger would bust a few. People were cheering. Even the band seemed quite entertained. After the next song *Goin' Down the Road Feeling Bad* was over, the four of them, in unison hurrahed, then hugged, then started heading back to Bernard.

"Alright! How 'bout a big hand for our *feel good* dancers right here!" The bass player called. "Where you all from?"

Ranger and Schalk and Sara and Sam all looked at each other.

"Here!"

"Here!"

"Right here!"

"She's from Australia!" Schalk called back, pointing to Sam.

"Alright ... Australia! Thank you for visiting us way out here ..." The band members smiled, with their gray hair, and their gray beards.

Grateful.

"Welcome to California."

The five of them ended up staying a little while longer, taking in all the sights and sounds as sundown gave way to a crystal clear night, the stream of traffic into Terrapin Crossroads continuing to pick up.

Then, Sara and Sam stopped by the restroom on their way out.

"Wow, Sam's one-of-a-kind, my man." Schalk patted Ranger on the shoulder as the girls were returning from around the corner.

"I know ..." Ranger replied. He had the same thought when he was holding her moonstone.

The girls arrived into the foyer, giggling about something.

And, a guy bumped into Sam.

"Oh ... Sorry. Excuse me." Sam glanced up at him.

His back was to Ranger.

"No problem." The guy was tall and well-built, and he turned to face her.

Then Ranger saw his face.

And recognized him.

It was the guy who had made the move when he went to get Lwazi's necklace back.

The one Ranger knocked down first.

"No problem at all … *Australia*." He smiled, then turned to the guys.

His smile disappeared.

Sam nodded graciously but uncomfortably in return, then made her way over to Ranger, who stared the man down as a couple other guys he did not recognize joined him.

The big man grinned once more before Ranger and Sam reversed and headed for the door, Schalk and Sara and Bernard in front of them.

Back at Liberty Dock, Schalk and Sara gathered their things, and leashed Kurtley and Rob who had been excited in their kennel.

"Tonight was fun." Ranger said Schalk, helping him with his bag. "Thanks again."

"You got it."

They all hugged and said goodbye.

After that, Ranger went and prepared the upstairs bedroom for Sam. His room. He and Bernard would stay in one of the rooms downstairs.

That felt safest to him.

Sam was so appreciative.

She melted into his arms as they stepped out onto the first floor lanai, taking dessert -- Humphry Slocombe Malted Dulce de Leche ice cream and fudge chunk brownies -- a blanket, a bone for Bernard, and pulling the lounge chairs together in front of the Bento fire pit to watch the stars.

It wasn't until after midnight when they finally decided to turn in.

For the morning, Sam had brunch planned with Naomi to talk about a new project Naomi had planned.

But, as excited as she was about it, she didn't really want to go. Not yet.

Not as she was crawling into Ranger's bed.

I never want to leave him, she thought to herself.

And, she wasn't alone on that. Downstairs, Ranger was feeling the exact same thing too.

The morning would be the first time in four days that they were apart …

Since Ranger had arrived on that bike with the flowers New Year's morning.

They met for brunch in Tiburon, which was about the cutest, most picturesque town you'll ever see, right next to Sausalito, with the prettiest views of the bay and San Francisco across the way. They were eating at Luna Blu, a waterfront eatery owned by Renzo from Sicily, who'd originally come stateside to work for the winery owned by Francis Ford Coppola, of *The Godfather* fame. The restaurant manager Pippa was from Oxford in England.

Naomi loved the place. Her husband had taken her there her first time.

"Hi, Sam … It's so good to see you." They hugged.

"Hi, Naomi."

Renzo and Pippa came to greet them in the anteroom.

They took their seats outside, ordered *paninis* and *piadinas*, and caught up. Then, Naomi told Sam about her project idea. She wanted to start one at a school near Twin Peaks in San Francisco, then connect it with a Noongar indigenous school in southwestern Australia, near Sam's hometown. The Noongar were Oola's aboriginal people; Naomi had remembered everything Sam had told her about her best friend that day at Alice's Restaurant, and Twin Peaks was one of Owen's favorite places to visit.

Naomi said she had already made all the contacts.

Sam was so excited. "Oh, my gosh, Naomi. This is the greatest thing ever." She felt herself on the verge of tears, again.

Naomi, really for the first time since they met, appeared overflowing with joy. It was wonderful to see.

When brunch was finished, Renzo and Pippa came to say goodbye. They all hugged and kissed, then Naomi and Sam walked out to the parking lot overlooking the small harbor in front of the restaurant.

Sam held her friend's hand in her own.

"Thanks, Naomi. I'm really honored to do this … for you, for Oola … and for Owen."

"Me too," Naomi replied.

Neither of them at all noticed the man in the sedan there watching them.

Officer Murray met Sally at the coffee shop across the street. They were ordering when the unlikely third member of their party arrived.

Damien.

The woman who'd attacked Sally, and Sam twice, had been transported from California to the mental health facility right there outside the shop's front windows.

Sally cringed as she saw Damien walking up.

"I know this is unusual." Murray started off, stirring his cortado. You could tell right away that the officer was a good guy, one of those who was both friendly and businesslike at the same time, serious but kind.

"Just figured we might find some understanding here, and possibly heal some wounds this way."

Damien and Sally looked off in opposite directions, avoiding eye contact with each other.

"So, she's said a couple things over there ... We're trying to piece them together to get an idea maybe ... about why all this happened." Murray's tone was rather comforting as he sipped, glancing back and forth over the top of his cup.

Sally looked at him.

"So, here it is ..." Murray continued. "She's been repeating your name, Damien, over and over ... And then something ..." Murray peeked into his notepad, "Something about the words ... *for life*."

Damien looked puzzled.

Sally shot him a disgusted look.

"And we found a bunch of these matchbooks in her purse from this place ... *The Griffon* ... with your name written in them."

Murray showed it to him.

"You know anything about that?"

"Uh ... no." Damien responded resolutely.

"The Griffon. You know the place, downtown, right? ... With the dollar bills all over the walls?"

"Yeah ... yeah."

Damien froze as Murray slid a mugshot of the woman from his portfolio onto the table. Sally, still with bruises along the side of her face, turned away.

"Do you remember her?"

After a moment, he responded, "Yeah ... actually. I think I do."

The officer waited for him to continue. "What can you tell me?"

Damien's expression turned pale a bit. Uncomfortable.

"Yeah, well ... My buddy Teddy and I were there one night, at The Griffon, and we saw her ... but her back was turned."

"Okay ..." Murray replied. "Then, what?"

"Then, I don't know ... I said something to her ... about her shoes, I remember." Damien stared off into the half-empty restaurant. "Those red high-heeled shoes."

Both Murray and Sally were looking directly at him now.

"What happened then?"

"Then, she turned around."

The photo of the woman lay there on the white pine table, between all the coffee cups.

Spine-chilling.

Haunting both Sally and Damien apparently now.

It was about half a minute before Damien spoke again.

"And, we left, immediately ... I never saw her again."

When Sam got home, Ranger was out on the lanai. He'd already given her a key and the code to the security system. When she came through the wide sliding glass doors to meet him, it was a totally welcomed surprise.

He hugged her.

Longer than usual.

"How was your brunch?"

"Really great ... Naomi's starting a new project at a school in Twin Peaks in San Francisco." The excitement in Sam's voice was just one more thing that made Ranger crazy about her. "And they're paying it forward to a school near my hometown in Australia ... Isn't that cool? Close to the caves and that Gnarabup Beach I was telling you about."

She was so hoping she could walk with him on that beach one day.

"And, they want me to lead it ..." Sam finished.

They held each other's hands as they stood.

"That is *really* cool!"

"Yeah." Her voice cracked.

He was so proud of her.

"Anyway, she said the view is beautiful up there too ... from the top of Twin Peaks."

Ranger looked up into the sky, the sun was still high. His eyebrows raised. "You wanna go?"

"Now?" Sam bubbled up.

"Yeah."

"Yes!" she answered.

It was a great time, Ranger thought ... There was nothing else planned for the rest of the day.

The drive to the peaks took Sam and Ranger across the Golden Gate, through the Presidio, Golden Gate Park, and onto twisty Twin Peaks Boulevard. They parked and climbed the steps to the top of the north summit, called Eureka Peak (the south one being Noe Peak), where the view really was spectacular.

They gazed east down Market Street to the Financial District and the Bay Bridge, Yerba Buena, Treasure Island, the port of Oakland, Alameda, Berkeley and the hills beyond. Then to the north, Alcatraz and Angel Islands, Sausalito, Tiburon, the Marin Headlands; and finally towards the Golden Gate, the Sunset, Ocean Beach and the Pacific behind them to the west.

"This is really beautiful." Sam snuggled close to Ranger as a trace of breeze blew her hair across her face. "Being here with you."

He held her in both of his arms, and they stood there, appreciating it all. The moment and the feeling. Just like the peaks ... together.

They had found it.

"You know, Ranger ... it's strange. Naomi says when the fog comes in here, you can't see a thing."

"Yeah ... That's hard to imagine." Ranger rested his chin on the top of her head.

"But, she also told me she was up here once ... with her son, and the fog was all around below them while the sun was still out, and it felt like they were floating, on the clouds."

Ranger breathed in deep, and Sam placed her head on his chest.

She sighed.

"I see why she said Owen loved it so much up here."

It took a second for it to register.

It was the first time Ranger had heard that name ... since those guys had called it from the car that day at the high school. When they were chasing him.

"That's his name ... Naomi's son?" he asked.

"Yep ... Mmm hmm." Sam glanced up, then back out to the Pacific in the distance. "I know ... it feels strange saying it, with him being gone and all."

It was silent for a breath there as Ranger rewound in his head. He realized he'd missed Naomi's presentation altogether New Year's Eve night at the Ritz-Carlton while he was backstage, and nobody else had said that name anywhere else around him.

But, he knew it almost instantly ...

It was the same Owen.

20 THE CALIFORNIA MISSIONS

"Things are tough all over, cupcake, an' it rains on the just an' the unjust alike ... except in California."

Watchmen

Detective Skelton was a short man, late 30s, balding in the front, but his hair was neatly cut. Otherwise, there were no frills about him.

Jacket off, his narrow shoulders failed to fill up the pinstriped button-down he was wearing, or hold his suspenders very well, but his manner was strong as he roamed the room, circling his desk, then over to the window, and back again. Outside, the belltower of the Mission San Rafael Arcángel rose above the trees adjacent to the law enforcement station, so resplendent you'd never know anything of the mission's turbulent past.

American pioneer Kit Carson had spent time at that mission; Skelton studied him in school. About five years back, he even visited the Sierra Nevada town named in Carson's honor -- there on the north shore of Silver Lake, California, just up the road from Tragedy Springs.

Carson was a man Skelton admired.

A man who stood for what was *right*, and pity you if you stood in his way.

Kit Carson was a legend of the frontier ... mountain man, wilderness guide, Army officer, and hero of the Old West. Dime-store novels celebrated his adventures. Carson wasn't a big man either, height-wise, but he was strong, stout and broad shouldered with a barrel chest. He was here at the mission in 1846 when a small group of settlers, under the command of Army Brevet Captain John C. Fremont, used it as the headquarters for the Bear Flag Revolt, taking California from Mexico and declaring it as their own independent republic.

And, Carson killed men. Lots of them. Savages, hostiles, threats to his livelihood. Indians.

Reports say he killed as many Indians as he could get his hands on, taking his first scalp when he was just nineteen years old.

Of all his adventures, one Carson story that always stuck with Skelton particularly, though, was about him and ... a girl.

In 1849, Carson guided soldiers on an expedition to track the trail of one Mrs. Ann White ... an American who'd been captured by the Apache. When they found her, she was dead. Abused, mutilated, with an arrow through her heart.

From Carson's memoirs:

> *Mrs. White was a frail, delicate, and very beautiful woman, but having undergone such usage as she suffered, nothing but a wreck remained; she was literally covered with blows and scratches. Her countenance even after death indicated a hopeless creature.*
>
> *Over her corpse, we swore vengeance upon her persecutors.*
>
> *In camp was found a book, the first of the kind I had ever seen, in which I was made a great hero, slaying Indians by the hundreds ... I have often thought that Mrs. White read the same ... [and prayed] for my appearance that she might be saved.*

But, to Carson's dismay, he was not able to save her.

William Tecumseh Sherman, Civil War general, author of the *scorched earth* total war philosophy, and namesake of the General Sherman Tree, met Kit Carson in Monterey, California, 1847.

He wrote:

> *His fame was then at its height, ... and I was very anxious to see a man who had achieved such feats of daring among the wild animals of the*

> *Rocky Mountains, and still wilder Indians of the plains ... I cannot express my surprise at beholding such a small, stoop-shouldered man, with reddish hair, freckled face, soft blue eyes, and nothing to indicate extraordinary courage or daring. He spoke but little and answered questions in monosyllables.*

Skelton always appreciated that bit of history. This story.

General Sherman's words.

He could see himself in them.

"Let's get some pizza ... Do you feel like it?" Sam asked.

"Yes, I do."

Ranger squeezed Sam tightly, and the two of them descended the steps to the Malibu, which was parked in the small lot between the two peaks.

The message alert on her phone suddenly went off in her bag.

It was a message from Sally ...

> *She was stalking Damien. Really creepy. Guess she thought you were with him. Call you soon. Driving to Boston with Mom & Dad. Love ya,*
> *Sammy*

She peeked at it as Ranger held her door open, and it sent a chill down her spine.

As Ranger came around to the driver side and got in, she grabbed onto his hand, looking into his eyes.

"Where do you wanna go ... for pizza?" she said softly.

Ranger looked back at her, the light disappearing outside.

"Umm ... Right down there, I think." He pointed north down by the water. "It'll be a surprise."

Ranger and Sam turned left onto Grant Avenue, one of the oldest streets in San Francisco, part of the old colorful Barbary Coast where the land originally ended and the bay began, where Gold Rushers from around the world abandoned their ships, the empty vessels ultimately becoming part of the landfill where the city's Financial District is built now.

The red lanterns strung across the main street all through Chinatown were already aglow, and as Ranger crossed over Columbus Avenue, he looked to park.

They got a spot just up from Caffè Trieste, famous among other reasons as the place where Italian immigrant *Papa Gianni* Giotta first brought espresso to the West Coast in 1956.

There was a group performing old Italian music along the back wall. Looked like a family, three or four generations, grandma singing, grandpa on the accordion, and kids dancing.

"That's where Francis Ford Coppola would sit and write the screenplay for *The Godfather*." Ranger held Sam's hand as they strolled west down Vallejo back towards Columbus ... a sedan passing them slowly with the windows down.

"Wow ... That's my grandfather's all-time favorite movie." Sam snuggled in.

There was a chill coming up in the air which hadn't been there the past several evenings.

"And Kerouac and Ginsberg and the Beat Generation guys hung out here in the 50s."

Sam stared down at their feet as they rounded the sidewalk corner. So cool, she thought, how their steps mirrored each other, his left with her right, and their two feet on the inside going back and forth together perfectly alongside each other.

"Yeah? We read that book in school ... *On the Road*," she answered without lifting her head. "Never did really understand how being so lost was considered so cool."

They made their way by all the sidewalk cafes and pastry shops, Italian-American and Tuscan eateries, to Tony's Pizza Napoletana there on the corner of Stockton and Union, kitty-corner to Washington Square, where North Beach locals gather, across from Saints Peter and Paul Church, whose steps were the backdrop for slugger Joe DiMaggio and Marilyn Monroe's front-page wedding back in '54.

"Well, here it is." Ranger smiled. "Some say *The Best Pizzeria in America*."

Sam's eyes got all big. She was excited.

He put their name in with the hostess.

"So, the owner," Ranger continued, "this guy Tony Gemignani, who's from here in the Bay, is like the 12-time world pizza making, pizza tossing world champion ... He's in the *Guinness Book of World Records* ..."

"Yeah? ..."

"Yeah," he said. "And apparently, when he won his first title over in Naples, the home of pizza as you know, the police had to escort him from the stage. They thought the native *Napoletanos* were going to attack him."

"Oh, my gosh!" Sam chuckled, putting her hand over her mouth.

"Yeah, they couldn't accept his victory."

They stepped back onto the sidewalk, among the patrons dining at the small outside tables and the other people standing along the street. Then, the hostess called their name.

"Sam and Ranger, your table is ready."

5:00 pm.

The plain manila file folder on Skelton's desk lay there unopened, as there was no need to open it. He knew every detail of what was inside.

What you had was a guy who didn't have many friends, and his family had no idea what he was doing. Hadn't in a long time. There were no co-workers to speak of, as he was one of those independent contractor-slash-entrepreneur tech types you find all over the Bay Area these days.

Basically, he gets dressed up one night, then ... that's it.

Ends up floating out in the ocean.

Since he got the case, Skelton had been asking around what events transpired in the area, most likely on a Friday or a Saturday, a couple or three weeks ago, and he'd found a few. Just today he discovered that a private affair had been thrown at the Pelican Inn over in Muir Beach two Saturday evenings ago. Problem was: the individual whose name was on the rental agreement was in Abu Dhabi, half a world away.

Until tomorrow.

So, he would wait.

Because he didn't think he was dealing with an accident here, or some unfortunate mishap.

Detective Skelton was investigating what he believed to be a murder.

Ranger and Sam sat in the back of the place at a booth next to one of the ovens and watched the artists toss the dough. They skipped *antipastos* and went straight for the pizza, Sam ordering the World Cup winning *Margherita*, and Ranger the coal-fired *New Yorker*.

It was heaven.

"Hey, I …"

"Sam, I …" Ranger started at the same time.

"Oh, go ahead."

"No, sorry. You go … You first, honey." She reached across and grabbed his hand, again, almost instinctively, the word *honey* enough to send him clear over the moon inside.

"Alright …" Ranger cleared his throat. "I …"

"I wanted to tell you … I think I know Owen."

"What? … Really? … Naomi's Owen? How?" Sam swallowed and took a breath.

A man walked by and entered the booth next to them.

Ranger told her the story. Lwazi, the golden heart necklace, the guys in the car.

She looked stunned as she took it all in. "So … it's gotta be him."

"I think so," Ranger answered. "I mean … I have a strong feeling it is."

"At brunch this morning, Naomi told me … Owen sent her a message a couple days ago … She asked me not to say anything."

Ranger listened. It seemed to get quieter in there for a second.

"It said *Happy New Year* … and that he hoped to see her soon."

"Did she call him back?"

"Yeah, she said the number didn't work … It was an 850 area code."

Ranger paused, then picked up his phone.

"Florida Panhandle …" Sam filled him in.

Ranger had been worried that Sam might be, say, *disenchanted* by the way he had handled the whole Owen situation, and the guys in the car, but got the sense now she wasn't at all. In fact, it seemed just the opposite. Like they were instantly, without a doubt together on this. Just like everything else.

Each could see it in the other's eyes.

"What do you think he was doing at the statue that day?" she asked.

"That's a good question."

"And, why were those guys chasing him?"

"Right."

"And, what's he doing in Florida, or at least with a Florida number?"

"Don't know."

They sat and contemplated it.

"Well, looks like we might be finding out real soon."

Nearly every emotion possible ran through each of them in that moment there in the booth … with the pizza in between them.

Man, they loved being with each other.

Sam and Ranger finished their dinner then headed across the park to the lit church steps, and back up Columbus by Z. Cioccolato, Stella Pastry, and The Stinking Rose. Music was pouring out of Caffè Trieste now and patrons were dancing and singing inside, so they decided to dip in for an espresso.

With people passing up and down the sidewalk behind them, Ranger opened the door for Sam.

It was 7:30 in the evening.

They had so much fun, they ended up staying until closing at 11:00.

Tucked high into a broad wooded hillside overlooking the rocky coast of the Pacific Ocean, buried deep in an area some of the locals called *Devil's Palisade*, was a villa ... A dark place, all dark on the inside as well, except for a candle shining through the picture window of the first floor withdrawing room. The woman of the house was there, recessed away from the candlelight, watching as headlights wound their way up to the compound through the mass of trees. The car ... the sedan from the parking lot at brunch in Tiburon this morning.

Upstairs, the man with the sharp teeth and the scar across his face sat, and waited.

21 STEEP RAVINE

"Before the fire to pass peaceful, contented days while the rain outside pours down … We tread the icy path slowly and cautiously, for fear of tripping and falling." Vivaldi, "Winter" of *The Four Seasons*

You know what they say about when it rains.

Skelton was well on his way to the Millennium Tower by the time Ranger and Sam had left for Steep Ravine.

All the rain that had fallen over the previous couple months caused Webb Creek, part of the Mount Tamalpais watershed, to be really flowing. As they hiked down from the Pantoll Station trailhead, Sam was blown away by the place's beauty. Steep, lush canyon walls and towering moss-covered redwoods, some fallen over the path so you had to duck under, were everywhere. Wooden and stone staircases, two waterfalls, and a precipitous 14-rung wooden ladder alongside one of them that hikers must be careful to descend.

This was where Ranger had wanted to bring Sam, almost from the moment he saw her out on that deck at Alice's Restaurant.

It was Wednesday morning.

"Ranger, this is just …"

"I know … Sam, stop right there." Ranger had been following her on the trail when they came to the first wooden bridge crossing over the creek.

"Yeah, do you wanna …"

He spun her into his arms and kissed her.

She almost fell over. "… take a picture?"

"Yeah …" he smiled.

They laughed, then took the cutest picture, on that first bridge.

And kissed on every single bridge that came after that.

At the end of the descent through the ravine, the water had calmed, forming a stream with pools and little fish, and the dense, fern-filled forest gave way to open grassland with sagebrush and coyote bush. They were still a ways up, so as they ascended a ridge and emerged onto the chaparral beyond it, they got their first gasp-inspiring view of the Pacific, the strand of Stinson Beach below them, and Point Reyes beyond in the distance.

"Ranger …"

It was perfect.

The Millennium Tower had already been an epicenter for controversy for some time before Skelton even stepped foot on the premises.

Several years back, residents of the blue-gray condominium high-rise at the corner of Mission and Fremont Streets, south of Market in San Francisco, were informed that their 58-story luxury home was … sinking.

And tilting.

Developers and lawyers had been sparring ever since over how to fix it.

Ever the optimist, Julian purchased his grand residence on the 45th floor about a year after the frightening news broke, at a steal of a price, and was hoping for the best.

He loved it here.

Skelton was waiting in the hallway as Julian exited the elevator, coming in from the airport, suitcase in hand.

"How are you doing?" Skelton offered, sizing him up and down.

Julian already looked notably different than he had a couple weeks ago at the Pelican Inn, the pompadour and moustache gone, replaced by messy fringe bangs, a scruffy beard, sunglasses, and a proper turban-tied headpiece ... a present from a new friend over there, to be sure.

"*Ana bekheir, shukran* [I'm fine, thank you], brother ... Can I help you?"

Skelton smiled before removing his badge from a jacket pocket.

"Perhaps."

The detective just had this way about him. To control a situation with the subtlest of tactics, to make you feel uncomfortable, ill-at-ease, self-conscious.

Julian stopped and set his bag down onto the marble, the front door to his apartment, Skelton, and himself forming a pretty even equilateral triangle out there in the hallway. Skelton looked up at the larger man, at least a foot-and-a-half taller and thrice as brawny, completely unfettered.

"What exactly ... can I do for you, detective?"

Through the blue-grey windows at the west end of the hallway, up there on the 45th floor, you could see the thick clouds coming in on the horizon.

"How was your trip?"

It took a moment before Julian answered.

"It was fine."

Skelton stared at him, then held out the photo of Michael Roman.

"Do you recognize this man?"

Sam and Ranger made their way down the rest of the trail, passing hikers on their way up, and arrived in the hamlet of Stinson Beach. When they reached the sand, they took off their shoes, and barefoot, walked out into the crisp, cool knee-deep surf.

"Whew!" A wave crested up to waist-high, and Sam leaped onto Ranger's back.

They stood there, watching the water, the ocean rolling back and forth, and Ranger's feet sinking further and deeper into the wet sand.

"So, to clarify, you didn't see Mr. Roman leave, you never saw him again after that night, and nobody else has contacted you about him in any way ... You've heard nothing."

"Correct."

Skelton sauntered over to the floor-to-ceiling window at the corner of Julian's living room, took his notepad out, and scratched something down.

"But you might remember who he came with ... once you see the guest list?"

"Probably ... yeah," Julian replied.

The detective remained there, his back turned.

"Can you at least tell me what happened to the guy?" Julian inquired, a bit north of a little bit annoyed with the investigator's methods.

Skelton squared back to his burly host, suddenly appearing as serious as a lightning strike. "Let's just call it a *missing-persons*, for now ... I can let myself out."

With no further gesture, the detective made his way over to the entranceway door.

He reached for the handle, then hesitated, and without turning around, asked in an acutely cold and sober voice: "How long do you think until I have that list?"

Julian replied, *soon*.

"Oh, and," Skelton added as he eased the door open, "I'd advise you not to speak to anybody about this, at least for now …"

The bigger man just watched him.

"Let's just keep it between you and me," Skelton said.

And, he walked out.

Sam and Ranger shared a yummy blueberry pastry and a chocolate-vanilla swirl soft-serve cone from the local Parkside Cafe before starting back up Mount Tamalpais to the Siata. Then, they trekked, up the road, across the Panoramic Highway, and into the winding cover of the willow and California bay trees, twinberry, hazelnut and currant.

"I wish Bernard could have come," Sam said as they emerged back onto the chaparral.

Neither had noticed, but a tuft of dark grey clouds was following them right up the foothill. And, it began to sprinkle just as Ranger spotted the coyote.

"Oh, look!" Sam saw it too.

The coyote stood there and watched them passing on the open trail, approximately twenty-five yards away. It was alone.

"Aww … Where are his mates?" Sam asked. "Where's his family?"

The tan-grey coyote stared as the rain began to come more heavily now, and it made no sound. As Ranger and Sam reached the crest of the knoll leading down to the old dam and the boundary of the canopied ravine ascent, it really started to storm.

They looked back and the coyote was still there.

It was fun hiking back up the ravine in the rain, and Sam kissed Ranger, drenched, as they crossed over every bridge again. When they arrived back at Liberty Dock, Bernard was overjoyed, and they washed up and spent the rest of the afternoon playing with him.

Until Naomi called.

"Hey, Richie!"

"Jules … you guys are back? How was it, my friend?"

"Yeah, we landed this morning. Man, we almost lost Danny-boy to one of those boat crews, they loved him so much … He wanted to sail off with them!"

"What else would you expect … Of course he did."

"Right. It was awesome. Dubai for New Year's?! C'mon, man … *Mudhahal*! That means *cool* … And, how was your guys' escape to the backcountry?"

"Really inspiring. They call that Milford Track *the greatest walk in the world*, and they're right. When Liz and I were standing there under Sutherland Falls, all by ourselves … under 2,000 feet of water …" Richie smiled over to Liz, who was listening.

"Wow!"

"Hi, Julian!" Liz called from the background. They'd gotten back just last night and she was still unpacking.

Julian hollered back *hello*.

"So, what's happening, man? Anything?"

"Yeah, I actually have a sort of serious question for you …" Julian started in. "So, I get off the elevator this morning at home and I've got this detective standing there outside my door in the hallway. Shows me a photo of this guy … who was at our Christmas party."

Richie went quiet on the other end, drawing his wife's attention.

"Says he went missing."

"What?" Richie reacted, alarmed. "Who? Who was it?"

"Michael Roman." Julian answered. "Do you know that name?"

"No … I don't think so. Did you remember him?"

"Yeah," Julian went on, "I recall seeing him, but I don't remember who he was with."

Liz fixed on Richie, concerned.

"Hey, man … You still have the guest list from the party?" Julian asked.

"Uh … yeah. Yeah, I'm sure I do."

"Alright. Well, the detective … who wasn't the friendliest guy in the world, and I really didn't care too much to help the guy … He wants to see it."

"Okay … Let me grab my computer." Richie went and got it and pulled the list up. "Let's take a look and see if we can figure out … something." He began scrolling through the names.

Michael Roman's wasn't on it.

"Yeah, I don't see him on here."

Silence.

"But, remember, Jules, there were all those last minute people we never put on the list." Richie read through it again.

"Right ..." Julian replied.

"Yeah, looks like," Richie counted in the background, "there are about fifteen people we invited who never RSVP'd the guest they were bringing."

"Okay ... Who were those?"

"Alright ..." Richie read. "We have Codie, he was one of Danny's boys. And Laura, and Karl."

"Of course. That guy never knows what he's doing the very next minute."

"Tania. You know Tania. And Kotaro, Siren, and Malcolm. Antoine, Ardie ... Your guy Hooper. Anne-Marie, and Kahena."

"Uh huh."

"And Caterina, you know, from the catamaran." He paused. "And, Ranger's friend Carolijn."

"Hmm. Really?" Julian paused for a second. "Okay, I still have no idea who it could be."

"Yeah, me either ..." Richie looked over to his wife.

It was quiet once more for about a quarter minute before Richie spoke again. "Okay. Well ... maybe we just get the list over to the detective and let him, you know, do whatever it is he does with it."

"Yeah, I guess you're right." Julian said. "Okay, will you send it to me? And, I'll pass it on."

"Roger that … Sending it now, buddy."

They were about to wrap up the call when Julian added one more thing.

"Hey, Richie … That detective, Skelton, he *advised* me to not talk to anybody else about this … What do you think that's all about?"

"Hmm … Not sure. Maybe he thinks it might interfere with the investigation."

"Or …" Julian added, "… maybe if I knew something and I started talking, he would find out, and it would make me look … you know, suspicious."

"Yeah, right."

"He seemed like the type of guy that would do something like that."

Richie thought about it. "Maybe we keep it between us, then, like the detective said."

"Yeah … I think so."

Liz stood there, a pair of Injinji hiking toe socks hanging from her hand, waiting for Richie to fill her in as the guys wrapped it up, said goodbye, and Richie hung up the phone.

He shrugged.

And asked his wife if she could keep a secret.

They met Naomi at the Buckeye Roadhouse, a lively Aspen lodge-style place in Mill Valley with vaulted dining room ceilings and a great river-rock fireplace, at about 7:00 pm.

"Thanks for coming," Naomi hugged Sam and Ranger as the hostess waited to seat them. She realized she hadn't seen Ranger since he came to find her in the grand ballroom of the Ritz-Carlton that night, but she felt like she knew him well anyway.

She smiled gratefully as they made their way to a table in front of the fireplace.

"This okay?" the hostess asked.

"Great."

They all took a deep breath.

"So, Naomi, tell us ..." Sam started in.

"So ... I talked to him."

That's as far as she got before the server came to greet them. "Hi, my name is Charlotte." Her name tag said *Rose*. "I understand you're all having dessert tonight, huh? ... Yum."

"Yes ..." Sam smiled at the young girl.

"Well, *hon*, they're all fabulous. Let me tell you ... I'll be right back for any questions."

"Alright, thanks."

Charlotte bobbed away, and Naomi went on.

"Yeah, so he called a couple of hours ago ..." She choked up for a second, but then smiled.

"Yeah ... Did he say where he was?" Sam asked.

"No."

"So ... what did he say?"

Before Naomi could answer, Charlotte returned.

"What'll it be, guys?"

Ranger straightened, and Sam kept her eye on Naomi as she cleared her throat.

"Um, I'll have the baked lemon pudding," she answered.

"And I'll have the chocolate caramel tart," Sam went next.

"I will try … the s'more pie," Ranger said, then gathered the menus and handed them back to the server.

"Fantastic!" Charlotte announced. "We'll have those right up for ya."

Naomi readied herself to speak, but then sort of broke down again.

"Is he in trouble?" Sam scooted closer to her.

"I think so."

"What did he say?"

"Well, he said he missed me … And that he's okay … And something about how he was trying to do the right thing … I don't know, I couldn't hear him very well."

Ranger and Sam just sat there, silent.

"Then, he said he wanted to meet me … somewhere." She wiped her eyes with her napkin. "Very soon."

Sam placed her hand on Naomi's shoulder as her countenance turned a bit hopeful.

"Is that everything?" Ranger asked her.

"He told me he'd call back … and to erase the number. Then, the phone clicked off."

The glow of the fireplace illuminated Naomi's face, and Ranger could see the sadness in it. Behind him, the fire crackled rambunctiously.

Just then, a man's face appeared in the darkness outside the big window to Sam's left, Naomi's right, barely visible if they'd have looked over.

And, another man entered the restaurant.

He was seated a couple tables away.

Ranger caught him out of the corner of his eye.

At the same time, Charlotte returned with the desserts, and her big, spunky smile.

"Here you go! ... Can I interest anyone in a coffee or anything else to go along with these?"

They all looked incredible.

"No, thank you, Charlotte." Naomi smiled. "They look so good."

"Yes ... thank you."

"Alrighty. Enjoy."

As Charlotte (or Rose) turned away, she noticed the man standing outside there in the dark.

They watched each other for several seconds.

A short time later, the man in the restaurant got up and left ... just as Charlotte was coming back inside the front door. She took stock of him. A little after that, a freckle-faced busboy with the shadow of a red beard came in from outside, spoke a couple words to Charlotte, and handed her a small slip of paper.

Ranger could see all this, as Sam and Naomi were busy comparing desserts.

Charlotte arrived back at the table. "Okay, is there anything else I can get for you wonderful folks tonight, then?"

She and Ranger met eyes.

"I don't think so." Sam smiled.

"No ... thank you, Charlotte." Naomi looked in much better spirits.

"Yep ... Everything was great."

She could tell Ranger knew something out of the ordinary had just happened.

And, that she had just taken care of it.

She winked at him.

"Excellent! If there's nothing else, I will get your check ... And, maybe we'll see you guys in here again sometime, soon."

"I definitely think it was good that we didn't tell Naomi about your ... encounter with Owen." Sam surfed her hand up and down out of the window of the Malibu as they got off the 101. "Not tonight."

"Yeah, you're right."

They pulled into the Liberty Dock.

As they crossed the parking lot, Ranger glanced down and saw the message alert glowing blue on his phone. He had a handful of messages ... from Lwazi, and Schalk, one from Dan, a couple from business associates, and one from an old friend by the name of TJ.

"What?! ... TJ!" He read it.

TJ was one of those guys you meet only once in a lifetime. The best storyteller with never-ending stories to tell. Brilliant and super-talented, TJ had been living "off the grid" since high school. He'd spent a few years in the fishing village Koh Panyi in the Phang Nga province of Thailand, and worked at the floating market at Bang Nam Phueng selling boat noodles. Then, he ended up in Cape Verde, in the Atlantic, recording bossanova and Cuban charanga music with the great Teófilo Chantre. After that, he hiked across Iceland.

Range! Long time, brother. Will be in your area Sunday 1/10. Would love to see you.

You can message me here.

"Wow! That's so exciting …"

"Yeah, it is." He smiled. "Okay, here's the deal … We're having a get-together, next week when TJ is here … for everybody to meet you. And, at midnight, we're celebrating your birthday. Just you and I." She could see the no-holds-barred joy in his eyes as he said it, and it just sent her over the moon.

"We'll contact everyone tomorrow."

Sam was ecstatic.

As they reached the walkway to the house, she thought about whom she would eventually introduce Ranger to … Sally and her *Nonno* and *Nonna* were the only ones to come to mind, and that was okay. She was so excited becoming part of his life … and leaving hers behind. All that emptiness, void of love.

They went in, and Bernard jumped all over them.

As Sam went to set her things down, she remembered that Sally was supposed to call soon. So, she checked her messages.

There wasn't one from her yet.

But, there was one … from Abby.

The young girl from Cape Fear.

"He said to find out everything about her."

The man parked in the marina lot in Tiburon spoke to the rest of them around the table. The room was dark, a single lamp hanging down above their heads somewhere in the middle of the city. Polk Gulch or the Tenderloin, perhaps.

Another man, the one outside the window at the Buckeye Roadhouse, was there as well. And, the one who came into the restaurant.

They were the same two who had followed Sam and Ranger to Twin Peaks the day before, and down to North Beach when they went for pizza.

The younger, taller guy from Monday at Terrapin Crossroads, the one Ranger punched out Christmas afternoon, was in the room too, along with a couple other hard-looking types who didn't say a word.

"We know it's Owen's mom ... And, we know he's coming to see her. That's it."

"Do we want to get their cell phones?" The one from inside the restaurant asked.

"No ... That will ... *alarm* them," the Tiburon one directed. They called him Toner.

"It's *okay* ... Next time they meet, we just follow *her* ... *Naomi*," the one from the window said with an accent of some sort, really creepy in the face as he said it.

"Boss wants *Romeo* ... Mr. Ranger ... and *Australia* followed at all times," Toner made it clear; the big, young guy tightening his fists as he heard Ranger's name.

The one from inside the restaurant grinned.

"Shouldn't have lost her the first time." The tall one mumbled it, not looking up.

"And, no rough stuff. Not yet. That's the order." Toner made eye contact with each of them, especially window man, and the big one, who looked to be the connection to the other two, the mutes.

He took in a long breath, the light swinging back and forth above his bald head.

"He wants Owen. That's it."

It was 12:15 am.

Thursday morning.

Bernard was up first monitoring the activity in the air off the lanai of the floating house ... He could tell another storm was coming in.

Rar Rar Raaar Raaaar!

The seagulls watched as he made a fuss.

Ranger woke a little after that, then Sam. They both slept well.

Sam made tea and joined Bernard and Ranger on the lanai.

There was a regatta going on.

"Good morning," she offered, and they all hugged.

The sailboats were right there off Harbor Point, in the protected part of the bay directly behind Ranger's place, where the wind is usually not too strong. But, it was blowing today. They were the heavier of the Olympic class dinghies with one crew in each. Single-handed, they call it. Team boats with their crew motored all along the race course boundary, watching the competitors intently, and as far as most of them could tell, the dinghy with the Union Jack pressed onto its sail was in front, its captain darting beam-wise under the boom, which swung back-and-forth often, waves lapping over the windward edge of his bow.

But, the Hungarian looked to be giving it all he had as well.

"Wow!" Sam cheered as they crossed the imperceptible finish line side by side.

"Yeah. Wow ... That looked intense."

They stayed out a while longer then decided to cook breakfast together, the three of them. They had some stuff for a good Australian *brekkie*, so Ranger helped Sam whip it up ... bacon, *snags* [sausage] from the Ferry Building, and fried eggs and *bikkies* [biscuits] with marmalade.

After, they got shoes on and got ready to take Bernard for a walk.

"All this ... could not be any better, Ranger." Sam gazed up into his eyes as they embraced, then they started off from the front porch, Bernard tickled pink on his leash. They clunked along the dock boarding, then turned and headed through the parking lot to Gate 5 Road.

Sam enjoyed it as they passed the string of delightful little places to eat along Bridgeway, the main route through Sausalito, like Saylor's, Napa Valley Burger Co., and Angelino.

"We should have our party there." Ranger pointed to the turn-of-the-century yacht club turned 1960s-style restaurant on the water, The Trident.

"How fun ... I love it." Sam smiled big, taking the place in.

"As a matter of fact, I think we should send the invitations out right now, while we're here." Ranger held up his phone and looked to Sam. "Let's get a picture."

"Oh, my gosh." Sam was so happy to do a picture, totally unconcerned with how she looked considering they had just been walking and she hadn't done herself up at all this morning.

That's just the way she was.

They positioned themselves in front of The Trident sign at the entrance to the restaurant, got the festive Bernard between them, and took a handful of the most darling photos they'd taken yet.

Ranger called inside to secure the reservation, then they selected their favorite photo ... and Ranger created the invitation.

Dear, Friends

We would love to invite ... especially You

To come meet ... joyfully Us

The Trident Sausalito

Sunday, January 10, 6:00 pm

Love, Sam and Ranger

This time Sam did start crying, just for a moment.

Ranger hugged her, then scrolled and check-boxed his closest friends from his contact list, and hit *send*.

Sam got herself back together.

"This is such a great idea ... I'm so excited." She held onto him, the stirred-up waters of the bay out ahead of them beyond the restaurant, the view of San Francisco across the way, and the shops with the hillside of charming homes above them along the street.

"Can we take a few more pictures? ... It just feels so special here to me."

"Of course, my lady."

So, Ranger held the camera out in front of them as Sam spun them slowly and they giggled, and they took more pictures with all the various backdrops behind them.

And, with Bernard.

It was early afternoon by the time they got back to the house, and the rain had arrived.

But, it was nice because they didn't have anything planned.

Ranger removed his wet Under Armor HOVR running shoes and set them on top of the washing machine. "Do you want to shower up, then maybe make some lunch?"

"Yes ... Absolutely!" Sam removed hers too and headed upstairs.

Ranger had just settled into the roomy couch, a fire percolating in the wood-burning stove, and oolong tea in the *kulhads* he'd received as gifts at the Pelican Inn, when Sam came back down and around the corner from the top floor.

"Hey ... What ya guys doing?" She plopped down next to them.

"Just made these." Ranger handed her a mug.

Rar raaaaar raar. Bernard welcomed her too.

"Oh, my gosh. He's so funny ... Thank you."

Ranger had his device there so they could look at the photos they had taken.

Something about the graying of the sky, and the locale, and perhaps the reason they were taking the pictures in the first place made them seem ... really special.

"These are ... *so good*." Sam scrolled through.

He smiled.

"Can I send them to myself ... so I can show a couple to Sally, and *Nonno*?"

"I would love that."

Sam got up to go get her device. "Okay ... I'm ready." She looked Ranger in the eyes and gave him a soft peck on the cheek. "It'll be like they get to meet you too."

Sam chose all the photos she wanted to save, and send off, and as the fire flickered away and the storm poured down, she composed a couple of greetings.

First:

> *Hi, Nonno and Nonna. It's your granddaughter*
>
> *I miss you so much and hope you are well*
>
> *I'm in California, looks like for a while*
>
> *And I met someone*
>
> *His name is Ranger, and he's wonderful. Really wonderful*
>
> *Just wanted to send you some pictures*
>
> *And say, amo voi due*
>
> *Always! Sam*

Next:

> *Hey, Sal. You're never going to believe it*
>
> *Can't wait to tell you*
>
> *Love you!*
>
> *P.S. His name is Ranger*

Then one more:

> *Hi, Abby. Good to hear from you.*
>
> *And hello to you from the west coast*
>
> *Here's a photo especially for you.*
>
> *See ... Moving on, no fear*
>
> *You can do it too!*
>
> *Your friend, Sam*

"Okay, done." She smiled and hit the send button.

Sam and Ranger finished their tea, sunk deep into the giant Donegal tweed couch pillows, Bernard falling asleep on the edge of the ottoman.

"Let's see about that lunch ..."

About an hour later, Sam's phone rang, one half-eaten plate of grilled gruyère sandwiches and roasted sweet potato salad on the serving tray in front of them.

It was Sally.

"Hey, Sal," Sam whispered, getting up so as to not fully wake the other two.

"Hey, Sammie!"

"Sal, how are you?"

"Good ... just got in to Boston."

Ranger heard the front door open and Sam's voice disappear outside. The rain had eased, and Bernard watched with one eye as Ranger moved over in front of the sliding glass doors, watching the riplets in the plunge pool and the bay beyond.

It's strange, the feeling you get. When you don't want to be away from someone, not even for a minute.

The past couple of days had been so amazing, here at home.

He went back over and brought her picture back up on his device.

She's just the most beautiful thing I have ever seen.

Then, he noticed something.

It was a man, dressed in dark clothes, standing there in the background across the street … across Bridgeway. He looked like the man from inside the restaurant the previous night. And, there he was again, in the background of a second picture standing with another man. Looking into the camera.

Ranger got to his feet immediately and went outside until he heard Sam's voice at the end of the dock, by the water.

She waved to him enthusiastically.

And, he waved back.

Skelton was down to the last few names on his list.

"Hello."

"My name is Detective Skelton, may I speak with Malcolm?"

"This is."

"I have a couple questions … Do you know a man by the name of Michael Roman?"

"Uh … no, I don't think so."

"Did you attend the Christmas party on December 19 at the Pelican Inn in Muir Beach?"

"Uh … yes."

"What was the name of the guest you brought, please?"

"Uh, sir … what's going on?"

"This is an investigation … The name of your guest please?"

"Uh, it was Francesca … Can I ask what this is all about, please?"

"No. This is an investigation. If you have any other information, reach me at this number. It's the police department. And, I strongly encourage you not to speak to anyone about this call until further notice. Understood?"

There was silence on the line.

"Sir, do you understand?"

"Yes."

"Thank you … good afternoon." He dialed the next number.

"Hello, Hooper here."

Who are these guys? … And, what are they doing?

Ranger could hear Sam telling her friend all about him. About them. She was so excited.

Still standing on the front porch, Ranger searched the number for the Buckeye Roadhouse on his phone

"Buckeye Roadhouse …"

"Hi, yes … is Charlotte working today?"

"This is Charlotte."

"Hi, Charlotte. My name is Ranger." He slipped back in the front door. "I was there last night ... with a couple of ladies. We ordered dessert."

"Oh, yeah. I remember ... Hi."

"Hi, good. Listen, this may sound strange, but I thought I saw you, maybe, dealing with ... some sort of situation while we were there ... Possibly with some man in the restaurant."

"Yeah, that's right."

"Charlotte, I'm going to tell you this quick. I think I saw that man today ... with another guy ... Kind of like, *What are you doing here? Are you following us?* ... You know?"

"Well, mister ... that sort of makes sense."

"What do you mean?"

"Yeah, there was a man outside looking in the dining room windows ... and he was with the other guy inside. I told the one outside to leave, or I would call the cops."

Ranger froze for a second, and listened to see if he could still hear Sam's cheery voice.

He could.

"They tried to stay in the lot, until one of our busboys went out there and started writing their license plate number down."

Ranger paused ... "Did he get it?"

"He thought he got it, pretty sure he did, but they drove off pretty fast, with their lights off, and it was dark."

"Hmmm."

"Yeah, I could tell right away there was something obviously going on."

Ranger could hear Sam's voice coming closer.

"Uh, Mr. Ranger, is it?" Charlotte asked. "Are ... you in trouble or something?"

"I don't know."

Sam was wrapping up her conversation with Sally; she was at the front porch now.

"Listen, Charlotte ... Will you do me a favor? Can you send me that license plate number? ... Please?"

"Umm ..."

Ranger confirmed she had his number and hung up the phone just as Sam came back in.

As the rain started up again.

22 CARMEL-BY-THE-SEA

"Men must know their limitations."

Clint Eastwood, Mayor of Carmel

It had been a long, lazy Thursday afternoon at Liberty Dock.

For the first time in a long time, Sam thought, she almost felt *at home*.

"So, how is Sally?"

"Surprisingly good." Sam answered. "Considering, you know, everything that's happened."

It seemed Ranger could just swallow her up into him, standing there in the entranceway with both arms around her like a custom-made cover, her face buried into his chest.

"She asked me to send her the picture with the Golden Gate Bridge in the background … The one of you and me … She's always wanted to go there."

"Sounds great. It'll be nice to get her out here one day," he said.

With the rain coming down outside, she sat back down on the couch, picking up her tablet to send Sally that photo.

"Hey," Ranger said, "while you're doing that, I'm gonna run up front for a minute, okay?"

"Okay," Sam answered.

"Be right back … then we can plan our night."

"Sounds great." She turned to look over the top of the couch with the glow of the fireplace lighting up the smile on her face.

He put his hand out to wave, then put on his rain cover and headed out.

Plunk, plunk, plunk, plunk, plunk. The rain thumped down on the wood of the dock until Ranger reached the cover of the front entryway and the parking lot beyond it.

Then, all of a sudden, his phone lit up.

7BLK100

Dark sedan

It was Charlotte.

"Okay …" Ranger said to himself.

He scanned the parking lot, going up one aisle then down the other, then noticed a car drive off from the other side of the trees, heading towards Bridgeway.

He could not see the license plate.

Then, the strangest thing happened.

The sun broke through, shining a patch of light onto the pavement. Deep yellow and orange. About fifty feet across on Gate 5 Road right in front of him. And, a car came into it.

With three men inside.

It was the big one, from Terrapin Crossroads … with the two other thugs.

The looks on their faces, harmful.

The tall guy smiled, then that quick, the sun disappeared.

A chill came over Ranger's being and he withdrew back towards the entryway, realizing now … they knew where he lived.

But, who were they? And were they working together, the two from the restaurant and these three?

A bunch of thoughts flooded his mind.

"Hi ... Sam," Ranger smiled as he came back in through the front door.

Sam blushed inside ... "Hi!" she responded excitedly.

"I've got a great idea."

Ranger tossed his raincoat aside and entered the living room.

"Yeah?" she said.

"Yeah ..." Ranger said back. "Let's go to Carmel."

Skelton sat at his regular table at the coffee shop down the street from the mission.

It was 5:00 pm, but he was not done working yet.

He'd found what he was looking for, talking to Hooper, the guy Julian had invited to the Christmas party because his boss was seeking a connection to the start-up he was with.

Hooper had invited Michael Roman.

He also found that Hooper didn't know Roman very well. In fact, he hardly knew him at all. They'd met just a couple times at a few high-profile parties in the city recently and had had a pretty good time together.

This is what Skelton found out:

1. Hooper and Roman had arrived at the Pelican Inn separately that Saturday night, but at about the same time. 7:45 pm

2. Hooper drove, Roman came by ride service
3. Hooper left the inn at about 10:30 pm, and had no contact with Roman after that
4. Roman told Hooper he was staying at the party. To pursue a girl
5. The girl had not come to the party alone

Skelton took a final sip of his ristretto.

After, he'd need to head back to the office to track down some more phone numbers.

"You mean tonight?" Sam was surprised.

"Tonight," Ranger said.

"What? ... My gosh, Ranger ... Yeah. I'd love to go to Carmel."

"There's nothing we have to do anyway, not until Sunday."

Ranger walked over to the sliders and looked outside. He estimated there to be about an hour of daylight left, and the sun was making attempts to punch through the overcast.

He made a quick call, then another, then smiled to Sam.

"Okay, put on some layers, baby. Let's go."

Sam's eyebrows raised.

Ranger winked to her, and she went upstairs to get ready. He packed a few things as well, layered up too, and they were ready.

"See you in a few days, boy." They hugged Bernard, who was fired up because he knew that when Ranger had a bag, it meant Kurtley and Rob were coming over to stay with Schalk.

He loved that.

Ranger locked up, and they made their way up the dock.

"You're not going to tell me why I'm in these L.L. Bean's, are you?" Sam smiled and reached for Ranger's hand. Hers was warm, and soft.

Ranger had his long johns on too, underneath.

"Is it colder in Carmel-by-the-Sea?"

"Um, no … We just have a stop to make before we go."

They got on Gate 5 Road and took a right at Bridgeway, with a couple cars behind them. Ranger watched the mirrors as they merged onto 101 North and exited on the first ramp for the Shoreline Highway. He slowed down at the little bridge crossing over Coyote Creek, just before entering the little area of Tamalpais Valley Junction, with a diner on one side and coffee shop on the other, the San Francisco Running Company and Proof Lab Surf Shop, among other establishments, down the street.

Ranger pulled into the automotive garage on the right, and the two of them went in.

"Ranger! Good to see you, my friend!" The man greeted them with his big, thick fingers, hairy arms, and what looked to be a prematurely balding head.

"*Gulliver* … you big teddy bear!"

That wasn't his given name. Mamuka was; he was Georgian.

"Gulliver, this is my *girlfriend* … Sam."

Gulliver stood there silent for a second. "Ahhh … yes. I can see it."

"Hi, Gulliver … It's great to meet you."

Ranger smiled, then whispered in Gulliver's ear.

"Got it, brother. Not a problem." He walked, and waved them into the garage out back. There was a door there that led to a retail shop next door where he began thumbing through a rack of Aerostich riding suits, eyeballing Sam for a fit. In seconds, he had one. "You can change there." He said, pointing to a dressing room.

"Ranger …" Sam whispered.

"It's okay. Just put it on, on top of everything," he said, walking her over to the door.

When she came out, his was already on and he was holding their boots.

"Come this way …" Gulliver led them to the next room. "And, here you go."

"Oh, my gosh." Sam gasped.

It was a motorcycle.

A Thunder Black Smoke *Indian* Chieftain Dark Horse.

"You can put your bags in here," Gulliver said, lifting the cover of one of the slammed saddlebags.

"What do you think?" Ranger smiled.

"It's unbelievable …" she smiled back.

Gulliver returned with a couple of black helmets, which Sam and Ranger slipped on for size, then he directed them to the back of the shop. "The road is yours, my friends."

"You're the best, my man." Ranger gave him a hug, and Sam gave the big man a hug too.

Then, they rolled the bike out the door.

"We'll be back Sunday."

Their boots crunched along the gravel out behind the row of

warehouses and businesses that lined the main drag. The ground had already started drying up, but there was a gleam on the pavement, still moist from the last rain, which was headed towards Richmond on the other side of the bay.

Now on the side road a block to the east of the main route, Route 1, Ranger got on the bike, and Sam jumped up behind him onto the gunfighter seat.

"You ready, babe?" he asked.

"I'm ready!"

In the dim light, they slipped around back to the Shoreline Highway and to the 101 South, and headed for the Golden Gate Bridge.

The heater in Sam's suit helped to keep her warm, and her arms wrapped around Ranger's waist the entire trip did the same for him. He kept his elbows pressed on top of her arms ... to make her feel safe.

Ranger pulled off at a gas station just short of Carmel, checking his rear view.

He was pretty confident no headlights had followed them down.

It caused butterflies seeing Sam's long blonde hair fall out of her helmet as she removed it, and the same for her watching him stand there in his suit. Neither of them could believe it. How, in this great big universe, these two humans, enraptured in each other's presence, unquestionably one thousand percent in love at first sight, found one another.

It was unbelievable.

"What do you think about just picking up some goodies here and staying in for the night?" Ranger asked as they headed into the station mart.

"Maybe curl up with a good movie?" Sam beamed, holding onto his arm.

"Yes! That sounds perfect."

They walked in, Ranger glancing back over across the lot once more as they did.

The attendant at the counter barely noticed them entering, her head buried in a textbook. Her name tag read Amélie.

Musak was playing in the background.

Sam grabbed some popcorn and put it in the basket, and Ranger got ginger ales and water, then they found the candy aisle.

"Psst ..." Sam held up two packs of *Fun Dip*, and Ranger smiled, giving her the *thumbs up*.

Amélie looked up and noticed.

"Psst ..." Ranger then raised a pack of *Sugar Babies*, pointing to the label, and then to Sam, making her giggle and blush.

The clerk noticed that too.

"Ahem ... " Sam got Ranger's attention again, her eyes big and playful, then lifted a box of *Milk Duds*, shook her head slowly and put it back. Then, a box of *Nerds*, wagged her finger and put that back ... And, finally, with a big smile, picked up one of those roasted peanut and honey nougat *Big Hunk* bars, nodded her head, and pointed her finger back at him.

They both cracked up.

Amélie did too.

"Hi ... Will that be all?" she smiled as Sam and Ranger stacked their items on the counter.

"Hi ... Yes, we think so." They smiled in return.

"Oh, wait. One more thing ..." Sam said, looking at each of them.

She grabbed a pack of *Life Savers*, the 5-flavor ones, and set it on top of the pile.

Ranger hadn't made a reservation prior to arriving, so he pulled up to a hotel he knew, engine rumbling on the *Indian*, and asked if they had a room for the next several nights.

It was *The Vagabond's House*, a couple blocks off the main street, Ocean Avenue.

"Our Room 5 is available ... Would you like it?"

"Yes, please."

Room 5 was great. A large king bed, with a twin bed set in the nook of the window overlooking the camellias and the waterfall in the courtyard. There was a fireplace, and hardwood floors, jetted tub in the marble bath, and a pair of comfy crimson leather sitting chairs just inside the Dutch front door.

"Wow," Sam said, peeling off her layers.

"Yeah." He hugged her, in his black thermals and knitted socks, her in her off-whites, the fireplace going.

"I just wanted to say *thank you* again, Ranger." Sam looked him in the eyes.

"Yeah?"

"Yes ... for saving me."

They stood there silhouetted in the warm glow, arms around each other.

"Twice."

She removed a red cherry candy from the roll and placed it between his lips, then took a green one for herself.

"Sally told me Damien met that woman at a bar and she had been stalking him ever since. And, I guess she thought I was in her way …"

"Makes sense." Ranger listened.

Sam dropped her head and buried it into Ranger's chest with the sound of the waterfall murmuring outside.

"And, you've given me … a second chance." Sam's voice cracked as she said it.

"How do you mean?"

"I mean …"

He brought her in close to him, snug.

"I wasted a part of my life in something I knew wasn't right. It never was … And now, you've given me a second chance."

"Yes …" Ranger comforted her. "Now, all we have to do is appreciate it."

"Yeah …" Sam sighed.

They hugged and kissed.

The roll of *Life Savers* clutched in her hand, inside of his.

For the rest of the evening, they cuddled up atop the king-sized bed and watched what they thought was the cutest little movie ever, about an oddball type of guy living in the town of Oceanview, Washington, who places an anonymous ad in the newspaper classifieds looking for a partner to time travel with him, and the perfect outsider oddball girl who shows up to do it. The classified read:

WANTED:

Someone to back in time with me. This is not a joke. You'll get paid after we get back. Must bring your own weapons. I have only done this once before.

SAFETY NOT GUARANTEED

It was so fun.

As they crawled into their individual beds, Sam wondered if she would even care to go back. Erase the mistake. *No ...* she thought.

Ranger had no regrets anymore either.

But, he was worried about the things from home that he still had to tell her.

It was the best night of sleep Sam had had in a long time.

Maybe it was the waterfall sound in the courtyard, or the motorcycle ride, or the bed ... or the fact that Ranger was there in the middle of Carmel in the room with her.

When they were both up, they put on sneakers and walked to breakfast down Dolores Street a handful of blocks to the Tuck Box, a hobbit-like tea cottage built back in 1927. Ranger chose the Tuck Box benedict: two poached eggs, Canadian bacon and seasoned cheddar Welsh rarebit sauce on an English muffin; and Sam took the jack cheese and avocado omelet.

They both had scones with the famous Tuck Box marmalades, and tea.

After breakfast, they decided to go for a walk, heading south further down Dolores, ending up at the Carmel Mission. From there, they followed the *Rio del Carmelo* (Carmel River) through the marshland, sea lions and other wildlife, west to the beach and the ocean. From there, they went north, passing poet Robinson Jeffers and his wife Uma's 1918 Tor House, which they called their *inevitable place*, passing Carmel Point, and emerging onto the mile-long white sand of Carmel Beach.

"Sam, there's something I need to tell you," Ranger said, holding onto her hand as she watched her toes going through the sand.

"Yeah, honey?"

"We have a little problem."

She stopped, turning to face him.

"Yeah?"

"Well, you know the guys I told you about ... the ones who took Lwazi's necklace?"

"Yes," she responded.

"One of them saw us at Terrapin Crossroads when we were with Schalk and Sara."

"Okay ..."

"Yeah, it was the guy who bumped into you when you came back from the restroom, as we were leaving."

Ranger could see the uneasiness build in Sam's expression.

"And, it looked like he might have followed us home."

It was sometime between noon and 1:00, and the sun was brilliant out there. Warm. And Sam's cheeks were already rosy from the walk and the light marine breeze kissing them.

"And?"

"He was outside our house yesterday, in a car, with some other guys."

"What?!"

"And, there's something else," Ranger went on.

Sam held onto his hands, tighter.

"Looks like there were a couple other guys following us Wednesday night too at the Buckeye Roadhouse, with Naomi."

Sam swallowed hard.

"I saw them again in a couple of the pictures we took yesterday at The Trident … standing in the background."

"Ranger …"

"I know … That's why we got the bike and got out of there last night."

"What do you think …?"

"Don't know for sure." He drew her in close and surveyed the beach around them. "I'm sure it has to do with … Owen."

The beach was picture-perfect. Framed by cypress trees and the crashing waves, and the Pebble Beach Golf Links out in front of them. Kids and families, and dogs, and the surfers in the waves, and couples all enjoying themselves.

Sam and Ranger stood stationary in the middle of it all.

Eventually, Sam raised her head to look up into Ranger's face.

"So, what are we going to do?" she said.

Skelton had a feeling it was going to be one of these.

Call it a hunch.

A woman who didn't disclose the name of the guest she was bringing to a party? Good chance there was something in that.

He looked at the paper. Last name on the list ... Carolijn.

Pictures of local hero Clint Eastwood were all over the walls, and the crowd was good at the Hog's Breath Inn this Friday evening, so it felt like a safe place to talk. Sam and Ranger took their table for two back away from the windows, under the big photo of *Dirty Harry* and his .44 Magnum, and the hog's head over the mantle.

"So, are we going to tell her?" Sam asked about Naomi, biting into one of the restaurant's popular beer-battered sidewinder french fries.

"I really don't know."

"Well, at least we know she's okay now, from her text." Sam had texted her earlier, as they were getting ready.

"You know, they might not even know who she is." Ranger thought. "You know? They've been looking for Owen, but she hasn't noticed anything out of the ordinary."

"Right."

"I mean, why would they be following us again yesterday if they knew who she was?" Ranger asked, sipping his local Castroville artichoke soup.

"Yeah ..."

All of a sudden, Sam's face turned troubled.

"Ranger. You don't think they want to ... hurt you, do you? ... That one."

"I don't think so ... I mean, why wouldn't he have given it a shot already?"

"Right."

"I think we're dealing with something ... way bigger."

Dinner arrived.

Sam had ordered butternut squash ravioli with egg pasta, brown butter and sage, and Ranger decided he had to try the *Dirty Harry* New York strip steak with garlic mashed potatoes, mushrooms, chef vegetables and whole grain mustard sauce.

"Do you think we should call the police?" Sam asked, as the waiter walked away, back across the bustling little inn.

Ranger sat there and thought for a second.

"What would we tell them?"

The Hog's Breath ended up being a fun place, and Sam and Ranger stayed for a while.

After that, they walked the block-and-a-half back to the hotel, the long way.

"What if Owen was in trouble with the police?" Sam asked.

They thought maybe they'd hold off contacting law enforcement until after they knew more. They also decided they should probably stay away from Naomi, at least for now. For her safety.

The rest of it, they thought, they would take as it came.

Ranger gave Schalk and Sara a call to make sure everything was okay on the Liberty Dock, which it was. And Sam messaged Naomi again to let her know that she'd be out of town, but to call right away if she heard anything from her son.

It had been a wonderful day in Carmel, considering.

"Wanna get out on the water … Maybe do this today?"

Sam held up a brochure for whale watching.

"Yes," Ranger replied. He was all for it.

Both of them had awakened a whole lot earlier today than yesterday morning. Surely because of the stuff on their minds. What was waiting for them when they got home tomorrow.

So, it felt like a good idea to just get away and not think about it.

They got ready, hopped on the Indian, rumbled down Ocean Avenue towards the beach, and took a right onto San Antonio for the entrance to the 17-Mile Drive.

The boat would be leaving Fisherman's Wharf in Monterey at 10:00 am.

The 17-Mile Drive is one of those places -- you know, so magnificent it takes your breath away.

Sam had read:

Follow 17-Mile Drive's red-dotted line to arrive at an enchanting world of dramatic coastal cliffs, snow-white beaches, mystical forests and iconic golf courses. Discover one of the most scenic drives in the world as you meet the inspiring Lone Cypress, ponder the giant trees at Crocker Grove, digest the untouched beauty at Fanshell Beach, behold the power of the Restless Sea at Point Joe, stroll the boardwalk above the beach at Spanish Bay, and much, much more.

It sounded magnificent.

They motored past all of these sites, and the mansions, Sam pointing nonstop as they went. They would stop and see a few of them more closely on the way back.

The weather was sparkling again, as is customary for this part of California in the winter, and the sun shone into their visors as they came around on Sunset Drive past Point Pinos, Lover's Point, the aquarium, and onto Cannery Row. They parked in the large lot adjoining Old Fisherman's and Municipal wharfs, then headed out onto the docks.

There was a relatively healthy crowd roaming around, even at this early hour on a Saturday, because there was so much to see. The glass bottom boats and sailing outfits were running, the other whale watching outfits, and the Wharf Chocolate Factory was already open.

Sam flashed Ranger a look as they passed by, he nodded, and they ducked in.

"Thank you ... Thank you. These look great!" They told the nice lady behind the counter, re-emerging onto the wharf with gigantic apple pie and chocolate caramel apples on sticks.

"Oh, my gosh ..." Sam laughed. "Are we really doing this?"

They bit in, caramel ending up at the tips of both their noses.

As they continued, they followed behind a family walking, eating, and tossing their trash onto the dock as they did.

It got Ranger's attention immediately.

He was about to say something when Sam stepped forward.

"Hey, guys ... Good morning. Let me get this for you." She smiled to the two younger ones, picking up their discarded wrappers and bags. "We want to take care of our environment, just like we want to take care of each other ... You guys have a great day."

She flashed the warmest smile to the parents, who, though they looked a bit bewildered, smiled back at her.

"Thank you …" they said in return.

"Oooh, look. Here it is."

Sam grabbed onto Ranger's arm as they arrived at the boat.

Monterey Bay has a canyon system underneath its surface that is every bit as impressive as the Grand Canyon itself. Steep canyon walls over a mile high, extending 95 miles out to sea, almost 12,000 feet deep, Monterey Canyon has been studied continuously by research, laboratory and oceanographic institutions because of its endless wonder.

Nobody knows exactly how a canyon so long and deep, the largest of any on the western North American continent, without the presence of a major river flow like those for the Amazon or the Mississippi, could have formed here.

Perhaps, some theorize, it was the Salinas River, or the Colorado, that created the feature. But, then again, maybe the source was some ancient river outlet that existed before. A mighty force that was around long before any of this was ever here today.

Sam and Ranger watched the gray whales migrating southward to Baja California, on their way to mate, and give birth, the heart-shaped spray of their spouts in the air everywhere … A few even breached.

Oooooh! Aaaahhh! The crowd on the boat cheered as the whales burst upwards, then crashed down, surfacing a couple times more, and their tail flukes going vertical as they dived and disappeared.

"You know, Sam, I need to thank you too." Ranger held Sam from behind, watching the indigo blue water where the whales had just gone under. In a couple months, it would be different for them here, returning from Mexico with their calves, having to traverse this Monterey Bay, the only open stretch back to Alaska taking them away from the safety of the coastline and putting them at risk of attack by great white sharks, and worse, orcas.

"What do you mean?" Sam asked, the sun reflecting off her salty cheeks.

He looked at her with a tenderness she really hadn't seen until right now.

"For being there when I needed you ..."

Before he could say another word, she gave it to him ...

One of the biggest kisses one could ever imagine.

Awww, a little older lady tugged at her husband's sleeve. He smiled too.

As they came back, it seemed that all of the otters and dolphins and sea lions, pelicans and everything else were happy to see them coming in.

Back into the harbor from over the expanse of the canyon.

23 POINT REYES STATION

"In the end, all we want is somebody who chooses us, over everyone, under any circumstance."

Anonymous

After the wharf, Sam and Ranger rode through town then decided on lunch at the Red House Cafe in Pacific Grove, taking a seat at a little table near the stairs on the wraparound porch. The adorable, chic 1895 establishment was bustling with the Saturday afternoon brunch crowd.

"Isn't this the most adorable place?" Sam beamed as they watched all the action.

"It really is … Good eye finding it, co-pilot."

"Here you go." The server brought their orders out, a Red House frittata with fresh spinach, artichoke hearts, roasted red peppers, and parmesan and jack cheeses, and buttermilk pancakes with mixed berries to share.

After brunch, they got back on the motorcycle, then stopped for a walk on the beach along wide open Spanish Bay all the way to the Restless Sea. Then, as the sun set, they went to see the Lone Cypress, a well-known single tree on a rocky outcropping, turn blazing red in the glow of the red, orange and purple early evening sky. It was stunning.

Owen rode by his mom's house in Sleepy Hollow, a wood shingle two-story with a deck and a stone walkway that meandered through the fern pines and rose bushes in the yard.

In the hills above San Rafael, the street was quiet.

So, it certainly looked like they hadn't figured out where he lived, or any more about him.

Just that he knew Finn ... And, that Finn knew where the money was.

But, Finn was still nowhere to be found.

Sam and Ranger decided to go see a play their last night in Carmel.

It was an outdoor one at the Forest Theater, heading down towards the mission. They were reprising the story from the first production performed there, July 9, 1910.

The story of King David.

"Hey, this place opened on your birthday," Sam commented about the July 9 date, reading the production notes. The two had settled under a blanket they'd borrowed from the Vagabond into the wood-backed bench seats near the proscenium stage, which was surrounded by tall pines and lit up bonfire pits on either end.

"Yeah, look at that."

The crowd had nearly finished shuffling in as the lights went down for the 7:30 start. The stars had come out in the sky, and the air was really pleasant with the fire crackling off to the left of them.

"This is romantic ..." Sam whispered in Ranger's ear, cuddling in as the music began and some of the players arrived onto the stage.

Vrooooom!

They danced a ebullient number, then a young woman performer came forward.

"This is the story of mighty King David," she announced. "Second king of Israel ... Shepherd boy and Goliath's slayer ... Musician, noble warrior, and lover of God ... Ancestor to the coming Messiah."

Booooom!

The music thundered through the forest.

"But, beware, oh King ..." she finished. "... Your secrets will have their consequences!"

"Wow ..." Sam took a breath. "Now that's an introduction."

The show was spectacular, and afterwards the performers lined up so the audience could meet them as they exited.

"Have a great night ..." The girl who had done the introduction and played *Bathsheba* smiled to Sam and Ranger.

"Good night. Thank you for coming." The *Absalom* shook both their hands.

"What a story ..." Sam commented. They walked down Mountain View Avenue towards Junipero Street.

"Yeah, sure opens your eyes."

They stopped in for dinner at the Forge, a 1944 metal-works outfit where many of the hand-wrought hinges, door latches, sign holders, and other hardware you see in Carmel still today were crafted. It was a place where artists and writers hung out, like Steinbeck (*The Grapes of Wrath*, *Cannery Row*, *East of Eden* and *Of Mice and Men*), and drank and told stories. Quintessential Carmel.

They shared the Forge hamburger and the Valencia paella.

"I'm really looking forward to tomorrow night, Ranger." Sam took a bite into the bacon, caramelized onion, avocado, roasted jalapeno and grilled mushroom burger. "Meeting everyone."

"I know ... I've been thinking a lot about it too."

"It's funny ... We've only known each other, coming up on nine whole days, tonight." The big stone and brick fireplace near where they were sitting in the courtyard and the twisted branches and roots of the foliage that meshed into the low patio roof over their heads made the place feel really authentic. Nostalgic.

Sam paused there in the glow, appreciating it all. "Now, look where we are."

Sunday, January 10.

It was early, about 7:30 am, when a message came across Ranger's phone.

Ranger, it's Carolijn. Please let me know when is a good time to talk. It's important.

It wasn't much after that Detective Skelton and Ms. Elodie-Jane, Ranger's little old neighbor, arrived in the parking lot at Liberty Dock at almost exactly the same time.

She watched as the stranger approached, scanning the area as if he was taking a bunch of mental notes.

"Can I help you with something, sir?" Ms. Elodie asked, never missing an opportunity to be the first one on the dock in the know.

"Perhaps ..." Skelton replied, making no eye contact, looking past Elodie the whole time.

Which immediately didn't sit well with her.

"Are you ... the manager here?" he said.

"Yes, I am, young man." She was not, officially.

"Detective Skelton." He flashed his badge. "Have you seen a ... Mr. Ranger Gabriel at all this morning?"

Ms. Elodie held up a hand to block the sunlight reflecting in her face.

"Nope."

The brevity of her response got Skelton's attention, and he looked her directly in the face, thinking he might have even caught a smirk.

Which he didn't like.

She knew Ranger wasn't there.

And neither was Schalk, because she'd already run into him on his way out this morning.

"Which way to his house?"

Skelton raised a sheet from his notepad, which had Ranger's address clearly written on it, slowly to the level of his nose.

What a boorish, and particularly annoying man this is ... Elodie-Jane thought to herself.

But, she was no cinch.

At the side of her dearest Higginbotham, she'd experienced a whole lot over the years. Forever the swashbuckler, Higginbotham had taken her on adventures all over the world. One evening at one of their social gatherings she hosted, she showed Ranger the photos ... A young, long haired Elodie and bearded Higginbotham jeeping across the Serengeti Plain. The two of them sporting snowshoes and sunglasses trekking the Karakorams of Pakistan. Her with a curly perm, him a gringo moustache, motorcycling through Soviet Russia.

They were perfect together.

Ranger never knew exactly what it was that Higginbotham did for a living, but he knew it was Ms. Elodie who went to rescue him one time from a top-secret something in Vietnam, February of 1975.

Just before the war ended.

She looked Skelton right back in the eye.

"I'm sure you can find it yourself."

Ms. Elodie-Jane picked up her bags and strolled off to her own floating home.

Down near the end of the Liberty Dock.

A couple doors away from Ranger's.

Sam woke up first and watched Ranger stir for a while in the double bed nestled in the alcove overlooking the courtyard.

It looked like he was dreaming.

"Good morning, honey. I got you something." She sat up in the oversized king with a pillow across her lap and a tray of chocolate croissants and hot cocoa in front of her.

"Good morning, honey." Ranger rubbed his eyes, standing up to stretch.

"I got them from the little French bakery down the street."

"Honey …" Ranger paused, glancing over to the door, a shade of concern coming to his face.

"Don't worry. I was careful … Very careful. I saw everything." She smiled and winked, pointing two fingers at her own eyes then at him.

He smiled back.

"I have us covered …" she said.

Sam and Ranger enjoyed their breakfast then took one last little stroll down by sea. When they got back, as Sam got herself into the shower,

Ranger checked his phone and saw the message from Carolijn.

Why would she be contacting me? He thought to himself.

There were also a couple missed calls from a number he did not recognize. 7:15 and 7:18 am, respectively.

They were on their way back home this morning. Schalk had already left the house; he and Sara were going to a fitness leadership seminar in Tampa, Florida, this week, so Bernard would be alone.

The ride was two-and-a-half hours, plus they still needed to get their car.

And, there was the party tonight.

"It's all yours," Sam smiled, emerging from the bathroom in a big, fluffy robe and her hair rub-dried, tumbling down.

"Thanks ..." Ranger kissed her on the cheek and went in. After he was finished, they suited up and went outside.

"Okay, let's do it."

The *Indian* Chieftain Dark Horse rolled past the Fort Ord Dunes State Park on Highway 1 and the scenic mounds overlooking the limitless ocean there just before 11:00 am, then the Summit Road-Highway 35 intersection along Highway 17 an hour after that, crossing over the San Andreas Fault again.

By 1:00, they'd reached the Golden Gate.

As they came to the Coyote Creek bridge leading to Gulliver's shop, Ranger scanned the street to see if he recognized any of the cars or license plates parked there.

He did not.

"Hey ... Hey. How was the trip?!" Gulliver was outside around back to greet them with his customary gargantuan grin.

"So good." Ranger flipped his visor up, Sam flipping hers up right after. "Thank you, thank you, my man."

"Yes, thank you. It was even better than I thought it would be ..." she echoed.

"Good, good. Come on in and get changed." Gulliver waved them inside.

He pointed Sam towards the dressing room then turned to Ranger.

"So, I pull Malibu into shop after you leave other day, and I watch outside, and *pow*, about half hour, guy start looking into window. I go around side and surprise him, you know, ask him if he need help or something ... *Pow*. He just walk away."

Gulliver gestured for Ranger to follow him over to behind the shop's sales counter. "Then, I do check on your car, and look what I find."

It was a GPS tracker.

Sam had come back from the changing room to see all this, and Gulliver stopped, not sure if she was supposed to.

"It's alright ... She knows everything." Ranger assured him.

Gulliver looked to Sam and nodded.

She nodded back.

2:30 pm.

The Malibu veered off the 101 at exit 445A towards Sausalito and headed for the Liberty Dock, Sam staring at the plastic bag with the tracker in it sitting in front of them on the dashboard.

"Maybe we should call the police." She looked to Ranger, who was deep in thought, staring straight ahead.

"Yeah …"

They came around on Bridgeway, then turned left at Gate 5 Road and parked.

Quickly, each scanned the lot, then together they headed towards the house, the sound of their sneakers on the docks echoing on the water.

Then, Ranger felt his phone buzz in his pocket. It was Carolijn again.

> *Ranger. Not sure where you are, but I need to talk to you.*
>
> *Call me, please.*

As Ranger unlocked the front door through the keypad, he pivoted to see somebody else coming down the dock behind them. A serious-looking man dressed in a suit and hard-soled shoes with a badge at his waist.

"Looks like somebody already did," he said.

Naomi pulled out of her Sleepy Hollow driveway just before 3:30 pm, turned right, and headed down the hill towards Sir Francis Drake Boulevard.

The Piaggio Typhoon 50 followed her, three cars back.

Weaving through traffic, stopping for several lights, the black scooter tailed her white Grand Cherokee for 15 minutes.

Waaaaaaaaa … wooooooooom!

The motor revving up and down was the only sound as the scooter kept a steady distance behind, until the Jeep pulled into the upscale Corte Madera Town Center.

It parked several rows away.

Naomi exited her SUV and walked over to the complex, then into one of the stores, and the driver followed, watching her from the opposite side of the breezeway.

When she was out of sight, he pushed up the dark-tinted face mask of his helmet.

"Mom."

It was Owen.

And, tonight would be the night, he decided, he would finally see her.

"Are you Ranger Gabriel?" Skelton asked, straight-faced, holding his badge up into Ranger's eye level.

"Yes. What can I do for you, detective?"

"You're a difficult man to catch up to."

Sam stood there quietly in the half open doorway as Bernard began barking behind her in the background.

"I was hoping to speak with you about a case I'm investigating."

Right then, Ms. Elodie appeared out on the front porch of her floating home, flashing Skelton a dirty look as he turned to see who it was. She waved to Ranger, and he waved back.

Bernard was still barking.

"Not sure this is the most confidential place to talk, Mr. Gabriel, know what I mean? Would you mind too much following me down to the station?" Skelton requested.

"Right now?"

"You have someplace else you need to be?"

"Not yet ... but in a little bit, we do." Ranger looked over to Sam, who had the GPS in her hand.

Skelton eyed them both, extending Ranger his card. "Won't take but a few minutes. I'll have you out in no time," he said. "Address is on the card."

After that, he turned and walked away, Ms. Elodie watching him closely as he made his way down the dock past her.

Bernard stopped barking.

The detective could see the door through the oversized sound-proof glass window separating his office from the waiting room, and he watched Ranger as he came in, surprised to see Sam following him in. He intercepted them before they sat down. The place was quiet, uncannily so for a police department, but it was a Sunday afternoon and hardly anybody was working.

"Detective, this is Sam. She knows everything that's been going on." Ranger spoke, but was nearly cut off.

"What do you have there?" Skelton noticed the plastic bag with the small device in it in Sam's hand.

"It's ... a GPS tracker," Ranger answered.

Skelton stared at them both, then turned and motioned them to follow into the office where they took the two seats in front of a large mahogany bureau situated in the middle of the room.

The Mission San Rafael Arcángel towering there above the trees in the picture window opposite them on the back wall.

"So, how do you two know each other?" Skelton inquired, standing behind his desk.

They hesitated, then Sam responded, "We met New Year's Eve ... in Half Moon Bay."

"I see." The detective took a seat. "And, what's with the GPS? Is there somebody ... following you?"

"Yes."

"Who?"

"We thought you were going to tell us that," Ranger answered for the both of them, sounding a bit confused.

Skelton stuck out his hand for the plastic bag, and Sam obliged, handing it to him.

"We'll have it run for fingerprints."

Skelton tapped a pen to the bare desktop for what seemed like a quarter-minute before he spoke again. "Mr. Gabriel, would you mind waiting in the lobby while I ask Sam a few questions first?"

"Uhh ..." Ranger replied.

"We like to interview witnesses one at a time ... It's standard procedure."

"Okay."

Ranger looked to Sam before getting up and walking out, taking a seat in the waiting room where he could see only Skelton's face and the back of her head through the glass in between them.

"Alright." Skelton managed a smile, removing the notepad from his jacket pocket. "Sam ... May I ask your full name?"

"Amaris ..." she responded. "Samantha Amaris."

The detective took it down.

"So, if you would again please, enlighten me as to how you two are acquainted ... you and Mr. Gabriel." Skelton opened a drawer, removing a single manila folder and placing it on top of the desk.

"Okay, well ... basically, we met this past New Year's, right after midnight ..."

"Uh huh," he muttered.

"Ranger, he kind of saved me from someone."

"And, who was that?" he inquired.

"Umm ... That's all been documented already. Do you not have that information?" Sam started to appear uncomfortable.

"Right ... Sure I do, but I'm not looking at the file right now. So ... from whom?"

"From ... that woman," Sam said.

"Right, but the GPS here, that's something completely different, as far as you know. Totally unrelated."

"Yes."

"And, you have no idea who it is who's following you now. Correct?" Skelton went on.

She turned to look at Ranger.

"You know, detective, I think maybe you should ask Ranger about that."

Skelton paused and studied her, looking her up and down for a couple of seconds, the manila folder with the photograph of Michael Roman from the Christmas party in it at his fingertips.

"Of course." He smiled at her. "I'll do that then."

Skelton had Sam return to the waiting room and asked Ranger to come in.

As the two passed each other, she looked at him like ... *What the heck was that?*

Ranger took one of the two seats in front of the desk.

"So, Mr. Gabriel, you saved Ms. Amaris ... New Year's?" Skelton started in.

"Excuse me ..." Ranger said.

"Talking about how the two of you met ... It's all documented."

"Yes, there was somebody after Sam, and I helped stop it ... That's right."

"Right." Skelton analyzed him closely. "Okay ..." he said, putting pen to the notepad, "Tell me about the people who are following you now?"

"Uhh ... I don't know very much." Ranger looked back at him.

Skelton stood up from his chair, both he and Ranger glancing at the unopened manila folder. "Have you seen them?" he asked.

"Yes."

"What did they look like?" Skelton pressed on.

"Well, there were several of them ..." Ranger answered. "Big guys. Pretty rough."

"Did you speak to them?"

"One of them, yes." Christmas afternoon at the high school passed through Ranger's mind really quickly, as did Owen.

"Good, Mr. Gabriel." Skelton cracked a little smile. "What did he say?"

"Not a whole lot."

Skelton took a few steps towards the window at the back wall then removed his jacket and hung it on the coat rack before returning to the desk. Like he was finished with his warm-up.

"You know, with all due respect, detective, you still haven't told me why I'm here," Ranger said to him.

Skelton stood for a second behind his desk, seriously, adjusting his suspenders. Then, he opened the manila folder revealing the 8½-by-11 of Michael Roman.

"Have you seen this man before, Mr. Gabriel?"

Ranger looked surprised. Caught off-guard.

"Mr. Gabriel?"

"Yes … I met him at a Christmas party a couple weeks ago." He figured then that was probably the reason Carolijn had been trying to reach him.

"Uh huh …" Skelton uttered. "Please tell me everything you know about him."

Ranger thought for a second. "Um, he was harassing people at our Christmas party, so I asked him to leave."

"I see …"

The detective circled around the room, around his desk and behind Ranger slowly, glancing directly at Sam as he did, then back towards the big window and the trees, and the mission.

"That's it? …" he said. "That's all you know about him?"

"That's it."

"Do you think, Mr. Gabriel ... this man has anything to do with who is following you?"

"Definitely not."

"Then, why are you being followed?"

It was the way Skelton was looking at Ranger, his eyes beginning to bore into him, that made things feel particularly awkward in there now. Sam could see it too.

Ranger thought for a second again.

"I was sticking up for this old man after these guys took his gold necklace from him, and one of the guys following us is ..."

"One of those guys ..." Skelton finished for him.

"That's correct," Ranger said.

"Did you ... take him out?" the detective asked abruptly.

"What does that mean?"

"You know ... did you have a *confrontation* with him?"

"I took the necklace back."

Ranger turned to check on Sam, who snuck him a wave, and as he turned back, Skelton was now standing almost on top of him there at the front edge of the desk, with the beautiful California mission in the window behind him.

"Did you know, Mr. Gabriel ..." the detective said to him, holding the photograph, "that this man, Michael Roman, went missing the night of your Christmas party at the Pelican Inn, December the 19th, and was found by a fishing boat a few days later floating face down in the ocean?"

Ranger's expression went blank.

"No ... I didn't."

"Now, I've already spoken to your friend ... one Ms. Carolijn ... earlier on the phone, and I know there was some sort of *confrontation* between you and Mr. Roman that night at the Pelican Inn as well."

Ranger listened silently.

"So please, again, if you wouldn't mind too much ... everything you know."

"Am I a ... a suspect here, detective?" Ranger asked. "Is that what you're telling me? ... Do I need to call a lawyer?"

"Why? Do you have something to hide?" Skelton returned.

"Absolutely not."

There was a weird noiselessness in the office for a second as Skelton moved back to the window side of the desk and took a seat in his worn leather chair. From Sam's view, he was completely blotted out by the figure of Ranger's significantly larger frame.

The detective stared his subject right in the eye.

"Mr. Gabriel ... What happened to the man, then?"

Ranger took a deep breath ... "I don't know."

It was nearing 4:00 pm, and Skelton noticed as Ranger glanced at the clock posted to the wall, one of those that clicked as the second hand circled its way around the dial.

And, it seemed to be getting progressively louder.

"Look, Mr. Gabriel ..." Skelton set a phone-sized voice recorder on top of the desk, the round red record light lit up bright and the time ticking silently on at 15:03 and counting now. It had been running the whole time. "We have a bit of a problem here … You've admitted to stopping someone from following Ms. Amaris there a little over a week ago … You took matters into your own hands against someone whom you report took an old man's necklace. And now, a woman at your Christmas party informs me that you were *protecting* her when you, by yourself, personally escort a man out of the Pelican Inn … The last time, very conceivably, anybody sees this man alive … And now, I have a dead body on my hands."

"Listen. I don't know what happened to this guy. Like I told you, I asked him to leave, and I walked him to the parking lot, but that's the last I saw of him." Ranger paused. "Are you arresting me, detective? … Am I under arrest right now? … Because if not, we really have someplace we need to be … soon."

The detective watched him.

"No … You're not. Not today, Mr. Gabriel. You're free to go." Skelton flashed a smile. "But, I'll be seeing you again. Real soon."

Ranger got up, turned, then reached for the worn brass handle to the door separating him from the waiting room. As he reached Sam, she hugged him.

"You know, Ms. Amaris … You really have to be careful."

The two of them looked back to find Skelton there standing in that doorway.

"Sometimes … the hero isn't who you think he is at all."

Sam clutched onto Ranger's hand as they walked out of the station. "That wasn't about Owen at all, was it?" she said as they descended the steps outside.

"No, it wasn't."

"What did he want, then … And, what did he mean about a *hero*?" She looked up at him.

"Missing persons. A guy from our Christmas party nobody knew who was harassing people. I asked him to leave, so he thought maybe I knew something more than I did."

"Oh …" They didn't say too much else the rest of the way home. Just held each other's hand.

"Let's have some tea and sit out on the patio upstairs for a while … before we get ready," Ranger proposed as they got to the house.

"That sounds good," Sam smiled. "I'll make it."

"Okay, meet me up there then?"

"You got it."

Several minutes afterwards, Sam showed up there on the balcony, kulhads in her hands, Ranger and Bernard sitting, waiting for her. He had started a fire and pulled the lounge chairs together under the humongous Pendleton Yakima blanket, and on the table in front of them … their stones.

There was a candle, two small gift boxes, and a card on the table too.

"Ranger …" Sam sighed as she set the tea mugs down. "What are these?"

He spread the wool blanket over them both.

"Early birthday present, I guess you could call it … Let's open them."

She smiled, looking into his eyes, then picked up the first box.

"Wha …" she stirred.

It was a ring, made of dark and shiny wood with a band of bright blue and brown stone inlay around it.

"It's redwood," Ranger told her. "With moonstone and sandstone mixed through the middle. Here, let me put it on you."

"Ranger ... It's absolutely beautiful."

"This box has a matching one," he smiled.

She put it on him.

Sam and Ranger held their hands out towards the fire pit, hers in his, and watched the bright stone in their rings flicker. It was almost halfway dark now out on Richardson Bay, lights from the houses and passing boats popping up all around them on the water. They snuggled under the blanket and pillows as a cool night began to settle in.

"Sam ..." Ranger half-whispered.

"Yes."

"I want you to know something ... "

"What?" Sam quickened.

"That no matter what ... I am forever with you."

"Ranger ..."

"Yep ... I want you to know that."

The fire popped and crackled loudly. Maybe it was the slightly more penetrating, cold air requiring more from the flame than it usually gave.

Ranger picked up her card and handed it to her. She opened it.

Happy Birthday, To Our Future, the envelope read. An inside, a poem by Carl Sandberg ...

> *I love you for what you are, but I love you yet more for what you are going to be.*
>
> *I love you not so much for your realities as for your ideals.*
>
> *I pray for your desires that they may be great, rather than for your satisfactions, which may be so hazardously little.*
>
> *A satisfied flower is one whose petals are about to fall.*
>
> *The most beautiful rose is one hardly more than a bud wherein the pangs and ecstasies of desire are working for a larger and finer growth.*
>
> *Not always shall you be what you are now.*
>
> *You are going forward toward something great.*
>
> *I am on the way with you … and therefore I love you.*

Under the blankets, tears in Sam's eyes, they held onto each other.

Bernard watching it all.

It was 5:30 pm.

Almost time to go, and Sam was excited. She was about to meet all these people Ranger had been telling her about the past week-and-a-half.

Richie, Dan and Julian. Duane, Frans, Tanaka. Elodie-Jane, Lwazi and Anna-Lena. Wives, girlfriends, TJ and others. Everybody she hadn't met yet.

Schalk and Sara wouldn't be there, as they had left for Florida, and neither would Naomi. So, they wouldn't have to worry about anybody following her from there, home.

"See you later on, my boy." Ranger hugged his dog as he lounged there in his lap on the couch, as if he didn't want to allow him to get up this time.

"You're such a good boy." Sam kissed Bernard on the head. "See you later tonight."

They left him there in the front entryway and headed up the dock to the car.

The Trident was all glittered up, illuminated in strings of pretty off-white lights outside and in as Sam and Ranger pulled up to the valet booth.

What a place, they thought.

With its 1960s-painted walls and ceilings, and famously rounded archways, dinner booths and picture windows, the restaurant was a jubilant gathering space. Built in 1898 as the home of the San Francisco Yacht Club, the musicians The Kingston Trio owned it in the '60s, hosting guests like Janis Joplin, Jerry Garcia, Joan Baez, Bill Cosby, the Smothers Brothers and the Rolling Stones. A young Robin Williams was even a busboy here during that period of time.

All this made for fun conversation among the night's party guests.

"I just knew this would happen soon." Elodie-Jane couldn't take her adoring eyes off of Sam, who sat there blushing. "Now, I'm Ranger's grandmother around here, and I'll be yours too. You call when you need anything, okay dear?" She had Sam put her number in her phone then kissed her on the cheek.

Ms. Elodie loved Sam already.

"Sam! You know you're one of the boys now!" Julian called from in front of the big windows, the lights of San Francisco behind him. "Come on up here and get in this picture!"

He, Dan, and Richie posed with Sam and Ranger for a handful of goofy photos.

"Sorry, Tanaka ... Bears rugby only!" Dan yelled.

"Awww ... Cold-blooded, man!" Tanaka laughed.

"Ranger, she's gorgeous, and so unbelievably genuine ... and really nice." Liz and Krystyna complimented as Sam joked around with Tanaka and the boys over by their table.

"Thank you, thank you ... She sure is. I'm really lucky," he smiled.

"Sam, I want to introduce you to some very special people I've known almost my whole life," Ranger said, moving over toward a booth by the little four-piece orchestra that was playing. "This is Frans and his fiancé Sophie, and Frans' very wonderful parents, Hansen and Clare ... who are like my second parents."

"It's such a pleasure to meet you ... I've heard so much about you all." Sam smiled big.

Frans' mother hugged her, tears of joy in her eyes, and Hansen looked so proud.

They stayed there and talked for a while.

"Hey, Grandpa Hank!" Ranger hugged Heyneke as he entered with the hostess to be seated, Duane and Libby right behind him.

"*God kveld (good evening), my sonn!*" He pulled Ranger in for a bear hug.

"Hey, everyone! So, so grateful you could make it." Ranger hugged them all. "This is Sam ... Sam, I love these people!"

Their eyes were all so big, as were their smiles. Everybody was so happy for Ranger.

And delighted to meet Sam. Heyneke pulled her in for a big mountain-style bear hug too, then flashed Ranger a thumbs-up and a discreet wink of the eye.

They gave Sam and Ranger all the updates on what was going on up in redwood country.

"Hi, Ranger, meet the newest proud employee of Marin General Hospital …" a woman's voice declared.

Ranger and Sam turned around to find Anna-Lena standing there behind them, with Lwazi beside her dressed all the way up in a sky blue plaid three-piece suit and bow tie.

"Hey! You're here!" Ranger was excited to see them. "Sam, this is the one-and-only Lwazi and Anna-Lena."

"Oh my goodness, I am so happy to meet you two," she said. "I feel like I know you already."

"Working now with Anna-Lena, huh, buddy?" Ranger said.

"Yes, sir, my friend, and you never guess what … Cecil too! He visit the kids in there."

"Really, that is … the best!" Sam and Ranger were both elated to hear it, and Anna-Lena looked honored to have helped set it all up. "Anna-Lena, you did good."

"I can't even tell you how proud I am of you both." Ranger said. "And, Lwazi, you look so much better than the last time we saw you at the hospital."

"Ha, thank you," Lwazi chuckled. "I know, it's the suit … I buy it myself with first paycheck. Working man got to look good, you know."

They all laughed.

"Ranger, hey brother."

TJ walked into The Trident with a big smile and a backpack strapped around his shoulders.

"Thomas Junior!" Ranger called out. He grabbed his buddy, clenching fists in a handshake that looked like the start of a bout of arm wrestling.

They were both extremely strong looking guys.

"How are you, my friend?" Ranger welcomed him.

"Good, good ... It's been a long time."

"Yes, it has. TJ ... this is Sam."

It was 7:45, and the party was well under way. People were finished with dinner, their clam chowders and pan-seared scallops, cioppinos and roasted garlic mashed, cheeseburgers and ribs, and a new band had taken to the small performing area, playing numbers from The Trident's glory years ... among them, *I Can't Help Myself (Sugar Pie, Honey Bunch)* by The Four Tops, Ben E. King's *Stand By Me, Louie Louie* by the Kingsmen, *When a Man Loves a Woman*, Percy Sledge, *Stuck in the Middle With You* by Stealers Wheel, *Ain't No Mountain High Enough*, Marvin Gaye and Tammi Terrell, *God Only Knows (What I'd Be Without You)* by the Beach Boys.

Tables cleared for dancing in front of the big windows overlooking the water.

It was a lot of fun.

At 9:30 pm as it was all winding down, Sam and Ranger stood before everyone and said a few words.

"Sam and I appreciate you so incredibly much for being here with us, everyone!" Ranger said. "You all are truly family to us, and we love every single one of you!"

Awwww!

"And, meeting every one of you ... whom I feel like I've known already," Sam added. "It's been like .. the greatest day of my life."

She started to cry.

"Until the wedding!" somebody shouted, sounded like Dan.

Woooooo! Hoooo!

The crowd cheered, and Sam and Ranger laughed.

"Would you like me to take a photo of you all?" One of the young servers came over and asked as Sam stood there drying her eyes.

"Yes, thank you ... That would be fantastic."

The group assembled in front of the arched windows with the night behind them, and the server took some really memorable pictures.

"We'll send all of these out to everyone ... tomorrow!" Sam announced.

Then, everybody went on their way.

"I'll meet you at noon for lunch then tomorrow, my friend." Ranger gave TJ a big hug. "Tommy's Joynt?"

"Yep, looking forward to it."

TJ was staying one more night in San Francisco tomorrow, then he was heading off, north to oppose some illegal seal and whale hunting going on undercover up there.

"Ranger and I learned all that stuff together, when we were kids," he told Sam, talking about the things they believed in.

Fighting for them.

"Let's go for a walk ... Want to?" Ranger asked.

"Sure do." Sam responded.

They walked out the front door then across the planks of the pier the restaurant sat on to the main street, Bridgeway, and slipped off into the night. There were lights, and cars, and people all around them.

And, Ranger was sure they were out there.

"Can I help you?" Elodie-Jane, who had just arrived home, offered as a woman she didn't recognize approached the Liberty Dock.

"Uh, hi. Yes, as a matter of fact. Would you happen to know which house is Ranger's ... Ranger's and Sam's?"

"Yes ..." Ms. Elodie answered.

"Oh ... my name is Naomi. Naomi Jacobs ... I'm a friend of theirs. Well, Sam mainly. It's her birthday tomorrow, and I wanted to leave a gift at their doorstep."

"Ohh ... How very sweet." Ms. Elodie smiled. "Well, I'm the manager here, Elodie-Jane, and I'd be more than happy to drop it off for you," she said.

"That would be great. Thank you!"

Elodie could see it was a basket of goodies: treats from Philz Coffee, See's Candies, bath soaps, that sort of stuff. Balloons and a card.

"Glad to." Elodie extended her hand, and Naomi gave her the basket.

"Good night, then, Ms. Elodie-Jane," Naomi said. "It was nice to meet you."

"Likewise, Naomi ... Have a lovely evening."

As Ms. Elodie made her way towards the house, Naomi walked back to her car. And, a dark figure followed, towards his.

By the time Sam and Ranger returned to Liberty Dock, it was 10:30 and pitch black.

There weren't as many stars out tonight.

They scanned the area by the dock quickly and headed in.

"Hey, what's that?" Sam said, spotting the basket under the light of their porch from a few houses down.

"Birthday balloons ..." Ranger said.

Sam picked up the basket, sorted through it, then found the card.

"How nice," Sam smiled. The envelope read:

> *To Sam, my friend. Thanks for everything!*

Then, her countenance changed as she opened it.

"It's from Naomi ..." she said.

"Oh, gosh ..."

Sam had dialed her number ten times before Naomi finally answered.

"Sam ..." she said.

"Naomi ... Where are you?"

"Uh ... I can't really say, Sam."

"Naomi, what do you mean?" The gravity in Sam's voice was clear.

"I'm driving ... Sam. Owen told me not to say anything ... to anybody."

Naomi sounded ruffled too.

"He even told me not to answer the phone ... for anyone."

"So, he called you? ... Are you going to meet him?"

"Yes ..." Naomi answered. "I'm on my way right now."

"She's going to meet him," Sam whispered to Ranger, her hand over the microphone on her phone.

"Where?" Ranger mouthed the question back.

"Naomi, where are you meeting? When?"

There was a pause on the line, like she didn't want to say.

"Naomi ..." Sam said again. The reception began to crack and break up.

"I know, Sam ... I'm so scared right now."

"Naomi, just tell us where and when ... Somebody needs to know where you are."

Ranger hung there for the next words to come from Sam. Then, she hung the phone up.

"Point Reyes Station ... midnight."

24 ALCATRAZ

"To go it alone, or to go with a partner? ... Do I need someone who, when the heat gets hot, has my back? ... I do."

Kenneth Calloway

"She didn't say anything about where exactly, did she?"

"No ... she didn't, and now she won't answer."

"Or, she turned her phone off." Ranger opened Sam's door for her into the Malibu.

"Right."

"This time, let's hope we see headlights behind us ..." he said. Ranger pulled slowly out of the parking lot, eyes fixed on his mirrors.

It was just over a 45 minute drive to the small, unincorporated former port and railroad junction called Point Reyes Station, a town of about 350 residents now, located just south of where the San Andreas Fault submerges under Tomales Bay forming the eastern boundary of the Point Reyes National Seashore.

"What's our plan?" Sam asked, her mouth barely visible in the dark passenger seat, her voice a bit on the nervous side.

"Well, if we notice anybody tailing us out there, then we take them on a wild goose chase ... Far away."

"And if we don't ..."

"If we don't ... then we need to find Naomi."

Ranger checked the rear view again.

Their route took them north on Highway 101, then west on winding Sir Francis Drake Boulevard, through the village of Fairfax and the deep redwood preserves, and finally onto Point Reyes-Petaluma Road to Highway 1.

The time was just shy of 11:30 pm when they rolled into town.

"Okay, let's try her one more time?" Ranger said.

There was nothing. The phone went straight to voicemail again.

"Nothing ..." Sam said.

"Yeah, she's going to do what Owen told her to."

They made the left where the Shoreline Highway turns 90 degrees and becomes the main drag through town and searched for the white Jeep, but it was dead quiet, nobody outside and no movement around. They passed a couple arts and crafts boutiques and bakeries, then Cheda's Garage and the post office and farmer's market buildings across the street. The first people they saw were a couple of bar patrons outside the Old Western Hotel on the corner of 2nd Street, and a couple walking kitty-corner up from there across the street by the Station House Cafe. Besides that, there wasn't anything else besides a handful of small businesses and restaurants and the Point Reyes Surf Shop before the highway swung a right and headed out of town, either south towards Stinson Beach, Muir Beach and San Francisco, or west, towards the peninsula, the beaches and the lighthouse.

"What do you think?" Ranger made the right, crossing the bridge at Lagunitas Creek, which drains right into Tomales Bay. At the intersection with Sir Francis Drake Boulevard, he turned around.

"Maybe we try one of these side streets, or we could ask someone at the bar if they saw anything," she said.

There were two side streets that ran parallel to Highway 1 through Point Reyes Station --- Mesa Road to the east and B Street to its west, and

Ranger hung a quick left onto the latter. At 2nd Street, he made the right towards the saloon.

And, there it was.

The white Grand Cherokee parked on the side of the road behind the big abandoned brick building they'd driven by just a few minutes before, across 2nd Street from the bar.

At that same moment, Owen slipped through the bar's front door, under the overhanging sign that read *The Old Western Saloon*, and the one beneath it forbidding anyone under 21 on the premises. He moved past the bar up front and the besottedly occupied stools, beyond the parquet dance floor and stage, and into the adjoining salon where the piano and pool tables were, and, without anybody noticing, squeezed through a small off-limits doorway leading to a secret passageway.

It was a hallway, a narrow corridor that led to a Prohibition-era underground tunnel connecting the saloon to the large abandoned brick and mortar building across the street, the old Grandi Hotel.

The place he had arranged to meet his mom.

The building was just like out of a scary movie. Long, dark hallways with cement floors and the studs in the walls and ceilings exposed as you wandered by them. Ornately designed, dusty rooms flanked by haunted-looking staircases leading to nowhere, it seemed. Doorways with no doors, and graffiti-ridden boarded up windows around every corner.

Upstairs, waiting in the faint light of the old dance hall ballroom like Owen had instructed, Naomi stood there quietly next to the dilapidated grand piano in the middle of the floor, which had been there since the place closed down in 1950.

A single candle on a glass tray burned on top of it.

It was 11:55 pm when she thought she heard a noise.

A door had been left open out back of the two-story structure, and Ranger headed for it.

"Should we call the police?" Sam asked as they reached it.

"I'm starting to think maybe we should ..." Ranger said back.

But, they didn't ... Instead, they entered the Grandi, heading right down a lengthy hallway, the heavy slab floors dampening the sound of their footsteps, Ranger raising a finger to his lips as a signal to move along quietly.

On one side of the building, Owen came up from the tunnel to the bottom of a set of stairs. On the other, Ranger and Sam reached the staircase at the entrance along the main street. As they did, they heard a *bang*, like somebody had just dropped something onto the floor, then a gasp.

Naomi ... they both thought.

Sam followed Ranger up the steps. Down the hall, they could now see the candlelight in the dance hall, and they went towards it, passing some of the old guest rooms that had been part of the grand hotel before it closed. The hallway was dark, so when they saw a figure entering the ballroom from the doorway opposite them, it didn't see them in return.

"Mom ..." the figure said.

"Owen ... baby."

Hunched in the near dark, Ranger and Sam looked at each other.

As they approached, they saw Owen and Naomi hug, then at the opposite end of the room, left of where they were and opposite the legless grand piano from Owen and Naomi, another figure came rushing in.

"Naomi ..." Sam shouted.

And in a blur, Ranger met the shape in the middle of the room and put him down.

But, three others were right behind.

"Mom, run!" Owen shouted as Naomi hesitated there behind the piano.

"Sam, you guys get out of here!" Ranger turned to her, his face almost invisible in the candlelight. "I'm right behind you!"

It all slowed down that second as Sam looked over the room really fast.

Owen was gone.

And she could hear the blows, and grunts and groans as Ranger engaged the three men.

She didn't want to run.

Her instincts told her to stay with Ranger no matter what, *come hell or high water*.

Huh! Ranger ducked, then struck the first one, rendering him unconscious and crashing him down to the hardwood floor. The second tried tackling Ranger but was jettisoned headfirst, careening off the piano, almost toppling over the light.

The third, one of the thugs from inside the car outside Ranger's house, squared up next.

Trample! Trample! Three more large figures appeared in a couple of the other doorways leading into the room.

"Sam ... go!" Ranger shouted, facing the one remaining open door.

She took Naomi and ran.

The thug swung and grazed Ranger just before he returned four or five blows of his own, and the thug was down.

Then, the three who'd just arrived circled into place, surrounding Ranger. Then three more, and several after that.

Two had taken off in pursuit of Sam and Naomi.

Owen had disappeared.

As Ranger scanned the room, he noticed one of the guys was the tall one from the school. From the concert by the water down at Terrapin Crossroads ... He was smiling.

"Alright, then ..." Ranger said, and they closed in.

Naomi was surprisingly more athletic than perhaps one might have thought she'd be.

Owen called from where he was beyond the end of the hallway, and she was there by the time Sam had turned her head back around. Sam had been looking back to the glow of the doorway where Ranger was, but ran as she heard the two men coming.

"This way," Owen whispered, guiding them both to the trap door leading back to the tunnel. Seconds later, they emerged back on the other side of the street, several saloon patrons glancing over as they climbed through the concealed exit.

"I'm calling 911." Naomi punched the numbers into her phone.

"Mom ... I have to get out of here," Owen said. He hugged his mother one more time.

Then, he glanced at Sam for a second, like ... *Thanks for your help, but who exactly are you?*

"Stay here and wait for the cops," he said to Naomi. "I'll be in contact."

"I love you ..."

Then, out the back door, he vanished.

It wasn't but three or four minutes before sirens were right outside the front entrance and four or five law enforcement officers were inside.

"Where were they exactly ... the last place you saw them?" one of them asked in a hurry, shotgun in his hands. Sam told them.

"And, how many were there?" another said.

"I don't know."

One of the officers stayed there in the saloon with Sam and Naomi ... But, as the others secured access to the big building across the street and made their way through it, it appeared everybody who had been there just minutes prior were already gone.

Sam stayed for hours after the officers let her go, well past sunrise, looking for Ranger.

Before they left the Grandi, officers had found his phone in that dance hall, all smashed up. They kept it for evidence. Sam continued to search for a while for anything that might help, but all she found were cigarette butts, shards of the broken candle tray by the grand piano, most likely the result of a thrown body, a restaurant business card in one of the stairwells, and a folded scrap of paper with a bunch of numbers written on it in the lot out back near the door where she and Ranger had entered about six hours earlier.

Naomi had left Point Reyes Station as well, the sheriffs taking her somewhere undisclosed as her house was no longer a safe place for her to be.

"Everything will be alright. Have faith, Sam," she tried to console her friend before she left. But, Sam was not okay.

It was well past the start of breakfast in the little cafes when Sam finally got into the Malibu, using the key Ranger had given her a few days ago. A single shiny key on a black keychain with two little copper-colored handcuffs swinging from it, each engraved with a word.

Alcatraz

Ranger picked up the souvenir when he visited the island penitentiary a couple years back.

They were planning to go there again soon, together.

Face in her hands, she sat there in the lot behind the big brick building and cried.

Not sure for how long.

What a horrifying night it had been.

And birthday.

The room was relatively dark, where Ranger was, though afternoon was fast approaching.

He wasn't able to see where the voices were coming from.

Or how many people were there watching him either.

He stood, tied to some piping, his hands and legs bound by the same thick zip ties police use to bind perpetrators. There was a small gash above his right eye, above the eyebrow, blood coming from his nose, and his lip looked like it had been cleanly sliced all the way through.

Like a razor had gone through it.

There was a light shining in his face.

"Mr. Gabriel, can you hear me?'

Ranger opened his eyes.

"Mr. Gabriel, please understand what I'm telling you … It is imperative that we find Owen." The man in the suit stayed behind the light, just his silhouette visible from where Ranger was.

"And right now, you are all we have … Why were you there last night?"

Ranger said nothing.

"Mr. Gabriel?"

The man went back and whispered something to one of the others at the back of the room. Then, he returned.

"Do you know Finn, Mr. Gabriel? … Do you know who Finn is?"

Again, nothing.

"Mr. Gabriel, please don't make me …"

"No." Ranger looked away as he said it, and the man turned again towards the others.

"Well then, I will tell you, and then perhaps you will understand how … important all this is. How critical it is for you … that you help us."

The man spoke coolly. Portentously.

"You see, Finn is one of ours … and he betrayed us."

Ranger squinted, keeping his eyes away from the light.

"Do you hear me, Mr. Gabriel?"

"Yes," he answered.

"He betrayed us, because his … *friend* … Owen told him to."

Ranger heard the door open but couldn't see it. A couple more people entered the room, and the one who was talking went to meet them. They exchanged words and he came back, faster than he had come the first time.

"Mr. Gabriel, are you going to be able to help us find Owen, or not?"

The man's image was closer than it had been before behind the light, Ranger could see.

"I hope you will ... Because the boss is coming here today."

Ranger remained silent.

"And I'm not sure he'll have any further use for you if you cannot ... Do you understand me, Mr. Gabriel?"

Another minute passed, then the man in the suit recessed to the other end of the room, back away from the light.

He said a final few things to one of the others, then opened the door and left.

And a couple of the rougher ones moved forward.

"I just can't do it ..." Sam sobbed, driving east along Sir Francis Drake Boulevard into the beautiful San Geronimo Valley.

She couldn't go home without Ranger.

Passing by the historic Papermill Creek Saloon, she pulled over and took out her phone. The only local number she had saved besides Naomi's was Ms. Elodie's, so she called.

"Ms. Elodie ..."

"Sam, darling ... Are you okay?" Elodie asked, hearing Sam's voice shake.

"No …"

"Sam, what's wrong?"

There was a delay on the line.

"Ranger is … gone."

Ms. Elodie asked Sam to explain to her what had happened, which she did.

"Where are you right now, dear?" Elodie-Jane was already on her feet.

"In front of a place called … the Two Bird Cafe."

"Okay … Go inside and stay there. I'll come meet you right away, honey," Elodie instructed. "Can't be sure some of them won't be waiting for you here still."

"Okay … Ms. Elodie."

They hung up.

Elodie wrapped herself in her shawl and took off.

And, Sam went into the cafe and took a seat.

In the smaller dining area next to the bar and the piano, and the stage where they perform music in the evening after dinner, tucked high up on a wall above the rafters in beautiful, resplendent color, was a mosaic painting of the Apache warrior Geronimo.

Geronimo, who warred against Mexico after they killed his wife, mother and three children. The brave Chiricahua who came to Arizona's desolate, inhospitable San Carlos reservation in 1877 in chains, but escaped three times only to raid the American settlers who had captured and imprisoned him. Geronimo, who fought for 30 years alongside his people, and in the end was hunted by 5,000 U.S. soldiers, nearly a quarter of the standing army, and 3,000 Mexicans, as he roamed free on the frontier. Until 1886 when he surrendered.

The last of his kind to do so.

The painting caught Sam's attention. Maybe it was his pose, armed with his rifle.

Or, the determination in his eyes.

She ordered something to drink and waited for Elodie, who showed up half-an-hour later.

"He's gone …" Sam sobbed into a napkin in her hand. They were the only two in the homey, wood-ceilinged room.

"Oh, Sam …" Elodie did her best to comfort her.

"I didn't know what else to do …" Sam wiped the tears from her face.

"It's alright. We'll stay here for now and wait to hear from the police." Ms. Elodie bundled her arms around Sam and walked over to one of the tables to sit down. "In the meantime, I've contacted everybody from your party last night to let them know what's happened … and to tell them that we're here."

Sam buried her face in the silver-studded shawl over Elodie's shoulder and cried.

And, Ms. Elodie watched through the restaurant's open windows.

Sitting there under the fearless fighter.

It was absolutely breathtaking, the route they had taken.

North up Highway 1 past Nick's Cove and Ocean Roar, through Tomales and Valley Ford, along the rugged and remote Sonoma Coast.

Ranger had been this way many times with his dad, and the Tsunami

Rangers, exploring places and dropping into the water to kayak.

And at home on the Liberty Dock, he had an article saved about this stretch of coastline, written for the *New York Times* by a guy named Kirby, who had driven the highway recently with his parents after they moved here from the southern half of the state.

Tumultuous and wind-swept. Wild and moody. Taciturn.

That's how he described it.

He wrote:

The Sonoma shore, it is a temperamental realm ... fogbound bluffs and tortured cypress trees, bent perpetually landward by stiff gales that howl in from the restless sea.

Winding country roads carried us over oak-covered hills and past expansive cattle ranches, and down to the wharf-side fishing village of Bodega Bay, a weathered but charming collection of wooden structures clinging to scrubby cliffs that surround the tranquil harbor.

At breezy Bodega Head, a favorite of whale watchers in winter and spring, the views up and down the rugged coast were magnificent. Beneath ocher sandstone cliffs, harbor seals napped on smooth black rocks or cavorted in the flourishing kelp beds, engulfed in seawater that alternated from aquamarine to indigo like a marine patchwork quilt.

The headland and harbor create an extraordinary topography, an unsettling reminder of the danger that lurks beneath: The deadly San Andreas Fault passes right through here. It shears Bodega in half, with the mainland on one tectonic plate, moving westward, and the headland on another plate, moving northward.

Sonoma's beaches are striking, mostly empty, and sometimes very treacherous. These are not beaches for swimming. There were signs everywhere warning of crumbling cliffs and dangerous "sleeper waves," which rise from nowhere and sweep the beach with gushing white water.

"Few survive," the sign says.

Eleven miles north of Bodega, we hit the mouth of the Russian River, where the hamlet of Jenner climbs the steep hillsides. The place has a faraway, edge-of-the-earth feel.

Jenner is unavoidably romantic.

We zigzagged north, hundreds of feet above the crashing surf, often without so much of a guardrail. I gripped the armrest as Dad negotiated the curves. Mom, in the back, read the paper. She couldn't look.

We wound our way past steep gulches with fresh creeks cascading into the ocean, until we arrived at Fort Ross State Historic Park, where the Russian-American Company, commissioned by Czar Paul I, operated an otter hunting outfit from 1812 to 1841. The weathered wood fort and fur-trapping center, where Russians and native Alaskans struggled but ultimately failed to survive, is perched on a picturesque promontory above the sea.

Past undulating vineyards of pinot noir and chardonnay that climbed the steep forested ridges ... I caught glimpses of the blue Pacific stretching out far below the redwoods. The crisp air was heavy with the scent of wildflowers and evergreens and the sun glowed warm and pure.

The landscape was peaceful and deserted, a world away from the crowded coast to the south.

A winding and scenic route.

This was place Ranger loved so much.

And it was here, up Highway 1 in an underground bunker on Black Mountain Ridge that they had taken him.

The driver of the Lincoln closed the door and followed the dark sedan down the driveway.

No noise in the Town Car, no radio, no talking.

Just the sound of the tires on the road.

The car followed the sedan, through the tanbark oak and Bishop pines of the Coast Range, the blackberry and the poppies.

Right then left, then right, left and right ... around the twisting curves of *Devil's Palisade*.

The ocean was right in front of them, visible through the windshield just beyond the sedan each time it emerged from the flora. The sun was there too, its position in the sky signaling about 2:45 pm.

After a few minutes, the sedan passed the campground, sparsely populated today considering how pleasant the weather was.

Then, it arrived at Highway 1 and turned left.

Rrrrrrrrrrr.

The Town Car engine growled as it accelerated away from the stop sign.

The two cars came around a couple wooded bends, then by some houses and a bar and grill, and finally by a general store and the entrance to the larger campground at Ocean Cove.

They were right on top of the Pacific now.

There was a little inlet, and the cars hair-pinned right past a gorgeous little beach, but the man with the scar on his face didn't look.

How could anyone not have?

The driver of the Lincoln continued on, by the resort and boat launch, the lodge and store, past another dramatic little gulch, *7BLK100* in his view. At Fort Ross, the sedan turned left, and the cars headed back up, into the hills.

Ranger grunted this time when the big man hit him, but like before, he didn't say a word. He looked worse now than earlier, blood trickling from his mouth and above his right eye.

Just then, the two cars pulled up and one of the men outside banged on the door.

Crack! Crack!

It opened and a shoulder-width streak of light flooded in and lit the floor up orange.

Four men walked through, large dark silhouettes Ranger could see lifting his head. Then the boss entered, his shoes clicking slowly across the cement until he reached the spot behind the lamp shining in Ranger's face.

"Hello ... Mr. Gabriel." His voice was strange. Soft, wheezy. Ranger could hear the breathing. A couple of the figures shuffled about in the background. Otherwise, it was dead quiet ...

"When I say *hello* ... you say *hello*," the strange man hissed.

Two of the thugs moved forward striking Ranger in the mid-section, one on each side.

Ugghh ... ugggh.

After that, it was still again.

Heeee ... heeee ... heeeee.

The breathing resumed, then the lamp swung around into the man's face.

It was obvious that the scar from his forehead to the side of his mouth had damaged the one eye pretty severely when it happened because the cornea was now thick and opaque, covering the pupil completely, greyish-blue in color, not blackish-brown like the other eye. And his teeth looked like they had been filed to points, but they were natural.

His face was pale and his expression chilling, to say the least.

The boss had turned the light towards him because he wanted be certain Ranger saw exactly what is was he had to say.

"Do you know what happens next, Mr. Gabriel?" he moaned. Ranger looked up at him as his shoulders heaved up and down with the breathing.

"You talk ... or die."

He stared Ranger in the eye for a few seconds then turned and started away.

"One hour ..."

The long coat of the grotesque head man cast a long shadow onto the cement as the door opened and the light came back in. Then, the big guy came forward again and checked the time ... It was 3:13 pm.

Time came to a standstill, or pretty close to it after that in the room, Ranger standing there, thinking about it all. If he could just get free of these ties, he felt like he still had a chance.

So, he pulled.

All those days, he thought, traveling and laughing with his friends, were they all for nothing? He scraped the ties up and down the back of the pipes to see if they would wear, but it made a noise and he sensed they might detect it, so he stopped.

All the times, when he stood up against these people. Was it worth it? If he could get his legs free, it would probably help him free his arms, so he began to pull, the pressure reverberating in the concrete beneath him.

He thought about family. His sisters. His mom and dad. All the years they spent together. And how he learned so little about the most important things. Could they hear him pulling? He thought they just had.

Maybe it was all for nothing now ... this thing he'd found with Sam.

Without condition. No turning back. With everything he had.

Even if this was it, he thought ... *Love never ends*.

Either way, he kept on trying.

4:00 was upon them, and the tall one checked his phone. He and thirteen or fifteen others were there in the dim room, waiting. The bald-headed one, Toner, was one of them too. He'd stayed behind after the man in the long coat had left.

Beep ... Beep.

His phone rang and he listened for a second.

Then, he responded ... One word.

"No."

Several minutes later, there was the sound of tires pulling up in the gravel outside.

The guards moved, and the door opened, and the one with the scar came in, along with three others ... A shorter muscular one with dark hair and a medium-length, dark beard. Another taller one with sunglasses. And a woman.

The one who had been downstairs by the window in the house on *Devil's Palisade*.

She looked rough. Not a trace more pleasant than any of the others.

The three met briefly with a few of the others in the back, then the bearded one flipped open a knife, and alongside the boss, approached the light.

Ranger couldn't see anything, but he did hear the metallic snap of the blade.

And the footsteps.

Click ... Click ... Click.

Then, they stopped.

"I love you, Sam ..." he whispered.

The one with the sharp teeth gritted slightly, then gave the go-ahead.

Then, exactly a split second after, the locked door across the cold floor burst open, and as the light poured in, Ranger looked over to see Richie in a cocked and ready stance.

He rushed in immediately, followed by Julian and Dan, TJ, Duane and Tanaka.

Ranger squinted, adjusting to the sunlight. He couldn't believe his eyes.

Boom! ... Crash!

Richie hit the first guy fast, then the second, who doubled over but wasn't all the way down, so Dan crunched him with a right hand as he sprinted by, putting him down and out. Julian ran into the big guy who had just arrived, and they squared up, but Julian was way too fast, dropping him in a heap, the giant's designer sunglasses sailing across the floor. And there was TJ, firing punches off so quickly most likely none of the thugs he encountered saw any of them coming.

One, two, then three guys down just like that.

Haaaaaaaaaa!

Then, like a lightning bolt across the half-lit room, Tanaka went flying onto Toner's back. Toner had gone to help with Duane, who was busy bulldozing a couple guys into the wall, but he fell in Tanaka's choke hold.

Crack! ... Bang! ... Arghhhh!

It was mayhem in there.

And in the middle of it all ... Sam appeared in the doorway.

"Ranger!" she called out, and he saw her.

The one with the beard and the knife, and the other tall one, had turned away when the door was kicked open, shielding the boss from the brawl and looking for a way out. Together with the woman, they started making their way to the door.

"Sam!" Ranger called back.

Sam didn't see them as they were coming towards her.

The bearded man lifted his knife.

Right then, Frans bolted in, flying by Sam through the door with arms above his head, and cracked the thug with the hard, dark object he had in his hands ... And down he went. However, so did Frans, unable to stop his momentum, he tripped over the man and went crashing headfirst into the wall.

Thwunkkk!

As the boss and the woman stepped back away from the door, Sam ran by them to Ranger, clinching onto him.

"Over there …" he said, signaling to the knife lying on the sunlit floor.

Sam ran over and picked it up and cut his arms and legs free.

"Stay right here …" Ranger said, then kissed on the lips and darted off into the fray.

It wasn't more than a minute later that all the rest of the thugs in the room were down.

"That's it … Let's go." Richie waved to everyone.

Dan and TJ helped Frans up, and with only a couple torn shirts and a few cuts and bruises, they all walked out.

Sam under Ranger's arm.

The police arrived in force just as the nine of them descended the dirt path towards the car. Sam recognized a couple of them from the night before, pointing them to the open door at the hillside. By now, the sun had made its way almost all the way over to the horizon, its colors unreal.

Purple and red, and orange, and gold … Beautiful, like you often get this time of year on the coast.

25 LIGHTHOUSE

"O, learn to love, the lesson is but plain ... And, once made perfect, never lost again."

Venus and Adonis

"Get yourselves checked out. We'll be in contact." The deputy from the Old Western Saloon who had the man with the scar and the woman handcuffed in the back of his patrol car directed Sam and Ranger as they walked by.

The man looked up and caught Sam's eye through the side window.

One by one, the other officers brought the rest of them out.

"You okay, buddy?" Julian opened the passenger door of his Suburban for Ranger and Sam, who climbed into the front passenger and middle seats.

"Yeah ... surprisingly."

Sam let a few tears of joy go.

Duane, TJ and Richie took the middle seats, and Tanaka and Dan helped Frans to the back.

"Frannie, you good?" Richie looked on as Frans held a towel pressed up to his face.

"Yeah. Maybe just a broken nose ... I think."

(From the wall.)

"You did it, buddy." Ranger turned to Frans. "You saved Sam, without a doubt."

A proud smile came to his face, underneath the towel.

Sam spun around and smiled at him too. "Thank you," she mouthed the words.

"Man ... how'd you guys even find me?" Ranger swung around to face everyone in the SUV.

They all turned to Duane.

"Unbelievable," Ranger said. They told him they'd share the whole story over dinner where Elodie-Jane and the rest of them were.

"Hey, let's go there." There was a clinic along the main road as they passed through Jenner, so they stopped to get everyone checked out. An hour later, the doctor released them.

No major injuries, except Frans' broken nose.

Back at the Two Bird Cafe, Elodie, Frans' parents Hansen and Clare, Liz and her pal Stacey, and Anna-Lena and Lwazi were waiting.

"So, a little while later, Richie came walking through the door." Elodie retold the events from the afternoon. "Then Dan and Julian ... And not long after that, Tanaka and TJ were here. They were both in San Francisco and drove up together."

"So, I ask what information we have," Julian went on. "Ms. Elodie tells us that Sam had found a business card for a restaurant in one of the stairwells and called it in to the sheriff's office. They tell her they'll investigate and get back to her."

Ranger took a bite of his chicken parmesan. He was hungry.

"The only other thing was this piece of paper she found behind the building you were in, with all these numbers on it."

"So, we say, *Do they make a any sense?*" Tanaka continued. "And everybody say, *No, not to me.*"

"We thought maybe they were lottery numbers or something."

"Then, Sam tells us that the police had found your phone inside the building … but it was destroyed."

"So, that probably meant they didn't want anybody to follow," Dan added.

"Right."

"So that made us think … *There's probably still a chance to … find him.*"

"Yes … That is right." Tanaka looked over to Dan. "We think … *Hey, that is right.*"

The group took up that whole portion of the dining area, and their tables were full now.

Drinking glasses everywhere.

"So we decide … *We need to do something.*" Ms. Elodie sat with her hand on Sam's shoulder.

"We were about to go to the restaurant on that business card."

"What's it called?"

Richie read the card:

Phoenix Supper Club

Bayview

San Francisco

415 - 222 - 1100

"We tried calling, but no-one answered."

"Then Duane, out of nowhere, with this scrap of paper and these random numbers, says … *Guys, I think I know where he is.*"

"Yeah!" Julian said. "He says to us, *Guys, these numbers ... I think they're coordinates.*"

Ranger looked over to Duane, and the whole table smiled.

"Right!" Dan said. "He looks at us and says, you know how he does ... *I'm relatively sure of it, guys. These numbers, I think they're code for geographic coordinates to some actual locations.*"

"You mean latitudes and longitudes?" Ranger asked.

"Yep. That's right."

TJ handed Ranger the paper. The numbers read:

19	*15*	*04*	*42*	*21*	*08*	*03*	*20*
08	*19*	*20*	*41*	*49*	*17*	*02*	*23*
10	*53*	*13*	*01*	*52*	*25*	*03*	*17*
07	*01*	*22*	*13*	*40*	*02*	*09*	*11*
12	*02*	*18*	*28*	*26*	*26*	*13*	*01*
19	*02*	*34*	*24*	*54*	*52*	*31*	*39*
06	*12*	*10*	*07*	*36*	*09*	*00*	*51*
28	*22*	*15*	*11*	*53*	*03*	*00*	*01*
04	*16*	*30*	*11*	*34*	*05*	*00*	*03*

"It *was* unbelievable."

"He figured out if you add up the first three lines, and you get the latitude and longitude of your house in Sausalito ... exactly."

"What?" Ranger appeared a little shocked.

"Then, the next three ... and it's where you guys were last night in Point Reyes Station."

"The old Grandi Hotel?"

"Exactly."

"And, the last one, Duane?" Julian turned and looked at him.

"Yeah, looking at the map, 38.505529° north latitude and 123.170055° west longitude ... That one was north of here, almost to Fort Ross, in the hills by Black Mountain Ridge."

"Precisely where you were." Ms. Elodie said to Ranger.

"So, we called the sheriff. They said they'd try to get someone up there as soon as they possibly could."

"But, we decided we couldn't wait."

"Right."

"Amen ... brother."

"We needed to go ... right now." Tanaka said.

"We all decided together ..." Elodie announced from her chair at the head of the tables ... "*We need to go get Ranger.*"

"Man ... I don't even know what to say," Ranger said back to them. "I just love you guys ... I really do. Each and every one of you."

It was pretty dark in there in that dining room by the fire, and there's no way of knowing for certain, but between all of them there -- Elodie-Jane, Clare and Hansen, Frans, TJ, Richie, Julian and Dan, Liz and Stacey, Lwazi and Anna-Lena, Duane, and Sam and Ranger too -- there probably wasn't a dry eye anywhere.

As dinner rolled on, a small band took the tiny stage in the room next door.

The room with the Geronimo where Ms. Elodie had come to find Sam.

"Oooh ... Higginbotham and I used to love this song," Elodie said to Sam. She sang along.

Name your price, a ticket to paradise, I can't stay here anymore

And I've looked high and low, I've been from shore to shore to shore

If there's a short cut I'd have found it, but there is no easy way around it

Light of the world, shine on me ...

It was late when they got back to the Liberty Dock, and Bernard was happy to see them.

Like he always was.

"I'll be right back ..." Ranger kissed Sam on the head and left her on the couch downstairs. About a minute later, he returned with a cake and a candle, and a small box gift-wrapped in black and gold.

"Happy birthday, my love." He looked at her, and they both took deep breaths.

That's what the cake said too, written in big red letters.

Happy Birthday, My Love

"Baby ..." Sam whispered to him.

"Go ahead ... open it." Ranger motioned to the box.

She did. It was a little book, like a small album.

"Cute ..."

On the first page was a photo of the two of them from the other day on Bridgeway down by the water. On the second, a fun one of them kissing on one of the bridges at Steep Ravine. And, the third, a photo of them at the top of Twin Peaks.

Then, Sam turned to the next page and … *Huh?* … held her breath for a second.

It was a picture of her favorite Gnarabup Beach back home, with images of big and small footprints labeled *Me* and *You* all around in the sand.

"Ranger …"

She turned to the next page and saw airplane tickets.

"You didn't …"

"I did," he smiled.

There were two tickets, departing from San Francisco International this weekend, on Friday.

"I figured let's go before we get back to work … Plus, it's summer down there."

She jumped up in his lap there on the big, cushy couch and hugged and kissed him all over.

"Ouch …" he said, holding a finger to his lip.

"Ohh! Sorry … sorry!" Sam proclaimed as Bernard looked on from his spot on the ottoman. "Sorry, I forgot."

"That's alright …" Ranger smiled. "On second thought, it actually makes it feel better."

She paused and looked him in the eye.

"I love you so much …" she said.

"One-hundred million percent the same here …" he said to her.

Tuesday.

Skelton continued to rifle through his morning's phone calls, taking copious notes as he did. Person by person, guest by guest, like Captain Erasmus had directed him.

"Did you happen to see anything out of the ordinary, an altercation or anything?" he asked.

"No ... not at all."

"Nothing?"

Everybody's answer was the same.

All he had was what Carolijn had told him ... And what Ranger had not.

But that, he believed, was enough.

By 10:00 am, the phone started ringing, everyone checking in to see how Ranger was doing.

"Feeling good, buddy ... No effects at all," Ranger let Schalk know, who had gotten word.

"You've always been amazing like that." Schalk sounded his usual happy self, and relieved.

"How's the weather over there in Tampa?" Ranger asked him.

"83 and sunny ... Matter of fact, we're heading over to some uninhabited island called Anclote Key right now. Gonna do some treasure hunting."

"Nice, I know Sara loves those seashells."

"You said that right ... She'll roll around all day with that mask and snorkel looking for just the perfect one."

Ranger looked up as Sam rounded the corner into the living room from upstairs.

"I'll see you soon then, buddy ... Thanks for checking on me. Love you, brother."

Sam sat down next to him.

"Schalk and Sara ..." Ranger set the phone down.

"Oh, how are they doing?"

"Great. They're heading out to some uninhabited key, and it's 83 degrees."

"Wow, that sounds so fabulous. I can't wait for the beach." Sam put her feet up.

"You know, honey, too bad we experienced Point Reyes the way we did the other day because the drive out there, and the peninsula, and the beaches ... Pretty awesome."

Sam smiled, raising her eyebrows.

Ranger smiled back. "You thinking what I'm thinking?"

By the time Sam and Ranger were ready and got all of Bernard's stuff together, it was noon. They packed a picnic basket together with salamis and cheeses, and pineapple and treats, and headed up the dock to the car.

"I'm so excited I get to drive you." Sam smiled big as they entered the parking lot.

Through the binoculars, Detective Skelton wondered how they could look so happy with Ranger having those cuts and bruises all over his face.

Mill Valley to the left ... Muir Woods to the right ... Route 1 straight ahead

As they began their descent into Muir Beach, parts of the highway appeared as if it were about to send you right off the cliff and into the Pacific.

"Wow! Look at that ..."

It was another one of those beautiful, warm winter days.

"Ooh ... There's the Pelican Inn," Sam said, looking out to the left at the bottom of the grade.

"Yep ... That's it."

The road climbed quickly up from there, past the hillside houses of Muir Beach and the impressive Muir Beach Overlook, then wound its way along the cliffs until it settled into Stinson Beach. From there, it hugged Bolinas Lagoon, ultimately making its way through the forested valleys around Five Brooks and Olema, and finally to Sir Francis Drake Boulevard.

The southern end of Point Reyes Station.

The arrow on the sign pointed to the left:

Tomales Bay State Park

Beaches

Lighthouse

They made the turn onto Sir Francis Drake and headed west into the quaint community of Inverness, by Vladimir's Czech Restaurant, the Point Reyes shipwrecks, and the adorable Sea Star Cottage on the water.

"Right now, we're right on top of the San Andreas Fault ... as we speak,"

Ranger told Sam. "The North American Plate is that way," he pointed out, "and we're driving onto the Pacific."

"Whoa. That's kinda scary." Sam spun her face around towards him in her sunglasses.

"Yeah ... exciting."

They went on. Onto the 71,000 acre peninsula headland called Point Reyes, past the turnoff to Tomales Point and the great white shark breeding ground there at the mouth of the bay, past Heart's Desire Beach, and through a handful of the historic cattle ranches that still function today as part of the national seashore.

In the distance ahead were some big trees standing all by themselves on the open land.

"Let's stop here," Ranger said. "It's pretty cool."

Sam slowed and steered right onto the narrow driveway.

"Oh ... wow. I think I've seen this place before ... in pictures."

It was the Cypress Tree Tunnel, a quarter-mile stretch of giant Monterey cypress trees planted here in 1929 that have grown to form a thick canopy over the road leading to an old maritime radio receiving station. A popular spot for tourists and photographers, especially those looking to catch the morning sunrise as it streaks through the branches.

They took the top down so they could see it all as they drove through ... It was gorgeous. Even Bernard enjoyed the view.

There are many beaches to visit at Point Reyes -- Drakes with its white sandstone cliffs and elephant seal colony, Abbotts Lagoon and the stream and bridge, the snowy plovers and peregrine falcons, Kehoe and its giant sand dunes, Limantour Beach and its harbor seals, the intense surf and tule elk up on the cliffs at McClures Beach, the rock formations and tidepools at pretty Sculptured Beach, and the 30-foot cascading tidefall called Alamere, which pours directly onto the beach below in between Wildcat and Palomarin.

And of course, the remarkable 11-mile uninterrupted sandy stretch, the Great Beach.

"Oh, my gosh." Sam jumped up onto Ranger's back when she saw it.

The sun was brilliant and warm, and the wind was nonexistent, so after a leisurely picnic, Ranger and Sam threw the ball with Bernard, took a few photos, then went off for a walk, pants rolled up to their knees.

"Look, you can see the lighthouse from here ..." She pointed to the cliffside in the distance, its bright light flashing on a regular pattern halfway down the rocks.

"Yeah ... that's it. The famous Point Reyes Lighthouse." Ranger held Sam's hand. "You know, we're 10 miles off the mainland here, the windiest place on the Pacific Coast, and one of the foggiest."

"So, that light's saved a lot of lives."

"Since 1870."

"Wow ... what a thought. Just that one little light."

Right then, Ranger tugged at Sam's hand and began rushing up the beach.

He noticed a wave coming up, much larger and thicker than the others that were breaking.

"Go, go ..." he said, Bernard running on the leash out in front of them.

The sneaker wave ended up reaching probably a hundred feet or higher onto the dry sand, washing tangled clumps of kelp up with it.

And, as it began to recede, Ranger saw that it had knocked down a woman and her child walking along the waterline in front of them.

They ran over, Bernard barking. As they got there, the woman was having difficulty getting to her feet and the boy, about eight, was being pulled backwards with the outgoing current. Sam got to her and helped her up, while Ranger plucked her son out of the rip.

"Oh, my gosh … Thank you, thank you," the woman repeated.

"You're welcome. Remember … Never turn your back on the ocean. Tell your friends, okay?" Ranger patted the boy on top of the head, and Sam smiled.

"Okay … I will," he said.

When they got back to the car, they drove the rest of the way to the end of the peninsula. Past the Sea Lion Overlook, down the footpath and under the wind-blown Leaning Tree, they reached the visitor center and the staircase.

308 steps down to the lighthouse.

As the sun went down, the critters started coming out all along the road back from the headland. Ranger had seen plenty of elk and deer, coyotes, roaming bulls, weasels, skunks, and even a bobcat on his trips out here before. This evening, they witnessed a badger in the Siata's headlights scurrying across the pavement into a little marsh.

"Whoa, what's that?!" Sam yelped, then started laughing.

They stopped for dinner at Fog's Kitchen on the water at Tomales Bay back in Inverness, who happened to be doing a special pet-friendly night, so Bernard was able to go along. They sat outside on the covered patio overlooking the sailboats in the harbor, Sam ordering the pesto linguine and Ranger the fish and chips, with a local cheese plank including a Marin camembert, the Achadinha broncha, and Laura Chenel chevre to share.

It wasn't until after 8:30 that they finally left.

Though they both were really tired, neither wanted to end the night and go home.

Sam flipped on her tablet before curling up under the covers for the night. She wanted to send the picture of her and Ranger at the top of the steps of the lighthouse to a few people.

Nonno and Nonna, Sally, Corinna and Agustin, and Abby.

> *Hi, Nonna and Nonno. Here's another lighthouse for us to visit one day together.*
>
> *I love you both more than you'll ever know.*
>
> *Sam*

> *Hey, Best Mate. How ya goin'? Thinking about you and really hope you can come visit soon.*
>
> *I love you so much for being such a great friend.*
>
> *Sam*

> *Hi, Corinna, Agustin and Family. How are my friends in Hot Springs?*
>
> *Corinna, the lesson you taught me really worked! I've found the FIRE!*
>
> *Agustin, I've seen so much nature on my trip. Today, I even saw a badger!*
>
> *Here we are at Point Reyes. I hope you get a chance to explore this place one day.*
>
> *Thanks for always being there for me when I needed you!*
>
> *Sam*

> *Abby, how are you? Hope all is well.*

Wow, it's so much different here than North Carolina. Just compare the lighthouses.

(This one was awesome but I still love Old Baldy the best.)

One thing I've learned since being here, though. You just have to go for it.

Decide what you want and make it happen. Otherwise, it might pass you by.

I'm so glad I came.

Keep fighting the good fight.

Sam

Downstairs, Ranger looked at the message he got on his tablet again:

Mr. Gabriel, please meet me at the station tomorrow at noon. Just you. Same address.

Detective Skelton

Morning came early.

Wednesday, January 13.

8:15 am, Skelton knocked on Captain Erasmus' door.

"I'm arresting Ranger Gabriel today," he said.

"What time?"

"Noon."

Erasmus looked up from the papers in front of him. "You have everything you need?"

"Yes, sir."

"Alright, then."

Erasmus watched the detective over the top of his reading glasses as he walked away, vanishing quickly to the other end of the office.

The Liberty Dock ...

Ranger and Bernard sat out on the deck, watching the boats and the birds.

Sam wasn't up yet, undoubtedly catching up on rest she'd missed the last several nights. Plus, Ranger kept the upstairs bedroom pretty dark, really good for sleeping in.

"What do you think, boy?" Ranger asked. He smiled, picturing how happy Bernard was going to be this week with Kurtley and Rob coming over.

Because he and Sam were headed to Australia. Two-and-a-half more days.

He was looking forward to it.

"Morning, babe." Sam tottered out through the sliders, still drowsy and hair all messed up. She crawled in next to Ranger under the blanket.

"Hey! Good morning, my little honey, badger."

They both giggled.

Sam set her head down onto the blankets in Ranger's lap and stared out over the water ... He brushed her hair with his fingers.

All types of boats were cruising back and forth on the San Francisco Bay this morning. Ferries going, and container ships out in the channel, sailboats, mainly keelboats and dinghies, an old-fashioned ketch flying all sorts of different colored flags, and a few yachts.

It was as lovely as it could be out there.

"Why do you think he wants you to come back?" Sam asked, watching it all.

"Don't know," Ranger said.

Rrrr Aaaa Arr ... Bernard warned the seagulls.

"Well, whatever it is, I'll be waiting for you outside."

They sat and listened to someone giving commands.

> *Ready about ... Helm to wind ... Jibe-ho!*

Ranger checked his watch.

"Wanna go for a run?" he said.

Sam, Ranger and Bernard parked on the west side of the bridge, crossing over through the noisy tunnel underneath with the traffic above their heads. Up the stairs on the other side, Ranger got his video ready, they stretched for a bit, then they went.

The Golden Gate Bridge: 1.7 miles across. Sam smiled big as she started down the sidewalk. Ranger filmed her, the sun coming in from the east lighting her hair up golden and illuminating the span's south tower 500 feet above. He panned up to its top.

"This is such a great idea!" Sam said into the microphone.

Their strides beat softly, rhythmically across the concrete.

Bernard ran, happy and well-trained out on his leash, and when the camera moved to him, it looked like he was smiling. He was excited.

The city was strikingly photogenic today, the skyscrapers south of Market rising above older San Francisco in the foreground.

They passed the tower and continued onto the main span, painted its international orange, 220 feet above the water.

"Look, waves." Sam pointed over to Fort Point beneath them as she took the video now. Then she filmed Ranger. He smiled ... busted lip, bruised face and all.

Out towards the Potato Patch, deep blue swells formed and a few of them were breaking. Sam swept the camera around and got everything.

They reached the San Francisco side and its vista point and took a few more photos.

After a while, Ranger asked Sam if she was ready to head back, and kissed her for what felt like thirty seconds on the platform.

"Ready when you are ..." she responded, thrilled.

"Okay then, I'll see you in a little bit ..." Sam said with a little smile. "I'll just go and park then. Text me when you're coming out." She watched him with those big eyes.

Ranger turned to her. "Okay ..."

Sam stood there by the Malibu as Ranger went in, and for some reason, she started to cry. Maybe it was everything they'd just been through, or just the morning together with him, but she had a sudden lump in her throat.

She watched as Ranger went up the stairs.

"Can I help you?" the receptionist asked.

"Yes ... Ranger Gabriel to see Detective Skelton."

She got on the phone. "Please have a seat. He'll be right with you."

After about a minute, a couple of uniformed officers came out to get him.

"Mr. Gabriel?" one of them said.

"Yes …"

"Please come with us."

The three of them proceeded through the glass and metal locking door into the interior of the station where Erasmus intercepted them. He said something to the officer in front.

"Uh, follow me, please, Mr. Gabriel." The officer led Ranger into an empty waiting room, closing the door behind them and they took a seat.

All of a sudden, Ranger had a really bad feeling.

All that had gone on the past two-and-a-half weeks. It all went through his mind again all of a sudden.

About ten minutes later, the door re-opened, with the other young officer standing there.

"Mr. Gabriel …" he called to Ranger.

Ranger got up and started for the door …

But, he heard the voice before he got to it.

"Well, it's not nice to ignore someone!" it said. "But, I guess we'll forgive!

He recognized it right away.

Ranger walked out of the room into the open space and saw Annie and Dee standing there.

"We know what we saw, though … Uh huh!"

"Dee ... Annie!" Ranger called out. "It's Ranger." He went over to them.

"Ranger!" Annie called back.

Dee, who was looking a bit nervous and uncomfortable, cracked a little smile.

"Hi, Ranger ..." she said.

Ranger hugged them both. "What are you guys doing here?"

"Mr. Gabriel, hello. I'm Captain Erasmus." The chief stepped forward and introduced himself, shaking Ranger's hand. "I'll be happy to explain all that."

Ranger looked over and noticed Skelton standing off to the side. He did not look happy.

"Ladies, I'll tell you," Erasmus turned to them again. "It's been a real pleasure to meet you. You're both very exceptional and very delightful young ladies."

"Well, thank you, captain. Glad to be of service!" Annie stood proud in her Hawaiian floral print muumuu and sunglasses.

"You're welcome," Dee said politely.

"Have fun in ... Bora Bora," the captain said. "Wow. Lucky."

"We sure will. Woo hoo! *Otea* all night long! That's the dance they do down there, Captain." Annie swung her hips around in circles like the island girls do.

"Annie ..." Dee shook her head.

Ranger, Dee and Annie shared a word together then made a plan to get together for dinner when they returned from their vacation. They were all really glad to see each other again, and Ranger was excited for them that they were doing so many fun things.

They deserved it.

"See you real soon then, Ranger!" The girls followed their driver to the door.

"For sure."

"Right this way, Mr. Gabriel," Erasmus said to him.

They walked through the open area to the captain's office.

"Have a seat, please."

"Thanks ..." Ranger said.

"So ..." Erasmus started, "We got a break on that Michael Roman case."

Erasmus closed the dark wood door behind him and proceeded to explain it all to Ranger. He told him about how the case first came across Skelton's desk, and how Skelton had discovered there'd been the party at the Pelican Inn that Saturday night. He told him how he'd secured the guest list from Julian, and how he'd found Carolijn had the run-ins with Roman. He then explained that Carolijn had informed Skelton that Ranger asked Roman to leave, and that there had been yelling outside the front door, and that he'd assumed it was between Roman and Ranger, but it was not. Roman was yelling because he had stumbled. Annie and Dee's driver remembered seeing him there, and the three of them all heard it.

He went on.

About a half hour later, Dee and Annie ran into Roman again. This time on the beach. Annie had wanted to put her toes in the water. And as they stood there, they'd told Erasmus no more than half an hour ago, barefoot in the dark, Roman literally ran into them.

The party was a dud ... Dee remembers him saying, so he was going to do something fun. Take a swim. Dee and Annie both recalled his name clearly. At least his last name … *Roman*. Because when he dared the ladies to come in, Annie for a second thought about doing it. *When in Rome …* she'd said to Dee. But, as they stood there, toes in the sand, unable to see, they began to hear splashing.

He kept on going, farther and farther away, Dee told Erasmus. *Until we couldn't hear him anymore.*

Eventually, the girls decided to leave, but they were both a little concerned about the guy. They were shocked when they heard what had happened to him.

Then, Erasmus told Ranger that Skelton had contacted everyone on that party guest list, asking if they knew Roman, or experienced any unwelcomed attention, or saw any conflict. Everyone except Dee and Annie.

Because the guest list had noted that they were blind.

The captain said he'd apologized for Skelton. The way he had treated people throughout all of this. He confessed that the detective was just a little too aggressive sometimes. But, Ranger already knew that … His friends had told him a couple nights ago in San Geronimo, after they had rescued him.

But, it might have taken a while to sort all this out had Erasmus not called those final two guests himself this morning, and Skelton had made the arrest.

"We don't stand for that kind of stuff here … Those girls were extremely valuable. Shined the light on everything." Erasmus stood to his feet.

"Right." Ranger got up from his chair as well. "Thank you, detective."

Annie the Unstoppable … he thought to himself and smiled.

On his way out, Ranger texted Sam, then glanced up and saw Skelton outside his office. Ranger extended a hand to him, and they shook. *No hard feelings.*

Back at the car, Sam looked at her phone.

I'm ready. Where are you?

She called him, and he told her where to meet him. He was taking her to lunch in Fairfax.

Excited, she pulled out and turned north on A Street, the mission right there in front of her. It was so beautiful, with the hillside just behind it.

And there stood Ranger. She pulled up and greeted him with a gigantic hug and a kiss.

"Hi, handsome!" She was so happy to see him. "How did it go?"

"Case solved ..." he answered, squeezing her tight.

She held on too, and didn't let him go.

PROLOGUE - THE CALL

When it comes calling, make sure you're ready.

Finn H.

That's what was scratched in the blue metal of the back of the camera.

Owen scrolled through the photos, sitting there on the sand in the warm Gulf of Mexico air.

There they all were, all those guys ... and now they were all in jail.

Click.

Toner.

Click.

The disturbing-looking one from outside the window at the Buckeye Roadhouse restaurant. They had called him *Earls*.

Click ... Click.

The tall, young one.

And, the woman.

Click.

And, the one with the scar.

Click ... Click ... Click.

All of them ... Except for this one.

Johnny.

"You're almost twenty-one years-old. I guess I shouldn't worry." Abby's mother couldn't hide the concern in her eyes.

"Yeah, you were right, Mom," Abby sighed. "I need to get off this island, for the first time in my life."

Her mother watched as she packed her things.

"Don't worry ... I'll be fine." Abby said, managing a little smile.

She placed her sunglasses on top of her head, like you do when you're not using them right at the moment, but you're about to.

"How long do you think you'll be gone?" her mother asked.

"A week or so. I'm not sure ... I guess it depends on how it goes?"

Abby's mom poked her lip out, conceding. She was positive that Abby could take care of herself, and it would probably be really good for her, considering how the past year had been and all, however she was still apprehensive about it, quite a bit, like any good mother would be.

It would be her first time away from home.

For the end of May, it was already warm outside. Over 90 degrees.

Which was hot for Cape Fear.

"Where are you planning on going first?" Ellen said.

"Not sure." Abby looked up, stuffing the last of her things, her two bathing suits, into her bag.

"Venice, maybe."

Point Reyes. Just before sunset.

The three men had counted their steps from the entrance of the

Cypress Tree Tunnel precisely 180° to the south, towards Schooner Bay.

995 ... 996 ... 997 ... 998 ... 999

Just like the map told them to.

And they started to dig.

Clunk ... Clunk ... Clunk. "There it is."

The one watched as the other two cleared the dirt away from the top of the big silver case.

"Open it ..." he said.

With a crowbar, they pried the lock off and lifted the top.

Breathing heavy, the two looked up at Johnny, who stood over them, for what to do next.

It was empty.

ABOUT THE AUTHOR

G.T. Rodrigues (Greg) and his wife Lou are from California but now live in Florida. They are special educators by trade and really enjoy supporting students. Greg and Lou have a son and a daughter, wonderful young people who enjoy helping others as well, and they come from big families – awesome parents, brothers, sisters, nieces nephews, and pets! Together, they enjoy traveling (just visited all the baseball parks across the Major League), good food (Mexican, Italian, cooking Canadian donairs and Nanaimo bars), and getting together for family gatherings. They also love sports (rugby, sailing, hockey (Go, Bolts!), surfing, NASCAR, cricket, footy), birdwatching, live plays and opera, music, sharks, classic cars, and being on the water. (They even dived to touch the hand of the Christ of the Abyss on a coral reef at the bottom of the open ocean.)

Whatever they do, being together is the best part!

Greg was inspired to write traveling romantic thrillers by learning about fellow University of Notre Dame alum and romance novelist Nicholas Sparks (*The Notebook*) and reading *The Walk* adventure series by Richard Paul Evans (which he did on a cruise ship from Venice to Istanbul).

Greg and Lou are thankful for the love God has given them, and realize that especially in today's world, it is so important we remember to love each other. Like in *The Meeting* with Sam and Ranger, we are called to do many things -- be kind, patient and brave, trust, persevere, grow, have faith, hope and love. And the greatest of these is to love. Blessings and all the best to all of you!

Made in United States
Orlando, FL
22 February 2023